TAMESIDE LIBRARIES

3801601943327 7

one

www.**Tameside**.gov.uk

TAMESIDE CENTRAL
LIBRARY
0161-342 2029

ASHTON LIBRARY
0161-342 2029
0161-342 2031

and other
stories

KT-238-681

WITHDRAWN FROM
TAMESIDE LIBRARIES

Also by Paige Toon

Lucy in the Sky
Johnny Be Good
Chasing Daisy
Pictures of Lily
Baby Be Mine
One Perfect Summer
One Perfect Christmas (eBook short story)
The Longest Holiday
Johnny's Girl (eBook short story)
Thirteen Weddings
The Sun in Her Eyes
The One We Fell in Love With
The Last Piece of My Heart
A Christmas Wedding (eBook short story)
Five Years From Now

Young Adult

The Accidental Life of Jessie Jefferson
I Knew You Were Trouble
All About the Hype

paige toon

one perfect christmas

and other stories

SIMON &
SCHUSTER

London · New York · Sydney · Toronto · New Delhi

A CBS COMPANY

First published in Great Britain by Simon & Schuster UK Ltd, 2018
A CBS COMPANY

Copyright © Paige Toon, 2018

The right of Paige Toon to be identified as author of
this work has been asserted in accordance with the
Copyright, Designs and Patents Act, 1988.

1 3 5 7 9 10 8 6 4 2

Simon & Schuster UK Ltd
1st Floor
222 Gray's Inn Road
London WC1X 8HB

Simon & Schuster Australia, Sydney
Simon & Schuster India, New Delhi

www.simonandschuster.co.uk
www.simonandschuster.com.au
www.simonandschuster.co.in

A CIP catalogue record for this book
is available from the British Library

Paperback ISBN: 978-1-4711-7944-0
eBook ISBN: 978-1-4711-7945-7

This book is a work of fiction. Names, characters, places and incidents are
either a product of the author's imagination or are used fictitiously. Any resemblance
to actual people living or dead, events or locales is entirely coincidental.

Typeset in the UK by M Rules
Printed and bound by CPI Group (UK) Ltd, Croydon, CR0 4YY

MIX
Paper from
responsible sources
FSC® C020471

Simon & Schuster UK Ltd are committed to sourcing paper that is made
from wood grown in sustainable forests and support the Forest Stewardship
Council, the leading international forest certification organisation. Our
books displaying the FSC logo are printed on FSC certified paper.

For Helen Brookes,
my beautiful, amazing, inspirational friend.
I love you to bits.

Contents

Introduction

Ever since writing *One Perfect Christmas* back in 2012, I've been asked repeatedly why my ebook short stories – which now include *Johnny's Girl* and *A Christmas Wedding* – haven't also been released in paperback. As they're only around a third of the length of my usual novels, it just hasn't been feasible. And even though I've explained to people who don't own e-readers that ebooks can be downloaded onto any device (smartphones, laptops, etc.), many of you just don't fancy reading anything that isn't printed on actual, tactile, smells-like-heaven paper.

Back in 2014 I launched *The Hidden Paige*, a club designed to give my readers exclusive extra content featuring characters from my novels – DVD extras but for books, if you like. In the last few years, I've delivered mini sequels, bonus scenes, extra chapters and standalone short stories direct to your inboxes.

I've shown you what happened when Rose from *The One We Fell In Love With* went on a night out with Lucy and Nathan from *Lucy in the Sky*; what was going through the mind of *Johnny Be Good*'s Johnny when he discovered that he had a teenage daughter and had to break it to Meg; how Lily from *Pictures of Lily* felt when she met *One Perfect Summer*'s

Joseph Strike and his fiancée Alice; and you've also heard what happened next for Daisy and Bridget from *Chasing Daisy* and *The Last Piece of my Heart*.

Now, with so many stories under my belt, including a mini sequel to *The Longest Holiday,* which I've penned especially for this collection, I am thrilled to be able to finally give you what you've been asking for: all of my ebook sequels, together with the extra content from *The Hidden Paige*, in one full-length, physical edition. (Note: we're also releasing this as an ebook for anyone who wants the full collection at their fingertips – *hello, ebook readers! No discrimination here!*)

In case you've forgotten what happened and when, or you would like a little more insight as to why I decided to revisit certain characters, I've written an introduction to each story featured.

Although existing readers of my books will get the most out of this collection, I hope those who are new to my work will still enjoy these stories as standalone pieces. If you choose to read my novels afterwards, you'll still find plenty of twists and turns, but I'm sure you understand it's impossible to avoid certain spoilers here.

If you're not a member of *The Hidden Paige* and would like to be, you can sign up at paigetoon.com – it's completely free and there will no doubt be a brand-new mini story winging its way to your inbox in the near future.

Until then, I hope you enjoy catching up with some old friends and making some new ones – I certainly did.

Lots of love,

Paige x

Twitter/Facebook/Instagram @PaigeToonAuthor
#TheHiddenPaige
www.paigetoon.com

One Perfect Christmas

After One Perfect Summer *came out in May, 2012, so many readers wrote to me demanding a sequel that I feared I might have to put aside my plans for* The Longest Holiday *to give them what they wanted. My editor has always encouraged me to write the book that's in my heart, and at that moment in time, I couldn't wait to get stuck into Laura and Leo's story.*

However, when it was suggested that I write an ebook short-story sequel to One Perfect Summer *to come out in time for Christmas, it felt like the perfect solution. I could give my readers what they were asking for — more to the story — without having to delay my next book.*

Although the ending of One Perfect Summer *felt right to me at the time, when I've read this book in subsequent years, I'll admit, it hasn't felt very satisfying. I'm so glad my readers pushed me to write this sequel because I loved being able to give Alice, Joe and Lukas the resolution that they needed.*

Over to you, Alice…

I have a spring in my step as my boots crunch through the freshly fallen snow. It's eight o'clock in the morning and I'm almost too excited to breathe. The anticipation of the last few weeks – no, *months* – has been killing me. How I will sleep tonight… Who am I kidding? I *won't* sleep.

But first I have to get through today. The smile grows wider on my face and I actually giggle. Out loud. Like a proper nutcase.

'Morning!' I chirp to a lone passer-by.

'Morning,' he replies with a slightly wary look in his eye.

The streets are almost deserted at this hour on a freezing Saturday morning in the middle of December.

I practically skip over Magdalene Bridge, glancing fondly at the punts moored down to my right. There's a thin layer of ice on the river and the buildings and streets are coated with fluffy white icing, all shimmering under a perfect blue winter sky. I don't think I've ever seen Cambridge look more beautiful.

Today is the day that two of my favourite people in the whole world – Jessie and Emily – get married to each other. I met Jessie when I was a student at Anglia Ruskin University, here in Cambridge. He worked as a punter on the River Cam – he taught *me* how to punt – but that wasn't the only way he brought joy back into my life. When I met him I was a mess. But enough of that.

Emily was our housemate in my second year. She was as meek as a mouse when we first met, and Jessie and I hardly ever saw her. But, eventually, she came out of her shell and we became good friends. Then she and Jessie became much more than that. They've been together for nine years and now, today, they're finally tying the knot.

When Jessie revealed he'd proposed to Emily, I thought they'd get married in Scotland, where she's from. But they delighted me by deciding on Cambridge. After all, this is where they met, and I'm about to arrive at the house Jessie grew up in.

Jessie's parents, Judy and Andrew, live in one of the gothic terraces on Mount Pleasant, at the top of the hill. They spent some time in America while we were at university, permitting Jessie to rent out the two spare rooms to students – namely, Emily and me.

I open the gate, walk up to the heavy, intricately carved wooden front door and knock. The door swings open almost immediately, and then I'm beaming up at Jessie. His red hair looks wilder than usual, and his face a little paler. I realise with building hysteria that he has a slightly manic look about him.

I burst out laughing. 'You're freaking out!' I exclaim, unable to offer him the calm, sympathetic shoulder that I probably should, given the circumstances.

'Yeah, yeah, alright,' he snaps good-naturedly, pulling me into the house and closing the door.

Then I throw my arms around him and he lifts me off my feet, squeezing the air out of me before starting to laugh too. He puts me down and I look up at him.

'Today's the day, Weasley,' I say gently, using the nickname that I came up with for him when we first met a decade ago, because he reminded me of Rupert Grint, AKA Ron Weasley from *Harry Potter.*

'Sure is, China,' he replies with a grin.

My name is Alice, but he calls me China because my grandmother was Chinese. I have her long, dead-straight black hair and her almond-shaped eyes, although mine are green like my mother's.

We only started using our nicknames again about eight months ago. We hadn't used them for years. We grew apart when... No. I'm trying not to think about that too much today.

Jessie brings me back to the present. 'Am I glad to see you. How's Emily?'

'Cool as a cucumber,' I reply. I left her in her hotel room on the other side of Cambridge. It's only a small city, so it didn't take long to walk.

I'm one of her three bridesmaids, and I arrived at her hotel this morning to find her calmly checking through the contents of her small suitcase before realising that she must have left her tiara at Jessie's place. I offered to walk here to collect it, seeing as I know Cambridge better than bridesmaids number one and two: Amy from Scotland and Ruth from London. I should do. I've lived here for over ten years now.

'Really?' Jessie asks with surprise.

'Yep. So you'd better get yourself together.' I notice the tiara sitting on the hallway table. 'Ah, good. You found it.'

'Yeah.'

I realise with surprise that I can't smell the pancakes and bacon that I would expect to be able to on a Saturday morning after a night at the Pickerel Inn, the local pub where we used to hang out. We went there for a few drinks last night for old times' sake with a few of our punter buddies from the past.

'Have you eaten?' I ask Jessie with a frown.

'No, I'm not hungry.'

I gape up at him. '*What?*'

He shrugs. 'I'm nervous.'

'You? Too nervous to eat?' I manage to splutter. 'Never, never, *ever* did I think I'd hear that. Where are your parents?'

'Mum's in the shower, Dad's still in bed.'

I check my watch. I have time – Emily won't mind if I don't rush back. 'Right,' I say with determination. 'I'm making you breakfast.'

He follows me reluctantly down the hallway to the kitchen. I pull out a chair for him and then set about getting the ingredients for Scotch pancakes out of the fridge and larder.

'What time are Chris, Jacob and Tom arriving?' They're his groomsmen. Chris is one of our old punter pals, and Jacob and Tom are friends of Jessie's from London, where he and Emily now live. Emily is a social worker and Jessie is a manager at a gastropub.

'Nine-ish.'

Good. They'll be able to take his mind off things, but for now that responsibility falls to me.

'How's the house?' Jessie asks.

My smile threatens to break my face. I only moved in a week ago.

'That good, huh?' He gives me a weak smile. He must be feeling faint.

'When are we allowed to see it?'

'Any chance you'll have time on Monday before you set off?' I ask hopefully. They leave for their honeymoon on Monday afternoon.

He frowns. 'Aren't you at work?'

'Oh yeah.' Trust me to forget about that.

He smirks. 'Bet you wish you weren't. When does he arrive?'

I catch my breath. 'Tomorrow night.'

'Excited?' he asks with a wry grin.

I nod quickly and can't stop my feet from jumping with delight on the kitchen floor.

Jessie laughs affectionately. 'I love seeing you this happy.'

I smile and decant some flour into a measuring cup. 'What about you, Weasley? How are you feeling? This is supposed to be the happiest day of your life.'

'I feel like I'm going to throw up.'

We hear quick footsteps on the wooden floorboards overhead and both glance upwards. His mum must be out of the shower. She sounds like she's racing around like a rocket, and then we hear her squawking at Jessie's dad to wake up.

'She sounds even more stressed than you,' I comment.

Jessie is an only child so this, effectively, is *her* big day.

'That'd be right.' He rolls his eyes and I turn back to the job at hand. 'What are you doing?' he suddenly snaps.

'I'm spooning sugar into a bowl,' I reply slowly, as though he's a bit thick.

'You haven't sifted the flour!' He sounds outraged. 'Budge over,' he snaps with a loud, overdramatic sigh as he gets up from the table. He pushes me down into his empty chair and I grin. Weasley making breakfast – order has been restored to the world. And, I think with amusement, I've managed to take his mind off things. Double result.

❄

By the time his groomsmen arrive, Jessie's mum and dad are downstairs; the former fussing around, while the latter reads the paper as though this is an ordinary day.

Jessie sees me to the front door. 'Don't forget to give her these,' he says, handing me a paper bag containing three Scotch pancakes wrapped in aluminium foil.

I didn't have the heart to tell him that Emily was ordering a champagne continental breakfast as I was leaving.

'Oh, and I'd better remember this!' I grab the tiara from the hall table.

'Give her my love,' he says, touching me on the arm.

'I will.' I smile warmly up at him. 'Good luck.'

'Thanks.'

'See you on the other side,' I add.

He snorts with derision and shoves me out of the house.

❋

The morning passes by in a blur of hair, make-up and beautiful dresses, and when we finally go downstairs where the cars are waiting to take us to St Mary's church in the city centre, Emily looks absolutely gorgeous. She's wearing a long, cream-coloured velvet gown with a matching coat to protect her against the winter weather. We wouldn't normally expect snow this early, but no one is complaining – it's magical. Her dark hair has been piled up on top of her head, underneath the glittering tiara. A few loose tendrils hang down. Her make-up is pretty and neutral – she looks very, very different from the goth chick who moved into Jessie's house all those years ago, with her heavy make-up, black clothes and nose ring. She stopped dressing that way when she got her job in London.

As for us bridesmaids, we're wearing floor-length smoky-grey velvet gowns and high heels. But even with our matching jackets, it's hard to keep our teeth from chattering as we pose for a few photographs. And then the show is on the road.

I'm nervous as the doors to the church are opened, so I can't imagine how Emily feels. Jessie is standing up at the altar with his friends and we exchange shaky smiles. As Emily's third bridesmaid, I have to lead the way in. Ruth is behind me, Amy, the Chief Bridesmaid, follows her and then it's Emily and her dad. The music starts up and my feet take me on autopilot up the long aisle.

Concentrating on walking slowly and not rushing, I reach the altar and stand off to the left. Breathing a small sigh of relief, I turn around to watch Emily. The church is quite full, and it's hardly surprising – Jessie has always been enormously popular, and Emily is a far cry from the shy girl she used to be at university. Jessie is standing sombrely as he watches his wife-to-be approach. It's the look on his face that does it. My eyes well up and with blurry vision I see Emily smile back at Jessie as she reaches him. Mercifully, a tissue appears out of nowhere. I smile gratefully at Ruth as the priest starts his address, and then we're instructed to sit down. I turn to take my seat in the front pew, but do a double take as my gaze falls to the far left corner of the church.

My heart skips a beat as his dark eyes meet mine.

He has a beard now, a bushy black beard, but it's definitely him. He smiles a playful smile and then gives me a look, nodding his head meaningfully. He's trying to convey that everyone else is sitting down so I quickly do the same, but his stare burns into the back of my head as my heart beats wildly. And then happiness floods me and I can barely contain myself. *He's here. He's here. He's here.*

It's hard to concentrate on the service. The next time we have to stand up, I look around to catch his eye, just to check it's really him. It is; he's unmistakeable, even with his new facial hair.

Joe. My Joe.

Of course, he isn't just *my* Joe. He's Joseph Strike, A-list actor and Hollywood's hottest rising star, so millions of women around the world feel like they own a little piece of him too. But they don't. Not really. He's mine, all mine. My heart is so full it feels like it could burst.

How did he get here without being recognised? It must be the beard. I suddenly have an uncontrollable urge to guffaw and I seriously consider stuffing Ruth's tissue into my mouth to stop myself, but luckily it's time to sing so we all stand up again. This time he grins back at me – he knows I'm close to losing it. I really need to concentrate but I see him begin to sing with such animated, over-the-top gusto to make me laugh, and it works.

Amy flashes me a look so I quickly turn to face the front of the church but glance back at him to see him mouth 'sorry' for getting me into trouble. I purse my lips then try as hard as I can to sing the words on the order of service in my hands. What if he leaves because he knows he's distracting me? Panicked, I look back, but he's still there singing more calmly and watching me. He gives me another meaningful nod and after that I force myself to concentrate.

The service is beautiful and when Jessie finally kisses his bride I have a valid excuse to clap so hard my hands sting. It's also blissfully quick, with two short readings and hymns that are uplifting and only a few verses in length.

The congregation follows the wedding party out of the church, and I know that Joe will wait until the end to leave so I have time to congratulate my friends. Jessie sweeps me up in a big bear hug and I whisper in his ear: 'He's here.'

He puts me down, a stunned look on his face as he scans the crowd.

'Inside,' I add quietly with a grin.

'What's this?' Emily asks, sensing something is going on. The three of us put our heads together.

'Joe is here,' I whisper.

Her eyes widen. 'Is he? Is he coming to the reception?'

'Oh. I don't know.' I hadn't thought about that. 'There won't be room, will there?'

'It's a buffet!' Jessie exclaims. 'Of course there's room.'

'He might worry about being seen,' I quickly add.

'He'll be alright,' Jessie tries to convince me. I know he's dying to meet Joe.

'Definitely!' Emily urges. She can't wait to meet him either. I suspect she's a bit of a Strike Stalker at heart, not that she'd ever admit that to Jessie.

'Come on, you three,' Jessie's mum Judy interrupts in a chiding tone. 'Let's get these photos over with. Everybody's freezing.'

Thankfully, the snowy roads have mostly been cleared, so it's not too hard for us bridesmaids to make our way in high heels through the narrow medieval streets to Garret Hostel Bridge. I wish Joe were next to me, keeping me warm, but I know he'll be staying out of sight for now. The bridge has a very steep incline, but it has been well gritted, so we make it to the top without slipping. The female photographer shoots some quick shots of the wedding party while we grin and bear the cold.

We all cheer as Jessie and Emily climb into their waiting punt beside the bridge, which Jessie's groomsmen decorated earlier with silver tinsel and shimmering garlands made out of tinfoil. We shower the couple with rose petal confetti as Jessie punts his laughing bride away to the reception venue further down the river. The rest of the congregation sets off, but I pause for a moment as my eyes fall on Trinity Bridge. I can't help but feel melancholic as I remember Lukas sitting there many summers ago, reading his book. Lukas. My tall, blond, good-looking, almost ex-husband. I try to close my mind off to him because I don't want to feel unhappy, not today.

I shiver and turn away, coming face to face with Joe.

I throw my arms around him and he hugs the breath out of me, warmth radiating from his body and engulfing mine.

'I can't believe you're here.' My voice is muffled against his chest. He pulls away and I look up at him.

'I wanted to surprise you.'

'You did.'

His smile fades as his gaze falls to my lips, and then he's kissing me. The world around us shrinks as shivers travel up and down my entire body. I can't believe he still has this effect on me. He holds me tighter and I press my body against his, sliding my hands inside his suit jacket to get close to him. He feels broader and more muscled than the last time I saw him, which was an unbearable three months ago. I suddenly, *desperately*, want to get him undressed. And then I remember myself and pull away, gasping for breath.

His dark eyes flash and he takes my face in his hands and stares down at me.

'I could get seriously carried away,' I say with meaning, touching my hand to his. I know I should be at the reception venue to welcome Jessie and Emily and the rest of the guests.

'Later,' he replies in a low tone. Then he tugs me to him and we walk down the bridge arm in arm.

I reach up and stroke his beard. 'What's this?'

'Had to grow it for the part.' He grins down at me. He's been filming on location in the Brazilian rainforest. We've had to talk via satellite phone over the last three months because the mobile reception has been practically non-existent. 'I'll shave it off when we get home,' he promises.

Home. The thought sends a thrill through me.

When I separated from Lukas at the beginning of the year, I moved into a house share, which was the only thing I could afford on my teacher's salary. It was a lovely little house, and my housemate Lisa was easy enough to live with, but I still felt like I'd returned to my student days. Joe wanted to buy a house for me – he went on and on and on about it – but I resisted, until about two months ago, when he said he was coming to Cambridge to spend Christmas with me. Our first Christmas together.

The sale went through last week. In my head, of course, it's his house and I'll look after it for him when he's not here, which sadly will be often. But he keeps insisting it belongs to both of us.

His filming schedule has been jam-packed this year, and next year doesn't look to be any better. His base is in LA – I went over there for the summer holidays, but it felt very surreal. I'm not sure I liked it very much. After that, Joe vowed to spend more time in the UK. It still astounds me that we've managed to keep our relationship under wraps. I love that I can have a normal life with a normal job, even if I do have to listen to my colleague Roxy going on about Joseph Strike all the time. Honestly, she's obsessed. Every piece of salacious gossip comes directly my way. It's the thing I find hardest to deal with.

'This place is amazing,' Joe says, looking around at the historic college buildings as we walk along the narrow streets, the Christmas lights twinkling prettily over our heads. I can see Amy and Ruth up ahead, so we're not too far behind everyone.

'It's even lovelier than usual with the snow,' I say. 'I'll show you around at some point.'

'Don't forget you also promised to take me punting.'

I laugh. How does he remember me saying that? It was almost a year ago! 'I haven't punted in donkeys' years.'

'I bet you'll pick it up again quickly.'

'I'll make you try it,' I reply.

'Now that will be a good way of drawing attention to ourselves,' he says with amusement.

'No doubt you'll be an immediate pro, just like you are with everything else.'

He laughs and squeezes me and happiness once more courses through my body.

We reach Magdalene Bridge just in time to see Jessie and Emily arrive at the punting station.

Everyone cheers and claps as Jessie helps Emily off, and then they begin to lead the way to the reception venue a little way down the river.

'You will come to the reception, won't you?' I ask Joe urgently as we hang back a bit.

He glances up ahead. 'I don't know, am I invited?'

'Of course you are. But are you worried about being recognised?'

'Ah, it should be alright, shouldn't it?' he asks.

'It should be,' I reply hesitantly. 'Anyway, it's all about Jessie and Emily today, isn't it?'

'Exactly.'

'They can't wait to meet you!'

We walk hand in hand for the last hundred metres or so, but neither of us speaks. I know we're taking a risk. When our relationship eventually goes public, everything will change. I won't be able to keep my job, a job I love. Sure, teaching six- and seven-year-olds can be stressful at times, but it's also fun and often very rewarding, and even more importantly, it's normal. I know where I stand with it. The idea of being constantly scrutinised and harassed – even hunted down – by everyone from snooping hacks to obsessive girls riddled with jealously and hatred… I shudder.

'We don't have to do this,' Joe says in a low voice, sensing my anxiety.

'No, it's okay.' I grip his hand more tightly, but inside I feel slightly sick. He puts his arm around me and gives me a quick, comforting squeeze, and then we're at the venue. We're the last ones to arrive, but Jessie and Emily are waiting for us, their eyes shining with anticipation. They know all about Joseph Strike. It's hard *not* to know about him. But they've seen all of his films too, and I know they're huge fans. It's enough to make my nerves temporarily dissipate.

'Hello!' I cry.

'Hello!' Emily squeaks, her eyes darting to Joe.

'Hey,' Joe says warmly, shaking Jessie's hand and patting him on his upper arm. 'Congratulations!'

'Thanks,' Jessie replies, blushing a deep beetroot colour.

'You look stunning,' Joe says to Emily, bending down to give her a kiss on her cheek. She also blushes furiously and mumbles a thank you, but I notice now she's unable to look Joe in the eye.

'Thanks for letting me come,' Joe says earnestly to them both.

'Of course.' Jessie shifts on his feet.

'No problem,' Emily adds. They both seem a little lost for words, but Joe doesn't appear fazed by their reaction. I guess he's used to the effect he has on people.

'Here,' Jessie says, swiping two glasses of champagne for us from a passing waitress's tray.

'What about you?' Joe asks, noticing their near-empty glasses.

'Oh yeah.' Jessie grabs another two.

'Cheers!' I exclaim and we all chink glasses. Jessie downs half of his champagne in one gulp.

'It was such a lovely ceremony.' I try to break the ice.

'It was,' Joe agrees. 'Where are you going on your honeymoon?'

'Austria,' Jessie replies. 'I'm going to teach Em how to snowboard.'

Emily rolls her eyes. 'Good luck with that.'

He chuckles and kisses her temple. She blushes again.

'I wish I knew how to snowboard,' Joe muses.

'Haven't you ever been?' Jessie asks with surprise.

'Nope. Never got a chance.'

'You should come with us sometime!' Jessie exclaims.

'That would be great,' Joe replies sincerely. 'You teach it, don't you?'

'I used to.' Jessie nods. I'm impressed Joe remembers this, actually.

'Maybe you could teach me.'

Jessie looks pleased. 'Absolutely. I'll get some practice in on my wife, first.'

Emily smacks him on his arm. 'You'll be lucky.'

'You guys are MARRIED!' I suddenly squeal, and they both laugh. They've visibly relaxed, thankfully.

'Are you looking forward to seeing your new house?' Jessie asks Joe.

'I can't wait. Is it alright?'

'I don't know. She wouldn't let anyone else see it until you had.' He gives me his best unimpressed look.

'Aw, really?' Joe peers down at me, his eyes twinkling.

'But now that you're here…' I say, giving Joe a look. He nods and I turn back to Jessie and Emily. 'You could pop over tomorrow, if you'd like to?'

'We'd love to!' Emily gushes eagerly.

'That would be great,' Jessie agrees.

'Jessie! Emily!' We all look over to see Judy waving. She spots me and comes over. 'I should have known I'd find you three together, again.' She glances at Joe.

'Mum, this is Joe,' Jessie introduces them.

'Hello!' She smiles brightly, but there's no trace of recognition. One down, ninety-odd to go.

'Can you and Emily come and chat to your Great Uncle Gerard, darling? I don't know how long he'll last before he'll nod off.'

'Sure, Mum,' Jessie replies in a resigned tone. 'See you later,' he says to us, taking Emily's hand and leading her away.

Joe smiles at me.

'Shall we find a dark corner?' I ask him.

He raises one eyebrow at me. God, he's sexy.

'Oi,' I gently berate. 'Enough of that.'

He looks past me and nods to the far corner of the room, where there's an empty booth. 'Over there.'

He leads the way, and I'm intensely aware of every glance, but no one does a double take. The beard is an excellent disguise, and who would expect Joseph Strike to be here anyway?

I slide into the secluded booth and he joins me, our thighs pressing together under the table. Suddenly the air between us is charged with electricity. I turn to face him and we stare into each other's eyes for a long moment, before he kisses me tenderly on my lips. It's over far too quickly. This is not the time or the place, and we both know it.

'I missed you.'

These words come out of our mouths at exactly the same time and we both laugh. He touches his hand to my cheek.

'You look so beautiful.'

I smile back at him. 'You look pretty damn sexy yourself.'

'Even with the beard?'

'Even with the beard,' I confirm. I place my hand on his chest, which definitely feels bigger than it was before. 'Have you had to bulk up for this part?' I ask curiously.

He looks a bit embarrassed. 'Yeah. It's been pretty full on.'

'Dodgy macrobiotic diets?' I ask with amusement. I've teased him about this before.

'Unfortunately, yes.' He rolls his eyes. 'But not anymore.'

He's just finished filming an action thriller called *The Darkest Side*. All that's left for him to do now is record some voiceover stuff in LA in January.

'Done with all those bare-chested shots on location, then?' I say playfully.

'Yep. The only place you'll see me bare-chested anytime soon is in the bedroom,' he replies with a raised eyebrow.

'Only in the bedroom?' I pretend to be put out. 'We have a very nice rug in front of a very nice log fire.'

He smiles and kisses me on my lips. 'I like that you just said "we".'

I giggle. 'Actually, I brought the rug with me from my last place, so technically it's mine. But I'm very happy to share it with you.'

'As long as you don't share it with anybody else,' he warns.

His brow furrows and he looks away. There's an immediate change in the atmosphere.

'What's wrong?' I ask with confusion.

'Nothing. Just ignore me.' He takes a sip of his drink, but doesn't meet my eyes.

'I can't just ignore you. Tell me.'

He looks hesitant. 'Did you and… Lukas… ever…'

'No!' I cry, horrified. The thought of making love to Joe on the same rug as I did with my husband… 'No! The rug is new,' I clarify. 'I bought it when I moved in with my housemate.'

'Oh.' He exhales loudly. 'Okay.'

'Hey.' I take his hand and squeeze it, then try to think of something to say to change the subject, but I'm not quick enough.

'Have you seen him recently?' he asks.

'I saw him about a month ago,' I reply quietly. 'He came back to help sort out our things.'

I couldn't persuade Lukas to sell our house at first, so we let it out on a six-month rental. The tenants vacated the property at the beginning of November, and Lukas finally agreed to put it up for sale. We received four offers in its first weekend. Newnham is a very popular area of Cambridge – properties don't come up that often. We're due to exchange this week and complete the week after. The new owners want to be in in time for Christmas.

Joe's jaw has tensed. I can see this, even under his bushy beard. 'Why didn't you tell me?'

'That I'd seen him?' I check.

'Yes.'

'I barely got to talk to you in Brazil. I was hardly going to ruin our conversations by bringing up Lukas.'

He lets go of my hand and takes another drink, trying to feign nonchalance. 'Fair enough.' But I can see straight through him.

I can't actually believe that Joe told me once that he would still want me, even if Lukas had taken me back. The idea of secretly slipping away from my husband for passionate trysts with Joe on the rare occasion that he's not filming… Even if Lukas *were* blissfully unaware of what was going on, Joe gets so jealous. I think we can safely say that staying married to Lukas would never have worked, even if I'd wanted it to. Which I didn't. I would never have done that.

But I could have if I'd wanted to.

Seven months ago…

There's a pounding on the door. I'm upstairs getting ready for bed and Lisa, my housemate, is out at the movies with her new boyfriend. It's pouring with rain outside – I can hear it pelting against the windows. Who would be calling at this hour? I consider ignoring it, but the pounding starts up again. I pull on my dressing gown and traipse down the stairs.

'Who's there?' I shout, not wanting to open the door to a stranger. We don't have a peephole.

'Open up!'

Lukas! I wrench open the door and see him standing there. Rain runs off his dark blond hair and down his chiselled face, which is tanned, even in early May. His blue eyes look desperate as he regards me with misery.

'Can I come in?'

At least he has the decency to ask this time.

Guilt washes through me, my unwelcome companion whenever Lukas is around. I take a step backwards and he enters. 'Let me get you a towel.'

He's still standing in the hall when I return.

'You're soaked through!' I exclaim, seeing the full extent of the rain's damage. I recognise that jacket. It's his light-grey Hugo Boss one – my favourite – but thanks to the rain it looks charcoal-coloured. He's trying to shrug it off, but the wet fabric is sticking to his shirt and making it difficult. I help him out of it and notice that even his white shirt is transparent.

'Oh, Lukas,' I murmur with dismay. 'Did you walk here?'

'Yes.'

I look up at him, but he's steadfastly staring at the floor.

'Have my dressing gown.' I take it off and hand it over. I'm only wearing my PJs underneath.

He says nothing as he puts it on the banister and starts to unbutton his shirt.

'I'll make you a coffee.'

I hurry out of the room, turning the heating back on as I pass the boiler cupboard. *I wonder what he's doing here?*

Lukas is in the living room when I return with his coffee. He looks so unfamiliar. It doesn't help that he's wearing my fluffy white dressing gown.

'Where are your clothes?'

He nods towards the table. I take the pile and start to lay them out on the radiators.

'Have a seat,' I direct him.

He slumps onto the sofa. I pass him his coffee and sit in the opposite armchair. He doesn't speak for a while, so I have to prompt him.

'What are you doing here?'

His blue eyes fly up to penetrate mine, and the agony I see in them in unbearable. 'I miss you.'

I avert my gaze. 'Lukas—'

'Alice,' he interrupts. 'Why are you doing this?'

'You know why, Lukas.' I sound resigned. We've been here before. Many, many times.

'Have you seen him yet?' he asks, a look of hope flitting across his features.

I swallow. 'Yes.'

He visibly slumps. 'I wasn't sure. I hadn't heard anything.' I know one of his greatest fears has been the idea of reading about us in the papers. 'Did you go to Australia?' he asks.

'Yes.'

Joe has been filming on location Down Under. I couldn't go during half term, and the distance was agonising, so I went there during the Easter holidays. I hadn't seen him since New Year's Day when we said our goodbyes at Wareham train station in Dorset. After that he had to fly home to LA and then on to the outback, and I had to return to Cambridge to sort out my screwed-up life.

'When did you get back?' he asks.

'At the weekend.'

'What was it like?' Lukas's voice is pained.

'It was… fine,' I say carefully.

The truth is, it was difficult. More difficult than I had imagined. Of course, at first it was blissful. Making love to Joe in his trailer after months apart, feeling with absolute certainty that I was doing the right thing in leaving a husband who loves me. But it was hard, too. Joe spent most of his days, and several of his nights, filming. Rumours had been flying around about him and his beautiful co-star for weeks, and I hated seeing him with her. And because we were trying to keep our relationship under wraps, I had to pretend to be his personal masseuse. We joked at my job description at first but it started to feel wrong. Sordid, in a way.

Joe didn't want it to be like that. He wanted to tell everyone that I was Alice – the Alice that he spoke about on live television back in December. His first love, the girl that he could never get over.

My friend Lizzy saw that interview and called the TV station. That was how we got back in touch. I hadn't been able to forget him, even though I had married Lukas. And when Joe became a superstar, it was even harder to put him out of my mind, because he was everywhere. I needed to know why he never came for me all those years ago.

We met in Dorset when we were both eighteen – lost ourselves in each other, *to* each other – and then we were torn apart. The next time I heard anything about him was years later when Lizzy showed me a DVD on my wedding day. A kick-boxing documentary called *Strike*. She'd watched it the night before and recognised Joe – she'd come to visit me in Dorset for a couple of days. But this man was called Joseph Strike – he'd changed his name and I felt like I didn't know him, that that part of my life was over. But it wasn't. Even after I married Lukas, I never stopped thinking about Joe, wondering what had happened to him.

Running away to a cottage in Dorset together was supposed to be about getting answers and finding closure, but even after nine and a half years, we fell so deeply in love again that we knew we could never let each other go.

Lukas found us at the cottage. He was so angry. I believed he would never forgive me. But Joe thought otherwise. He thought Lukas would want me back, and he was scared that I'd choose an ordinary, private life with a normal man, instead of a relationship with one of the most sought-after people in the world.

What sort of a life would that be? I knew it would be challenging. But once I'd found Joe again, fallen for him all over again, my decision was set in stone.

Joe was right about one thing: Lukas did want me back. Even after everything I had done to him.

I couldn't believe it. I still can't believe it. He quit his job in Germany – he had moved there a couple of months earlier, while I'd stayed in the UK to teach – and got another research placement at the University of Cambridge where he had studied and later taught. I tried to convince him not to do this, that it was futile – I wanted a divorce – but my words had no effect.

'*You didn't want to go to Germany, and I should never have left you… I'm sorry.*'

I never thought I'd hear him say that. I wish he hadn't. It would have been less painful if he'd hated me.

He violently opposed the idea of me moving out of our home, but he couldn't stop me. He also violently opposed a divorce, and as he was the one who had to file for it under grounds of infidelity (mine), my hands were tied. I knew it would take time to convince him. I was still trying.

Lukas speaks quietly. 'Do you still love him?'

'Yes.' My eyes well up with tears. I hate myself for hurting him like this. I wish he could accept that it's over between us.

'What about his co-star?'

I know he – along with millions of others – has been glued to the tabloids for news about a romance between Joe and Michelle Bleech, the stunning Australian actress who he's been sharing a lot of time with on set. Lukas's reasons for his interest are very different to the rest of the population.

'They're just friends.'

Even *I* know this sounds weak. I was riddled with jealousy when my colleague Roxy kept going on about them. But Joe insisted they were just friends. However, it was only when I saw them together first-hand that I could accept it as the truth. I still couldn't stand the sight of the woman, though. She was far too touchy-feely for my liking.

'Alice…' He gets up from the sofa and tries to approach me.

'No. Don't.' I put my hand up to ward him off. He hesitates for a moment. 'Lukas, please. Don't do this,' I beg. I get to my feet and step away from him.

He stands up, but ignores my protests. 'I still love you. I will always love you.'

'I can't…' I go to walk into the kitchen, but he grabs my hand, pulling me back to him. His dressing gown has fallen open, revealing his body beneath. He's wearing nothing but boxer shorts, and I inadvertently glance at his chest. I immediately regret it, because suddenly he *is* familiar to me. So familiar my heart clenches.

'I know you still love me, too.'

'I don't!'

But it's a lie. And he knows it. I do still love him. I still remember falling in love with him, with this gorgeous, intelligent German student who was studying Physics at Trinity College. I remember making love to him in his room, above the bookshop opposite Great Gate on Trinity Street, with the Christmas lights glowing outside his window. I remember him proposing to me at the top of an Austrian mountain, kneeling on the purest of snow. I remember him telling me that I was his first love, his only love. He disappointed his parents – his austere, mega-wealthy German parents – by choosing me instead of his childhood sweetheart, who was from a very good family, as I heard time and time again. To my knowledge he still hasn't told his parents we've separated. He made sacrifices for me because he loved me. And I loved him. I still love him. Just not as much as I love Joe. For me a choice *did* have to be made. So I made one. But it appears Lukas still believes he can change my mind.

'Enough. You've got to stop this.' I shake my hand free.

'Why haven't you made your relationship public?' he asks me quietly.

'I don't want… We don't want… I want…'

'You want a normal life,' he finishes my sentence for me.

I look away from him, because he's right, of course.

He steps forward and puts his hand on my arm. I stare up at him. 'Alice, you know you will never get that with him. You'll have to quit your job, you won't be able to live in this house, or any house without security and bodyguards. You won't be able to go anywhere on your own, ever again. And how will your children live? Presuming you *want* children with *him*?' I know the thought of this must hurt him very much. He had been wanting to try for a family for ages. He continues.

'You're stealing away every chance of a normal childhood. You're effectively entering yourself – and your children – into a prison sentence. Is that really what you want?'

No! No, it's not what I want! He's preying on my greatest fears and I hate him for it.

I remove his hand from my arm, give him my fiercest glare and try to keep my voice steady. 'You're not going to change my mind.' I take a deep breath. 'I want a divorce.'

He stares at me for a long moment, but I don't waver. And then I see his eyes fill with tears before he closes them. I lose my resolve and my bottom lip starts to wobble.

'I'm sorry,' I whisper. His eyes fly open and suddenly I'm in his arms, my cheek pressed against his bare chest as his arms crush me to him. I struggle to free myself, but he holds me tightly.

'Don't,' I protest, but then he's holding my face in his hands and forcing me to look up at him. His lips are on mine before I know it, but it feels wrong, so wrong. All I can think about is Joe. I'm frozen. I can't kiss him back. I think it's in that moment, when I don't melt under his touch as I'm sure he expected me to, that Lukas finally accepts that it's over.

He flings me away from him, hurt and anger distorting his usually perfect features.

'You will regret this,' he promises darkly, snatching his still-damp clothes from the radiators and pulling them on. 'There's no going back this time.'

And much as it pains me, it's what I want to hear.

He returned to Germany after that. His former employer at the University of Munich took him back. He still couldn't bring himself to talk to me about selling our house, though. So we rented it out. The next time I would see him would be when we went there to clear out the last of our belongings. It was then that he finally consented to my request.

❋

'He's agreed to a divorce,' I tell Joe now. His dark eyes light up.

'Really?'

'Yes.'

'*Really?*' he asks again, almost unable to believe it.

'*Yes.*'

With utter relief, he pulls me to him. I breathe in his scent as I press my face into his neck.

'Why didn't you tell me *this*?' he asks as he jerks away, staring at me with confusion. This topic certainly wouldn't have ruined our conversations. It's what Joe's been after for months.

'I knew I'd believe it when I saw it. I didn't want to get your hopes up. But the divorce papers came through yesterday.'

'And he's signed them?' he checks warily.

'Yes.'

'So it's over?'

'It's been over for almost a year.'

'Yes, but now it's official.'

I nod and his face breaks into an enormous grin. 'So now you're *my* Alice. *Just* my Alice.'

'I've always been *your* Alice,' I say softly as he hugs me to him once more.

'I'm so happy,' he murmurs into my hair.

'Me too.' Another surge of joy passes through me.

❄

We eat, drink and dance the night away, and although we get a few odd looks, I'm pretty sure Joe's identity remains safe. For one more night, at least. At nine o'clock, he goes off to get his suitcase from a nearby hotel. His PA checked him into one so he could have a shower and leave his belongings somewhere, but he returns within half an hour, giving me just enough time to have a dance with Jessie and Emily.

By eleven thirty, Joe is seriously flagging. He only flew in from LA this morning after an all-night flight, and even in First Class he says he barely slept. Jessie and Emily are showing no signs of calling it a night any time soon, so we go to say goodbye.

Emily throws her arms around me and I hug her tightly.

'Thanks for letting me be your bridesmaid.' My tone is serious, but Emily snorts.

'As if I wouldn't have asked you!'

My eyes brim with tears and I hug her again. The truth is, I didn't expect to be asked. Emily wasn't one of my bridesmaids when I got married. And I had five. My face burns with shame as I remember how I allowed Lukas to convince me that it was all about politics. I didn't even know one of my bridesmaids – I met her for the first time the day before we got married. Plus, I hardly saw Emily back in those days. But I should never have allowed that to happen. I'm beyond delighted that we've become good friends again this year.

I turn to Jessie. 'Come here,' he slurs drunkenly, hauling me into his arms. He presses his lips to my head. 'My little China. Look after her,' he tells Joe, and it's almost a warning.

'I fully intend to,' Joe says, gently pulling me to his side. 'So we'll see you tomorrow?'

'Oh, yeah!' Jessie exclaims. 'Phew, forgot about that. I was about to get all emotional.'

I smirk at him. 'Call me when you're ready. No rush,' I add, giving Emily one last peck on her cheek. 'Have a good one,' I say to her with a wink.

'You too,' she says brazenly back, glancing at Joe.

I laugh and lead the way out.

'We should be able to catch a cab out here, but if not we'll walk up to the taxi rank.' My teeth start to chatter. It's even colder than before.

Joe chuckles and vigorously rubs my arms in an attempt to warm me up.

'What?' I ask him over my shoulder.

'Nothing,' he replies.

'You're used to having a driver,' I realise with amusement.

'I haven't had to hail a cab in years,' he admits.

'Well, for the next few weeks, you're just little Joe Strickwold, so get used to it,' I tease.

'I'm very happy to.'

A cab appears around the corner and he steps out onto the street and whistles loudly. It screeches to a halt.

'Bloody hell!' I exclaim. I've never seen anyone do that, other than in the movies.

Huh. But of course he's been in plenty of movies…

'I lived in New York for a bit,' he tells me with a grin, opening the door for me. I climb in and tell the driver where to go. Joe puts his suitcase in the boot and then slides in after me.

'I didn't know you lived in New York,' I say. There are still so many gaps to fill in. Thankfully, we have time.

'For a year after I first moved to America,' he explains, glancing across at me.

'Wow. Did you like it?'

'Loved it. Might buy an apartment there one day. Have you ever been?'

'No, funnily enough. It's one of those places I always wanted to go,' I reply.

'I'll take you.'

I smile at him and rest my head on his shoulder, draping my arm across his waist.

'How far away is home?' he asks.

'About fifteen minutes,' I reply.

He slides his arm around me and we stay like that for the rest of the journey.

Eventually, the taxi driver turns into a sleepy village, dark except for the occasional light glowing through the cracks in curtains. I chose this village, not only because it's quiet and private and we have plenty of space, but because most of its occupants appear to be nearing ninety. I'm pretty sure that they won't be bothered – if they ever become aware – that there's a celebrity in their midst.

'Take a left here,' I tell the driver, extricating myself from Joe as he pulls into a narrow lane. 'We're at the end.'

'This is a bit tucked away,' the driver comments.

'It sure is,' I reply, flashing Joe a grin. His posture has changed. He's sitting upright and he looks eager and full of anticipation, like a child on Christmas morning.

Joe didn't even have access to email in the rainforest, so I couldn't send him the estate agent's particulars. I described the house to him, although nothing would have prepared him for what it's like in real life. The 'wow' factor will have to wait until the morning, though, because it's so dark right now that all we can see are the tall wooden gates in the car's headlights.

The taxi driver reverses back out of the road while I lead Joe to the gate's keypad.

'Five, seven, zero, two,' I tell him as I punch in the code. 'Fifth of July, 2002.'

'The day we met,' he says quietly.

We gaze at each other in the darkness for a moment before I push open the gate.

The sky over our heads is bursting with stars and a new moon hangs yellow above the rooftop. As we walk across the snow-crusted gravel driveway, I feel the familiar flutter of butterflies as they take flight in my stomach. I push my key into the lock and flick on the hall lights as I go inside. I'm suddenly intensely aware of Joe's presence behind me, the warmth of his frame. I turn around to face him and see that his expression is as serious as mine.

He takes me in his arms and kisses me passionately. Shivers travel up and down my spine, but I'm no longer cold. His kiss deepens, and then his lips move to my neck. I gasp and arch my back. I want him so much.

'I take it you don't want a tour?' I ask breathlessly.

'Only to the bedroom,' he replies, scooping me up. I laugh lightly. He's so strong, he makes me feel weightless. He grins at me, making my heart flip. 'Which way?'

I nod at the stairs. 'Up.'

'I like what you've done here,' he comments jokily, nodding at the heavy-aluminium mirror over the hallstand, mixing modern with old.

'Thanks,' I reply with a grin, my arms looped around his neck.

'Nice rug,' he continues when we reach the landing.

'The one in front of the hearth is nicer,' I reply mockingly and he raises one eyebrow at me. 'Right here,' I direct him with a jerk of my head.

He's kissing me again before we reach the bedroom. Frantic, desperate kisses. There's no more laughing, no more talking as we undress quickly, not taking our eyes from each other. There are no witty remarks about the super-king-size bed with its sculptured mahogany bedhead and white Egyptian cotton 600-thread-count duvet cover. All I want is him. Inside me. Now. We fall onto the bed and as his warm, hard body presses against mine, I inhale sharply with ecstasy as I get my wish.

He kisses me lightly all over my face when it's over. Soothing me. Loving me. Once more I was overcome with emotion at the end – sometimes Joe just does that to me. I take a deep, shaky breath and he rolls off me, turning on his side to stroke my face and brush away my tears. My nose is still prickling and there's a lump in my throat.

'I love you,' he whispers.

'I love you more,' I reply.

'It's not possible.'

We smile small smiles at each other.

'Please can we go public?' he begs. 'I hate being without you.'

I sigh, my tears abating. 'Let's talk in the morning.'

He nods and I reach across to switch off the bedside light.

'Nice bedhead, by the way,' he murmurs as I snuggle into the crook of his arm.

I swear I'm still smiling as I fall asleep.

❋

I wake up to the sound of him shaving. I sit up in bed and peer through the gap in the door to the en suite. Sensing movement, he pauses for a moment and peeks out at me.

'Morning,' he says with a grin.

'Morning,' I reply sleepily.

'Sorry I woke you.'

'What's the time?'

'Nine o'clock.'

That's pretty good for me, actually. I've been struggling to sleep recently. I nod at his electric razor. 'Are you sure that's a good idea?'

'You think I should keep my disguise?'

'Might be an idea?'

'Nah,' he says. 'It's too damn itchy.'

I smile at him. 'I prefer you clean-shaven anyway.'

'You'll have me that way in ten minutes.'

'Promises, promises,' I tease.

But he stays true to it.

It's even more blissful kissing him when I don't have a beard to contend with. I could stay in bed with him all day, if I weren't so excited about showing him the house.

'Come on,' I urge.

He climbs out of bed and I pause for a moment to admire the view as he gets a T-shirt and cargo pants out from his suitcase. He must've brought it upstairs while I was asleep. He is definitely broader. Hang on, what's that?

'Is that a scar?' I ask with concern as he drags his T-shirt over his head.

'Where? Oh, there,' he replies, looking over his shoulder at his lower back. 'Just a scratch.'

'That is *not* just a scratch,' I say, climbing out of bed and going over to study it. It's about ten centimetres long, jagged, and looks quite deep. 'Did you need stitches?'

'A few,' he replies, stepping away and pulling on his cargo pants. I bloody knew it. 'It's not a big deal,' he adds.

'How did it happen?'

'I fell out of a tree.' He looks a bit self-conscious.

'Are you still doing your own stunts?' I ask accusatorily.

'Don't start that again,' he warns.

'I'm serious, Joe! You shouldn't do that! It's dangerous!' My voice has climbed an octave and I hate that I sound whiney, but I can't help it. He hurt himself in Australia, too, when he slipped and fell down a rock face during a thunderstorm. He still has the scars on his ribs to show for it.

'I've always done my own stunts,' he says firmly.

'Yeah, well, that was before you had me around to nag you,' I point out. 'It's not just you that you have to think about anymore,' I add.

'I guess we'll have to add this to our list of things to talk about,' he says meaningfully.

That shuts me up.

He leans forward to give me a quick peck on my lips. 'Don't worry about me. I'll be fine.'

I give him a wry look and then go to the curtains. 'You ready?' I ask.

His brow furrows. 'Yes?' he replies uncertainly, not knowing what I'm going on about.

And then I pull back the curtains.

'Wow,' he says.

The view out of our window is stunning, gently undulating snowy hills reaching for miles. There are no leaves on the trees at the moment, but I can already imagine how beautiful it will be in the spring. I hope he's here to share it with me.

'Come and see downstairs,' I say eagerly.

Home is a large thatched house, dating back to the mid-sixteenth century. It was once a farmhouse and is still set within five acres of land, with barns that have conversion potential should we ever need the extra space. Joe could probably do with a high-tech gym and a kickboxing studio to work out in, keep his famous martial arts skills up-to-scratch. Then again, we could just get a bunch of animals. You know, for fun. Joe would *love* a puppy. I still remember how much he loved his late dog, Dyson. I wonder if I could get him a dog as a Christmas present? I am *so* tempted. Obviously, I'd have to look after it... Hmm, might not be very practical.

Joe's amazed at everything I've managed to do in such a short space of time. But I did have movers and packers to help me, and I have been walking around interior design shops for weeks, using the credit card Joe's PA Melanie sent me. I'm so relieved he likes everything. It's all for him.

We sit at the kitchen bench table and I make him a freshly ground coffee while our croissants are heating up.

'Now, are you sure you can eat these?' I tease, bringing the pastries out of the oven.

He rolls his eyes, but chooses to ignore me. 'What time do you think Jessie and Emily will come over?'

'I don't know. Sometime this afternoon, I imagine.'

'They seem nice,' he comments.

'You were very good with them,' I reply. 'Do you find it weird, people reacting to you like that?'

'It still freaks me out sometimes,' he admits.

'In that case, you're a good actor.'

'Well, thank you.' He smiles at me, then his face becomes thoughtful as he sips his coffee.

'What is it?' I ask.

He reaches for a croissant, trying to play it down. 'Nicky thinks I could be up for an Oscar this year.'

Nicky is his agent. I spoke to him once, years ago, when I tried to track down Joe. I still haven't met him in person.

'No way!' I squeal excitedly. 'For *Magnitude Mile*?'

'Yeah.'

'Well, I'm not surprised. It's the best movie I've ever seen.'

He laughs with embarrassment. I was in LA with him during the summer holidays when it came out. I went to the Hollywood premiere, and it was one of the most surreal moments of my life, walking down the red carpet and hearing people chanting his name. But after that I felt a bit lost, because not only could I not arrive with him, I couldn't even sit next to him. Naturally, I felt incredibly proud of him, but overall it was quite a lonely experience. Not that I told him that.

'Ooh, does that mean you'll get to go to the Oscars?' I ask.

'Yeah.' He tuts. 'At long bloody last.'

His last two films, *Night Fox* and *Phoenix Seven*, were both nominated for various awards last year. People thought it was a travesty that he wasn't nominated for Best Actor for at least one of them, so it seems 'Oscar' might put that right this year.

I feel a sting. How I would love to go with him – actually *with* him – but that would mean letting go of almost everything else in my life.

'So…' he says, and I know exactly what he's going to say.

'No,' I rebuke him. 'I don't want to go public yet.'

He takes a deep breath and exhales loudly. 'Then when?'

'I don't know. I can't stand the thought of losing my privacy – my family's privacy. Imagine how this will affect Mum and Dad?'

'Don't think I haven't worried about that, too.'

'And I have nightmares about your crazed fans hunting me down…'

'We'd have to get you some security—'

'You think I want to have bodyguards following me around?' I interrupt, my voice rising.

He stays silent, brooding.

'And I still love my job,' I add more calmly. 'I don't want to leave it.'

He sighs before speaking. 'I wish you didn't have to go to work this week.'

'Me too.' I manage a laugh. 'I don't love it that much.'

He smiles at me. 'So what does Miss Simmons get for Christmas from her pupils?'

I wince. He clearly doesn't know I'm still using my married name at work. But he's going to find out on Friday when I bring Christmas cards home from the children.

'It's still Mrs Heuber, I'm afraid,' I tell Joe.

'Oh.' He looks away from me, distinctly unimpressed. 'When are you planning on changing it?'

I shift on my seat. 'I don't know. I'm not sure I want to confuse them all halfway through the school year.'

'But you're divorced,' he points out. 'Finally,' he adds under his breath with a touch of sarcasm.

'I'll speak to the head teacher about it,' I promise him.

'What was he like?' Joe swallows and turns to study my face. 'When you saw him?'

I know he's not talking about the head teacher. We're back on the subject of Lukas. 'He was... detached.'

'Did he try to convince you to go back to him?'

'No, actually. No. I don't think he'll do that again.'

God, it was awful. Lukas was so cold, so distant. He informed me very matter-of-factly that he's seeing someone else, a fellow professor at the University of Munich. She's German, and also a physician.

I tell Joe about her. 'He'll be able to discuss metaphysics and quark structures till his heart's content. I could never understand what he was going on about.'

I try to brush it off, but the truth is it hurts to think about Lukas with someone else. Even though I know it shouldn't. Deep down I'm glad he's happy. I just wish he didn't hate me so much.

❄

The next morning it's with a heavy heart that I kiss Joe good-bye. I have to return to school for my last week before we break up for the Christmas holidays. I promise him I'll come home as soon as I can, but he assures me he'll be happy just chilling out in our new home and maybe going for a walk.

When I get home there's a snowman on the front lawn. Joe comes out of the house and stands next to it with his arms crossed, looking very pleased and proud of himself. I crack up laughing.

'You doofus,' I say.

'Don't you like it?' he asks, pretending to be hurt.

'I've seen better,' I joke.

He tuts at me and shakes his head. 'Now you've done it.'

'What?'

He scoops up a handful of snow.

'Don't you dare!' I warn as he packs it into the shape of a ball. 'Right!' I turn to scoop up a handful of my own, but his snowball hits me on my bum as I'm bending over. 'Oi!' I shout, turning around and hurling a ball at him. He ducks and it flies straight past him. Another one comes my way. This time I block it. I chase him, laughing, around the side of the house. But he stops suddenly and comes towards me.

'How was your day?' he asks, his eyes twinkling.

I screw up my nose, but don't let go of my snowball. 'Actually, it was a bit rubbish.'

His face falls. 'Why?'

'Roxy told me something.'

He groans and rolls his eyes. 'Not her again.' He's never met her, but he's not her biggest fan. The feeling, however, is far from mutual. She's a self-confessed Strike Stalker, the person who fills me in on all of the gossip relating to Joe, whether I want her to or not. I never told her that I knew Joe when I was eighteen – it was a subject I kept close to my heart. It still is.

I drop the snowball and dust off my hands. I don't feel like playing anymore.

'What did she say?' he asks warily.

My heart sinks. I have a horrible feeling that Roxy might be onto something with this one. 'It was about Michelle Bleech.'

Joe keeps steady eye contact.

'Is it true that you're going to be starring with her in another film?' I can't keep the hurt from my voice.

He sighs again. This is not good. 'Nicky wants me to, yes.'

'Why didn't you tell me?' My voice sounds small.

He gives me a pointed stare. 'I didn't want to ruin our conversations.'

It's the same argument I used on him.

I turn and walk away from him, my head down.

'Alice!' he calls out. He runs after me and tries to pull me back, but I shake him off.

I hate Michelle Bleech. Okay, so I know there's no truth in the rumours. She and Joe have a very tactile relationship and there's definitely sexual chemistry between them on-screen, but off it there's nothing going on between them. I saw that for myself in Australia.

'Please don't be upset. You know I don't feel anything for her.'

'I thought she was your best mate,' I spit bitterly, jealousy coursing through my veins as I go inside the house.

Joe follows me, his shoulders slumping.

I still remember that argument with Joe very clearly. It was one of our worst. The tabloids had been riddled with rumours about Joe and Michelle's steamy sex scenes. Even my best friend Lizzy had been in touch, asking how I felt. The truth was, I had been feeling sick and humiliated.

Ten months ago...

'I just don't understand why they'd keep printing this stuff if there's no truth in it.'

It's the middle of February and I'm on the phone to Joe. His filming schedule is so tight that we barely have any time to talk, and I hate myself for ruining our first conversation in a week by bringing up my insecurities.

'There is no truth in it,' he reiterates firmly, the satellite phone sounding less crackly for a change. 'She's good fun, we have a laugh, but that's it.'

Every word hits me like a bullet. 'She's good fun, is she? You have a laugh?' I despise how jealous I sound. I was never like this with Lukas. But then Lukas didn't need to have sex with other women. Okay, so I know film sex isn't real sex, and supposedly it's really uncomfortable and anything but titillating for the actors, but *still*.

Joe sighs loudly. 'See, *this* is why actors date actresses.'

My mouth gapes open in shock. 'Did you really just say that to me? Go off and bloody well date her, then!'

'I didn't mean...' he splutters. 'Alice! What's got into you?'

Hot tears prick my eyes.

'Alice?' His voice is quieter, more concerned.

'It's hard, Joe.'

'I know. It's hard for me too, thinking about you still living so close to Lukas,' he says bitterly. 'How's that divorce coming along?'

'He still won't agree to it,' I reply miserably. 'But he will eventually. And at least you don't have to listen to everyone going on about what we're getting up to all the time.'

'Just ignore them!' He raises his voice. 'None of it is true! We think one of the make-up artists is leaking stories to the press. It won't go on for much longer.'

'Leaking stories implies that there actually *is* a story that needs to be leaked!'

'Alice!' he raises his voice. 'There is *nothing* going on between Michelle and me. We're just friends.'

'*Friends?*' I erupt bitterly.

'Yes, friends,' he replies calmly. 'You surely can't have a problem with that?'

I surely can. Stupid, beautiful *cow*.

❄

I storm into the kitchen and flick on the kettle. Joe follows me. 'You and Jessie are friends,' he says calmly. 'I don't give you hell about that.'

'What?' I splutter. 'I've known Jessie for years!'

'So? I lost count of the number of times he hugged you and ruffled your hair yesterday…'

'Please don't tell me you're jealous of *Jessie*!' I interrupt, outraged. 'He's just got married!'

'Yes, and how do you think Emily feels about your touchy-feely relationship?' he asks.

'Don't be ridiculous!' I snap.

Does she mind? Jessie and I have *always* had a very tactile relationship. Okay, so we lost that a bit when Lukas came on the scene, but I've been so happy to be close to him again. I've never even considered that it might bother Emily, but maybe it does. Maybe I need to be more sensitive.

I stand there at the kitchen counter in horrified silence as these thoughts go through my head. The kettle boils and Joe makes me a cup of tea.

'Does it really bother you how Jessie and I are with each other?' I ask, slightly astounded.

'A little bit,' he admits.

'You really are quite a jealous person, aren't you?' I can't keep the surprise from my voice.

'Only when it comes to you,' he replies, flashing me a smile. 'I never used to be.'

'Well, you don't have to fret about me.'

'And please don't fret about *me*,' he begs, pulling me into his arms.

I go willingly, but my heart sinks at the thought of him kissing Michelle Bleech, tongues and all. Suddenly I hate the fact that he is an actor. How the hell am I going to cope when that movie comes out and I have to watch them getting naked and steamy together on the big screen?

'I hate her,' I say in a muffled voice.

He exhales loudly and holds me at arms' length. 'You know, this would all be very different if you and I went public.'

I look up at him.

'Alice, I know you'd be sad to leave your job, but you could try something else?' he says in a pleading voice. 'We could go travelling for a year, spend some proper time together.'

'Travelling?' I say with confusion. 'But what about your filming schedule?'

'I don't have to agree to anything.'

'But won't Nicky be pissed off?'

'Who cares?' he says simply. 'It's not up to him.'

'So you wouldn't do the film? With Michelle?'

'No. Not if you don't want me to.'

My heart soars. 'Really? You would do that for me?'

'Alice,' he says firmly. 'I would do *anything* for you. Remember?'

I do remember. I do remember him telling me that a year ago in Dorset.

'You could still do one film,' I say, thinking for a moment. 'I could definitely cope with that.'

'How about an action film? I've read the script. There's no kissing.'

'Really?' My heart threatens to burst, but I keep myself in check. 'You can't avoid sex scenes forever.'

'I can if I want to.'

I snort with laughter. 'I'll probably get used to them eventually,' I muse aloud. 'But if you could avoid them for the foreseeable future it would be very much appreciated.'

'Done.' He laughs and squeezes me hard. 'Now. What about your job?'

❄

It's with a heavy heart that I go to work on Friday morning. It's the last day of school. My pupils will return after the Christmas break. I sadly, will not. On Tuesday, I told the head teacher of my decision to leave. I explained – to his bewilderment and absolute astonishment – what was going on. I think he was worried I'd lost my mind, that I'd invented a relationship with Joseph Strike the movie star, but I managed to convince him that it was fact, not fiction. He agreed to line up a temporary teacher for the next term. We both knew that we couldn't put the children at risk by allowing me to stay.

I say goodbye to my class with tears in my eyes and a lump in my throat. I know that I will treasure their cards and gifts forever, given to me by the last children I will ever teach. I can't stop crying once I reach my car. I sit there at the steering wheel, sobbing my heart out. A loud knock startles me and I look up to see Roxy standing there, white-faced and anxious. I quickly brush away my tears and wind down the window.

'What's wrong?' she asks with horror.

'I... I...' I can't tell her. Not yet. Not until it's official. 'It's personal,' I manage to say.

'Oh, okay then,' she replies, a little put out. We're really only colleagues – we've never spent time together outside of work. I'm not sure I can trust her with this.

I take a deep, shaky breath. 'I'm not coming back after the holidays,' I tell her.

'Why not?' she gasps.

'I can't go into details right now,' I manage to say, reaching for a pen and a piece of paper. 'But will you call me in the New Year? We could go out for a drink?'

'That would be great,' she says warmly, taking the note with my telephone number on it.

I sniff loudly and smile up at her. 'Have a good Christmas.'

'You too,' she replies, patting me on my arm. 'Drive carefully!' she calls after me.

What I wouldn't give to be a fly on the wall when the news of my relationship with Joe breaks... She'll want to kill me for not telling her beforehand. But I'll introduce her to him one day to make up for it.

My parents are coming to spend Christmas with us. They still haven't met Joe in person. Well, not since he became famous, and not in the last year since we found each other again. They knew him over ten years ago when I fell head over heels in love with him. I still remember coming home from Dorset on New Year's Day almost a year ago. I had just said goodbye to Joe at the train station in Dorset after Lukas had discovered us at the cottage. I felt like my train was travelling at light-speed as it raced me back to London. I didn't want to go home, to have to explain to my parents and Lukas what had been going on. But it was something I knew I needed to do.

Just under a year ago...

The hall light is on, but I can't tell if my parents are in when I heave my bags up to the white-painted-brick terraced house where I grew up in East Finchley, north London. It's six o'clock in the evening, but it's the middle of winter – New Year's Day, in fact – and the sun sank a couple of hours ago. I scan the streetlamp-lit road with my heart in my throat to see if Lukas's silver Porsche is parked up somewhere, but it's nowhere to be seen. I don't know if he's still in the UK or if he's gone back to Germany. The thought of trying to track him down there... Of returning to the country house belonging to his cold mother and father... I'm filled with fear. I need to find him. But first I need to face my parents. I know from the voicemail messages I forced myself to listen to on the train that they've been worried sick.

I put my key in the lock and turn it, pushing the door open. At the far end of the long corridor is the kitchen and, right at the end, eating their dinner at the little white table, are my parents. They meet my eyes with shock in theirs. My mother's mouth falls open and then they're on their feet and rushing towards me.

'Alice!' my dad shouts.

'Where on earth have you been?' Mum shrieks, pushing past him to get to me.

I drop my bags with a thud onto the wooden floorboards as she reaches me. She checks my face with her hands to see if I'm unharmed, and comes away, finding nothing.

'I'm sorry, I...'

My voice trails off. This is going to be the first of a very long line of apologies.

Where do I start?

'Why did you lie about being in Germany with Lukas?' Dad asks accusingly. 'We were out of our minds with worry when Lukas turned up looking for you! He said you told him you were staying with us!'

'Shall we go back to the table?' I suggest. I know I've interrupted their dinner.

'No, no, I've lost my appetite,' Mum hastily replies, pushing me into the living room. My dad looks a bit grumpy as he follows. Thank goodness for microwaves – he can reheat his food later.

'Where have you been?' Mum repeats her question the moment we're sitting down.

'Dorset,' I reply, averting my gaze.

'Did you go to see Joe?' she continues.

At least they know that much. I nod. 'Yes.'

'Bloomin' heck,' Dad mumbles. 'After all these years. How on earth did you find him?'

'Didn't Lukas tell you anything?' I ask warily.

'No, he stormed in here looking for you, asking if we had any clues as to where you might be. Then we remembered you'd mentioned the cottage and before we knew it he was gone. We guessed afterwards that this might be about Joe.'

'Why didn't you call us?' Mum asks.

'I'm sorry. I had my phone switched off. I didn't want to be contacted.'

'We've been worried sick!'

'I'm sorry.'

'Tell us what happened,' Dad interrupts. 'Did you see Joe? What was he like?'

'He… He's the same. Only different. He…' I try to explain. 'He looks just like he does when he's on the telly—' They won't have seen his films; they don't go to the cinema much.

'On the telly?' Dad interrupts.

With disbelief, I stare at their faces.

And then it dawns on me. They still don't know. They still don't know who he's become. Lukas didn't even tell them that. Why would he? Wasn't his pain enough to deal with, without adding a heavy dose of humiliation?

I find my voice. 'You know he's not Joe Strickwold anymore, right?'

Bewildered, Dad sits back in his seat. 'Who the hell is he, then?'

'Joseph Strike.'

My eyes flit between them as confusion, recognition and finally shock register on their faces.

'Joseph Strike?' Mum asks, her voice unsure.

'The actor?' Dad double-checks.

I nod, but figuring they'll want firmer confirmation than that, I reply, 'Yes, that's him. The Joe I met in Dorset is now Joseph Strike, the movie star.'

Both of them slump back in their seats, utterly flabbergasted.

'You did tell him to go and make something of himself,' I find myself muttering.

❄

'They're here!' Joe shouts from the living room. He's been looking out the window, waiting for my parents to arrive. I go to press the buzzer for the gate to let them in. Joe joins me in the hall. I realise he's shaking slightly.

'It's okay,' I say tenderly, touching Joe's arm.

'I'm freaking out,' he replies.

'Don't.'

He flashes me a look. 'This is your dad we're talking about.'

'Things are very, very different now,' I remind him, opening up the door. I take Joe's hand and lead him outside. As my dad drives the car into the driveway, I catch sight of him and Mum. They look like rabbits caught in the headlights.

They climb out of the car simultaneously, but I choose to get the Dad part out of the way first. I jog towards the car and throw my arms around his neck.

'Hi, Dad.'

'Hello!' he exclaims.

I turn and beckon Joe forward. 'Dad, you remember Joe.'

'Er, yes, of course.'

'Hello, Mr Simmons,' Joe says quietly, stepping forward to shake his hand.

'Jim and Marie, *please*,' Dad insists. Even back in the day, Joe referred to them by their first names. It's funny to think of him feeling all formal now.

'Jim,' Joe repeats shyly with a smile.

I drag him away to the other side of the car, where Mum is trying to busy herself so she doesn't stare at the great big elephant on the driveway.

'Hello!' she says, looking all flustered.

'It's nice to see you again,' Joe says genuinely. She was always kind to him.

'Come inside for a drink,' I urge. They'll chill out after a few sherries, I'm sure.

'Let me help you get your bags in from the car,' I hear Joe say. I lead Mum towards the front door, but she pauses for a moment to look up at the house.

'Alice, this is beautiful.'

I beam widely.

'Does Joe like it?'

'He loves it,' I tell her, looking back at him as he carries a suitcase across the drive with such ease that it looks like it must only weigh a few kilos. It still amazes me how fit he is. He did fifty press-ups this morning without even breaking a sweat.

'What do you think, Jim?' my mum asks.

'Truly special,' Dad replies, shaking his head with amazement. 'How old did you say it is?' he asks.

'Mid-sixteenth century,' I reply. 'Come and see inside,' I urge.

Joe and I take them on a quick tour before settling ourselves on comfortable sofas in the living room. The room is vast with old stone floors, but it still manages to feel quite snug thanks to its low Tudor ceiling beams, enormous fireplace and cosy rugs. As Joe puts two more logs on the fire, I glance down at the rug he's standing on. We christened it last week, and repeated the experience last night. My cheeks heat up as I remember what he did to me there. Joe gives me a quizzical look as he returns to the sofa. I can't believe I'm thinking these dirty thoughts in front of my parents!

As the evening wears on, Joe becomes more and more chilled out. I think my parents' initial discomfort put him strangely at ease, and in turn, they begin to relax, too. So much so that they quite happily quiz him about what it's like being a big Hollywood star.

'I read something in the papers last week about your new film,' Mum says as we sit around the big oak dining table. 'You're going to be teaming up with Michelle Bleech again?'

I tried to play down my dislike for the actress earlier on this year, but I'm still a bit taken aback that my mum is mentioning her over dinner.

'No,' Joe says firmly, shaking his head.

I glance at him. 'That's not definite though, is it?'

I mean, I know he told me he wouldn't take the part, but if his agent is going to put pressure on him...

'It absolutely is,' he replies, giving me a look. 'I told you I wouldn't take it.'

'What if Nicky insists?' I'm aware that my parents are watching this exchange with enormous interest, but I can't not pursue an answer now that we're back on the subject.

Joe laughs. 'He can insist all he wants, but what I do is my business. And yours,' he adds, reaching across the table and squeezing my hand. He turns back to my parents. 'I'm going to take some time off this year so Alice and I can be together more. This last year has been a bit crazy.'

I take a deep breath. 'I'm not going back to work in the New Year,' I blurt out.

'What?' my dad splutters.

'Why not?' Mum asks with alarm.

'We've decided to make our relationship public. We imagine it will be quite big news. I can't put the school or my pupils at risk.'

'But what about your job? Your salary?' Mum asks, flashing my dad a concerned look.

'I'll look after Alice,' Joe interjects.

'Yes, but…' Dad's voice trails off, but he looks disapproving.

'She'll never want for anything,' Joe adds, staring across the table at me. His voice is quiet, but strong. 'I'm never going to let her go, ever again.'

I squeeze his hand. And considering our past, how Dad insisted Joe leave me ten years ago, my parents remain respectfully silent.

❄

It's Christmas Day, and when Mum and Dad are snuggled up in front of the fire watching an old movie on telly and sipping their sherries, I take Joe to one side.

'I have one more Christmas present for you,' I say to him.

He raises one eyebrow. 'I have another one for you, too,' he says in a low voice, 'but it's not really appropriate to give it to you in front of your parents.'

I whack him on his arm and try not to giggle. He grins at me.

'How do you fancy coming into Cambridge with me?' I ask him.

His eyes light up. 'I'd love to.'

'It shouldn't be too busy, with it being Christmas Day. I thought I might take you punting.'

His face breaks into a grin. 'Could this day get any better?'

'Wait until you see if I can remember how to do it.'

'I have faith in you,' he replies.

❄

Last week after work I popped by to see my old boss at the Silver Street punting station. He agreed to let me borrow a set of keys so I could unlock one of the punts, as they're not open on Christmas Day.

We drive into the city and park on West Street, which is deserted. I take Joe across the road and there in front of us behind a field dotted with speckled brown cows is King's College Chapel, Cambridge's most famous landmark.

'Whoa,' Joe says, staring at it in the not-too-far-off distance. The snow has mostly melted and there are blue skies today, so the sun lights up the roof of the chapel in a spectacular fashion. It's a perfect day for the river.

It's still freezing cold, though, so we've wrapped-up warm. Joe is wearing a beanie hat, but I worry it's not much of a disguise. I'm hanging on for dear life to these last few days of anonymity – we've decided to put out a press release in the New Year. It's for this reason that I'm choosing to take Joe on a proper tour of the Backs – the backs of the colleges – rather than upriver towards Grantchester where it's quieter. This might be the one and only time that we can do it. I wonder if I can still remember my script.

Joe settles himself into the low seat facing me, while I stand on the back of the punt. Familiarity floods me as I let the pole slide through my fingers and hit the river bottom below. I push away and we're on the move. We pass under Silver Street Bridge and the words come back to me in a flood.

'The Mathematical Bridge is the only wooden bridge on the Backs,' I adopt a professional guise as I relay this to Joe with a playful smile. 'Popular fable is that the bridge was designed and built by Sir Isaac Newton without the use of nuts or bolts, and at some point in the past, students or fellows attempted to take the bridge apart and put it back together. But they couldn't, and had to resort to fastening the bridge with nuts and bolts. This story is false: the bridge was built out of oak in 1749 by James Essex the Younger to the design of the master carpenter William Etheridge, 22 years after Newton died. The bridge you see today is a replica of the original bridge. It was rebuilt using teak in 1905.' My memory serves me well. I'm pleased.

Joe nods with amusement. 'Hmm. Interesting.'

We pass Queen's College, Clare College, King's College and Trinity Hall, and then finally we're on the approach to Trinity. I open my mouth to regale Joe with tales about Cambridge's wealthiest college. I want to tell him how some people say – completely untruthfully – that you can walk all the way from Cambridge to Oxford on land owned by Trinity. But words fail me. All I can see is the place on the bridge where Lukas used to sit, reading his study books. It was on the bank there that he once helped me when I bashed my head on the underside of the bridge and nearly knocked myself out, much to the hilarity of my colleagues. It feels wrong to tell Joe about Trinity, to *joke* about Trinity. Trinity – and Lukas – will always have a special place in my heart, whether I want them to or not.

Joe, who has been looking up at me with delight, realises that something is wrong. But to his credit, he turns his attention to the other side of the river and lets me be.

We pass under the bridge and I try to swallow the lump in my throat as I point at the Wren Library.

'It has some original *Winnie the Pooh* manuscripts,' I blurt out. I used to be able to say this far more eloquently.

'Fucking ace,' Joe says to make me giggle. It works. I take a deep breath and nod towards St John's on the other side of the river, continuing the tour in full.

'Do you want to have a turn?' I ask him after we've passed under the Bridge of Sighs. We're almost at the Magdalene Bridge punting station.

He hesitates before making to stand up. 'Sure, why not?'

I carefully step down from the back of the boat and we swap positions. He follows my directions as I say them out loud. 'Stand sideways to the edge, looking forward. Bring the pole up until it's almost clear of the water. Keep it vertical!' I tell him. 'Now, shift your weight over your front leg and let the pole drop through your fingers until it hits the bottom.'

He pushes along naturally.

'Let the pole float up and use it as a rudder,' I direct him. 'You're doing really well!' I say with glee after a minute or so.

He flashes me a grin, but he's trying hard to concentrate.

'Did you like the tour?' I ask, relaxing slightly now that I can see he's got the hang of it. Much quicker than I ever did, that's for sure. But I knew that he would.

'Loved it,' he tells me. 'I can't get over the history of this place – and the fact that you still remember it all! It's awesome. No wonder you wanted to stay.'

'I love living here,' I admit.

'Would you ever want to move to Dorset?' he asks casually.

I cock my head to one side. 'I've never really thought about it. I'd like to spend more time there, for sure. It would be nice to go there for part of the summer holidays again.'

We went there in the summer half term last year, after

he'd returned from Australia. Things hadn't been brilliant when I'd left him at Easter in the freakishly stunning hands of Michelle Bleech, and then there was that interaction with Lukas at my house, when I had to admit to myself that I still loved him. My next few satellite conversations with Joe had been tense. We agreed to meet in Dorset after he'd finished filming, just for a week to get away from it all. And it had been bliss. Just what we'd needed.

'So you think Dorset would be a good place for us to get a holiday cottage, then?' he asks, glancing down at me as he lets the pole slip through his fingers once more and rhythmically pushes away.

I screw up my nose. 'I think I'd miss *our* cottage if we bought another one.'

He grins. 'I hoped you'd say that.'

'Why?' I'm confused.

'I bought *our* cottage. For you.'

'*What?*' If I were still standing up on the back of the boat, I think I would have fallen into the river. 'But I thought the owners didn't want to sell?' I called them a year ago to ask.

'They didn't,' he replies nonchalantly. 'But I got my lawyers involved like you suggested, and it appears they could be convinced after all.'

I abruptly close my mouth.

'Happy Christmas,' he adds with a grin that warms the cockles of my heart.

'I really want to hug you right now,' I say.

'Come on, then.' He opens up his arms to me and I get to my feet, gingerly stepping onto the back of the boat. We wobble slightly as we embrace, but it's the happiest I've felt, possibly ever.

'Do I get a Christmas kiss?' he asks me with a twinkle in his eye.

'You'll get more than that later,' I promise, tilting my face up to him.

We break apart, slightly out of breath.

'I love you,' he murmurs. 'Thank you for giving me the best Christmas day I could ever have wished for.'

'I nearly bought you a puppy,' I tell him with a cheeky grin.

'No way!' he cries.

'I figured it wasn't the right time, though. A dog is for life and not just for Christmas, and all that.'

His face falls. 'You're probably right.'

'But we'll get a dog one day. Won't we?'

He grins again. 'Absolutely. Maybe once we're married and have a houseful of kids.'

'Marriage *and* kids, hey?'

He frowns. 'Of course.'

I beam up at him and he kisses me again.

I see them out of the corner of my eye as Joe lets me go, the three teenage girls on the bridge. I freeze, feeling Joe's confusion as he witnesses my reaction, and then he follows the line of my vision just in time to hear their screams.

'It IS him! It's JOSEPH STRIKE!'

'AAARRRRGGGGHHHHHH! JOSEPH STRIKE!'

'IT'S JOSEPH STRIKE!'

Joe's grip on me tightens as he holds me to him. More people appear on the bridge, keen to see if the girls, who are pointing and jumping around like lunatics, are right. The look on their faces when they recognise Joe… It's almost comical. But then I see some camera phones come out and I can't help but give Joe a panicked look.

'It's okay,' he says calmly, rubbing my arm. 'It's going to be okay.'

I take a deep breath and look up into his eyes, which are somehow smiling now. 'Are you ready for this?' he asks with a raised eyebrow.

'As I'll ever be.'

And then he takes my face in his hands and kisses me, while camera flashes go off over our heads.

Johnny's Girl

I probably hear from my readers about Meg and Johnny more than any other characters I've created, so it may surprise some of you to know that Johnny Be Good *is my lowest-selling adult title. It didn't make much commercial sense to write the sequel* Baby Be Mine, *but I'm lucky to have an editor who encourages me to follow my heart, allowing me the creative freedom to really enjoy my career – hopefully, this comes across in my writing.*

The idea for my young adult series about fifteen-year-old Jessie sprung from something Meg says in Baby Be Mine: *that, considering the number of women Johnny had slept with in the past, it wouldn't surprise her if he had more children out there that he didn't know about.*

Johnny's Girl *is a short story that bridges the gap between* Baby Be Mine *and* The Accidental Life of Jessie Jefferson, *which is told from Johnny's daughter's point of view.*

I loved being inside Jessie's head – it didn't make any difference to me that she's a teenager. The only thing I found slightly weird is that, even writing as Jessie, I myself still fancied Johnny. Er, he's her dad!

But I'm getting ahead of myself. We're still with Meg for Johnny's Girl *– take it away, Nutmeg…*

His kisses start at my ankles and trail all the way up my legs, over my back and up to my neck.

'Mmm,' I murmur sleepily, rolling over and coming face to face with him. His green eyes are piercing in the morning sunlight spilling through the floor-to-ceiling windows. He kisses me slowly, deeply, and I feel that very familiar and *very* delicious spark of desire as he settles over me, his tanned, toned arms trapping me and keeping me exactly where he wants me.

Which is exactly where *I* want to be.

'I love you,' he says in a low voice, pulling away and staring at me seriously.

'The feeling is very much mutual,' I reply with a smile.

And then he's kissing me again.

What a lovely, lovely way to wake up.

Johnny is brushing his teeth when I come out of the shower. I dry myself off and he spanks my bum as I join him at the sink.

'Oi!' I laugh, wrapping my arms around him from behind and staring at his slightly fogged-up reflection. He rinses his mouth out and turns around to face me, wearing nothing

more than a pair of white boxer shorts and his tattoos, which
decorate his arms and part of his torso. I glance down at the
small one that he had done recently on his left pec, in swirly
black writing: *Nutmeg.*

Nutmeg is the nickname he gave me when we first met.

I run my fingertips across it with amusement.

'I still can't believe you did that.'

He strokes his thumb down my jaw, tenderly. 'You are a
part of me,' he says gently. 'And now,' he adds with a grin,
spanking my bum again, 'you will *always* be a part of me.'

I giggle and slap his stomach, then I go and pull my blue,
orange and pink block-coloured maxi dress out of my suitcase. Possibly for the first time in my life, I didn't want to
waste time by unpacking.

'Do you have to wear that?' Johnny asks, wandering out
of the bathroom.

My face falls. 'Don't you like it?'

'I prefer you naked,' he replies with a twinkle in his eye.

I tut good-naturedly and get dressed. 'Well, I'm hungry.
And sadly, you haven't brought me to a nudist resort.'

'Damn. That idea didn't even occur to me.'

I grab a rolled-up T-shirt out from the suitcase and chuck
it to him. He catches it and pulls it over his head, accepting
my clothing choice without a second thought.

God, I love being married to this man.

'What are you smiling about?' he asks me with a raised eyebrow.

'I love being married to you,' I tell him softly.

'The feeling is very much mutual,' he repeats my earlier
phrase with a smile. 'Now throw me my jeans, Wife.'

❄

One year and four months ago, I married the love of my life: rock star Johnny Jefferson. I fell for him when I worked for him as his personal assistant. He was a nightmare back then – a proper bad boy: womaniser, drink and drug problems… Urgh, I still hate thinking about it. But, allegedly, he fell for me, too, even though he struggled to show it at times.

Well, that's a bit of an understatement.

I thought I'd made the biggest mistake of my life when I fell pregnant. These days I can't believe I ever regretted it, because we have Barney – our beautiful blond-haired, green-eyed boy.

And of course, now we also have an eight-month-old baby, Phoenix. But he arrived after marriage. Just. I'm pretty damn fertile, as it turns out.

We have left our two gorgeous boys with my parents in a beach house in Malibu for one night – which is the longest Johnny could persuade me to get away. I know they'll be safe and sound – I miss them, but Johnny and I needed this break together.

I'm back in America for the first time since leaving it two and a half years ago. Johnny has had to come back and forth for work recently, but he's kept his trips short and sweet. He always asks me to join him, but Phoenix has been so young. That's the excuse I've used, at least, but Johnny knows the real reason. The truth is, I've been in no hurry to return to this country after the way I left it. Too many bad memories. They still haunt me.

✳

'Why don't we have breakfast here?' Johnny asks suddenly.

'Oh, I didn't think of that.' I just assumed we'd walk to the restaurant. 'Do you think it's too late?'

'I'll call them,' he replies casually, wandering over to the desk phone.

Silly me. This is Johnny Jefferson we're talking about. He always gets what he wants.

In the end.

Yep, he got me too, eventually. But I made him work for it.

I slide the glass door open and step out onto the private deck, which is suspended over the grass-carpeted cliffs below. The ocean stretches out before me, cool and deep blue underneath a pale-blue, cloudless sky. I sit down on a sun-lounger and pull up the hem of my dress, letting the warm morning sun soak into my legs. It's been a bitterly cold winter back in England. It feels like it's gone on and on and on. It was pouring with rain when we left – absolutely bloody miserable.

I take a deep breath of the cool spring air and slowly exhale. We're in Big Sur at my favourite resort of all time, the Post Ranch Inn. I came here for the first time with Johnny when I had only recently started as his PA. I stayed in a Tree House then, with views of trees and the Santa Lucia mountains beyond, while Johnny stayed in an Ocean House. Now we're in a Cliff House, with a secluded terrace and our own private spa tub. I glance at it now and smirk as I remember how... er... *hot,* we got in there last night.

We flew here by helicopter yesterday morning. Johnny usually prefers to drive the mountain roads, but he doesn't have any of his supercars in America anymore, and anyway, we didn't want to use up our time travelling when we're only here for such a short stay.

My parents have been wanting to come to America for years, so they jumped at the chance when Johnny offered to fly them over from the South of France for a three-week holiday in return for babysitting the kids for a couple of days. We had to put it to them like that, otherwise they would have felt as though they were taking advantage of his generosity. They still offered to pay for their own flights, but Johnny wouldn't hear of it.

'Drop in the ocean, Nutmeg, drop in the ocean.'

He teases me with this catchphrase anytime I think twice about buying anything.

❋

'All sorted,' Johnny says as he steps out onto the deck behind me.

'Cool, well done,' I reply.

He touches my cheek and then comes to sit on the sun-lounger next to me. Raking his hand through his dirty-blond hair, he looks out through the glass surrounding the deck at the water beyond.

I smile at him. 'Nice, eh?'

He keeps his eyes on the view. 'Not bad.'

'You alright?' I ask, sensing his thoughtful mood.

He glances across at me and narrows his eyes. 'Don't you miss it?'

'What? Big Sur?'

He shrugs. 'Yeah. LA. America. The weather.'

'No...' I reply hesitantly. 'I mean, I love *this*...' I indicate our surroundings and the sunshine. 'But, I don't know...' My lips turn down. 'It *has* been nice coming back,' I say carefully. 'It's been better.' I flash him a small smile and he looks momentarily pained, but then he leans across and presses a kiss to my temple.

'I love you,' he says, staring into my brown eyes.

'I know,' I reply with a wry grin.

'Come here.' He tugs on my arm and pulls me on top of him. He pushes my light-blonde hair off my face and cups my face with his rough fingers, which are calloused from years of playing his guitar. 'Happy anniversary,' he murmurs.

'Happy anniversary,' I reply with a smile.

We couldn't get away for our actual anniversary because Phoenix was still so small. This is our belated celebration, and it was worth waiting for.

'You make me so happy,' he says. My insides swell with happiness and contentment and I slide down a little so I can lay my face against his chest. His strong arms encircle me and I bask in his warmth.

The feeling, as we keep saying, is very much mutual.

After breakfast, we go for a wander through a forest of enormous redwood pines soaring over our heads. The last time I was in this forest, I gave myself a hot flush imagining Johnny and I together. I come clean to him about this now.

'Did you?' he asks with a flirtatiously raised eyebrow, pausing for a moment and leaning back against a huge tree trunk. It's dark and quiet in here, the only noise coming from birds singing in the high tree tops. He takes my hands and pulls me closer.

'I remember you going for that walk, actually. I thought about coming to find you.'

'You didn't?'

He nods, seriously. 'I did. After that night in the hot tub…' His voice is deep and sexy. 'I wanted you.'

Even now, even after all this time, I blush at his intonation.

'You should have come to get me,' I tell him.

'I thought you were into Christian,' he replies, and it

have sex three times a day occasionally. Sometimes more.'

'Not straight after Phoenix was born,' I correct him. 'And not when you're away.'

'Phone sex doesn't count?' he asks hopefully.

'No,' I tell him firmly. 'Let's call it once a day on average.'

'That's being extremely cautious.' He stares back at his fingers, then looks back up at me with confusion. 'I'm not good at maths.'

I laugh out loud.

'Bollocks,' he mutters.

'We must've had sex well over seven hundred times,' I chip in, waiting for his response.

'Erm…'

'Have you slept with more than seven hundred groupies?' I ask with surprise.

His brow furrows and he looks away from me. 'No, I don't think so.'

'Don't lie to me,' I warn, all humour gone from my voice.

'I am *not* lying to you,' he says seriously, firmly. 'I'm *thinking*. And I don't *think* I've slept with that many women. *Seriously*,' he stresses. 'But I can't be completely sure,' he adds, his shoulders slumping. I know that he's telling me the truth.

'Sorry,' I say, feeling bad about letting my green-eyed monster take over again.

'Never apologise,' he mutters, taking me in his arms and holding me tightly. 'I love you,' he says into my hair.

I bury my face in his neck and kiss him there. He pulls away and kisses me again, and I don't stop him even when we become more passionate. But I'm not quite ready to 'live dangerously', as he put it, so we reluctantly break away from each other and walk hand-in-hand through a field full of wildflowers back to the privacy of our cliffside room.

❋

'Look! There they are!' I cry gleefully as I peer out of the helicopter window at the small figures of Mum, Dad, Barney and Phoenix below. They're standing on the front garden near the swimming pool and Mum is holding Phoenix in her arms, pointing up at the helicopter as it flies in to land on the roof of the Malibu beach house we've hired for this holiday. Barney is jumping up and down on the spot, waving like a little lunatic. I am so excited to see them again. I'm out of my seatbelt well before the rotor stops moving.

'Hang on a sec.' Johnny puts his hand on my arm. He's happy to see the boys too, but I don't think he would have minded if we'd stayed away for another day. As for me, much as I loved my precious time alone with my husband, I wanted to be back to put our children to bed. Phoenix is not even nine months old and I'm still doing the last feed of the day. I missed our ritual last night, even though Johnny did his best to keep my mind occupied with *other* things... Hmm, I'm thinking maybe we should get a hot tub of our own.

As soon as I'm allowed, I climb out of the helicopter and run down the roof steps to the front lawn where my parents and children are waiting.

'Mummy!' Barney shouts, waving around a tube of M&Ms with a little battery operated fan at the top. 'Look what Grandma bought me!'

'Wow! That's amazing!' I exclaim, raising one eyebrow at my mum. She looks guilty. 'It had a helicopter on the top,' she says defensively. 'Like the one Mummy and Daddy went away in.' She has a tendency to spoil him with treats, whereas I try to steer clear of too much sugar. For Barney, not me. I've got a ridiculously sweet tooth. Yep, I stick by my double standards.

I sweep him up into my arms and give his little body a big squeezy hug, then I pass him to Johnny who has just appeared behind me.

'Hey, buddy!' he says, while I take Phoenix. He's blond with brown eyes, like me, and he has an exceptionally toothy smile. Exceptional, because there's just the one tooth at the moment. I tickle him under his chin and he giggles up at me. They're both wearing their PJs and are ready for bed.

'How was it?' I ask Mum and Dad as we wander back inside.

'They were as good as gold,' Mum says.

'Fine,' Dad replies nonchalantly.

'Did you have a good time?' Mum asks us both.

My face breaks into a grin and I look up at Johnny and smile. 'Yeah, it was great.'

'Thanks,' Johnny says meaningfully to them both.

'Anytime,' Mum replies, patting him on his arm.

We wander back inside. The three-storey, cube-like house is on stilts overlooking a sandy beach and the Pacific Ocean beyond. It's styled like a beach house – despite its size suggesting it's more of a beach mansion – with painted white weatherboarded ceilings and sanded floors with cream-coloured shaggy rugs underfoot. The outdoor deck is modern with a fantastic view, but inside it's a little bit twee, and not really to Johnny's minimalist taste. But it's secluded and safe, and it counts dozens of other A-list celebrities as neighbours. The price for renting it reflects that. Ouch.

'*Drop in the ocean, Nutmeg, drop in the ocean…*'

We sit in the living room on huge, comfy light-grey sofas dotted with dozens of muted-coloured cushions and catch up on the last thirty-six or so hours. After a while, Phoenix starts to grizzle – it's well past his and Barney's bedtime – so Johnny and I excuse ourselves and take the boys up to their bedrooms. Johnny goes next door with Barney to read him a story, while I feed Phoenix in an armchair overlooking the ocean, listening to the low murmur of Johnny's voice next door. After a while, Phoenix falls asleep, exhausted. I hear Johnny come out of Barney's room, just as I'm laying my baby boy into his cot.

'Okay?' Johnny whispers from the doorway.

I nod my reply.

I step out of the room and join him in the wide corridor as he takes me in his arms. This first year with Phoenix has been a very different experience to the first year I had with Barney. That year was full of uncertainty and fear. I loved being a mother, but I was living in doubt. I didn't know if Barney was Christian's or Johnny's. I was *with* Christian – I hadn't seen Johnny since I fell pregnant. And when I found out that I was, I hoped the baby would be Christian's, a good, kind man who wasn't into drink, drugs and shagging around. But months after Barney's birth, my son started to resemble his rock star father, and I found myself living in a nightmare, knowing that the truth would destroy Christian – and hurt my baby. I didn't think Johnny would step up to the plate and become a father. But when the truth came out, he did. And devastating as it was for Christian, over the next year we found a way to be a part of each other's lives again as friends. Now Barney calls him Uncle Christian, and I thank my lucky stars each and every day that he found a way to forgive me – and Johnny. But I still haven't forgiven myself. I don't think I ever will. As mistakes go, this one is hard to top.

❄

Johnny pulls away and looks down at me. 'I'm so glad you're here. I hate being away from you.'

'We'll be able to travel with you a bit more now. It'll be easier,' I promise, staring up at him earnestly.

'I've gotta go in for a meeting tomorrow,' he says. It's with the execs at his record label. 'Do you want to hitch a lift and go shopping while your parents are still here to help out?'

I look thoughtful. 'Actually, Mum might be up for having a look around, too.'

'I was going to take the bike,' he says.

'Oh!' I laugh lightly. 'Fair enough. No, I don't think Mum would be up for squeezing on the back of that.'

Johnny still keeps his Ducati motorcycle in LA. He uses it when he's here.

'I'll organise a car for you,' he says with a shrug.

My instinct is to tell him that I'll sort it, but I zip my lips.

We have a PA in Henley, where we live. Her name is Marla, but she's a mum of three and she only works part-time. I still sort of feel that it's my job to look after Johnny, even though I haven't been able to do as much of that as I would have liked, recently. Anyway, Marla's on holiday with her family while we're here, so Johnny has been trying to help out with organisational stuff. That's another indication of how much he's changed in the last couple of years. He used to be a right selfish git.

'But I do want to get you on the back of my bike again soon,' he warns.

I feel apprehensive. 'Let me talk to Mum first. She might prefer to hang here.'

As it turns out, Mum does want to stay home.

'Go with Johnny! Your father and I will have plenty of time for shopping when we leave you.' They're heading to Las Vegas in a few days, and from there onto the Grand Canyon. 'You should have stayed in Big Sur for longer. I haven't seen anywhere near enough of my grandchildren recently,' she complains good-naturedly.

'Okay, if you're sure.'

'I won't organise a car, then,' Johnny chips in cheerfully.

❋

I'm nervous the next morning as I kiss the kids goodbye and go outside to the garage at the front of the property. My nerves intensify when I hear the loud roar of the Ducati engine as it fires up. I haven't been on the back of Johnny's bike for so long. Not since I left LA the first time.

'Here,' he says loudly over the engine noise, passing me the shiny, black helmet that was resting on the seat behind him. He nods to the bench-top nearby, where I see a brown leather jacket and gloves.

'Where did you get these from?' I shout with a frown.

'I keep them in storage!'

'Who for?'

'For you!' he shouts back, shrugging his frustration at me. As long as they weren't for anybody else...

I pull on the jacket and can smell the leather even over the fumes coming from the exhaust pipe. I screw up my nose and Johnny takes the hint, turning the ignition off.

'Thank you,' I say pointedly.

'Don't look so excited,' he replies with a grin.

'Are you sure you want to do this?' I ask.

'Get your arse over here,' he responds firmly.

I've become a bit of a wuss since the kids were born. I'm not sure I'm going to be able to handle this.

I zip up the jacket and hesitantly walk over to him, putting on the gloves as I go. He picks up the helmet and pulls it over my head, fastening it up.

'I won't go too fast,' he promises, his green eyes twinkling.

He flips his visor down to obscure his face and then does the same to mine, patting the seat behind him. I put my foot on the footrest and swing my leg over the back of the bike, clutching onto him for dear life as he restarts the ignition and drives out of the garage.

The first five minutes are absolutely terrifying. After that, I begin to relax and enjoy myself. I remember this feeling, actually. This feeling of freedom, of being able to go straight to the front of the queue of cars waiting at the traffic lights, and be the first off the mark as we leave them in our wake. Johnny used to easily escape the paparazzi this way. I can understand how much he loves to ride.

Being with him now, I remember how much I used to love riding *with* him. It makes me feel young again.

I laugh inwardly. I'm only thirty for crying out loud. But this is making me feel nostalgic for a time before I had to grow up and become responsible for two little lives. Not that I'd change a thing.

❄

Last night I called my friend Kitty to see if she was free to catch up for lunch. I don't need to go shopping. I haven't seen Kitty in person since our wedding, but we Skype fairly regularly. We became pals when I first started working for Johnny. She was also a CPA – Celebrity Personal Assistant – although she no longer works for actor Rod Freemantle. After quitting, she took a year off and went travelling, and when she returned, Rod helped her to get a job in the film industry. Now she works in PR for one of the Hollywood studios.

'I'll pick you up in a couple of hours,' Johnny promises, dropping me at the curb-side. 'I'll call when I'm setting off.'

'Cool, thanks. Have a good meeting.'

'See you in a bit.' He flips his visor down and zooms away from me. It's only when he's turned the corner that I realise my heart is fluttering. He still gives me butterflies. I take my helmet off and shake out my shoulder-length hair, then I turn and walk up the few steps into the white picketed enclosure that is The Ivy.

The waiter seats me outside at a table for four on the terrace underneath a white umbrella. I'm tempted to put it down so I can feel the sun on my skin, but I don't want to cause a fuss. I order a mineral water and pull out my Kindle, enjoying a rare bit of me-time as I wait for my friend.

'Are you Meg Jefferson?' I hear a slightly breathless voice ask.

I turn around, half expecting to see one of Johnny's potentially demented fans. I burst into laughter when I come face to face with Kitty.

I get up and throw my arms around her. She's wearing a horizontal-striped black and bronze mini dress with long sleeves, and purple slingbacks on her feet.

'You look amazing!' I exclaim. 'I love your dress.'

'Thanks!'

'Don't comment on what I'm wearing,' I tell her hurriedly. I feel completely underdressed in my black skinny jeans, T-shirt and trainers. My helmet is on the seat next to me, the jacket slung over the seat back. 'I had to dress appropriately for Mr Ducati,' I reveal.

'Did you come by bike?' she asks gleefully, pulling out a wrought iron chair and joining me at the table. She used to have a bit of a crush on Johnny. I presume she's over it now.

'I had no choice.'

'Great table, by the way.'

The maître d' knew who I was. 'I think he thought Johnny would be joining me,' I whisper.

She laughs. 'So when did you arrive?'

'Friday, but we went straight up to Big Sur on Saturday morning.'

'Nice! Was it amazing?'

'Even better than I remembered it.' I spot the waiter on his way over. 'What do you want to drink?' I ask Kitty as he arrives at the table. She glances at my glass.

'Mineral water?' she scoffs. 'Will you have a glass of wine with me?'

My lips turn down. I'm so tempted, but I can't. 'Better not,' I say, regretfully. 'You have one, though.'

'Um…' She hesitates, reluctant to drink alone. 'Okay, sure. House white will do, thanks.' The waiter goes off and she turns back to me. 'Why aren't you drinking?'

'Apart from the fact that I'm still breastfeeding at night—'

'Ohhh,' she says slowly, and I could have left it at that, but I'm already onto the second half of my sentence.

'… I avoid alcohol around Johnny,' I finish saying.

Now her expression tells me that she understands. Johnny used to claim that he didn't have a problem with alcohol – only drugs – but he's since accepted that he has issues with both. He regularly attends AA meetings, but it helps if the people close to him don't drink, either. I'm certainly not going to put him at risk by indulging myself, however much he tells me that my abstinence is not necessary. There's too much at stake.

'Fair enough,' she says, her dark brown ringlets bouncing as she cocks her head to one side. 'How's he going with it all?'

'He's amazing,' I say warmly, shaking my head because I still can't believe it. 'Did I tell you he's quit smoking?'

'No way.' She looks shocked. Johnny used to pretty much chain-smoke, so this is a huge deal. 'How did you manage that?'

'It was all him.' Well, sort of. 'It was when I was pregnant. He'd never smoke around Barney or me,' I'm quick to point out. 'But the smell of it on his breath used to make me feel nauseous. So he quit,' I say simply, although it was anything but simple. Talk about a bear with a sore head. He was a grouch for weeks. *Months*.

'Wow.' She smiles at me. 'I knew it was meant to be between you two. You're sickeningly happy, aren't you?'

'The happiest I've ever been.' Pause. 'But enough about me, otherwise you'll be throwing up in the bushes. How are you? How's it all going at work? Anyone on the scene?'

'Funny you should ask…'

'What? Tell me everything!'

'There's this super-hot new guy at work. And I love my

job, by the way. Anyway, this guy is sex on legs. Tall, slim, dark hair and the most intense blue eyes you've ever seen. He's been flirting with me a little.'

'Sounds gorgeous!'

'But he's only twenty-seven,' she points out, disheartened.

'So?'

'I'm thirty-six,' she says.

'And?'

She frowns. 'Don't you think that's a bit of an age gap?'

'Hell, no! Get in there. Do you socialise outside the office?'

'We've had a few tequilas. He's been working with me on an upcoming premiere. Oh, I meant to tell you!' she exclaims.

'What?'

'It's for a Joseph Strike film!'

I freeze.

❄

I first met Joseph Strike about three years ago when I came back to LA for the second time. Johnny wanted to spend some more time with Barney, so I agreed to move in with him, even though the plan was that we would lead separate lives. He was going out with Dana Reed, an absolute bitch of a girl who he met in rehab and got up to all sorts of grief with. So, when Kitty persuaded me to start dating again after I met Joseph at a film premiere after-party, I was only too happy to oblige.

Joseph was – *is* – divine. He's tall with short dark hair, dark-brown eyes and a body to die for. He'd only played a small part in the film we'd been to see, but I remember thinking at the time that he was destined for big things.

Turns out I was right. He's a major movie star now, and

every time I see his face on a poster, or hear him being inter-
viewed on TV or radio or being mentioned by any one of our
friends, I have to hope that Johnny isn't with me, because it
puts him in a vile mood.

✳

'You should come!' Kitty exclaims. 'It's this Friday.'

I laugh and roll my eyes. 'Johnny would go nuts.'

'What? Why?' She looks confused. 'He could come too,'
she says.

'Yeah, right!' I laugh. 'You know he's really jealous of
Joseph, right?'

She screws up her nose. 'Is he?'

'*Yeah!*'

'But he's *Johnny Jefferson*!'

'I know. It's absolutely ridiculous. And considering how
many women *he's* slept with… Don't get me started, it's
actually laughable.'

'You should come, then! Serve him right.'

'Nah,' I brush her off. 'I wouldn't hurt him like that. Can
you imagine if he went to one of Dana's gigs?' She's a singer,
but as far as I know, she hasn't put out anything new for a
while. She must be still battling her drink and drug demons.
'I'd go mental. He'd never do that to me.'

Kitty shrugs. 'Fair enough. Shame, though. I'd love to
hang out with you.'

'We could go to another premiere?' I say hopefully. 'One
where you're not working?'

'Okay, yeah,' she replies with a smile. 'I'll see what's
coming up in the next couple of weeks.'

'Great!'

'Shall I say hi to Joseph from you in the meantime?'

A flutter goes through me. Despite how much I love and fancy Johnny, Joseph Strike is undeniably hot. 'No,' I decide. 'He probably wouldn't remember me, anyway.'

'He does,' Kitty says.

My heart jumps. 'What?'

She grins. 'He does remember you. I was introduced to him for the first time the other day when he came into the office and he recognised me.' Kitty was with me when I first met him at the premiere party, and on another date when we all went to a Halloween party. That was the night we slept together.

'Did he?' My voice has gone up an octave.

'Yeah.' She giggles. 'He asked if we were still in contact and then said to say hi and congratulations. But I'm sure he'd like to say it face to face.'

'Congratulations? On what?'

'On your wedding!' She laughs. 'Have you forgotten you got married?'

'Oh!' Of course. Now I feel like a bit of a tit.

'You know he's totally in love now?'

'No? Wow! Sorry, every time anything about Joseph Strike comes on TV, I have to change the channel,' I say wryly. 'I thought he was a bit of a player.' That's the impression I got of him after he became famous, anyway. I've lost count of the number of women he's been papped with.

'Not anymore,' she says. 'Apparently, he's a changed man.'

'Well, I'm very happy to hear it,' I reply with a smile. 'But Johnny will still flip out if I go to his premiere.'

We giggle and then the waiter comes over again, so we have to focus on ordering.

Even with a longer lunch-break, Kitty has to get back to work before Johnny returns. I could walk up to Melrose Avenue and have a look at the shops, but I'm feeling too chilled, so I spend my last half an hour reading and drinking a coffee. I look up when I hear the familiar roar of his motorcycle engine. He pulls up right in front of The Ivy and flips his visor up.

'Shall I come in for a bit?' he calls to me.

I give him the thumbs up and he switches off the engine, handing the keys to a waiting valet. Before he's even taken off his helmet, a couple of paparazzi have appeared. He ignores them and jogs up the steps to join me at my table.

Sometimes I get recognised when I'm on my own, but those times are few and far between. It's been blissful today, basking in my anonymity, no one giving me a second glance as I've sat and gossiped to Kitty.

But now all eyes are on us. Johnny touches my shoulder and bends down to give me a kiss on my lips to a soundtrack of camera shots being clicked off. He puts his helmet on the other spare seat and pulls Kitty's chair closer to mine. The waiter is beside him in an instant.

'Can I get a coffee?' Johnny asks, glancing at me. 'You want anything else?'

'Go on, then, I'll have another decaf,' I reply. I turn to Johnny. 'How was your meeting?'

He shrugs. 'So so.'

My brow creases. 'What's wrong?'

'Nothing's *wrong* wrong,' he says, staring at me intently. 'They want me to start recording the new album around the middle of May. It'll probably take a couple of months.' Pause. 'They want me to record it *here*,' he elaborates.

'Oh. Really? You can't do it back at home?' I hate the

idea of him having to travel backwards and forwards for two whole months.

'They've lined up Mikky Tryslip to do it.'

I shrug. The name means nothing to me.

'Super producer,' he reveals. 'Afraid of flying,' he adds drily.

'Can't someone else produce you?'

'He's one of the best in the business.' He shrugs.

So that's that, then.

The waiter returns with our coffees. Johnny rubs my knee under the table. 'They're going to think we've had an argument if you look like that,' he says gently. He's referring to the paparazzi: they're still there, watching.

I smile a small smile. 'I suppose we could come with you?'

His face breaks into a grin and he reaches over and tucks my hair behind my ear. 'I love you,' he says seriously, cupping my face. Then he kisses me and I kiss him back, trying but failing to ignore those ever-present camera clicks.

❋

'Can we take a detour on the way home?' Johnny asks me as I climb onto the back of his bike later.

'Sure. Where?'

'Surprise.'

We lose the paps who are tailing us after a few blocks, and after a while Johnny starts to head up into the hills. I grow tense because I think I know where he's taking me. After a while, we pass through the gates into Bel Air, and continue to wind our way further into the hills, past high fences hiding enormous mansions belonging to the rich and famous.

Finally, Johnny pulls up outside familiar wooden gates. He reaches over and presses the buzzer, flipping his visor up to look into the camera staring down at us from high gateposts.

'What are you doing?' I ask with confusion. 'We can't just drop in.' And then I see the For Sale sign.

He doesn't say anything, just puts one gloved hand on top of mine to reassure me. My heart constricts as the gates begin to open and we ride along the long driveway to the two-storey, rectangular, white-painted concrete house that was once Johnny's LA base.

His shag pad.

His party pad.

Leafy trees partly obscure the impressive piece of modernist architecture, but the house and gardens still look exactly the same as I remember them. Johnny switches off the bike's engine just as the large front door opens and a well-dressed brunette in her mid-to-late forties steps out.

'Bear with me,' Johnny murmurs, indicating for me to climb off the bike.

'Mr Jefferson,' the woman says, coming forwards with a friendly smile as Johnny takes his helmet off.

'Hello again,' he replies, shaking her extended hand. *Again?* 'This is my wife, Meg.'

'Great to meet you at last,' she says. 'I'm Miriam. Shall we go in?'

How do they know each other?

'She sold the house the first time,' Johnny tells me.

'Oh.'

I hesitantly follow Miriam and Johnny into the hall, and then further into the large, double-height, open-plan living room. The house looks and smells the same – albeit with no furniture.

Whoever bought it after Johnny sold it has long gone.

The view still makes me stop in my tracks. Huge, floor-to-ceiling windows look down onto the city of LA, baking in the afternoon sun. A large infinity pool is on the terrace, behind an almost invisible glass safety fence that Johnny's last PA had installed when I moved here with Barney.

'I guess you won't need me to give you a tour?' Miriam asks with a smile.

'No,' Johnny replies, tearing his eyes away from the view.

'Would you like some time alone?' she asks.

'Sure.'

'I'll be outside if you need me.'

As soon as she's gone, I turn to Johnny. 'What are we doing here?' I ask uneasily.

There's something about his expression – he looks lost, torn, confused... And none of these emotions make me feel any easier. He puts his hands on my hips.

'I miss it,' he says, and I instantly feel a little sick. I *don't*. Not after the memories, the heartache, the misery... 'When I heard it was back on the market, I wanted to come and see it.'

'*Why* is it back on the market so quickly?' I ask.

'An Arab Sheikh bought it for his son. He wanted to try to make it in the film industry, but it didn't work out and he's gone back to Saudi Arabia.' His face softens. 'I want to buy it back, Meg. I want this to be our LA base.'

I pull away from him and walk towards the living-room doors. I flick the switch that unlocks the door and step out onto the warm terrace.

I remember this. I liked this – *loved* this – once. But I thought this part of our life was over. That we'd moved on. I'm happy in Henley, where we live. Yes, the weather has sucked recently, but I feel settled there. I don't want to uproot the whole family again.

'I'm going to have to be out here a lot for work this year,' Johnny says from behind me.

I want to sit down, but there are no sun-loungers out here anymore.

'I love this house,' he says softly. 'It's everything I ever dreamed of.'

I know that our house in Henley is not really to his taste. It's beautiful – a big old mansion – but Johnny has always been into minimalist, modern styles. I love that style too – all that light.

I don't say anything as I walk away from him, over to the pool gate. I open it up and go inside. I want to stand on the first step. I know that the water will be blissfully cool, and my feet are hot in these trainers. Johnny joins me, putting his arm around my shoulder.

'This place has good memories for you too, right?' he asks. He points to the left of the pool. 'That was where I saw you for the first time, lying there, fast asleep, in your skimpy bikini.'

'I remember it well,' I say wryly. 'I nearly jumped out of my skin when I heard your voice.'

'Look, they kept our table.' He nods at the polished concrete table with bench seating. We shared a pizza there on my first night in LA and he quizzed me about my love life.

'And they've still got the bar,' I say sardonically, spotting the outdoor bar that used to be stocked with just about every spirit under the sun. Whiskey was Johnny's drink of choice.

He lets his arm drop and I instantly feel mean. He hasn't had a drink in over two years.

'Sorry.' I turn around to face him.

'It's a fair comment,' he replies, his green eyes looking even more luminous with the light of the pool reflecting in them. Yes. I remember this sight, too.

'I love you,' I say seriously. 'I love you so much. I don't want *anything* to come between us.' I say this last sentence fervently and tears prick my eyes.

'Hey,' he says, looking crushed. He pulls me into his arms. 'Nothing is going to break us now. We're too strong. I would never do anything to risk hurting you, Barney or Phoenix. You guys are my *life*.' He squeezes me hard as he says this, then he pulls away to face the house. 'But I still love this place. It's *me*, you know? I mean, look at it. It's fucking awesome.'

I laugh at his enthusiasm, despite myself. 'It's pretty cool,' I agree.

'We could buy it back – in your name as well as mine,' he says pointedly. 'It could be *our* place. I like England, but I'm so pissed off with the rain,' he adds grumpily. 'And if you really hate it after a year or two, we could always move back.'

'Hang on,' I interrupt. 'Are you saying you want to move here permanently?' I'm taken aback. 'I thought you were just talking about a summer pad. Somewhere to live while you're recording your new album.'

He shrugs. 'I thought we could give it another go.'

My heart starts to beat faster. 'What about our place in Henley?' I ask. 'I love it there. The kids love it. And Barney really likes his nursery.'

'Barney is *three*,' Johnny says meaningfully. 'He'll adapt. He always does.'

Hmm. That's certainly true. His little life has been nothing but adaptation.

'What about me? I'm not sure I'm very good at starting afresh anymore. I've only just begun to feel settled with you at home.'

'Come on, Nutmeg. Christ, you're only thirty. And I'm thirty-six! Let's live a little. You knew when you married me that life wasn't going to be ordinary. I want you guys to come on tour with me next year.'

'Since when are you touring next year?' I ask.

'I was going to tell you,' he says wearily.

I have such bad memories of Johnny on tour… And he knows it. He can see it on my face.

'You have nothing to worry about,' he says firmly. 'Shall we go and see inside?'

Talk about a change of subject. 'Fine,' I reply bluntly. 'But don't go thinking this is a done deal, because I'm nowhere near convinced.'

'I know, I know,' he says flippantly. 'We've got lots to discuss.'

I've said it before and I'll say it again: He always gets what he wants in the end.

❄

Two months later, I find myself standing in the very same spot, looking down over the city of LA.

'Can we go in the pool?' an eager Barney asks.

'Of course,' I reply with a smile, looking behind him to see Johnny stepping out onto the terrace with Phoenix on his shoulders. I kick off my flip flops – this time I came prepared – and stand on the first step. The weather is much warmer now than it was in March and the water is the perfect temperature. Not too hot, not too cold. I sit down on the side of the pool and turn to take off Barney's shoes.

Once I agreed, Johnny had the house sale pushed through quickly, wanting it to be ours by the time he started recording his new album. In the last couple of weeks, while he's been in LA recording, he's been able to get the place ready for us. I, meanwhile, have sorted out our things at home, many of which are being shipped over on a big crate to arrive in a couple of weeks. We're hanging onto the house in Henley for the moment – we'll probably rent it out to keep it occupied – but there's no rush.

I tug Barney's shorts down and he sits next to me on the step while I lift his T-shirt over his head. He splashes the water with his feet. Beyond excited.

'I'll go and get our swimming costumes,' I say to Johnny, who has just joined us, poolside. 'You coming in?' I call over my shoulder.

'Sure,' he replies.

I walk back into the living room and step around the shaggy, lime-green rug and the enormous, brand-new charcoal-grey L-shaped sofas that Johnny bought last week before we arrived. I walk over to the concrete polished staircase and go up the one floor, turning left at the top to walk along the landing, which is open to the living room on my left. Our bedroom door is straight ahead.

We had a bit of a giggle when we went into the master bedroom at the viewing and saw that the last owner had papered the walls with red velvet and had chosen gold-embroidered carpet and curtains. Now every room has been redecorated – a couple in exactly the same style as Johnny had them the last time. The room which I used to stay in was nicknamed the White Room. I was touched to see it restored to its former glory after the last owner's opulent navy blue and silver colour scheme. Now its walls, ceilings and floors are pristine white, with white built-in lacquered wardrobes, and an en suite with white stone lining every surface. The children have the bedrooms next to the White Room and the decorators have done a gorgeous job, but I'm looking forward to putting my own touches onto them once the crate arrives with all of their things.

I reach our bedroom door and push it open. The room spans the width of the house, from front to back, with a floor-to-ceiling view over LA at the back, and large windows overlooking the trees at the front from inside the big en suite bathroom. To the left of the bathroom is a bright and airy walk-in wardrobe which I'd never been inside before. I can smell the fresh paint, though. Apart from the white walls, the master bedroom is very different to how it looked when Johnny lived here before. It's the one room he *didn't* have restored to its former glory. We chose the colour scheme together. New plush smoky-grey carpets, a yellow and grey geometrical pattern on the curtains, and a contrasting yellow and green patterned bedspread on the brand-new super-king-size bed. A modern, yellow chaise longue rests near the windows showing the main view. The bathroom overlooking the trees is fitted out with white stone, and we've even had flick-switch glass installed in the windows so the clear glass turns opaque at the flick of a switch.

It's stunning.

Fresh, shiny and new.

My toes dig into the plush carpet and I can't help but smile as I stand there for a moment and take in my surroundings.

Out of nowhere, the memory hits me of Dana lying sprawled out and naked on the bed while Johnny lay wasted in the bathtub. I squeeze my eyes shut and shudder. Then I steel myself.

I've got to move on. We will fill this house with happy memories now, more than enough to wash away the bad ones. The sound of my children laughing, the sound of my husband strumming his guitar and singing in the music studio next door. I'm back here as Johnny's *wife*, and I won't be bowed by bad memories.

I go and unzip my largest suitcase and dig out our swimming costumes.

❄

It surprises me how quickly I settle back into life in LA. I hire a new PA/occasional nanny called Annie, who's petite and pretty with twinkly eyes and a warm smile. But underneath her pixie-like features, she packs a hefty punch and she came highly recommended. Kitty heard about her on the CPA grapevine – she was working for an aged movie star who, to put it kindly, is a little bit of a diva. Annie decided that it wasn't unreasonable to desire a life outside of work, so she's here during normal working hours, although she has agreed to help out with after-hours babysitting sometimes. It's a far cry from the 24/7 of my CPA past, but it suits us, and we love having the house to ourselves at weekends.

We have two new maids, Sharon and Carly, who come in every morning. Johnny's old maid, Sandy, has moved to Indianapolis with her husband for work, so there was no chance of her returning.

As for our cook, I'm thrilled when Eddie – our American

cook who came to England with us – decided to join us on our return journey. We've even managed to persuade two of our old security/bodyguards to come back: Samuel and Lewis. I'm happiest to welcome back Davey, though, the limo driver who I have always had a real soft spot for. He's not long out of retirement, but he quit his other job for a company executive as soon as Johnny got in touch. Now he has a brand-new, shiny black Mercedes limousine to ferry us around in, with car seats for the kids at the back of a long bench seat that curves along one whole side of the vehicle. Opposite the bench seat is a mini bar, stocked with anything but alcohol.

I see Kitty occasionally while Johnny is at work, although I'm yet to go out with her over an evening. She asks me to at our next lunch date.

'It's a film premiere,' she tells me. 'Should be really good fun. The after party is at Chateau Marmont.' The notorious rock star hang-out.

'When is it?'

'Tomorrow night.' Which is a Thursday. 'Johnny could come too?'

'I'll ask him. Barney, stop wriggling.'

It's a warm, sunny day, and we're in a little café on Melrose Avenue – one of our haunts from the past. This time, though, I have *two* children, and Samuel is waiting outside the door. It still freaks me out to have a bodyguard. I accept that the added security is necessary when I have the kids with me, but sometimes I insist on going out alone if it's just me. It's a shame we can't sit outside today, but if there's one thing I hate more than the paps getting pictures of me, it's the paps getting pictures of the kids.

Kitty bounces Phoenix on her lap and makes him giggle. I watch on, half with amusement and half with dread because he's just had some milk and could throw up at any minute on her very beautiful and very pink Amber Sakai dress.

'I'm full,' Barney moans from beside me.

'Two more mouthfuls,' I insist.

'But I'm full,' he complains again, flopping back in his seat.

'Fine.' I give up. So much for being consistent. 'Do you want me to take him?' I ask Kitty, hopefully, nodding at Phoenix. *Give me the baby before he barfs…*

'No, no, he's fine!' she says breezily. 'So what do you think about the premiere?'

'Can I have an ice-cream?' Barney interjects.

'I thought you were full,' I say wryly.

'I am, but I really, really want an ice-cream,' he tells me seriously, his green eyes pleading with me.

I stare back at him, wavering. Kitty still can't get over how much he looks like his dad.

'Get him an ice-cream,' she butts in good-naturedly.

'Okay, but let me take Phoenix before he's sick on you.'

She laughs, but all-too-willingly hands him over.

'Can I?' Barney interrupts.

'Yes, okay,' I say wearily.

'Yay!'

'But only if you promise to eat your dinner!' I hastily add.

The baby hiccups, burps, and then vomits into the napkin I'm holding, ready and waiting. I really am too good at this.

Kitty grimaces.

'Sorry,' I apologise, then I smirk. 'You know what? Yes, to the premiere.'

As much as I love my children, I could do with a night off.

❄

Davey drives me to the film premiere on Hollywood Boulevard. I'm wearing a black Brochu Walker mini dress over black skinny jeans and ankle boots. I remember the first time I came to a premiere as Johnny's PA, I got all dolled up, and ended up feeling like a bit of an idiot when Kitty turned up in jeans. Now, there's every chance I'll get recognised, but I'd still feel a bit silly going the whole hog with a long evening gown. Maybe if Johnny were with me I'd make a bit more of an effort, but he wasn't interested in seeing the film or walking the red carpet. The movie is a romantic drama, which is totally not his scene, but he says he'll come along later to the after party.

Davey's voice sounds over the intercom. 'Johnny asked me to tell you he put a little something in the minibar for you.'

'Oh! Okay.' I reach across and open the small fridge. I spy the champagne immediately: Perrier Jouët Rosé. Very expensive and very delicious. My heart sinks.

'He told me to tell you not to worry,' Davey adds in a kind voice. 'He really was quite insistent that you go out and have a good time.'

Still, I hesitate. I would love a drink, but…

'He's a much stronger man these days, Mrs Jefferson.'

'Did he tell you to say that, too?' I ask wryly.

'No. That came from me.'

'And call me Meg, for crying out loud. How many times do I have to tell you?'

He laughs a deep laugh. 'I haven't heard a champagne cork popping.'

'Oh, alright then, you bully,' I joke.

I pull out the champagne and look down at the bottle with its pretty vintage flower climbing up the side. I suppose I've got to start trusting Johnny not to cave under pressure. I won't drink too much. I unwrap the foil at the top, just as we arrive at Kitty's house.

She comes out of the door – she's obviously been waiting. She's not working tonight. It's Dex's gig – the guy that she's been having an in-work flirtation with. Nothing has happened between them – yet. Maybe tonight will be the night…

Kitty looks gorgeous in a floor-skimming, burnt-orange maxi dress. Her curly hair is down and falling well past her shoulders. I'm wearing my hair down, too, but I've tonged it to give it a tousled look. I'm wearing shimmering green eye-make-up and lip gloss.

'Hi!' she exclaims, climbing into the car and calling back her thanks to Davey. She spies the bottle. 'I hope that's not all for me.'

'How about we share?'

'Yay! I'm so pleased you're drinking with me!' she exclaims, clapping like an over-excited child.

I laugh and pop the cork, and she takes the two champagne glasses from between my knees and holds them out for me to pour in some of the fizzy pink bubbly.

'Cheers!' she says as Davey pulls smoothly away from the curb.

'Cheers!' We chink glasses and I take a sip. Yummy.

'I love your dress,' I say. 'Making a bit more of an effort these days, hmm? Is that for the benefit of a certain someone?'

She laughs. 'Might be. Trust me, I need all the help I can get.' She takes a large gulp of her champagne.

'I'm looking forward to meeting him,' I say with delight.

Davey drives us right up to the red carpet. We climb out to the sound of deafening screams and the flashes of paparazzi cameras. This is the first premiere I've been to in years – since

I was last in LA – and I still remember that buzz of excitement that comes from walking down the red carpet. The celebrities take their time, signing autographs and posing for pictures, but Kitty and I wander along towards the cinema entrance without pausing.

Then I hear my name being shouted. I look over my shoulder at the pool of photographers behind the ropes, and a few more of them call for 'Meg' to come and pose for a few pictures. Kitty smiles and guides me back towards them, standing on the side-lines while I pose for the cameras, feeling incredibly surreal about how I'm considered a somebody these days.

'Meg Jefferson?'

I turn around to see a beautiful, blonde TV presenter with a microphone in her hand. A man holding a television camera stands to her right.

'Hi.' I try to appear relaxed.

'No Johnny tonight?' she asks with a friendly smile.

'He's coming along later,' I tell her.

'More of a party man, less of a film-goer?' she teases.

'Well, he's not really into partying much these days, either,' I reply with a wink. 'At least, not like in the old days.'

'Too busy being a husband and a father?'

I grin. 'You could say that.'

'Enjoy the film,' she says amiably, turning away to grab the next celebrity on the red carpet.

I walk over to Kitty, trying not to look too much like a rabbit caught in the headlights.

She giggles. 'You're a celebrity now, get used to it.'

'Never,' I mutter under my breath.

❉

The film is brilliant. Romantic and sexy with a dark, sinister side, and the edgy lead actor, Hugh Michael, is super-hot.

Davey collects us to drive us up the hill to Chateau Marmont.

'Do you know if Johnny still intends to come?' I ask him.

'I believe so.'

He was still in the studio when I set off. Annie is looking after the boys tonight. I send her a quick text to check that all is okay. She responds immediately to tell me that they're fast asleep. Next, I text Johnny asking what time he's planning to come. He doesn't reply, but that's nothing out of the ordinary. Sometimes he doesn't bother checking his phone for hours, and he certainly won't if he's having a late one at the studio.

I put my phone back into my bag and then Kitty and I pour ourselves another glass of Perrier Jouët.

Modelled loosely on a castle in the Loire Valley, Chateau Marmont is partly obscured by lush, green vegetation and is situated on Sunset Boulevard in West Hollywood. Davey drops us out at the front and we head straight through the opulent interior to the garden, where champagne and cocktails are already flowing freely.

We nab a spot near the door where the canapés are emerging and giggle as we swipe a few, then we go and find ourselves somewhere to sit down.

'Just like old times.' I laugh as I chink Kitty's glass of champagne and tuck into the few canapés I've collected on a paper napkin.

'Well, whaddaya know, it's Little Bo Peep.'

My stomach lurches at the sound of this voice and my eyes shoot upwards to take in Dana Reed, former Next Big Thing in Music and Johnny's ex-girlfriend.

She's wearing six-inch wedges, black hot pants and a see-through top. Her long, dark hair has been twisted into a messy topknot, her skin is as pale as ever, her eye make-up as dark and her lipstick as red. My instincts tell me that her appearance is not the only thing that has remained unchanged: she's still a total bitch.

'Wow, that's so classy of you,' she says sardonically, nodding down at the napkin of canapés in my hand. She's still stick-thin, but her face looks more gaunt than it did a few years ago. Still taking drugs, at a guess. Rage rushes through me. I hate her. Hate, hate, *hate* her! 'Meg Stiles,' she says slowly. 'I didn't think I'd ever see you again.'

'You mean Meg *Jefferson*.' Kitty finds her voice before I find mine.

Dana laughs a horrid, tinkly laugh, but her gaze is trained on me. 'Of course! I heard about your *nuptials*. Big congratulations. How's it all going?' Complete and utter sarcasm.

'Very well, so kind of you to ask,' I reply with no trace of a smile on my face.

'Give it time,' she warns with a devilish smile. 'That bad boy won't stay tamed for long.'

I literally want to kill her. It's a serious effort to reign myself in.

'Would you like a canapé?' I ask sweetly, offering up my napkin. 'You look like you're about to collapse.'

Kitty sniggers beside me. Dana's eyes narrow. 'You might think you've won—'

'It's not a competition,' I cut her off. 'But you'll always be a loser.' Now fuck off and leave me in peace, you pathetic piece of shit.

I have no idea how I manage to stop this last sentence from coming out of my mouth.

Her expression wavers, but then she forces another laugh. 'Give Johnny my love. I'm sure we'll see each other around, now he's back in LA.'

'Oh, fuck off and leave me in peace, you pathetic piece of shit.'

Whoops. Couldn't contain myself that time.

Kitty guffaws, Dana's eyes widen with surprise, and I defiantly pop another canapé in my mouth, even though I've lost my appetite.

'You heard the girl. Scat!' Kitty says to Dana, then: 'Hey, look, there's Joseph Strike!' She ignores a po-faced Dana, pointing straight past her to the tall, dark and utterly gorgeous film star that I once had a fling with.

Back then, Joseph proved to be a pretty good distraction from Johnny's evil ex, and here he is rescuing me from my foe again – in a different way this time, obviously. 'Let's go and say hi.'

Before I can object, Kitty stands up and pulls me to my feet. I have a choice: stay here with Dana or follow her over to Joseph. I would prefer not to do either – Joseph is in my past, and I know Johnny would hate it if he saw me talking to him. But his druggy ex-girlfriend made my life miserable. And, right now, my priority is to get away from her.

'He's with Dex,' Kitty says over her shoulder. No wonder she's in such a hurry to go and talk to them.

I follow Kitty, but while doing so, dig into my bag and pull out my phone. I call Johnny.

'Where the hell are you?' I hiss into the receiver as his voicemail picks up. 'Dana is here and I could really do with your support.' To my dismay, I realise I'm fighting back tears. 'I'm about to go and say hi to Joseph Strike, so get your arse here asap.'

I end the call, instantly despising myself for that pathetic attempt to make Johnny jealous. Dana makes me feel deeply insecure – she always has – but I should be over it by now, and I'm angry with myself that I'm not. I'll call Johnny back in a minute, I decide, watching Kitty as she greets Dex and Joseph. He's not answering his phone anyway – is he still in the studio? That's weird: it's so late.

'Hey,' I hear Joseph reply, shaking Kitty's hand and flashing her an easy smile, 'good to see you again.'

My heart is still racing with adrenalin after my encounter with Dana, but now it's racing in a different way. I'm about to face Joseph again, and so much has changed since I last saw him. A memory of our last date comes back to me: him naked and making love to me in the bedroom of his small, messy student-like flat. Now he's a full-on A-lister – Hollywood's hottest.

He looks much how I remember him: tall with short, dark hair and brown eyes. He's wearing a slim-fitting black suit with a white shirt covering up what I know is a perfect body.

This suddenly feels very wrong. I shouldn't be here. I don't want to be here. I want to be at home with Johnny, safe in his arms. Where *is* he? I want to turn and run, but then Joseph spots me and his eyes open wide and his face breaks into the biggest grin.

'Meg!' he exclaims, reaching past Kitty to grab my arm. 'How the hell are you?'

He seems so pleased to see me that some of my bad feelings dispel.

I force a smile. 'I'm good, thanks.'

He pulls me in for a quick hug, kissing my cheek. I register that his aftershave smells familiar. He stares down at me with dark-brown eyes. 'I heard you got married! Congratulations, that's so cool!'

I can't help blushing. 'Thanks,' I reply, wishing I could chill-out.

'Wow.' He shakes his head. 'And you have two kids, now?'

'That's right.' *Finally*, my smile is genuine. 'Barney and Phoenix. Barney has just turned four, and Phoenix turns one next month.'

'You've just moved back to LA, yeah?'

'Yes. Johnny needed to be here for work.' I shrug, finally pulling myself together. 'Am I right in thinking that you're with someone now?' I ask him.

'Yeah.' His eyes light up. 'Alice. My girl.'

'Have you been together long?'

'I knew her years ago, well before...' He looks around him. 'You know.' Well before he was famous, I'm assuming he means. 'We're engaged.'

'Oh, that is so lovely, congratulations!' I say in a high-pitched voice.

'Is that Dana Reed over there?' Joseph suddenly asks.

My lips turn down, but I don't follow the line of his sight. 'Afraid so.'

'Last time I saw her she was lit up like a Christmas tree.' He grins. 'Do you remember?'

I can't help but laugh. It was at the Halloween party and she went dressed as an angel. 'How could I forget. And you were rocking your Karate Kid look.'

That was the night we slept together. Argh! I don't want to think about that now! I take a small step backwards to include Kitty and Dex in our conversation. I haven't even said hello to Dex, yet. I rectify that now.

'I'm Meg, by the way.' I smile at him.

'Sorry, I should have made the introductions,' Joe apologises. 'Dex works at the studio.' I know this, of course.

'Nice to meet you,' I say, shaking his hand.

'Great to meet you, too. Kitty's always talking about you.'

'Likewise,' I reply with a raised eyebrow.

'I might grab another glass of champagne,' Kitty says smoothly. 'You want one, Meg?' She gives me a pointed look, warning me not to give away anything about her feelings for the office hottie.

'Okay.'

'You boys want anything?'

'Sure,' Dex says, affectionately touching her wrist. I can sense their chemistry from here.

'Nah, I'm good,' Joseph replies. 'I'm going to shoot off in a bit.'

I'm disappointed to hear this. Talking to him again has reminded me how much I liked him in the first place – and he doesn't seem to have changed much. It would be nice if we could be friends, but that will never happen if Johnny has anything to do with it. I don't imagine Alice would be too thrilled by the idea, either.

'Well, if I don't see you again…' I say regretfully.

'We'll bump into each other,' he brushes me off, his dark eyes full of warmth. 'LA is a small town.'

'It's good to see you, anyway,' I say sincerely. 'And I'm so happy to see you doing so well.' I feel compelled to tell him this, just in case I don't get another chance. 'I always knew that you would.'

'It's good to see you too, Mystic Meg,' he jokes.

I turn away before he can see me blushing. I love and fancy Johnny like mad, but Joseph Strike will always have something about him. Alice is a lucky girl, whoever she is.

Just as I think that thought, I see Johnny staring straight at me from across the terrace. And he does not look happy.

'Johnny's here,' I say as an aside to Kitty.

'I'll get the drinks. See you in a bit,' she replies.

He's not smiling as we make our way through the crowd towards each other. I cover more ground, because he keeps getting stopped by people wanting to say hi. He greets them distractedly then continues on his way, his green eyes locked with mine.

I'm on edge. Is he properly angry with me for that Joseph comment? I should have called him back, but now it's too late.

'Hey,' I say as he reaches me.

'Hi.'

He bends down and presses his lips to mine, sliding his right hand into the hair at the nape of my neck and holding me to him. I pull away with confusion.

'Did you get my message?'

'Just now,' he breathes, his brow momentarily furrowing. 'I was already on my way when you called.' His eyes flicker past me and around the room. 'Where is he?' he asks drily in my ear.

'I think he's gone.'

'Did you speak to him?' His eyes flash as they stare down at me and I curse myself as my face heats up. I don't know why I feel guilty.

'I said hi, yeah,' I reply defensively, meeting his direct stare. 'Have you seen Dana?'

He tenses and looks up, his gaze moving around the room again before stopping suddenly. 'Mmm.'

I never wanted Johnny to set eyes on Dana ever again, let alone speak to her.

'Do you want to speak to her?' I ask in a small voice,

desperately hoping the answer is no, but believing I owe him that because of my conversation with *my* former flame.

'No,' he says firmly. 'I have nothing to say to her.'

The relief is immense.

He gently kisses my lips. 'Can I take you home?' he asks.

'Um… Kitty.'

'She looks fine to me.'

I turn around to see her laughing with Dex. She has her hand placed flirtatiously on his chest and he's grinning down at her.

'I need to talk to you,' Johnny adds in a low voice and my eyes shoot back to look at him.

'What's wrong?'

'I'll tell you when we're in the car.'

'Is it the boys?'

'No, no,' he says hurriedly. 'Everyone's fine.'

But something *is* wrong. He didn't deny it. That wasn't anger when he walked in the door; it was something else entirely. And the fact that he hasn't even given me the Spanish Inquisition about Joseph tells me that whatever it is he's about to reveal is going to hit me like a tonne of bricks.

My heart is hammering as we say goodbye to Kitty. She doesn't seem to mind being left alone with Dex. I'll call her tomorrow for an update, but right now, I want to find out what Johnny wants to talk to me about.

Davey is waiting for us. I give him a wary look as he opens the door for me. I wonder if he knows what's going on.

'Thanks, Davey,' I say, as Johnny climbs into the car behind me. He punches the button by the mini bar to put the privacy screen up, then guides me to the back of the car. He sits down beside me and takes my hands. I have a very bad feeling in the pit of my stomach.

'Wendel called me,' he says in a low voice, not meeting my eyes.

'Right…' I say uncertainly. Wendel is Johnny's solicitor. It was because of him that I got the job of Johnny's PA in the first place. I was working for an architect at the time – Wendel was a client.

Johnny looks up at me and his eyes are full of sorrow. Whatever it is he wants to say, he's finding it extremely hard.

'Just tell me,' I urge him.

He swallows hard. *What is it?* 'Wendel spoke to a man earlier today, claiming to be the stepfather of a girl who…'

My imagination strikes me with thoughts much faster than Johnny can speak. Has he had an affair? Has he cheated on me since we've been married? Oh God, no. Please, no…

'… is the daughter of one of my first fans,' he continues.

Eh?

'Her mother passed away recently. She never told her daughter…'

My mind is still racing: *I don't understand. Where is this going?*

'… who her real father was,' he finishes.

He looks deflated and then it all falls into place. One of my worst nightmares has come true.

Johnny has a daughter. A daughter he never knew existed.

When Johnny first found out about Barney, the thought occurred to me that my son might not be Johnny's only child. He made a mistake with me, not using a condom – what was to say that he didn't make other mistakes with any of his *seven hundred or so* groupies? What was to stop one of *them* conceiving his child? I tried to persuade myself that they would have come forward by now – that no secret would have stayed hidden for this long. But maybe – like me – another woman felt the need to stay silent, the need to keep her child's identity a secret for who knows what reason. Now, the truth has come out – and I don't know why.

Johnny grips my hands tighter. I feel numb.

'I'm sorry,' he whispers.

'Tell me everything,' I reply in a dull voice.

✳

Wendel is based in London, and earlier today he spoke to an English man called Stuart Taylor, who claimed that Johnny was the father of his stepdaughter Jessica Pickerill. Wendel didn't want to alarm Johnny immediately, so he's worked through the night in the UK, checking as many facts as he could. He can confirm that Stuart's wife, Candice, was killed in a tragic accident just over five months ago, leaving behind an only daughter, Jessica. Stuart claimed that Candice – Candy – was one of Johnny's first groupies when he first kicked off his career with Fence, the band that would eventually make him famous. He said that Candy fell pregnant, but by then Johnny had gone on tour in Europe, and Candy, feeling sickened about being just another one of Johnny's many groupies, decided to raise the baby on her own. As the years went by, she became increasingly fearful that her daughter would choose to leave home and live with her rock star father if she should ever find out the truth. So Candy kept it hidden. Now Stuart has told Jessica everything. And she wants to meet her dad.

✳

All of the blood has drained from my face. 'Do you remember her?' I whisper. 'Candy?'

Johnny looks away, but nods. 'Yeah. I remember her.'

I feel like I'm going to throw up. 'So it's true?'

He doesn't answer immediately. 'There's a chance that it is.'

'But… But… What if she slept with someone else? What if this girl isn't yours?' My words come out in a rush.

'That's possible of course. Wendel is arranging a paternity test.'

I wrench my hands away from Johnny. He puts his hand on my shoulder, but I shrug him off. 'Don't touch me!' I blurt, violently edging away.

'Fuck,' he mutters, covering his face with his hands.

'Don't you feel sorry for yourself!' I all but shout. 'I should have known this was going to happen when I married you!'

'But you *did* marry me!' he raises his voice in return, his expression fierce. 'For better or for worse!'

My face crumbles and he takes me into his arms.

'I'm sorry, I'm sorry,' he murmurs against my hair as a lump forms in my throat and hot tears spring into my eyes. 'We'll know as early as next week. It might be nothing to worry about.'

Deep in my heart, though, I know that Johnny will always give me something to worry about.

The next day, Wendel confirms that the paternity test has been delivered direct to the girl's stepfather. They live in Maidenhead, in Berkshire. Jessica is only fifteen. I wonder what's going through her mind, having just discovered that her father is Johnny Jefferson, one of the most recognisable people in the world.

I can't even imagine.

It'll be a few days before the tests come back. But in the meantime, Wendel emails through a picture of Jessica.

My heart sinks. We don't need a paternity test. The evidence is right here in front of us. She looks just like her dad. And there's no doubt in my mind that said dad is my husband.

❆

My best friend Bess calls me on Tuesday afternoon when Johnny is at the studio. Despite the earth-shattering news, he's determined to continue recording his album.

'It's been a pretty shit few days, to be honest,' I tell her glumly when she asks how I am.

'What's up?' She sounds concerned.

It goes without saying that she'll never repeat anything I tell her in confidence. 'Johnny has a daughter.'

'*What?*' She's aghast.

'She's fifteen. Her mother died recently, and her stepfather has only just told her the truth about who her dad is.'

Silence. 'Are you sure?'

'Pretty much. The paternity test results will come back in the next couple of days, but I've seen a picture. She looks just like him.'

'In what way?'

'Same eyes, tousled blonde hair… I don't know, she just *looks* like him. She's very pretty.'

'Jesus. How's Johnny taking it?'

I hesitate. 'He's knocked for six, to be honest.'

❆

Last night I came downstairs after putting the kids to bed to find Johnny sitting out on the terrace, sucking the life out of a cigarette in much the same way as I'd imagine a vampire sucking the blood out of its victim.

'Oh, hon,' I'd said with disappointment.

'Just *don't*,' he'd snapped, holding his hand up to keep me at bay.

'It's okay,' I'd said gently, going over and taking his hand. It was shaking. 'Oh, Johnny.' I bent down and kissed him on the top of his head, then rubbed his rigid back, my heart going out to him. He inhaled a deep breath and exhaled unsteadily. I've rarely seen him so cut up. I'd been so hard on him the last couple of days, barely speaking to him, barely looking at him, too hurt and confused to consider that he might need consoling himself. Now I felt fiercely protective and horrendously guilty for pushing him away.

'It's going to be alright,' I said, sitting down next to him on the sun-lounger and resting my chin on his shoulder. He didn't look at me, taking another drag, but blowing the smoke away from me, so I knew he still cared. 'I'm sorry I've been so distant, but we *will* get through this.'

'I really want a fucking drink,' he replied under his breath and terror pulsed through me. 'I won't.' He glanced at me sharply before stabbing his fag out on the stone ground. 'But I really fucking want one.'

'We'll get through this,' I promised him again, more firmly this time.

✳

'He's going to a meeting tonight,' I tell Bess now. She knows I mean an AA meeting. 'I think he might start smoking again, which makes me so sad after everything he went through to give up.'

'Hey,' she says gently. 'What are you going to do if the test comes back positive?'

'I don't know. I'm sure it *will* come back positive, but it's really down to the girl. Her name is Jessica. I don't know what she'll want to do. Presumably she'll want to meet Johnny.'

I refrain from bitterly adding, 'Who wouldn't?' It's terrible of me to judge someone I don't know, but she's a teenage girl. How could she *not* be beside herself to discover that her dad is rich and famous?

And then I remember that she's lost her mum and I can't even imagine what she's going through. A wave of sympathy crashes through me. I'm all over the bloody place. I'm trying so hard to stay calm and objective, but it's difficult. Johnny and I have only been married a year and a half and now this huge damn curveball has been thrown at us. Our lives will never be the same again.

Johnny has a teenage daughter! Of course he's going to have to see her, to get to know her, to support her. But what will she be like? What if she's a boy-mad, badly behaved little shit? Seeing Dana again has reminded me how awful it was when she was with Johnny. I couldn't bear to be back in LA with another loose cannon living in our house.

Anger surges through me once more, but I try to control it. After last night, I know I have to be rock-solid for Johnny. That's the way it's always been. I can't risk him going off the rails again.

'Have you told your parents, yet?' Bess asks me.

'No. Just Kitty.' She called me the day after the premiere. She and Dex snogged each other that night at Chateau Marmont and they've since been on a proper date.

But as for telling my parents... 'I'll wait until the test results are confirmed.' Delaying tactics. I'm dreading how they'll react.

'Shit,' Bess says.

'I really wish you were here,' I murmur.

She sighs, then: 'Do you want me to show you something to cheer you up?'

'Show me something? You're five and a half thousand miles away, how are you going to do that?'

'It's on the internet, you ninny.' She instantly sounds more perky, and it has a knock-on effect of brightening my mood. 'I can't believe I've only just seen it,' she adds.

'Go on, then,' I say.

'Right. Go to YouTube and type in "Tom McFly's wedding speech".'

'Tom from McFly's wedding speech?'

'Yeah. Trust me, you'll love it. Hang on a sec, I'm going to watch it too, so I know which bit you're crying at.'

'*Crying?*' I ask with alarm.

'Just put it on,' she snaps.

I purse my lips and follow her directions.

'Are you ready?' she asks.

'Yep.' Then I spy the clip length. 'It's nearly fifteen minutes long!'

'Shut up. Okay, press Play on the count of three. One, two, three...'

Unconvinced, I press Play.

Fifteen minutes later...

'Oh my God, that is *SOOOOO* cute!' I squeal into the receiver, wiping away tears of emotion.

'I know!' Bess squeals back. '*I* want to marry him!'

'Me too! I think that is the cutest thing I've ever seen in my life!'

'Told you you'd love it,' Bess says with glee.

'Are you staring at pictures of puppies again?'

I jump at the sound of Johnny's voice, spinning around on my swivel chair to see him standing at the doorway, one arm resting on the doorframe.

'Johnny's back,' I tell Bess, sniffing loudly.

'Don't tell him about Tom, otherwise he'll get a complex,' she warns jokily.

Hmm…

'Better go. Thanks for cheering me up. Chat tomorrow maybe?'

'Sure. Call me anytime. Well, not in the middle of the night, obviously. Unless you really need to. If it's a proper emergency—'

'Bye, Bess,' I laughingly interrupt.

'See ya.'

We hang up. I look back at Johnny to see him standing there and I'm struck by an odd sense of déjà vu, remembering a time from our past when he would come into this office to chat to me, his employee. I was in love with him then and it hurt. It really hurt.

It still hurts…

'What were you watching?' he asks quietly, seeing the smile slip from my face.

'Tom from McFly's wedding speech,' I reply dully.

He screws up his nose and comes into the office, pulling up the chair next to mine. 'Tom from McFly?'

'Yeah.' I stare at him defiantly. Johnny has always picked on my taste in music, but I've always been a pop girl, not a rock chick.

He reaches over and presses Play. Tom starts to talk about

how doesn't know how to write a speech, but he does know how to write a song. And then he starts to sing his entire wedding speech and I love it all over again.

'Well, I'm glad he's managed to cheer you up,' Johnny says sardonically.

'I *adore* him!'

'Fuck me,' he snaps, reaching over and clicking on the pause button. 'Wasn't my wedding speech good enough for you?'

'I would have preferred it if you'd sung a song,' I tease him, even though, actually, his wedding speech was beautifully heartfelt and made everyone cry, including me.

'Fucking hell,' he mutters again, sitting back in his seat and eyeing me. 'So what do you want to do, get married again?'

'Are we getting a divorce first?' I shoot back, raising one eyebrow.

His brow creases. 'Don't say that.'

'I'm only joking!' I cry, reaching forward and taking his hands, hating how pear-shaped things have got between us.

'I've written you loads of songs,' he says crossly.

'I know, I know, and they were lovely…'

'*Lovely?*' He's appalled at the description and I can't help but laugh. His face softens. He runs his fingertips down the side of my leg.

I lean towards him and gently rest my forehead against his. My earlier tension and anger feels long gone. I don't know when it will return, but for now I just want to feel close to the love of my life again.

'It's going to be okay,' he whispers.

I've been saying the same thing, but something tells me our lives will never be this perfect, ever again.

❄

A couple of days later, we get the results back. Confirmed: fifteen-year-old Jessica Pickerill is Johnny's biological daughter.

On Friday night, Johnny fills me in on the meeting Wendel had with her earlier that day in London.

'She wants to meet me.'

Surprise, surprise.

'You can't blame her,' he says, seeing the look on my face.

'No, I know.' I shake my head, feeling bad for letting my bitterness seep through to the surface again. 'When?'

He shrugs. 'I don't know. The sooner the better, don't you think?'

'Isn't she at school? Oh, I suppose she's breaking up for the holidays soon.' I answer my own question. 'But what about *our* holiday?'

We had planned on going to a private island at the end of July, a sort of reward for all of the time Johnny's been spending in the studio.

'She can come afterwards,' Johnny suggests.

'No,' I say quickly. 'What about before? Just for a week?'

'Really?' He sounds hesitant. That would mean her coming out next week. 'Are you sure?'

'God, no, I'm anything but. But I don't want this hanging over us all summer.'

'Fair point,' he says quietly.

'Sorry, that sounded very selfish,' I apologise, remembering that there's a young girl's feelings to consider, not just mine and my immediate family's. 'I imagine she'd prefer to meet you sooner rather than later, too,' I add.

'I'll ask Wendel to speak to her on Monday.'

'Okay.' I think for a moment. 'I presume he got her to sign a confidentiality clause?'

'He asked her to keep quiet about it.'

'Johnny!' I exclaim. 'She's a teenage girl! How is she going to keep quiet about the fact that her dad is a famous rock star?'

'I don't know, Meg,' he replies with frustration. 'But I don't feel we can throw legal shit at her when she's only just found out about me! She *is* my daughter. It's not fair.'

My mouth abruptly closes. Johnny has a teenage daughter. The reality of our situation has belatedly sunk in, and its impact feels like a slap across the face.

The next day is Phoenix's first birthday and I've never felt less like celebrating. I've gone from feeling angry and tearful to just tearful. I feel like there's a perpetual lump in my throat that won't go away. I would give anything to be back in Henley, living in our own little world in our beautiful old house surrounded by my friends and their children. I returned to LA knowing that I would miss my mummy pals and our playdates, but I told myself that I'd make new friends, go to new playgroups. So far I've been too busy settling back into the house and researching schools and nurseries for Barney. Johnny is out all day, and right now I need him more than ever, yet when we're together, despite the front I'm putting on of being strong, all I feel is distance.

And so we have a little birthday celebration, just the four of us, and I've never felt so lonely. I'm fighting back tears when we sing 'Happy Birthday', overcome with emotion about this big milestone in my baby boy's life. I would give anything to be celebrating back home, surrounded by children and babies and our extended family, and be blissfully ignorant of a one-time groupie called Candy.

✳

Two days later, Jessica's flight is booked. She's coming to LA on Sunday.

I nod when Johnny tells me that night. I've now moved on to feeling strangely detached about the whole thing.

'Are you okay?' he asks warily. His fingers are fidgeting and I know he wants to smoke, but he's trying not to start up again.

'Did you ever manage to get hold of Santiago?' He was Johnny's pool boy and sometime gardener, and Johnny once went mental when I nicked a cigarette from him.

Johnny frowns. 'Why are you asking about Santiago now?'

'We've managed to bring back Samuel and Lewis, but what about him? I want him back. I liked him. He was a friend and I don't have many in this fucking country!'

My fury hits me like a wall. I'm up and down like a rollercoaster at the moment.

Johnny's jaw twitches. 'I managed to get hold of his mum. He's taken a year out to go travelling.'

I go back to feeling surreally detached again. 'Maybe we'll be able to re-hire him when he gets back,' I say in a monotone voice.

'Maybe.' He looks away from me, down at the city lights twinkling in the distance. We're sitting at the bench table, side by side, with our backs resting against the hard concrete. The baby monitors are glowing green on the table behind us, our sons fast asleep inside the house. The sun is just setting and the sky is orange, but there are no stars, yet. I can hear a far-off police car whizzing through the hills with its siren blazing.

We stay silent for a long time, then I feel his eyes on me once more. 'Are we going to be alright?'

I feel the tension radiating from him as I stare down at the view and ponder this question for a little too long.

I turn to look at him and feel physical pain at the sight of the apprehension in his eyes. I brush my thumb across his warm face. His stubble is prickly under my touch. He hasn't shaved for days.

'We've been through much worse than this,' I say, smiling through the sudden onslaught of tears. He exhales in a rush and I realise he was holding his breath, and then he's crushing *my* breath out of me as he holds me tightly.

'I love you,' I say into his shoulder.

'I love you, too.' His deep voice is thick with emotion.

'We're going to be okay. Of *course* we're going to be okay. I'll always love you, Johnny. I always have and I always will.'

He hugs me even tighter, and then he's kissing me as though his life depended on it. I passionately return his kiss and he pulls me to my feet, carrying me a few steps to the lawn sloping away from the house. He lays me down and covers my body with his, trapping me and keeping me exactly where he wants me.

Which is exactly where *I* want to be.

We make love there, on the grass, and it's like it's our very first time, raw and passionate and full of need and longing. Afterwards, he stays on top of me, both of us breathing heavily, as I stare past him to the newly shining stars in the sky beyond. I know without a shadow of a doubt that, despite his flaws, despite his past, Johnny is worth fighting for. And I swear to myself that I'll never let anyone come between us, whoever they may be.

✳

I spend the next couple of days getting everything ready for Jessica's imminent arrival. We're putting her in the White Room, which was my room once.

I remember the second time I came here with Barney; Johnny's PA at the time had filled the bathroom cabinets with all sorts of cosmetic goodies. I want to do the same for Jessica to make her feel welcome, so I go shopping to stock up, taking a strange amount of pleasure at the thought of seeing her excitement. I hope she *is* excited.

Johnny told me that she grew up in a small townhouse with no luxuries to speak of. He also told me how her mother died on Jessica's fifteenth birthday; struck by glass falling from a loose window on her way to pick up Jessica's birthday cake. We both get a little emotional when we think about that.

I hope I can be a friend to this girl. I hope my jealousy and insecurity don't get in the way. I want to be strong for her, to help her through this incredibly tumultuous time in her life. I hope she lets me.

✳

After lunch on Sunday, Johnny tells me that he wants to go for a bike ride.

'But she's going to be here in a couple of hours,' I reply with a frown.

'I need to get out,' he says. 'Just for a bit.'

I can tell from his expression that he needs his freedom to compose himself. I know how he feels.

I wish I could go with him, but it's Sunday and we have no help with childcare today. I'm relieved it will just be the four of us when Jessica arrives. I still haven't got used to having staff, and however much some of them feel like friends, I'm glad no one else is here to witness such a private event.

'Okay,' I say. 'Make sure you're back by three thirty, though. Just to be on the safe side in case she comes through immigration early.'

Davey is going to collect her from the airport. He didn't say anything, but I could tell from his eyes how shocked he was when I showed him the picture of Jessica. He probably would have recognised her without it.

Phoenix is asleep and Barney is watching TV in the living room, so I leave him to it and walk out to the garage to see Johnny off. I've always thought he looks hot in his biker jacket. He climbs onto the big, black Ducati and pushes his dirty-blond hair off his face before pulling the helmet over his head. My heart unexpectedly flips.

'What are you smiling at?' he asks me, and I wish I'd kissed him before he'd covered his face. I shake my head and shrug, but he must be a mind-reader because he takes his helmet off again.

'Come here,' he mutters with a grin. He kisses me gently on my lips, but I want more.

'Jeez,' he murmurs under his breath. 'You're making me want to take you on the grass again.'

We kiss each other, long and languidly, before I finally pull away. 'I'd better get back inside to Barney,' I say with regret.

'Just wait until I get you on that island,' he says in a low voice, still staring at my lips.

'Can't wait,' I say. We've just got to get through this week.

He pulls on his helmet again, flipping up his visor. His eyes look even greener when they're all I can see of his face.

'Don't be late,' I warn.

'I won't.'

I take a step backwards and he fires up the ignition. He flips down his visor and I watch with a heart full of love as he roars out of the garage and down the driveway, leaving a dust cloud in his wake.

Two hours later, my earlier warm and fuzzy feeling has been replaced with nervous anxiety. Davey has called me to say he's en route from the airport and Johnny is still not back. Where the bloody hell is he?

Phoenix is awake and the three of us are in the living room, playing with Barney's collection of cars. I'm so distracted, so on edge. I just want Johnny here. I try calling his mobile, but he doesn't answer.

And then he rings me back. 'Is she there yet?'

'Almost! Get your arse back here right now!'

'I'm on my way,' he promises, ending the call.

Argh! Still living in his own little world…

I'm pacing the living room when the buzzer goes to let me know that the gates have opened. Is it Davey or Johnny? Please, please, please let it be Johnny.

I hurry to the front door and open it in time to see Davey's limo pull up in front of the house.

Oh God, she's here. I try to compose myself.

What will she be like?

Please let her be a nice, friendly, easy-going teenager.

No, those words surely don't belong in the same sentence.

Oh, just please don't let her give us too much grief.

Davey gets out of the car and cocks his chauffer's hat at me, but I can barely smile back at him, because then he's opening the car door and one chunky, black boot is stepping out, followed by a slim, tanned leg, and a short silver swing dress which would be more at home in a nightclub. I stare with shock at the stunning girl with surfer-style, platinum blonde hair and eyes hidden by dark sunglasses.

She looks like a wannabe rock star.

She looks like trouble.

She's Johnny's daughter and she's here to stay.

Holy shit, what the hell have we let ourselves in for?

Johnny's Girl

Extra scene

Over the years, lots of you have asked me to re-write my stories from the point of view of my male characters. The only time I've written from the perspective of any of my guys was when I wrote Leo's chapter in The Longest Holiday. *But after writing* Johnny's Girl, *I was intrigued to know more about what was going on inside Johnny's mind, so I wrote this bonus scene for* The Hidden Paige. *Here he's about to break the news about Jessie to Meg…*

'I'll call you as soon as I know more,' Wendel says.

'Fine,' I reply, terminating our conversation and dropping the phone onto my desk with a clatter. I rest my elbows on the polished surface and stare in a daze at the dark computer screen in front of me.

My solicitor has just told me that I have a teenage daughter. Allegedly.

Fuck! How am I going to break this to Meg?

I rake my hands halfway through my hair and apply pressure to my skull with my fingertips. She's going to go absolutely mental.

'Johnny?' I jolt at the sound of Annie's voice and turn to see my PA standing in the office doorway. She looks worried. 'Is everything okay? Davey's on the drive if you want him to take you to the party? Or will you go by bike?'

'What's the time?' I ask dully.

'Ten thirty.'

Christ, I'm late. 'Better take the Merc,' I reply with a heavy sigh as I get to my feet.

My Ducati would be quicker, but I'll be bringing Meg home with me and the bike can stress her out. I'm going to be doing enough of that as it is.

'Is there anything I can do?' Annie asks with concern, taking a step backwards to let me pass.

'Ring Wendel. He'll fill you in. And let Davey know I'll be outside in ten,' I say over my shoulder.

'You got it,' she calls after me.

Annie doesn't normally work this late, but she's baby-sitting the boys tonight. Kitty persuaded Meg to go to a film premiere and I've been in the studio all day with Mikky, my producer. I only got home a few minutes before Wendel called.

I go upstairs to our bedroom and turn on the shower in the en suite before emptying the contents of my pockets onto the bed. I notice that a text message from Meg has come in, asking me what time I'll be there. I don't reply because she'll see me soon enough. And then she'll wish I'd stayed away.

*

Davey has worked for me for years, so he knows when I'm not in the mood to talk. He leaves the screen up and the intercom set to private once I'm inside the car.

It's not far to Chateau Marmont where the premiere after party is taking place. I know it well – it used to be one of my regular hangouts – but I'm in no rush to face my wife.

My head is all over the place as I sit at the back of the limo and stare out of the darkened windows at the lights of LA, lit up like a Christmas tree in the valley far below. I feel like there's a tiny person inside my stomach, tying my intestines into a giant ball of knots.

When we're nearing West Hollywood, my phone vibrates against my thigh. I dig it out of my pocket and tense at the sight of Nutmeg's name on the Caller ID.

The device carries on buzzing in the palm of my hand, but I can't bring myself to answer. I feel paralysed. Paralysed with fear. What can I say to her? I hope I can figure it out when I see her because I haven't got a freaking clue at the moment.

Her call goes through to voicemail, and at that moment, I totally despise myself. I'm such a coward. I suddenly have an overwhelming urge to drown my sorrows in a bottle of whiskey.

No.

I've been clean for almost two and a half years and I'm not going to screw it up now. A fag wouldn't go amiss, but I've quit smoking, too, goddammit. When Meg was pregnant with Phoenix she refused to kiss me because my breath made her queasy. That was incentive enough. It killed me not to kiss her. She's the love of my life.

I wonder if she drank the champagne I arranged for her. She avoids alcohol when she's around me, but I really wanted her to treat herself tonight. She's barely gone out since she had our little boys.

Curious more than anything, I lean forward to open the mini-fridge, and sure enough, there's a half-empty bottle of Perrier-Jouët Rosé inside. I'm happy for her, but then my demons are back and I'm fighting a fresh urge to take a swig.

Steeling myself, I swing the fridge door shut and slump into my seat.

What is my brown-eyed girl going to think of me? I feel downright nauseous. I love her so much. The thought of hurting her hurts *me*. She's *got* to forgive me for this. But I know it's one of her worst nightmares come true. She's always been worried that, one day, one of my groupies will come forward and say I'm the father of their child. I've been careful over the years, but clearly not careful enough. Nowhere near fucking careful enough.

For a moment, my mind is filled with memories of Candy, the girl in question. She was only seventeen when we hooked up – and that was nearly seventeen years ago. I can picture her laughing, her long, dark hair damp with sweat as she's bandied about in the mosh pit. I remember her being at the front when we did our slow number, and I can see her looking up at me with those big, caramel-coloured eyes of hers.

I saw her at the next concert, and the next, and the next… I wanted her, but she didn't give herself to me easily, which surprised me. She certainly got my attention.

I've thought about her a little over the years. She wasn't like so many of the others. I wouldn't recognise most of them if I saw them on the street, but Candice, I remember. I liked her. I liked her a lot. So I did what I always did and dicked her around when she tried to get closer to me.

I can't believe she's dead. Out of the blue, grief hits me like a wall. She was killed a few months ago when a loose window fell down on her from a four-storey height. She was just casually walking along the pavement…

What a terrible way to go. And she left behind an only child, a girl called Jessica, or Jessie, as she apparently likes to be known. Candy died on the exact day of Jessie's fifteenth birthday.

My chest feels constricted. *I have a daughter!* And she was completely clueless about me until a few days ago.

Her stepdad thought it was time she knew the truth. He was the one who contacted Wendel.

How could Candy have kept this to herself all these years?

She had a baby girl – *my* baby girl – and she didn't see fit to tell me?

So many emotions are swirling around inside me. I don't know what to think.

My phone buzzes again – once – snapping me out of my thoughts. I have a voicemail – from Meg, at a guess. I put my phone up to my ear and listen.

'*Where the hell are you?*'

Uh-oh, she's angry with me.

'*Dana is here and I could really do with your support.*'

Damn, my ex-girlfriend is there? She'd better not be harassing my Nutmeg…

'*I'm about to go and say hi to Joseph Strike…*'

WHAT?

'*… so get your arse here ASAP.*'

She ends the call.

What the fuck? Jealousy swiftly snakes its way into the emotions already wreaking havoc on my gut. Joseph fucking Strike? *Really*, Nutmeg? If I get there and see her cosying up to that actor bastard, I'll go mad.

And then I remember what I have to tell her, and my boiling blood cools to Arctic temperatures.

She might have had a fling with him once, but she's not interested in him anymore, I tell myself as the rational part of my brain kicks in. She's just upset about Dana. I put Meg through enough shit over my drug addict ex-girlfriend to last a lifetime. It's no wonder she's freaking out.

Needing a diversion, I press the button to bring the privacy screen down. I chat to Davey for the rest of the journey.

We arrive soon afterwards, pulling up right outside the venue. Davey opens the car door to clicks and flashes from the cameras of dozens of waiting paps. I can't be arsed to deal with the wolves tonight, so I ignore their shouts and head straight for the entrance. The party is in full swing and I can feel eyes on me as I make my way through the crowds, searching for my girl. A few people I know try to stop me, but I brush them off.

'I can't talk right now,' I tell them, one after the other. 'I'm looking for Meg. Have you seen her?'

When I find her, she's standing near Kitty on the other side of the terrace. She looks so beautiful tonight, even more so than usual. She's wearing a black mini dress over skinny black jeans and her blonde hair stands out against the colour. I dig black on her. She appears happy, which is weird, considering the tone of her message, but at least she doesn't seem to be angry anymore. And then she spots me and her eyes widen slightly, the small smile that was on her lips freezing in place. She says something to Kitty and begins walking towards me.

I keep getting stopped on my way over to her, which is damn annoying, but finally we reach each other.

'Hey,' she says.

'Hi.'

I bend down and kiss her, sliding my hand into her hair and holding her to my chest. God, I need her so much. I can't believe I'm about to crush her with my news.

She pulls away, looking up at me with a guarded expression on her face. 'Did you get my message?'

'Just now,' I reply, frowning as I remember the crap she was spewing about Joseph Strike. Did she talk to him? Is that why she was looking so pleased with herself? 'I was already on my way when you called,' I say, scanning the room. 'Where is he?' I ask when I fail to locate him.

'I think he's gone,' she tells me. She looks guilty, which gets my back up.

'Did you speak to him?' I know I sound jealous – I fucking *am* jealous – but I'm damned if I can help it.

She blushes. Great. That's a yes, then.

'I said hi, yeah,' she replies defensively, staring up at me with defiant eyes. 'Have you seen Dana?' she asks in turn.

Bollocks. Forgot about her. I scan the room again and spy her pretty quickly, pausing for a second to check her over. Jeez, she looks a state. She's been using again. You just can't help some people.

'Mm,' I belatedly reply to Meg's question, before dragging my eyes away from my crazy ex.

'Do you want to speak to her?' Meg asks, her voice wavering.

Aw, Nutmeg! My heart goes out to her. Of course I don't, baby.

'No,' I respond firmly, wanting to ease her pain. 'I have nothing to say to her.'

I lean down again and give her a tender kiss, and then a fresh bout of nerves pulses through me, reminding me of what I need to do. 'Can I take you home?' I ask in her ear.

She glances over her shoulder. 'Um… Kitty.'

'She looks fine to me,' I say. She's flirting with some dark-haired dude. 'I need to talk to you,' I add quietly, nerves washing over me again.

Her eyes dart up to look at me.

'What's wrong?' she demands, knowing instantly that *something* is.

'I'll tell you in the car,' I reply.

'Is it the boys?'

Jesus, I didn't mean to freak her out. 'No, no,' I quickly assure her, placing my hands on her shoulders. 'Everyone's fine.'

She still looks worried, and she should be.

We say goodbye to Kitty and the bloke she's with and get the hell out of there. Davey is still pulled up out the front, so we get in quickly and he closes the door behind us. I return the privacy screen to its up position and usher Meg to the back of the car. We sit side-by-side and I shift to face her, reaching for her hands.

You've just got to say it…

Okay, okay.

Okay.

I take a deep breath, but I can't look at her.

'Wendel called me,' I start.

'Right…' she replies uneasily.

I force myself to meet her wary brown eyes, but God, it hurts.

'Just tell me,' she encourages. She wants to know, now.

I push myself to continue, but as I speak, I can see the cogs of her brain whirring, ten to the dozen. 'Wendel spoke to a man earlier today, claiming to be the stepfather of a girl who is the daughter of one of my first fans. Her mother passed away recently. She never told her daughter who her real father was.'

I experience a pang as I watch her confusion transform into horror. She knows exactly where I'm going with this. I squeeze her hands tighter.

'I'm sorry,' I whisper, feeling like I could hurl at any given moment.

'Tell me everything,' she says flatly.

And so I bring her up to date, breaking into a cold sweat when I realise that her hands have gone limp in mine. She's looking pale by the time I finish.

'Do you remember her?' she whispers. 'Candy?'

I glance out of the window and nod. 'Yeah, I remember her.'

'So it's true?' she says.

I swallow. Nothing is definite yet. Wendel wants Jessica – Jessie – to do a paternity test. Maybe Candy lied to Stuart, Jessie's stepdad, back then. Maybe I'm not the biological father. Maybe...

But no, I have a feeling about this. I shouldn't give Meg false hope.

'There's a chance that it is,' I reply.

'But... But... What if she slept with someone else?' It hurts to watch her clutching at straws. 'What if the girl isn't yours?'

'That's possible, of course. Wendel is arranging a paternity test.'

To my dismay, she rips her hands away from me. I reach across to try to comfort her, but she shrugs me off. 'Don't touch me!' she yells, flinching away from me.

'Fuck,' I mutter, covering my face with my hands. I feel like the walls of the incredible life we had are crashing down around me. It's all going to shit.

'Don't you feel sorry for yourself!' she shouts suddenly, making me jolt. 'I should have known this was going to happen when I married you!'

'But you *did* marry me!' I raise my voice at her, the anger masking my fear. 'For better or for worse!'

And then her face crumples and I pull her to me and hold her against my chest, telling her I'm sorry, over and over again. 'We'll know as early as next week,' I murmur as she sniffs. 'It might be nothing to worry about.'

But even as I say it, I know it's not true. I have a strong feeling that a teenage girl called Jessie is about to become a permanent feature in our lives.

I wonder what she's like...

Daisy Says Goodbye

I tend to write my books in real-time, and then I get myself into all sorts of trouble if I try to cameo past characters in new stories — I literally get headaches trying to work out who would have been doing what at which time!

When I decided to touch base with Daisy and Luis for The Hidden Paige, *I considered writing about what they might be doing now. But, actually, what I really wanted to do was go back in time to soon after the end of* Chasing Daisy *and find out what happened next, so luckily I saved myself a headache with this one...*

Lots of you have asked for another mini sequel since reading this, and I do have some ideas, so stay tuned!

Even with my thick winter coat on, I can still feel the cold dampness of the stone bench seeping through to my skin.

I don't mind. It's worth enduring the temperature for this view.

I take a deep breath of the clean, crisp air and exhale slowly, gazing towards the pine-blanketed mountains. The sun has only just dipped below the peaks and now the land is cast in shadow and all around it's still and quiet. There are no goats in the small adjoining paddock these days, and no chickens. Since my nonna passed away, there's no one here to look after them, but we try to come when we can. This is still my favourite place in the world – and I've been to a *lot* of places.

When you've worked on the Formula 1 circuit, travelling goes with the territory. I no longer work on the circuit, but I still travel a lot. *That* goes with the territory of having a Formula 1 racing driver as a boyfriend…

Luis and I spent Christmas at his home in Brazil within the vast bosom of his enormous family, but now we have retreated to Northern Tuscany in the mountains near Lucca for an intimate New Year's Eve. It's getting increasingly cold and dark out here, but behind me, the little stone cottage nestled into the hills is cosy and warm. Just as I think it might be time to venture back inside, I hear the front door open.

'Daisy?' Luis calls, and there's concern in his voice.

I look over my shoulder to see him standing in the open doorway. 'I'm on the terrace,' I call back, getting to my feet.

'It's freezing out here!' he exclaims.

'I was watching the sunset,' I reply with a smile as I walk towards him. He still looks half asleep. I left him out cold on the sofa about forty-five minutes ago.

'You should've woken me,' he replies, kissing me gently on my lips and drawing me inside, pushing the door closed behind me. 'Now I'm going to be up all night,' he adds.

'Is that a promise?' I raise one eyebrow and he grins at me, sliding his hands around my waist and pulling me against his hard chest. He lowers his head and kisses the hollow of my neck, making me giggle, but then his kisses continue upwards to my jawline, and a shiver starts at my scalp and ripples all the way down my spine to my toes. I clasp his face with my hands and pull his mouth onto mine.

I will never get tired of kissing this man. It has been a whirlwind couple of years, but I swear I fall in love with him a little more every day. He lifts me and carries me through to the bedroom.

Dinner can wait.

❉

'Cheers.' We smile at each other across the small candlelit kitchen table and chink glasses.

'Happy New Year,' I say, taking a sip of fizzing prosecco before tucking into my meal: a warming lamb casserole that needed to be rescued with hot water earlier to loosen the gravy. It was in the oven for much longer than it needed to be, but it still tastes great, even if I do say so myself.

'Mmm.' Luis obviously agrees with me.

Cooking is my passion. I'm doing a culinary arts course and loving every minute of it. It's been a challenge trying to juggle my studies around going to the races with Luis, but so far I've just about pulled it off. I'm more worried about my upcoming sandwich year when I'll be working in a restaurant. I'm terrified my new boss will be a ball-breaker about me taking time off at the weekends. I might have to miss some of Luis's races and it's going to kill me to not be able to support him. He loves seeing me standing on his side of the garage, but I do feel like a nervous wreck most of the time.

'Are you okay?' Luis asks, sensing my apprehension. 'Is it the magazine?'

'What? No!' I exclaim with a grin. 'I told you I was fine about it.'

He looks relieved.

'Surely you know me well enough to know that,' I chide.

He shrugs. 'I thought I did.'

We picked up some magazines and newspapers at the airport and I was a bit taken aback to come across pictures of my ex boyfriend's recent wedding. Johnny is a famous rock star and he recently married his former personal assistant, Meg. I used to be his personal assistant, too, once, and I know from experience that he's capable of mixing business with pleasure with sometimes disastrous results. It used to hurt, thinking about him, but Johnny has nothing on me these days.

Luis and I actually met him and Meg last summer at the Goodwood Festival of Speed, a motorsport event in the UK. Luis helped to carry their baby son's buggy up some steps for Meg, having no idea of her connection to me. Later we saw them both outside on the lawn watching the fireworks. It was the first time I'd spoken to Johnny since I quit working for him, but I had seen him around, and each occasion had left me with a bad taste in my mouth.

This time it was different. *He* was different. He seemed happy and content, like he'd finally left his wild days behind him. We exchanged a few words and he was friendly and kind – very different from the selfish bastard who broke my heart years before. I felt at peace with it, with him, but seeing his wedding pictures still came as a bit of a surprise.

I think Luis will always worry that our history will come back to bite us.

'Are *you* okay?' I ask with concern, sensing that something is still troubling him.

He looks across the table at me, his brow creased.

'What is it?' I ask, feeling a flutter of panic in my stomach.

'It's nothing,' he replies with a small smile.

He's not a very good liar.

'Luis?' I say warily.

His face breaks into a sheepish grin. 'I wanted to wait until midnight.'

'Wait for what?' I ask with alarm as he pushes his chair out from the table and stands up, coming around to my side of the table. Now I'm really confused.

He crouches down in front of me so we're eye to eye. 'You know how much I love you, don't you?' he says in a low voice.

'Yes. I think so. But you're worrying me now.'

'Don't be worried,' he implores, but *he* looks freaked out, so why shouldn't I be?

'Just tell me,' I say.

'I'm not telling,' he says cryptically. 'I'm *asking*.'

I frown at him. And then he proffers up a small, velvet black box and everything becomes clear. I draw a sharp intake of breath as he opens it up, revealing a white platinum band, encrusted with an array of sparkling diamonds, large and small.

'I love you so much,' he says, emotion wracking his voice. 'Will you marry me?'

My eyes fill with tears and we both stand up, me throwing my arms around him and him holding me so tight I can barely breathe.

'Of course I will.' I squeeze my eyes shut, but a tiny potent memory pierces my moment of happiness, and just for a millisecond I imagine Will standing there in my nonna's kitchen, staring at us both.

❄

The next few months are hectic, to say the least. My clever, talented fiancé – it still feels strange to be calling him that – won the championship last autumn so the media attention goes into overdrive once the racing season kicks off again in March. I'm used to the cameras hunting me out for the pre-requisite supportive partner shots, but now the news of our engagement has hit, I'm even more of a target.

We've decided to get married in Brazil this August – Luis didn't want to wait a sensible person's length of time, and God knows, I'm all for living life in the fast lane.

Some would call me crazy, but I've handed over almost all of the organisational reigns to Luis's mother. I have very little time to plan a wedding and I actually don't care what happens on the day, as long as I'm married to the love of my life by the end of it. Judging by all of the ideas Mariana – Luis's mother – keeps emailing me, we're going to have one hell of a wedding.

All I have to sort is my dress and my shoes. It's June now and I am leaving it pretty damn late, as my friend Holly remarks when we go shopping together in London. She's my chief bridesmaid, and Luis's three sisters will step into the other roles. Four bridesmaids seems pretty excessive to me, but it was a much kinder option than having to choose between them.

'I can't believe you're so relaxed,' Holly comments as I hold one dress up in front of me and gaze at my reflection in the full-length mirror. 'Beautiful,' she comments obligingly.

'You've said that about all of them so far,' I point out.

'And I meant it. You could wear a sack and still look good.'

I roll my eyes good-naturedly and she smirks at me. 'What about you?' I ask. 'Have you found a dress yet?'

'Oh, I've got some pictures to show you, actually,' she says, pulling out her phone while I hand the dress to the waiting attendant and ask to try it on. She heads off to hang it in a changing room while I turn my attention to the photos on Holly's phone.

It's customary in Brazil for the bridesmaids to choose their own dresses as long as they're the same length (skimming the floor) and all of a completely different colour. Luis's sisters have already chosen their dresses, so Holly has to avoid blue, green and mauve.

'I like the yellow one,' I say, peering at the photos on her phone as she flicks through them. 'Definitely. It looks incredible on you.'

'Are you sure?'

'Absolutely.'

'I wish I could make snap decisions like you.' She shoves

her phone back into her bag. 'Seriously, how are you so laidback? I can't believe you're letting Luis's mum plan everything. Aren't you worried?'

'Not at all.' I shake my head. 'I'm just grateful she's happy to do it. Luis's sisters keep telling me that she's having the time of her life.'

Luis is a national hero in Brazil, and his entire family were beside themselves when we told them we were getting married in his home country rather than in America, where I hail from. My parents were less thrilled.

'Does your mum mind being left out of all the planning?' Holly asks carefully.

The corners of my lips turn down. 'She's not happy about it, but I think she understands. She hasn't exactly been there for me over the years. My father was more pissed off.'

'Why?' Holly pulls a face. She knows we barely speak, so she can't think why he'd care about my wedding plans.

'I've robbed him of his chance to blow his cash and impress his buddies,' I explain.

'Oh,' Holly says in a small voice.

'But hey, it could've been worse. At least we sent him an invite.'

My father and I have never been on the best of terms. He likes to control the people around him and has been incensed on more than one occasion when he's discovered that he can't control *me*. He got me fired from my hospitality job at the Formula 1 team that Luis drove for because he pulled the strings behind the scenes of one of our major sponsors. Luckily, I was ready to move on anyway. I'm over it now. When I didn't go running home with my tail between my legs, he had to admit defeat. Although he never actually apologised, my mother has been trying to mediate, and she has said that they will both be attending the wedding.

I haven't gone so far as to ask him to walk me down the aisle, but I'm not ruling it out completely.

Luis's mom has offered up any number of uncles to do the honour, so I have options. It's actually tradition for the groom to choose his groomsmen on the day of the wedding, so maybe I'll leave it that late, too, but I don't know, it could be time to lay the past to rest.

As I think that thought, I'm struck with another vision of Will, staring at me solemnly with his blue eyes.

I sigh and Holly looks up sharply.

I shake my head at her slightly. 'I keep thinking about Will at the moment,' I say quietly.

She gives me a sympathetic smile. 'It's only natural at this time of year.'

Will Trust, Luis's teammate and the man I once fell in love with, died in a racing accident at the British Grand Prix three years ago. It was the anniversary of his death last week.

'He was on my mind a lot the night Luis's proposed, too,' I admit heavily. 'In fact, I've thought about him more in the last few months than I have in the last year. I wish I could lay him to rest before I get married, you know?' I flick a glance her way. 'I've never even been to see his grave so that doesn't help.'

She looks concerned. 'Well, maybe you *should* visit his grave.'

'I can't. He's buried in his parents' local church graveyard, right next to Laura's parents' house.'

Laura was Will's childhood sweetheart, the girl next door and the woman all the press thought he was destined to marry. But Will broke up with her just before he died – mainly because of his attraction to me. Laura, for some reason, kept up the charade of them still being a couple.

Luis and Holly were the only ones who knew I lost him, too.

I shudder at the thought of how much that hurt Luis back then. He was in love with me, and I was mourning the loss of his teammate and biggest rival. And he was mourning the loss of his friend. It almost broke him.

'It's still a public graveyard, right?' Holly checks. 'Surely anyone can go to visit?'

'Yes, but I've always been terrified of bumping into Laura. Who knows when she'll be visiting her parents? I don't think Will's mother or father would look twice at me – you know what cold fish they were – but Laura would remember me, I'm sure. What if she put two and two together? I don't want to upset her like that.'

Holly frowns, deep in thought. 'You know what, I don't think she's in the country at the moment. Pete told me that she didn't go to Will's ball because she was in America.'

Pete is Holly's boyfriend's brother and he's a mechanic for a Formula 1 team, so we all still cross paths, even though we no longer work together.

The ball Holly is talking about is a charity event that Laura organises every year around the anniversary of Will's death. Luis and I donate money, but we've never attended. It would just be too difficult, too weird.

'She's definitely out of the country?' I ask, my mind ticking over.

'I can double check for you, but I think so,' Holly replies.

Later I head back home to our house in Hampstead, still no closer to buying the dress of my dreams. I did manage to secure shoes – gold ones, which are traditional for brides in Brazil – but that seemed to be of little comfort to Holly, who warned me how much time it takes to custom-make a wedding dress.

Luis was visiting team headquarters earlier – several of the Formula 1 teams are based here in the UK, so, thankfully, he doesn't have to travel far – but he's still not back when I arrive.

I get on with rustling up some dinner for us. I've become pretty friendly with Luis's nutritionist over the last couple of years, and between us we do what we can to keep Luis fit and healthy. You may not think that sitting behind the wheel of a car is physically challenging, but it takes a hell of a lot of stamina to be a racing driver, not to mention skill.

Luis arrives home just as I'm finishing up with the preparation. We're having Thai-inspired sea bass and it'll be cooked in no time once we're ready to eat.

'Hey,' he says wearily as I come into the hall to greet him.

'What's wrong?' I ask, seeing the look on his face as his arms snake around my waist.

'I missed you,' he murmurs, burying his face in my neck.

'You only saw me this morning,' I point out.

'And it's been a long day without you.'

'Are you okay?' I ask gently, pulling away to look into his eyes.

He pauses before continuing. 'I've just been on the phone with Holly.'

My stomach churns. Surely she didn't tell him that I want to visit Will's grave?

'She told me that you want to visit Will's grave.'

And there it is: our history coming back to bite us.

The blood drains away from my face and I take a step

backwards as a cold flush washes over me. Why would she do that?

'I texted her to ask how your wedding dress shopping was going,' he reveals. 'Don't be angry,' he adds. 'She replied that I needed to get you to, how did she put it? "Pull your finger out".' He sounds wry. 'I called her on speakerphone to find out what she meant and it just came out. She's worried about you.'

Holly and Luis have always got along well, ever since they worked together. It's not common for them to speak on the phone, but it's not completely uncommon either: Holly is Luis's go-to girl when it comes to my birthday and Christmas presents.

'Should *I* be worried?' he asks cautiously.

'Of course not!' I exclaim, trying to control my emotions. I know that Holly only has my best interests at heart, but I'm not sure it's in Luis's best interests to know that Will has been on my mind a lot lately.

'Because we can go, you know. The two of us. To Will's grave.'

I stare at him for a long moment, seeing the shine come over his eyes and then my own vision goes blurry. His arms close around me and I nod, then we stand there in the hall for a long time, just holding each other.

✳

Will was buried in a graveyard beside a small, old church in a village in Cambridgeshire. I duck out of my lessons the next day and Luis drives us both there, heading north of London on the M11 for about an hour before coming off the motorway. He found out in advance where the graveyard is, and I map-read to direct him. We could just plug in the satnav – in fact, he's so good with directions that he could probably find the village from memory – but I'm glad to have something to take my mind off things.

I've been remembering the last time Luis drove me up this way. It was for Will's funeral. The memorial service took place at one of the big university churches in the city, but his family laid him to rest near their family home.

I wasn't privy to the private service that they held, but I knew without a shadow of a doubt that Will would have wanted me there. It was incredibly painful to be left out in the cold.

Soon we're driving along winding, narrow roads, over tumbling streams, through tiny, quaint villages and past amazing, old thatched cottages with crooked walls and exposed beams. It's a perfect English summer's day with only a few fluffy clouds in the pale-blue sky. The trees are green and leafy and the fields are full of golden rods of wheat, bathed in sunshine. This is where Will grew up, a far cry from Luis's Brazil and my Manhattan.

There are very few houses in Will's tiny village and they're mostly set within large grounds and back behind brick and stone walls.

'I think that's Will's home, there,' Luis says quietly, slowing to a stop outside a gated driveway. The front garden is densely populated by mature trees and behind them is an imposing country house.

'And that must be Laura's,' I say, taking in the farmhouse to its right with its cream walls and red-tiled roof.

Further to the right, up a small hill, is a stone church.

Luis slowly drives towards it, pulling off the side of the

gravelly road. He climbs out and I turn around to pick up the bunch of white calla lilies lying on the back seat. My door opens and Luis is standing there, giving me a sad smile.

I take his hand and step out, noticing both of our wedding rings glinting beside each other in the afternoon sunshine. Diamond engagement rings like mine are not actually typical in Brazil – it's more normal for both the bride and groom to wear wedding rings on their right hands when they get engaged. During the marriage service they're swapped to their left hands. Seeing our rings together like this now gives me strength.

I give Luis's hand a squeeze and stand up, pushing the door of his navy-blue Ferrari closed behind me. We walk hand-in-hand up the hill towards the church where unstable-looking gravestones from decades past are crammed into every square metre of available space. My breath catches as I scan the scene before me, my eyes almost immediately seeking out the clean, straight lines of the most recent memorial, belonging to Will.

Luis tenses beside me, and I know that he's seen it too.

We walk towards it together and stand in silence, looking down at the inscription for William Henry Trust. There is a vase of fresh red roses sitting on the white stones covering his grave, and I wonder if his mother or father brings them here regularly, or if these flowers have just been placed here in honour of the anniversary of Will's death. I suspect it's the former. The flowers probably came from his family's rose garden.

I thought his parents seemed icy and aloof when I met them. Will said they showed no interest in his racing career when he was growing up. It was his grandfather who encouraged his passion, taking him karting from the age of seven and leaving him money when he passed away so he could fund himself. But his parents loved him and were devastated when he died. They didn't outwardly show warmth – Will and I had that in common. Luis, on the other hand, was raised in a crazy big household full of love.

For a moment, I can see Will clearly, staring at me in the darkness of his Chelsea home as we lay side by side on his bed. We had fallen asleep together and until that point had done nothing more than kiss. It was supposed to stay that way until he'd had a clean break from Laura, but in the very early hours of the morning we both woke up, and without speaking a single word, we made love to each other. A few short hours later, he was gone.

A lump springs up in my throat and I want to give myself over to my grief, but I don't want to upset the man standing beside me by losing it over another.

Did I really, truly love Will? I barely knew him. I was certainly infatuated with him, but what I felt for him pales in comparison to the depth of my feelings for Luis. That's a tricky word, though: comparison. It's hard to compete with a dead man.

I lean down and place the flowers on Will's grave, then reach over and touch my hand to his gravestone, looking up sharply at the sound of Luis's shaky breathing. His bottom lip is trembling dangerously and his eyes are about to spill over with tears.

'Oh, baby,' I murmur, my heart going out to him. And then he pulls me into his arms and we both let out a sob, holding each other tightly as we let go.

It is cathartic and liberating, and later when we return to the car, I feel lighter than I have in months.

'I didn't know that I needed to do that,' Luis says, staring across at me.

I grin and loop my hand around the back of his neck, drawing him in for a tender kiss. 'I'm so glad we're in this together,' I whisper. 'I love you so much. A million times more than I've ever loved anyone. You do know that, right?'

He grins at me, his dark–brown eyes twinkling. 'I do. Now can we please go and get married?'

'Hell yeah,' I reply. 'I just need to buy a goddamn dress.'

'Okay, let's go shopping then,' he says flippantly.

'As if!' I laugh.

'Why? It's not like I haven't bought a dress for you before,' he says with a smirk.

Yes, and it was absolutely stunning. The night I wore it was the first time we slept together.

'Your mum would go mental. It's bad luck!'

'Who gives a shit about that?' he asks.

I laugh. 'No way. I've got it covered. And I promise you can still take it off me at the end of the night.'

'Well, in that case…' he says with a cheeky grin, pulling back onto the main road. And just like that, we leave our past behind us and drive towards the bright future that lies ahead.

When Lily Met Alice

Bronte, from Thirteen Weddings, *first appears in* Pictures of Lily *as the magazine editorial assistant who Lily covers for. When I came to write* Thirteen Weddings, *I wanted to acknowledge Lily in turn, and, as Bronte now worked at a celebrity magazine in London – very much modelled on* heat *magazine, where I worked between 2000 and 2007 – it also felt like the perfect time to cameo film star Joseph Strike and his now-fiancée, Alice, from* One Perfect Summer.

To remind you of the scene from Thirteen Weddings, *Bronte hears that Alice and Joe have visited the conservation park where Lily works, and Alice's baby bump has been caught on camera – an exclusive and big news in celebrity-magazine world! Bronte calls Lily for the inside scoop.*

I wasn't sure whether to write this scene from Lily's or Alice's point of view, so I asked readers of The Hidden Paige *to vote. Lily won with 55 per cent of the votes, so* voila! *Here she is…*

I wake up alone. It's the early hours of the morning and Ben is not in bed beside me. This is not *that* unusual, considering, but I know I won't get back to sleep without checking on him.

I sit up and slide my feet out onto the cold floorboards, then find my dressing gown from behind the door and slip my arms into it, tying a knot across my no-longer-flat stomach. I pad quietly out of our bedroom and into the hall. The lights are off in the kitchen, so I take a left and head for the living room, coming to a sudden stop in the doorway.

My husband is fast asleep on the sofa, lying on his back with his bare arms cradling a tiny bundle to his chest. This is the third morning in a row that I've found him here.

'You need your sleep,' he told me yesterday morning when I berated him for not just bringing her into bed with us when he heard her crying.

'So do you,' I pointed out.

And now here he is again, *and* he has to work again today.

Poor thing, he must be cold. It's late March and the nights are drawing in, especially here in the Adelaide Hills. We still haven't upgraded the heating in our home, which once belonged to Ben's grandmother. She practically raised him and left this house to him when she died. We've been living in it for about three years now, but we can't afford much on his keeper's salary or my part-time junior keeper wage. If only I could make more of a living as a photographer.

'You can't expect it to happen overnight,' Ben keeps telling me.

Still, I wish it would.

I walk back down the hall and into the spare room, dragging the blanket off the end of the bed, before returning to the living room with it. Quietly making my way over to Ben, I lay the blanket across his sleeping body. He stirs and his eyes open, even darker blue than usual in this dim light. I can see now how red they are.

'Sorry, I didn't mean to wake you,' I whisper, squeezing onto the sofa beside him and touching my hand to his warm, stubbly face. 'You look exhausted,' I add with concern.

'I'm oka—' His sentence is cut off by the violence of his yawn. His broad chest rises and falls, the bundle moving with it. But still, she sleeps.

'Oh, sweetheart,' I murmur. 'Let me take her so you can go back to bed.'

He shakes his head and smiles up at me, sleepily. 'I'm alright. How was your night?'

'Better,' I tell him with a nod. I slept badly the night before.

'What's the time?' he asks.

'Six.'

'Lily, get back to bed!' he commands in a loud whisper.

'No, I'm awake now. You should go.'

'I've got to be up in an hour anyway,' he says, never one to complain.

'I love you,' I tell him, bending down to kiss him.

'Mmm,' he murmurs against me, the vibration tickling my

lips. I deepen our kiss and he returns my gesture with increasing passion. I really want him to put his arms around me, but he can't because they're otherwise engaged. It's very frustrating.

'Do you think she'll transfer?' I ask impatiently against his hot mouth.

'Let's try,' he replies with his own sense of urgency. He sits up, still cradling the bundle to his chest.

I'm rigid with tension as I watch him put her down. Her eyes open and she lets out a squeak.

No, no, NO!

He glances up at me, his face filled with regret and apology as she continues to cry.

'I'd better feed her,' he says.

No!

But I just nod, the disappointment crushing. A mean part of me wishes he'd let her cry, but I know that's not Ben.

If this is what he's like with a two-week-old infant koala, what's he going to be like when I give birth to an actual human baby in five months' time?

※

'Do you think someone else might like to take the joey tonight?' I ask Ben later, over breakfast. I try to keep my voice sounding casual so he doesn't think I'm a complete hussy who wants him only for his body.

God, I really do want his body, though.

He cocks his head to one side. 'Mike and Janine are still on holiday until Wednesday, but I suppose I could ask Owen.'

'Yes! Surely he'd love that?' Owen is quite new so he

should be overjoyed at the prospect of having a baby koala all to himself.

'I don't know,' Ben replies with a shrug. 'We'll see.'

He finds it hard to relinquish responsibility for the tiny orphans who are brought into the conservation park where we work. This little joey was knocked off her mother's back by a car while crossing the road. The mother was killed and her daughter was badly hurt – Ben was worried he'd have to euthanise her – but she's improved over the last couple of days. I know he'll struggle to give her up to Owen. And now I feel bad for asking him to. At least she'll soon be well enough to be relocated to the hospital room at work with the other hand-reared infants.

'What time's your lunch break today?' I ask, changing the subject and reaching across to adjust the collar of his dark-green polo shirt. He's wearing khaki-coloured shorts and brown boots. Soon it will be too cold for anything but trousers, but the weather is supposed to be nice today. Yesterday it rained practically from dawn till dusk.

'I'm doing the dingo talk at eleven and then I'm on koala duty all afternoon, so I'll probably have half an hour or so from noon. You planning on coming in?'

'Yes. I want to take a few more website pics while the weather's nice.'

I'm helping to overhaul the conservation park's website. I'm not getting paid for the photographs I'm taking, unfortunately, but I don't mind when it's something I enjoy doing so much.

'You really want to come in on your day off?' Ben asks worriedly. It's Sunday. Not that that makes any difference when you're a keeper. The weekends are our busiest days. 'Don't you think you should rest up a bit?'

'I'm fine,' I reassure him with a smile. Sometimes it's like he thinks I'm going to break. 'I'll go back to bed when you leave,' I say, although actually, I'm more likely to tidy the house.

'In that case, I'd better get moving.' He gets to his feet and bends down to kiss my forehead.

'Oi,' I say, tilting my face up.

He smiles and bends down properly to peck me on my lips, but it's not enough. It's never enough.

'I'll bring you a packed lunch,' I tell him. 'Meet you behind the café?'

'Okay. Love you.'

'Love you, too.'

❄

As I won't be officially at work today, I don't bother getting dressed in my uniform. Instead, I pull on my low-rise jeans, looking down at my stomach with surprise when I realise that I can barely do up the buttons. I'm four months' pregnant, and I've only recently started to show. Persevering with my outfit, I crack on with the housework, but my stomach seems to expand within minutes so after a while, I give up on my jeans and choose comfort instead. Even my yellow dress is quite snug over my small bump, but I decide to make the most of wearing it because it won't fit for much longer. I pull on my black cardi over the top, prepare a small picnic and then head into work.

The weather forecast was spot on: it's a beautiful autumnal day, with a chill in the air, but not a cloud to be seen. I put down the windows as I drive through the winding hills towards Mount Lofty and the conservation park. The scent of eucalyptus fills the car and I breathe in deeply and feel a rush of happiness.

I'm so lucky.

Behind the café, there's a grassy slope that crackles with the sound of brittle, dead gum leaves wherever you walk. Ben is not here yet, but he will be soon, so I put down my camera bag and spread out our picnic blanket. I wouldn't normally bother with one, but the grass is still damp after yesterday's rainfall.

In front of me is a big, old eucalyptus tree and I love staring up through its branches at the sky beyond. I remember when I used to think its brown-grey tree bark was ghostly – shredding from the trunk in long, thin strips. I still think it's eerily beautiful.

I hear his footsteps approaching and look over my shoulder to smile at my husband.

'There's a sight for sore eyes,' he says with a grin, coming over and flopping down beside me on the rug.

'Hey.' I smile as he smooths his hand over my tummy and kisses my bump.

'Hello, baby,' he whispers.

'Hello,' I reply in a silly, small voice. He laughs and glances at me with his gorgeous blue eyes, then lies down beside me, propping himself up on one elbow.

'You look beautiful,' he says seriously, his hand skimming my curves.

'You're not so bad yourself,' I reply, reaching up to run my fingers through his sandy blond hair. Sometimes I still can't believe that this man – the first and only true love of my life – is married to me.

He tilts his face and kisses my wrist, but I pull him down towards me so he kisses me properly. Honestly, I'm insatiable.

'Can't we sneak into the food store or something?' I suggest cheekily.

He chuckles against my mouth. 'Tempting as it is to give you a quickie, we'd probably get fired if we got caught.'

'Argh,' I mutter with fake annoyance, pushing him away.

He smiles at me as I unpack our food, trying to focus on something other than the screaming hormones raging around my body. I've been so turned on recently – even more than usual. I blame the baby.

It's a bit weird, really. What's Mother Nature playing at? I'm pregnant now, job done.

'What are you thinking?' Ben asks.

'You don't want to know,' I reply wryly, passing him a cheese sandwich.

After we've eaten, I pack away the remnants of our picnic while Ben lies on his back with his eyes closed, his breathing becoming slow and steady. As I pause for a moment to drink in the sight of him, a memory comes back to me of a long time ago, when we sat in this very place. I was in love with him, then, but it was a forbidden, illicit love.

The electrical charge that seemed to pass between us is still present now, but my feelings are even deeper, stronger, more irrepressible.

I don't want to wake him, but my craving to be held is hard to ignore, so I touch his hand, prompting him to jerk awake. *Whoops.*

I feel a stab of guilt, but then he opens up his arm to me and I snuggle in close, resting my face against his chest. His strong arm comes around me and he kisses the top of my head.

'I should get back to work,' he says in a deep, gruff voice.

'Five more minutes,' I plead, nuzzling my face against his warm neck and now stubble-free jaw.

'BEN! LILY!'

We jolt apart from each other at the sound of our names being shouted.

'You will never guess who's just walked in,' Owen says, practically buzzing with excitement as he jogs towards us.

Ben and I stare at him, fathomless, but he doesn't wait for us to speculate.

'Joseph Strike and his bird!' he erupts.

'No way?' I glance at Ben with delight and then back at Owen. 'Are you serious?'

'Absolutely.' He turns and runs off, not waiting for us to follow.

I scramble to my feet and Ben looks up at me with surprise. 'Come on!' I urge, beckoning at him wildly.

'Since when did you become a Strike Stalker?' he asks with a raised eyebrow, slowly standing up.

'Since *Phoenix Seven*,' I admit, blushing. I liked Joseph Strike as an actor before, but that film sparked a bit of a crush. Well, more than a bit, actually. Obviously I totally love and fancy and adore and desire Ben like mad, but *come on*! It's *Joseph Strike*!

Ben purses his lips. 'I've got to get back to work.' He reaches down to pick up the picnic rug, shaking off the dead leaves and folding it up. 'Do you want me to put this stuff back in the truck?' He nods down at our picnic things.

My eyes dart towards the entrance, but I imagine Joseph and Alice – his fiancée – will be well inside by now, so there's no point in *me* going to the car park.

'Actually, yeah, that'd be great,' I reply edgily.

'You're not going to follow him around like a crazy person, are you?' he asks circumspectly.

'Of course not,' I mutter, the colour on my face deepening as I pick up my camera bag and sling it over my shoulder.

'Lily…' He laughs under his breath. 'Come and hang out with me by the koalas,' he suggests steadily. 'Then you'll be there when they come by.'

Excellent plan! 'Okay,' I agree with a goofy grin.

He looks up at the sky and then back at me with weary but amused resignation.

'I'll get started on photographing the koalas in the lofts,' I say, trying to sound professional and less like a demented fan as I turn to hurry off. 'See you there in a bit,' I call over my shoulder.

I almost squeal when I see the crowd of people up ahead. There they are! I think I can just about make out Joseph Strike's dark-haired head over the sea of hanger-ons, but I can't see Alice. He's tall for Hollywood, but she's only small. Probably about two dozen tourists have surrounded them and are excitedly chattering and jostling against each other, trying to get closer to the superstar and his famous childhood sweetheart.

I suddenly feel dirty at the thought of joining them. With a sigh I decide to take an alternative route to the koala lofts and Ben.

❄

'Can we keep it down, please?' Ben urges the crowd with gentle authority. 'These little creatures have very sensitive hearing.'

'Sorry,' Joseph apologises in a low voice, his jaw twitching.

He is very, *very* good-looking up close. He's only about thirty – the same age as me – but he's well over six-foot tall with dark-brown eyes and short black hair. He's wearing navy-blue shorts and a slim-fitting cream-coloured T-shirt that reveals the definition of the much-admired chest it encases. His arms are tanned, lean and muscled.

Is it definitely autumn? Because it feels like high summer right now.

'It's alright, buddy, it's not your fault,' Ben replies kindly. I love that he's so unaffected by the famous actor standing before him. 'Usually, it's just these guys that are the ones getting stared at,' Ben adds, indicating the koala on the perch – his name is Bonty. Ben asked me to bring him over to his perch earlier, so I'd be standing here when the celebs arrived. Gotta love that man.

'How many koalas do you have?' Joseph asks.

'About fifty. They're only allowed to be handled for twenty minutes each a day, so we rotate them fairly regularly. Don't we, Lily?' He smiles at me at that point.

'Mmmhmm,' I reply, concentrating on keeping a straight face as Joseph and Alice look at me. I really am trying very hard not to jump up and down on the spot and scream like a lunatic.

'This is my wife, Lily,' Ben explains.

I jolt and my heart speeds up a little bit faster as Joseph and Alice say hello.

I smile shyly and say hello back.

'She's a keeper here, too, but it's her day off,' Ben adds.

'And you still came in to work?' Joseph asks me. Now my heart feels like it's pounding in my ears.

'I love it here,' I reply timidly, looking at Ben. 'This is where we met.'

'Aw,' Alice says, smiling at Joseph.

She's very pretty – about my height with shoulder-length dark hair and clear, green, almond-shaped eyes. No wonder he couldn't forget her after they lost contact as teenagers.

Practically everyone knows their love story.

'So, who wants to hold Bonty?' Ben asks, his eyes darting between Joseph and Alice.

'Al?' Joseph asks.

'I'd love to, but I don't want to freak him out with all these people around,' she replies nervously.

At that moment, a short, stocky man with greying brown hair breaks through the crowd being held back by security and runs forward with his iPhone held aloft.

'Whoa,' Joseph says, putting his hand protectively on Alice's tummy as the man clicks off a shot. A second later, a bodyguard is upon him.

'Daddy!' we hear a girl cry from the crowd, and are startled to see a ten-year-old holding her arms out to the man who's being restrained. He must be her father.

'He's fine,' Joseph calls to his bodyguard, who releases the man to be with his daughter. 'We should move on,' Joseph says regretfully to Alice.

'Okay.' She nods and I hear a small sigh escape her lips.

'Ben,' I interrupt quietly. 'Can I make a suggestion? Hospital rooms?'

He smiles and nods at me with understanding, before turning to Joseph and Alice. 'Lily's made a good point. Would you guys like a private tour of the hospital rooms? It's where we keep the injured animals and the orphans who are being hand-reared,' he explains. 'We've got a two-week old joey in there at the moment. You can hold her in peace and quiet if you'd like?'

Alice's face lights up as she looks at Joe. He smiles down at her, then at Ben and me. 'That would be fantastic,' he says.

I really want to kiss my husband right now.

Ben looks over his shoulder and beckons to one of our colleagues, Serena, who comes to take over.

'It's this way,' he says to the rest of us, nodding ahead. I walk beside him, fighting the urge to squeeze his hand as Joseph, Alice, three enormous bodyguards and half of the tourists here at the conservation park follow us.

When we reach the hospital rooms, one of the bodyguards comes inside the main door with us, leaving the other two with the hordes outside.

'There's no need for this, Liam,' Joseph says, putting an arm out to stop him from going into the actual hospital rooms.

'Sir,' the bodyguard replies firmly, and he doesn't look like he's the sort to back down.

'Joe, it's fine,' Alice murmurs, taking his arm. He steps aside.

'Sorry about this,' Joseph apologises once again to us, as Liam moves past him into the room. I guess he's scoping it out, checking it's safe.

'No worries at all,' Ben replies good-naturedly.

I get the feeling Joseph apologises a lot. He seems like a really nice guy, and I'm not just saying that because I fancy him.

A moment later, Liam exits with a decisive nod.

Alice thanks him as we file inside, leaving him out in the corridor.

'Here she is,' Ben says softly, his voice full of warmth as he goes over to the nearest holding cage and lifts out the little joey that's been keeping us company for the past few nights. He glances at me. 'Do you want to prepare a feed?'

'Sure.' I'm glad to have something to do as I mix a lactose-free formula from powder and water. Koalas are allergic to cow's milk.

'I thought you meant a kangaroo joey!' I hear Alice exclaim in a whisper at the little bundle of grey and white fur in Ben's arms.

'Whoa, she is so cute,' Joseph agrees in a low voice.

'Joey is the term for all marsupial infants,' Ben clarifies, passing her to Alice, who nearly spontaneously combusts on the spot as the tiny creature wraps its long black claws around her finger and looks up at her with warm brown eyes.

'Aw,' Joseph says, reaching forward to stroke her grey-white hair. The joey squeaks.

'Coming, little one,' I say, attaching a teat to a syringe. 'She'll use a bottle when she's older,' I explain, passing Alice the device.

The joey suckles immediately.

'Does she have a name?' Alice asks.

'Not yet, so if you have any ideas...' Ben replies.

'We're rubbish at names,' Joseph says. 'We still haven't come up with any for this one, yet, and he's due in four months.' He rubs Alice's belly.

'Are you pregnant?' I ask with surprise. I haven't heard they're expecting. They're engaged, but not married.

She nods. 'Twenty weeks.'

How could I have missed her bump? I can see it clearly now, with Joseph's hand smoothing down her light-blue maxi dress.

'I'm sixteen weeks,' I tell her with a grin.

'Are you really? Congratulations!'

'You too! We don't know what we're having yet,' I say.

'Are you going to find out?' Alice asks.

'We haven't decided yet.' I nod at Ben. 'I think this one wants a surprise.'

'I figured we'll have enough surprises when the baby arrives,' Joseph interjects.

'So you're having a boy?' I ask. I noticed he said 'he' a few moments ago.

'Yeah,' Joseph replies, and the look of love in his eyes as he regards his fiancée does a strange thing to my crush. It practically snuffs it out. It's hard to fancy a guy who is so completely and utterly devoted to another woman. I smile at Ben and the corresponding smile he gives me reignites the fire in my stomach.

There we go. Crush firmly back in place. But for the right person, this time.

'Shall I get Beryl out?' I ask Ben. 'For Joseph?'

'Call me Joe,' Joseph interjects.

'Sure,' Ben replies.

I go over to another holding cage and lift out Beryl, a two-month-old. I carry her over my shoulder like a baby, and pass her to Joe. His hands brush mine as he takes her from me.

Okay, maybe the crush isn't completely gone.

'Are you guys here on holiday or working?' Ben asks him, ever at ease.

'I've been filming,' Joe explains. 'But we're taking a break now, aren't we, Al?'

'A very welcome one,' she replies with a smile at the joey in her arms. She glances up at me. 'I don't suppose you'd grab my iPhone out of my bag and snap off a few shots of us, would you? It's in the front pocket.'

'Of course I can,' I reply, doing as she asks.

A few moments later, another idea comes to me.

'Would you like me to shoot some with my professional

camera, too? I could email them to you. I promise I wouldn't send them to anyone else,' I add quickly.

'That would be great!' she enthuses, grinning at Joe.

'Yeah, definitely! Thanks,' he adds warmly.

I suggest we go out the back under the eucalyptus trees. There's a fence, so it's private, but the shots will look much better with natural daylight.

Liam, the bodyguard, comes too. I'd almost forgotten he was there, he's so quiet.

'Ready?' I ask when they get into position. 'On the count of three: one, two, three!' I begin to click off shots of them looking straight to camera. 'How about a couple of natural ones, now?' I propose, continuing to shoot as Ben swaps Beryl with the joey to give the latter a break. I capture a particularly lovely one of Joe resting his hand on Alice's baby bump.

Afterwards, we go back inside and I show them the whole set, one after the other. I've relaxed now that I'm behind a camera. 'I'll delete this one,' I say of an unflattering angle, acting on it immediately. 'And this one,' I add of another where Joe has his eyes closed. 'Are you happy with these?' I double check, flicking through them again.

'They're fantastic,' Alice says. 'Are you a professional photographer?'

'I'm trying to be,' I tell her modestly.

'Yes, she is,' Ben firmly corrects me. 'She's *brilliant*,' he adds with pride. 'She's been taking photos for this place's website, but she's had her pictures featured in magazines and newspapers, too.'

'Have you really?' Joe asks, cocking his head to one side.

'I used to freelance at Tetlan, a magazine publishing house,' I tell him with a shrug. 'So I have a few contacts.'

'It's nothing to do with your contacts,' Ben says seriously. 'She took all of those,' he adds, pointing to the publicity posters on the walls.

Alice goes to take a closer look. 'They're excellent,' she says.

'Really good,' Joe adds.

'Thanks,' I reply, my face warming at their praise.

'Well you must let us pay you for these,' Alice says resolutely.

'Absolutely not,' I cut her off.

'No, we *will* pay for them, won't we Joe?' she says.

'I won't hear of it!' I interrupt indignantly. 'There's no way I'll take any money from you, so don't say another word.'

Joe chuckles and Alice raises her eyebrows at him.

'If you could do an autograph for my sisters, though, I'd be delighted,' I say with a smile.

'I can certainly do that,' Joe replies while Alice delves into her handbag and pulls out a stack of publicity shots.

'How many sisters do you have?' she asks me.

'Three,' I reply.

Joe takes three pictures and a silver pen from Alice and bends over the counter, writing while I tell him the names of my half-siblings: Kay, Olivia and Isabel.

'They are going to flip out when these come through the post,' I comment. 'They live in the UK.'

'Can I do one for you guys, too?' Joe asks, glancing at Ben.

'You may as well just make it out to *her*, buddy,' Ben replies wearily. I giggle and slip my arm around his waist, smiling up at him.

'You should get a photo with Joe,' Alice suggests.

'Okay!' I don't need to be asked twice. I hand my camera to Ben, then stand next to Joe, willing myself not to blush as he puts his arm around my shoulders and bends down to press his cheek to mine.

A slightly manic giggle escapes my lips, but everyone pretends not to notice.

'I saw the trailer for *Two Things*, recently,' I say, slipping firmly into fan mode. 'It looks amazing!' It's out in Australia at the end of August.

'I can get you tickets for the premiere in Sydney in August if you'd like them?'

'Oh my God!' I squeak, unable to contain myself. 'That would be incredible!'

'You might be a bit busy in August, Lils,' Ben points out reasonably.

I stare at him with confusion and he looks meaningfully at my belly.

'Oh.' Dammit!

Joe chuckles. 'Maybe next time.'

Alice smiles at me, ruefully. 'I know exactly how you feel,' she commiserates. 'I'd planned on going on the publicity tour with him this time, but I won't be able to fly either.'

'Aw,' Joe says gently, rubbing her shoulder.

What a sweet couple.

While I'm putting my camera away, I hear Alice say something to Joe in a low tone. Out of the corner of my eye I see him listening and then nodding.

'Sure,' he replies.

'Um…' Alice starts, turning to me. 'This might seem a bit weird…'

I'm instantly curious.

'… But would you like to sell these?' she asks. 'No one knows I'm pregnant yet, so you could sell them as an exclusive. I don't know, it might help a little.' She looks awkward as she's relaying this, clearly not comfortable with the idea of being famous, which makes what she's suggesting even more astonishing.

'I... I... *Really?*' I ask with amazement, my head spinning as Ben smiles encouragingly.

'Absolutely,' Alice reiterates. 'Maybe they'll help you get your foot in the door or something. Not that you should stop being a wildlife photographer,' she adds hastily.

'Not likely,' Ben replies on my behalf, reaching across to squeeze my arm. He looks really pleased for me.

'We could do a mini interview, too,' Joe chips in.

'*Really?*' I seem to have lost the rest of my vocabulary.

'Of course. Jeez, it's nice to be asked, isn't it, babe?' He glances at Alice.

'Rather than told,' she explains to us with a wry smile.

'But I have one condition,' Joe adds with a raised eyebrow. 'Would you call the joey Alice?'

Alice laughs and Ben and I do, too. 'Alice it is,' Ben says.

*

With all of the excitement, Ben forgets to ask Owen to take Alice the joey, so we have no choice but to bring her home for another night.

I get to work after dinner, editing the photographs and typing up Joe's words. I send the shots over to Alice, as well as the interview for her approval, even though she didn't ask for it.

To my surprise, she replies after only a short while to say the piece is great and that she loves the pictures. I can't believe she gave me her personal email address.

'Who are you going to contact about this?' Ben asks,

bringing me a cup of tea. I turn to face him and he pulls up a chair to sit opposite me.

'I was wondering about calling Bronte at *Hebe* in London.'

Hebe is a celebrity weekly magazine and Bronte is a friend of mine from when I used to live and work in Sydney. We met at *Marbles* magazine when I covered for her as editorial assistant. I was asked to apply for her job when she got promoted to the picture desk, but I moved back to Adelaide with Ben instead to pursue my first love. Well, first *loves*: Photography *and* Ben.

He nods and lifts my foot up onto his lap, proceeding to massage it.

'*Hebe* would be perfect.'

I'd love to give the exclusive to my friend, especially as she's bought some of my pictures from me in the past. It would be nice to return the favour.

'That feels amazing,' I murmur, closing my eyes as Ben continues to work away at my foot.

'Will you ring her tonight?' he asks.

I shake my head, sleepily. 'I don't want to call her about work stuff on a Sunday.' It's only Sunday morning in England. 'I'll wait until she's at work tomorrow,' I add with a yawn. It will be tomorrow night here with the time difference, but I'd rather not leave a message on her voicemail in case someone else picks it up.

He nods and takes my other foot. My eyelids are feeling heavier by the second.

'Come on, beautiful, let's have an early night,' he says gently, after my third yawn in a row. He stands up and holds his hands down to me.

'You were amazing today,' I say seriously, as he pulls me to my feet.

He looks confused. 'What do you mean?'

'You were so cool. So calm and collected around them. I was fighting the urge to bounce up and down like an idiot.'

He laughs gently and tucks my chestnut-coloured hair behind my ears. 'Well, I don't fancy Joseph Strike, so it was a bit easier for me.'

'I don't fancy him, either.'

'Don't you, now,' he says wryly, not even bothering to punctuate his sentence with a question mark.

'Not as much as I do you,' I correct myself with a grin, sliding my arms around his waist.

He chuckles under his breath and holds me against his chest, rocking me slightly.

'Can we go to bed, now?' My voice is muffled. I pull away and look up at him, hoping he can see exactly what I plan on doing to him once we get there.

A smile plays about his lips as he bends down to kiss me.

'Alice' starts to squeak.

Ben sighs heavily against my mouth and pulls away to rest his forehead against mine. 'I'm sorry. She's due a feed,' he says wearily.

'Okay.' I tenderly touch my hand to his jaw and he raises his head to look at me disconsolately. 'I'll see you in a bit,' I say with a poignant look.

But I'm fast asleep by the time he joins me.

We oversleep the next morning so it's a rush to get out of the house. Both of us are at work today – me as a keeper, rather than a photographer. I'm still on a high after the previous day's excitement and I can't wait for the day to end so I can go home and call Bronte.

In the afternoon, Trudy in the office gets a call from Joseph

Strike's PA to say that he and Alice want to make a huge donation to the conservation park. She goes straight to tell Ben, who is elated.

'I'm so proud of you,' I say.

'It's nothing to do with me,' he replies modestly.

'Yes, it is,' I insist, nudging him delightedly.

❋

Bronte starts work at 9.30 a.m. UK time, so I have to wait until at least eight o'clock that night before I can call her. I decide to give her an extra half an hour to make herself a cup of tea before I ring, but by eight fifteen, I'm chomping at the bit.

'Shall I email her first, do you think?' I ask him.

'It wouldn't hurt,' he replies.

'Actually, I'm not sure she has the same email address.'

'You could email and then call, too,' he suggests.

'Okay, I'll just nip to the loo.'

Just as I'm finishing up, the phone rings. Ben answers, and a moment later he calls out to me.

'*It's Bronte!*'

'No shit?' I exclaim, rushing back through to the living room. I bet she's heard Joe was at the conservation park yesterday.

'She was just about to email you,' Ben says to Bronte, grinning up at me.

I grab the phone from him and clamber onto the sofa beside him.

'Joseph Strike,' I say into the receiver. 'Am I right?'

'Yes, you freaking are,' my friend replies in her familiarly bubbly Aussie accent. 'Did you see him?'

'I got pictures,' I reply, bursting to hear how she'll react to *that* little piece of information.

'No!' she gasps. 'Does she have a baby bump?'

How does she know Alice is pregnant?

'Clear as day,' I reply, trying not to seem fazed. 'I got some brilliant ones of him with his hand on her tummy.'

'Wow! Can we buy them from you?'

Eek! This is so exciting! I beam at Ben, who's clearly on the same wavelength.

'Ooh, I don't know... How much do you think they're worth?' I ask cheekily, making Ben throw back his head and silently guffaw.

'Who would have thought you'd become a pap,' Bronte says with a giggle.

'I did ask their permission first,' I tell her, playing it down. The truth is, they *offered* their permission.

'Did you?' Bronte asks with surprise.

'Yeah. His chick and I compared baby bumps,' I say nonchalantly, making Ben chortle under his breath again.

'*What?*' Bronte exclaims in my ear. 'Are you telling me you're pregnant?'

Oops. I still haven't got around to spilling the beans to everyone.

'Yes,' I laugh happily. 'Four months.'

'Oh, that is so lovely!' she squeals. 'I'm so excited for you! Is Ben pleased?'

'Ridiculously.'

He reaches over to stroke my waist. I am *so* having sex with him tonight. Sooner rather than later, I hope.

Focus! 'Anyway, Joseph didn't mind having his picture taken at all. They're such a lovely couple.' And they really were. They're the sort of people you could imagine being friends with, but I bet everyone who meets them thinks that. 'So, do you want to see them?' I ask.

'Yes, please. Have you shown them to anyone else?'

'Don't be daft. You were the first person I thought of.'

'Aw. I really, really appreciate this,' she says with genuine warmth.

'My pleasure. Give me your new email address and I'll send 'em over.'

We end the call and I grin at Ben, who claps his hands and rubs them together with glee. 'She already knew Alice is pregnant,' I say with downturned lips. 'So it's not an exclusive.'

'Don't worry about it,' Ben reassures me. 'It's still a big coup.'

I go to my desk to send over a few of my favourite pictures.

The wait for Bronte to call me back is *agonising*, but it's probably only about ten minutes.

'Hello?' I feel slightly breathless as I snatch up the phone.

'Hey, it's me,' she says. 'We all absolutely love the pictures.'

'Do you?' Yay!

'Yes. I'm with my boss right now and he'd like to buy the exclusive worldwide rights.'

I feel lightheaded when she tells me what they're offering. It's way more than I thought it would be. She sounds more reserved than usual in the presence of her editor, but at some point I'll ring her back and scream down the phone.

'I did a mini interview with them, too, so I'll send that over,' I tell her to her delight.

I'm not going to reveal that they're expecting a boy. Joe didn't talk about it in our official chat, and it feels like too much of an invasion of privacy to mention it. I didn't even feel comfortable asking Alice for permission via email.

When we hang up, I turn to Ben and relay Bronte's offer.

'That's fantastic!' He pulls me onto his lap and hugs me so tightly I can feel my bump pressing against his stomach.

'Shall we upgrade the heating system now?' I say with a smile.

'Is that what you want to spend it on?' he asks with surprise.

'Yes, and *lots* of baby stuff.'

He laughs. 'Fine by me.'

'Oh, and babysitters for the future,' I add, playfully pushing him away.

We've had far too many interruptions over the last few days, and it's not like we'll have much family help once the baby comes. My mum lives in Sydney and Ben's mum is in Perth, but that's a bit beside the point because they're both pretty useless. I'm sure our friends, Josh and Tina, will help out, but I don't want to impose too much.

Ben takes my hand. 'I'm sorry you've had to put up with the joey over these last few days,' he says solemnly.

'You never have to apologise for that,' I chide. 'But with that said, I'm bloody glad Owen has her tonight.' I jokily jerk my head in the direction of our bedroom. Nudge, nudge, wink, wink.

He laughs and manoeuvres me off his lap.

'It would be good to still have a bit of time for the two of us,' he agrees, leading me to the bedroom. 'Although, I bet you won't want to leave her side once she's here.'

'Are we having a girl, are we?' I ask with amusement as he switches on the light.

'Do you really want to find out?' he replies, his eyes glinting under his grandmother's small but exquisite antique chandelier.

'I think I agree with Joseph Strike. Plenty more surprises once he or she gets here.'

'Okay,' he says. He pauses, as though wondering whether to mention something.

'What is it?' I prompt.

'Don't feel pressured,' he starts. 'But if it *is* a girl, do you think we could consider calling her Elizabeth?'

'After your nan?'

He nods uncertainly.

'Ben, I would *love* that.'

His smile lights up his whole face and fills my stomach with butterflies.

'Now will you make love to me?' I hastily shrug off my cardie.

He chuckles. 'You'd say anything to get me into bed.'

I crack up at that, but then he bends down to catch the hem of my dress, silencing me.

'Will you still love me when I'm enormous?' I ask as he eases the garment over my bump.

I can just make out him rolling his eyes before my vision is obscured by yellow fabric. 'Always,' he says firmly to my face as it reappears.

I shiver from the cold and step forward to help him with his shirt, but my hands get distracted feeling the contours of his chest so he has to take it off unaided.

Soon we're entwined underneath the bedcovers, skin on skin, with our body heat warming each other up. He moves to cover me, supporting his weight with his elbows.

'I love you,' I tell him breathlessly between hot, hungry kisses.

He breaks away to cup my face and stares at me steadily. Sometimes I think I could drown in these eyes of his.

'I love you, too, Lily. I always will.'

The sincerity in his voice makes me feel unexpectedly

emotional. My eyes prick with tears and then, on sudden impulse, I reach down and pull him into me. We both gasp at the raw sensation of our bodies connecting.

Enough of the sentimental shit. Let's get jiggy with it.

Rose's Big Night Out

I always cry when I finish writing a book, and The One We Fell in Love With *was no exception. It felt absolutely right to leave it there on the beach with Rose and Eliza, but I was curious to know what happened on their night out with Toby, Lucy, Nathan, Sam and Molly, so I wrote it up for* The Hidden Paige!

I loved hopping back into the triplets' world and also getting a chance to revisit the characters from my first book, Lucy in the Sky. *Although* The One We Fell in Love With *was told in alternating chapters from the points of view of the three sisters, I felt Rose still had more to say, so it is she who is talking to us now in this extra chapter.*

That night I find myself sitting between Eliza and Toby in the beer garden of the Beach Hotel, just across the road from Byron Bay's Main Beach and the glittering Pacific Ocean. The sun's rays are still potent, so we're all wearing our sunnies, and it's blissful being able to kick back and relax after the madness of Christmas yesterday.

Sam, Molly, Nathan and Lucy are squeezed onto the bench seat opposite, and we're hearing about when Nathan and Lucy first met.

'They used to tell silly jokes to each other *all* the time,' Molly reveals. 'Nobody else found them funny.'

'Bullshit!' Nathan exclaims. 'They were hilarious!'

'Mate, they were rubbish,' Sam chips in, shaking his head.

'What do you call an elephant that doesn't matter?' Nathan asks me directly.

'I don't know.'

'An irrelephant,' he replies.

I crack up laughing.

'See?' Nathan says to his brother.

'Toby and Eliza didn't laugh,' Sam points out.

'They will at your cheese jokes,' Lucy prompts her husband.

Nathan smiles across the table at me, his blue eyes twinkling. I'm already giggling in anticipation.

'Did you hear about the explosion in the cheese factory?' he asks as Sam and Molly groan simultaneously and bury their faces in their hands.

I shrug.

'There was de-Brie everywhere.'

'Oh God,' Eliza says despairingly while Toby seems lost for words.

'You see what we mean?' Molly turns to them wearily.

'What did the cheese say when it looked in the mirror?' Nathan ignores them, focusing only on me, his willing subject. 'Halloumi.'

I snort and Toby chuckles.

'A kid threw a lump of cheddar at me. I thought, *that's not very mature…*'

Even Eliza sniggers.

And so it goes on… 'What kind of cheese do you use to lure a bear? Camembert. What kind of cheese do you use to hide a horse? Mascarpone. What do you call a cheese that doesn't belong to you? Nacho cheese.'

'Enough!' Sam shouts eventually, thumping his fist on the table. 'I can't *camem-bear* any more of this!'

We all fall about.

I'm going to miss the banter of this lot when we part ways, but Toby and I have accepted an invitation to stay with Nathan and Lucy in Manly, the beach-side suburb of Sydney where they live. They haven't had many date nights since the birth of their eighteen-month-old son, Finn, but they've said they'll organise a babysitter so they can take us out in the city. They're certainly making the most of their temporary freedom tonight.

We've just finished our beer-battered fish and chips and will be heading inside to watch the band soon, but for now, the sun is still fairly high in the sky and we're all happily soaking it up.

'Another round?' Toby asks the table.

'I'll help,' I say as he gathers the orders.

I still can't believe he's here, I think to myself as I follow his tall, slender frame to the bar, both of us weaving our way through the packed tables. *And I can't believe he's mine…*

He is so gorgeous, his skin already tanned from the three-and-a-bit days he's been in Australia. He's wearing a pale orange surfer T-shirt and black jeans, and I'm not oblivious to the attention he's already been receiving from the opposite sex tonight.

We reach the bar and he turns to face me, resting one elbow on the bar top.

'You having fun?' he asks, his smile reaching his warm brown eyes as he tucks a stray strand of hair behind my ear.

'Yeah, are you?' I ask, grinning back at him.

He nods, still smiling at me as his thumb brushes my cheek.

This is the first time we've had a night out together since he arrived, and we haven't had much time alone. We're not alone now, either, but I'm still experiencing these sudden little thrills of anticipation at being at a bar with him. To be honest, anywhere other than the house at the moment feels like a treat – the house with its ten adults and four children crammed into it…

Toby and I are still staring at each other, and he's starting to make a move to kiss me when the bar girl interrupts us.

'What can I get you?'

He turns to give her his full attention and I squeeze his waist from behind.

'Just going to nip to the loo,' I say. He gives me a brief nod, but doesn't falter in reeling off his order.

I don't think Mum is convinced about Toby yet. I've

caught her giving us the occasional perplexed look, and I finally got it out of my sister that Mum was initially shocked to hear Toby and I were a couple – Eliza had to tell her what was going on when Toby flagged up the idea of joining us in Australia for Christmas. He and I are going to go backpacking together in the New Year.

'Well, *obviously*, she thought he was too young for me,' I said at the news of Mum's reaction. I wasn't surprised – he's just turned twenty-two and I'm pushing thirty – but I couldn't help feeling disheartened.

'Er, she did, yeah,' Eliza replied, before hurriedly adding, 'but she'll come around to the idea, don't worry.'

I hope she's right. Her daughters have given her a rocky ride recently when it comes to matters of the heart.

On my way back to the bar, I notice that the empty space to Toby's left has been filled by a modelesque girl wearing tiny shorts showcasing long, bronzed legs.

She picks up two of our beer glasses from the bar and raises one eyebrow sexily at Toby, leaning closer to demurely say something in his ear.

He practically recoils from her, quickly shaking his head, but she's seemingly unperturbed at his obvious rebuttal. She giggles, flicking her dark hair away from her face, and sloshing some of the liquid out of the glasses while she's at it. I'm close enough now to hear her say a giggling 'whoops', but I almost falter in my steps at the sight of her sexily licking the spilt liquid off her hand.

I glance in horror at Toby to gage his reaction, and thankfully he looks put out, but his frown transforms into a smile when he spies me approaching.

'Thanks, but we can manage.' He nods at me. 'Here's my girlfriend.'

Her face falls at the sight of me, but she shrugs and plonks the glasses on the bar before turning her back on us.

Jesus.

On the plus side, this is the first time I've heard Toby call me his girlfriend and it's a bit of a buzz.

'What did she want?' I ask with annoyance as we make our way back to the others.

Lucy didn't want a drink, so we're capable of carrying the six glasses between us.

'She offered to help me carry the beers to our table,' he replies.

'Oh.' Is that all? She looked like she was offering to jump his bones. Maybe she would've made that suggestion later – and if we weren't together, maybe he would have accepted. She was stunning, after all, and certainly much younger than me.

I hate it when my doubts creep in, but creep in they do.

What's it going to be like when Toby and I go backpacking together? Mum's response to our age difference was predictable, but other people will no doubt have a similar reaction. The thought makes my heart sink.

I'm already a fish out of water, taking a year out at twenty-eight. It's tempting to just lie to everyone we meet and claim to be younger... But no, that's not me. I wish I could be cool and confident about it. Hopefully, all it will take is a little time.

It's not long before we hear the rock band start up in the back room. We have our tickets already – Nathan and Sam came into town earlier to buy them – so we pick up our drinks and begin to make our way inside.

'You alright?' Toby asks me softly, his brow furrowing. 'You went a bit quiet after we got that last round.'

'I'm okay,' I reply, trying to smile.

He reaches forward and tugs on Nathan's T-shirt, prompting him to spin around.

'Hey, mate, can we grab our tickets from you? We'll catch you up in a bit.'

'Sure,' Nathan replies, nonplussed, digging into his pocket.

As soon as the others have gone, Toby leads me away from the crowded tables.

'What's wrong?' he asks, rounding on me. 'It wasn't that girl at the bar, was it?'

I sigh, deflated, and his eyebrows jump up.

'*Seriously?*'

'She was gorgeous, Toby, and so much closer in age—'

'Rose, for fuck's sake,' he says, throwing his head back with a groan and staring at the sky. He meets my eyes again and steps forward, placing his hands firmly on my waist. 'You've got to get over it. I love *you*. I want to be with *you*. I fancy you like mad, for Christ's sake, no other girl could ever stand a chance.'

His eyes burn into me with an intensity that makes me prickle all over, and then he bends down and presses his lips to mine. The sun in the sky, the people in the beer garden, the music – it all fades away as he deepens our kiss.

'Holy shit,' I breathe when he eventually withdraws. I look up at him with wide eyes.

His pupils are big and dark as he stares down at me. A moment later, our mouths are colliding again, even more passionately than before. I think he's made his point, but I don't mind if he wants to make it again…

We haven't kissed like this since our very first time, but the memory of that night in the club is coming back thick and fast. My knees have turned to jelly and I feel completely light-headed. I can't imagine how I had the willpower to ask him to stop once before, but I'm sure as hell not going to now.

By the time we join the others, my hair has come loose from its bun and my lips look thoroughly bee-stung. Eliza cottons on instantly.

'You two need to get a room,' she says with a laugh, rolling her eyes.

'Tell me about it,' I reply shakily. The thought had already occurred to me...

Toby has been sleeping upstairs on the living room sofa and I've been sharing my bedroom with Mum and Eliza. I've assumed that we'll be on our own, backpacking, before we can take our relationship to the next level, but after what's just happened, I'm not sure I'm going to be able to wait that long.

'Maybe you should splash out on a hotel room tonight,' Eliza says with a cheeky grin.

'I wish. But I couldn't cope with the look on Mum's face when we waltz in tomorrow.' My face burns even now at the thought.

She shakes her head good-naturedly and nods towards the band. 'Come on, let's go a bit closer.'

Toby stands behind me, his hand draped casually around my front, but after a couple of songs, his fingers slide under the hem of my navy chiffon top. He rests his palm on my stomach, his thumb stroking backwards and forwards. I can barely concentrate on the music. I feel intensely jittery as I lean back against his chest. He tightens his grip on me.

I notice the girl from the bar dancing sexily nearby, but I barely even bat an eyelid in her direction. The alcohol has loosened me up, and I'm exactly where I want to be. I turn around to face Toby. He doesn't waste a moment taking my face in his hands and kissing me senselessly. I don't think I've ever snogged anyone in public like this before, but I just can't seem to help myself. I think I could kiss him forever. Oh no, why is he stopping? He smiles down at me.

'Shall we go for a walk on the beach when we get back?' he asks in my ear, the vibration of his deep voice tickling my eardrum.

A thrill darts through me. Is he thinking what I'm thinking?

He raises one eyebrow at me and I nod, biting my lip.

No amount of alcohol I've drunk can curb my butterflies after that...

'Toby and I are going to go for a walk along the beach when we get back,' I tell Eliza later while Toby runs across the road to flag down a taxi. Lucy's driving tonight so she's taking the others home.

'A walk, eh?' she can't help teasing, but I'm grateful that she leaves it at the one comment. 'Go to Little Wategos Beach,' she suggests. 'It's smaller and more secluded than Wategos.'

'Remind me where that is again?'

'Head up the steps towards the lighthouse, but turn left to go down to the beach.'

'That's right, I know where you mean.' A group of us took a walk up to the lighthouse and Australia's Eastern-most point yesterday afternoon to try to burn off our turkey roast.

Luckily the moon is full tonight, but when we arrive back at the house to find the others getting out of the car, Sam still urges us to take a torch. Toby goes up to the house to grab one while I wait on the driveway alone, gazing up at the night sky and listening to the wind rustling the nearby palm trees. A black, winged creature flies over my head – whoa, that was a big bat.

I hear Toby's footsteps on the stairs and turn to look at him, feeling a shiver of anticipation as he joins me. He has a couple of beach towels draped over his shoulder.

'Grabbed them from the sun-loungers on my way out,' he tells me.

'Did anyone see you?' I ask.

'Er, yeah,' he replies awkwardly. 'Sam did. He started to give me an earful because the current is so strong. But then he realised that we're not going swimming.'

'How embarrassing,' I mutter.

He laughs under his breath. 'At least it wasn't your mum.'

We walk in silence for a little while down the steep hill towards the beach. The air is mild, but it's not humid like the night before last.

'Have you noticed Lucy hasn't drunk a single drop of alcohol since I got here?' he says casually.

'No,' I reply with a frown. 'I'm sure she was drinking wine the other night.'

'I reckon that was apple juice.'

'You think she's pregnant?' I ask with glee.

'I'd put money on it. I bet they tell us when we go to visit them in Sydney.'

'Aw, that's lovely. Finn is such a cutie.'

'Yeah, he is,' he responds warmly.

We reach the cliff steps and Toby leads the way as we climb upwards, pointing the torch at my feet and constantly reminding me to watch my footing. Occasionally, we catch glimpses of the ocean on our left. To our right is thick bush. I can't kick my butterflies, and they're certainly not helped by the thought of the creepy crawlies and critters that lie within the darkness.

Eventually, we reach the point where we have to turn left to go down to Little Wategos Beach.

'Be careful,' Toby warns, holding out his hand and leading me carefully, step by step. 'Your palm is clammy,' he comments, giving me a squeeze. 'Are you feeling alright?'

'I'm just a bit nervous,' I admit.

'Really?' he asks with a note of surprise.

'It's further than I thought it would be,' I say, pretending that my anxieties have nothing to do with what lies in store when we arrive at our destination.

The truth is I haven't had sex for over a year, since I broke up with my last boyfriend. Obviously, you don't forget how to do it, but the first time with someone new is always a bit scary. What if we don't click?

It's a relief to finally make it off the precarious steps and onto the beach. The ocean is glinting prettily in the moonlight and there's something timelessly romantic about the sound of waves crashing against the sand. We really don't need the torch down here. The stars are so bright – so much brighter here in the Southern Hemisphere than they are at home. We can see the whole of the beach stretched out before us, and a look to our left and right confirms that it's deserted.

We turn left and walk along the sand, my hand continuing to embarrass me with its sweatiness.

'Sorry,' I say, removing it from Toby's grasp and wiping it on my jeans.

'Are you sure you're alright?' he asks again, concern now apparent in his voice. 'We don't have to—' His voice trails off. 'I mean, it's nice to just get some alone time with you, to be honest.'

'No, I know, I know. I thought that too,' I say quickly, awkwardly. What is wrong with me? 'How about here?' I suggest, indicating a cluster of large rocks. We'll be shielded from view if anyone does come onto the beach. Toby lays one of the beach towels between two boulders and sits down. I sit down next to him, and he loops his arms around his knees and stares contemplatively at the water.

I cast him a sidelong glance. After a moment, he turns to meet my gaze, his eyes dark in the night. I think he wants me to make the first move. I'm not about to deny him.

Our kiss is gentle and tentative, very different to the heated passion from earlier. He caresses my temples with his thumbs and withdraws, kissing me softly once more on my lips.

'I love you,' he says quietly.

'I love you, too,' I reply.

His hands on my face freeze and he tenses. 'You do?' He's taken aback because it's the first time I've said it aloud.

I nod, sincerely. 'I've never felt this way about anyone before.'

'Me neither,' he replies, and I can hear the emotion in his voice. 'I think I fell in love with you when you came running after me, worried that my dad had given me that shiner.'

I cover my face with my hands. 'That was so embarrassing.'

'No, it wasn't,' he says with amusement, pulling my hands away. 'It was sweet. It showed how caring you are. I love that about you.'

We smile at each other, and then we're kissing again. My butterflies go into overdrive as we fall back onto the sand with a sudden sense of urgency. I want to be with him. In every way. And I don't want to wait any longer.

I pull him on top of me, desperate to feel the weight of his body on mine. I gasp as he moves his mouth to my neck, propping himself up with one arm as he unbuttons my top. I reach up and run my hand along his impressive bicep.

'Take off your T-shirt,' I urge.

He complies, sitting up and tugging it over his head.

'You are so fit,' I murmur, to which he laughs. 'Seriously, how did you get to be so fit?' I ask.

'Lugging huge sacks of flour around the bakery for years, I guess,' he replies with a shrug.

'Mmm,' I say appreciatively, stroking my palms across his chest.

'I'm not a piece of meat,' he jokes, batting me away. 'Now, let me see your tits. I've been after them for months.'

I crack up laughing.

'You think I'm joking,' he says with a grin, sliding his hands along my collarbone and down to the swell of my breasts. His fingers and thumbs close over my nipples and I gasp, all humour suddenly gone from my expression. He leans down to kiss me and after that, there's no going back.

❄

'Oh my God,' I whisper afterwards, pressing my face against his neck as I pant. I'm a little overwhelmed, truth be told. Turns out artisan bread is not the only thing Toby's hands are capable of working their magic on.

He presses a soft kiss to my lips and makes to move off me, but I hold him in place. I'm not ready to let him go yet.

'That was incredible,' he whispers, propping himself up on his elbows.

'*You're* incredible,' I say, gazing up at him in awe. His dark features are framed by starlight, like a paper cut-out in the sky. He kisses me gently again, but I deepen it, trying to pour all of the love and affection I feel into this one small gesture. He breaks away and rests his forehead against mine for a moment before moving to settle beside me. This time I let him go because I'm struggling to inhale.

He grabs the second towel and lays it across us like a blanket, pulling me into his arms as we gaze up at the night sky together. I don't want to go back up to the house yet. Maybe we'll stay and see in the sunrise. We'll be knackered today, but it will be worth it. I know I'll never forget this first time with him.

'You realise I'm not going to be able to keep my hands off you after this,' he murmurs. 'It was bad enough before.'

'The feeling is mutual,' I say with a laugh, holding him tighter. 'I think we're going to have to put your sofa to good use once the others are in bed.'

'Right outside Simon and Katherine's bedroom?' he asks with alarm, referring to my uncle and his partner.

'It's worth the risk, don't you think?'

He chuckles. 'Yeah, I guess it is. But I can't wait to have you to myself once we go backpacking.'

'I can't wait for that, either,' I say, pressing my lips to his jaw, which is rough now with stubble.

We stay there on the beach, staring up at the night sky and wishing on the occasional falling star until the sun starts to come up. Then we drag our weary bodies off the sand and traipse all the way back up to the house. Toby collapses on the sofa – he'll have all of half an hour, I expect, before the children wake up – and I sneak into my bedroom and quietly undress, trying not to rouse the snoozing bodies of my mother and sister. Eventually I slide under the covers and breathe a sigh of relief. We got away with it.

'Did you have fun?'

I freeze at the sound of Eliza's enquiry, spoken mischievously – but quietly, at least.

'Yes,' I whisper back. 'Night, night.'

'Was he good in the sack?' she asks.

'Shhh!' I urge, trying not to giggle.

'Was he?'

'Yes! Now shut it!'

She stifles laughter and then we both fall silent. I'm just dozing off when she says, 'I'm happy for you, Rose. I love you, Sis.'

'I love you, too,' I murmur, my heart so full of love and happiness as I drift off into a blissfully deep sleep.

Bridget's Beach Proposal

I think I enjoyed writing from Bridget's perspective more than any other heroine's — I loved writing her story so much that, weeks after I'd penned the final page of The Last Piece of My Heart, *I still couldn't let her go. I kept thinking about something she references in the epilogue, so I decided to go back and write up the scene. In terms of a timeline for those who have read the book, what follows should slot in after the last chapter, but before the epilogue.*

I bolt awake. Charlie is lying next to me, regarding me with amusement.

'Was I snoring?' I blurt with surprise. I'm pretty sure I've just woken myself up with the force of it. Either that or there's a pig in the room.

I don't think there's a pig in the room.

Charlie smirks and slides his hand under my neck. 'Just a bit,' he says as I go with him into the crook of his arm.

'Sorry.' I'm a little embarrassed. 'I never snore.'

'I'll be the judge of that,' he replies mildly.

I lift my head and stare at his face. 'I do *not* snore!'

He chuckles. 'I'm teasing. Anyway, I'd still love you even if you did.'

'Well, I don't.'

'No, you don't,' he concedes.

I relax back into his embrace.

'Hardly ever,' he adds, and receives a thump on his chest for winding me up. He laughs and kisses the top of my head.

'What's the time?' I ask sleepily, my cheek pressed against the warmth of his bare skin. I can't believe we've woken up before April. Frankly, it's a miracle, even if she was awake for two hours in the night. Charlie was zonked after trying to make a work deadline so he slept through it all.

'Ten thirty,' he replies.

'Ten thirty?' I exclaim, wrenching myself out of his grasp and sitting up. 'We're going to miss music!'

'Relax, Adam's taken her.'

'*What?*' I screech. 'Adam's taken April to music group?'

'That's what I said.'

'Why? How?' I ask in quick succession. I know I've gone on to Charlie's wayward brother about how entertaining the music man is, but we're talking about a *children's* group. I never in a million years thought he would take— '*Ohh,*' I say slowly as it dawns on me. 'Caitlyn.'

'Yep.' Charlie nods once.

Caitlyn is my friend Jocelyn's younger sister. She's just got back from a stint in Australia and is staying with Jocelyn and her family in their house across the road until she gets herself sorted. She joined Jocelyn, her son Thomas, April and me last Wednesday when we went to music. Adam got wind of it on Sunday when they came to ours for a roast lunch. He started salivating the moment he laid eyes on the blonde-haired, blue-eyed beauty.

'I cannot believe your brother is using our daughter to *pull,*' I say impertinently.

'Relax,' Charlie replies with a grin. 'He's still doing us a favour, remember.'

I humph and lie back down.

'I love that you call her 'our' daughter,' he whispers after a moment, and his tone carries such tenderness.

'I love that you let me,' I whisper in return as Charlie draws me closer and kisses me.

'When did they set off?' I ask as he presses his lips to my jaw.

'A few minutes ago,' he murmurs. 'I'd just come back to bed.'

'So we have an hour?'

'Ish.' He shrugs and gives me an impish grin.

I mimic his expression.

※

'We should get up,' Charlie urges around half an hour later when I'm lying in his arms, lazily drawing circles on his chest with my fingernails.

'What's the rush? They won't be back for a while,' I reply sleepily.

'No, but we've got plans.'

'What plans?'

'Lansallos for a picnic.'

My eyes light up. 'Really?'

'Yep. I've finished my job and it's a beautiful day. Adam's coming, too.' He slides out of bed. 'Come on, up you get. You can join me in the shower if you're quick,' he adds cheekily, stretching his arms over his head.

'Nice motivational methods,' I tell him with a smile, throwing off the duvet.

By the time Adam returns with April, we're almost ready to go.

'Hello gorgeous girl!' I exclaim, unclicking April from her pram and scooping her up for a cuddle. 'How was music group? Was it fun?'

She nods eagerly and stares back at me with her very blue eyes.

'Did Uncle Adam like it?' I ask, stroking my hand over her wild blonde curls.

Again she replies by nodding and grinning. She *can* talk; she's just being lazy. And cute.

'Would you like him to take you again?' I ask.

'Steady on,' Adam chips in, tickling his niece's ribs and making her squawk with hysterics. She wriggles to get down, but I kiss her temple before complying, watching fondly as she runs into the living room. *I can't believe she's just turned two...*

I turn back to Adam and give him a meaningful look. 'How was it?'

He shrugs. 'Good.'

'Are you seeing her again?' He knows full well I'm talking about Caitlyn.

'We're going for a drink tonight,' he replies with a grin.

'Don't you *dare* mess my friend's little sister around,' I warn, prodding his chest.

'She's hardly little. She's twenty-seven, for Christ's sake.'

'Ready?' Charlie interrupts, coming out of the kitchen with the hamper. 'You ready, April?' he calls into the living room. 'We're going to the beach.'

'Beach! Yay!' I hear her little voice reply, followed by the pitter-patter of her feet.

'Toilet first,' I prompt, catching her hand and leading her into the downstairs cloakroom. I move her stool into place and help her with her clothes, then kneel down on the wooden floor and offer enthusiastic encouragement as she goes about her business.

If someone had told me two years ago that I'd get real joy from seeing a two-year-old do a wee, I would've laughed in their face.

How my life has changed.

And it's entirely for the better.

❄

Adam carries April on his shoulders for the first part of the walk down to Lansallos Cove, stopping every so often to play with her on the wooden stepping stones, seesaws and other playground equipment we find along the way. It's a gorgeous September day, only a mild breeze blowing, and the sun is streaming down through the leafy canopy over our heads.

Often when we come here it's overcast and windy, but today reminds me of the very first time Charlie brought me. I can't believe that was over a year ago.

Charlie wraps his arm around my shoulders and pulls me close as we watch Adam help April walk along a balancing beam.

'Do you think he's feeling guilty for using her to get laid?' he whispers into my ear.

I laugh under my breath. 'He's certainly being a very doting uncle today.'

'What are you two sniggering about?' Adam calls over at us.

'Nothing,' Charlie replies innocently.

Adam is always lovely to April – it's just that today he's being *particularly* hands-on.

'You guys can go on ahead if you like,' Adam offers. 'Take some time just the two of you. We'll catch you up.'

I stare at him with astonishment.

'What?' he asks, slightly miffed at my expression. 'I'm just being nice!'

'Okay,' I reply. 'I mean, *thanks!*'

'Yeah, thanks, mate,' Charlie adds.

Charlie and I glance at each other as we walk on, pursing our lips. The sound of running water in the nearby stream merges with the crunch of our footsteps as we make our way along the wooded path.

Being a travel writer, I've seen a lot of beautiful places, but

Cornwall's beaches still take my breath away, and Lansallos is one of my favourites. You approach it via rolling green hills that slope downwards into an unusual stone path carved out of the rock. The cove wraps round into a semi-circular shape and the water by the sand and shingle shore is pale blue and perfect for swimming in on sunny days. The colours of the rocks that form the cove walls are also interesting: they shimmer with greens and blues and shades of grey.

Charlie and I unpack the picnic things and lay out a couple of rugs, but there's still no sign of Adam and April by the time we're done.

'Let's take a walk up onto the rocks,' Charlie suggests. 'Adam will work out where we've gone.'

'Okay,' I agree, following him.

There are big boulders by the shore, crusted with barnacles. Charlie climbs up first and then turns around to assist me. I don't need his help – if anything, I find it harder holding his hand than clutching onto the rocks myself – but I'm touched by these simple gestures that show me how much he cares.

I've never even come close to feeling about someone else the way that I feel about Charlie. It's been months since I moved in with him and April, but I swear I love them both more with every single day that passes. I have never felt happier or more content. I'm not sure I'll ever be able to convey how much he and April mean to me, but I hope he knows.

I squeeze Charlie's hand as he leads me over a rock pool.

He smiles at me over his shoulder, the sunlight catching on his dark-blond hair and making his eyes look even more golden than usual.

'Hang on a minute,' I say.

'We're almost there.' He nods across the crevasse to the small, dark, secluded cave I've become familiar with. He knows I like to sit at its entrance, staring across the water and getting inspiration for book ideas.

'Just stop,' I say again.

His brow furrows, but he does as I ask. 'What is it?'

'I need to kiss you.'

He chuckles but obliges, once, twice, three times, then he cocks his head towards the cave. 'Come on, let's sit down for a bit.'

We never get to come up here together because one of us always has to stay on the beach with April. Speaking of which, there's still no sign of her and Adam.

'Do you reckon they're alright?' I ask with a frown, scanning the beach before we jump over the big crack in the rocks and disappear from sight.

'They're fine,' he assures me.

We settle down in front of the cave and look out over the rocks to the vast blue ocean beyond. We're completely hidden from view here.

I take a deep breath and let it out slowly.

Charlie glances at me. 'You okay?'

'Pretty much perfect,' I reply with a smile.

'Phew.'

'Surely you know that,' I chide, gently elbowing him.

'You sighed.'

'With happiness,' I reply, meeting his eyes for a long moment.

He reaches across and smooths a strand of dark hair away from my face.

'*Are* you happy?' he asks, and I'm taken aback by the gravity in his tone.

'Happier than I've ever been in my life,' I reply with a frown. 'Can't you tell?'

He gently cups my face and his ensuing kiss is so tender and filled with so much love that it makes tears spring up in my eyes.

When we break away from each other, his eyes are shining, too.

My feelings for him are so intense – so strange, deep and profound – it amazes me that he might feel the same way.

'You're the best thing that's ever happened to me,' I say, a lump forming in my throat. 'You and April.'

He takes me in his arms and holds me close, resting his chin on the top of my head.

'Bridget?' he asks after a long moment.

'Yes?'

He strokes my hair, prompting me to look at him, but seconds tick by before he speaks. 'Will you marry me?'

My heart metaphorically leaps from my chest and slams back into place, winding me. 'Oh, Charlie!' I shake my head and throw my arms around him, squeezing him hard.

'I'm not sure if that was a no or a yes,' he manages to say with what little breath he has.

'Of course it was a yes!' I practically yell at his face, and then proceed to cry big, fat ugly tears all over him. He laughs and cuddles me close.

'I got you a ring,' he says after a bit, releasing me to dry his own eyes.

'Did you?' So this wasn't a spur of the moment thing?

'Do you want to see it?'

'Have you got it?'

He smirks. 'It's in my pocket.'

'Get it out then!'

He grins and digs into the pocket of his navy shorts, bringing out a small black box. He flips it open and I gasp.

'It's stunning!'

'We can change it if you don't like it.'

I shake my head rapidly. 'I love it. Shall I try it on?'

'I haven't had it sized for you, yet, just in case you wanted to return it, but give it a go.'

He slides the ring – white gold with three large glittering round-cut diamonds – onto my ring finger. It's slightly too big, but it looks so beautiful. I lean across and kiss his lips hard, and then stare down at the ring – my eyes for once, not drawn to the picturesque view.

'How soon can we tie the knot?' I ask.

'Next summer? Is that too soon?'

'No way, I'd marry you tomorrow.'

He grins, and then his expression becomes more sombre. 'I thought next summer would give everyone a chance to try to come to terms with it.'

A little chunk of my happiness is instantly snuffed out. He's talking about his late wife Nicki's family, of course.

Nicki's mother and sister came to April's second birthday party last week and things were still very tense and awkward between them and me. I just have to believe that, with time, they'll come to accept me. I really don't plan on going anywhere.

It helped that I had already driven to Essex a couple of months before to talk to them both. It was flat-out one of the scariest things I've ever done, facing them alone, but it wasn't so bad. They're not horrible people, they're just still grieving the girl they lost. I know it must be hard to see Charlie move on with someone else, but one day I hope they'll realise we're right for each other – that I'm good for April. The love I feel for her is unlike anything I've ever experienced. I would die for her – simple as that. I will always put her first.

I bite my lip, wanting to ask the question that's been on my mind for a while now.

'Charlie,' I say hesitantly, hoping this is the right time. 'Will you let me adopt April?'

His eyebrows pull together and then he nods, his golden-brown eyes brimming with emotion. 'I'd love you to.'

When we venture out from behind the rocks, Adam and April are already tucking into the picnic. Adam spies us immediately and jumps to his feet, throwing his hands up in the air.

'WAS IT A YES?' he shouts, his voice carrying across the cove.

I glance at Charlie, who gives him the thumbs up.

'Did he know?' I ask.

'Yeah.' He casts me a wry look. 'He was *supposed* to take April for a walk once we got here – I had to improvise.'

He jumps down onto the beach and turns around to face me.

'How long had you been planning this?' I scramble down the rocks a bit further before taking the leap myself – his legs are longer than mine.

'I've been thinking about it for ages,' he replies, steadying me as I land.

'Have you?'

He looks a little uncomfortable. 'I wanted to speak to Val and Kate first.'

That's Nicki's mum and sister. 'You spoke to them when they came for April's birthday?'

He nods. 'I hope you're not upset.'

'Of course I'm not. Why would I be?'

'I wasn't sure if you'd mind them knowing before you that I wanted to pop the question.'

'No, it's fine. I understand.' He was just trying to show respect to his former family-in-law.

'Have you been *crying*?' Adam asks with alarm as we approach.

April runs over to us and Charlie grabs her and swings her around like an aeroplane, making her squeal with delight.

I shrug and grin at Adam. 'Might've been.'

'Why? Aren't you happy?' He looks genuinely confused.

'Of course I am, you idiot!' I laugh at his expression. 'One day you'll get it.' I turn and face the ocean and hold my hand out dramatically. 'When you find *The One*...' I let my voice trail off and he shoves my arm with mild annoyance.

'So you're going to be my sister-in-law,' he says with a grin.

'Hell, yeah, bro.' I hold my hand up for a high five. He tuts, but obliges. 'Oh my God! I've never had a brother before!' I exclaim loudly. I'm an only child.

'It's overrated,' Charlie teases, plonking April back on solid ground. She wobbles left and right and then falls down on her bottom.

'Oi, careful what you say,' Adam warns him. 'Or I'll get you back when I do my best man speech.'

I smile with genuine delight and turn to Charlie. 'Have you already asked him?'

'It was part of the deal for me babysitting today,' Adam interjects.

'I can't wait to call my dad!' I say, diverted.

'He already knows,' Charlie reveals sheepishly. 'I spoke to him at April's birthday, too.'

My mouth falls open. 'Did you ask his permission?'

He shrugs. 'It's convention.'

'I'm thirty-five!' I crack up laughing, but I'm secretly *thrilled*. 'What did he say?' I'm expecting to hear some kind of joke about how it was 'about time someone took her off my hands', but Charlie is straight-faced when he replies.

'He said that he couldn't think of a better man for his daughter.'

My eyes well up again. How I love my dad for saying that.

'He's right,' I tell him softly, stepping forward to slide my arms around Charlie's waist.

He's the best person I know.

Beside us, Adam makes a vomiting noise. Charlie breaks away from me and pushes him over.

❄

Charlie and I usually take turns doing bedtime, but that night we do it together. We chat in the bathroom while April is in the bath. I perch on the toilet with the seat down and Charlie sits on the floor, his knees bent and his back resting against the closed door.

It's been the loveliest day. When we got back from the beach, I called Dad and emailed Mum – she's on a cruise at the moment so it can be hard to get hold of her – and I also rang Marty, my best friend, and asked her to be my chief bridesmaid. She almost pierced my eardrums when I told her Charlie had proposed.

'Where shall we get married?' I ask, my insides still bubbling over with happiness because I can't believe I'm actually engaged.

'Do you want to get married here or in London?' Charlie asks.

'Are you kidding? Here, definitely. This is home now.'

He smiles warmly at me and holds my gaze. 'I've been thinking about selling the house.'

'Really?' I'm surprised. This is the first time he's mentioned it.

'I wondered about finding a place together, making it ours.'

Having a fresh start...

This home may hold countless happy memories of the first two years of April's life, but it also holds devastatingly sad ones. Nicki collapsed beside six-week-old baby April's cot the night that she died. Charlie discovered her there.

'Are you sure?' I ask, filled with compassion.

He nods.

I feel a belated trickle of excitement. Buying a house together? I love the idea. 'Would you like to find somewhere to do up?'

He shrugs. 'I'd love to. If that doesn't do your nut in.'

'Ooh! Maybe we could borrow Hermie again and live in him for a few months!' I'm talking about my dad's campervan.

He smiles. 'I'd be up for that. Wouldn't it be great if we could get our own campervan and go on a bit of a road trip together?'

'We should do that for our honeymoon!' I exclaim. 'I'm sure Dad would lend us Hermie.'

His face lights up. 'That would be awesome! Europe, maybe?'

I furrow my brow. 'We would take April, too, though, right?'

'You don't want to go on honeymoon without her?'

I laugh and answer honestly. 'No.'

He grins at me and swipes my right foot, lifting it into his lap. 'Aw,' he says.

'I wonder if you can get married on Lansallos beach,' I muse out loud as he starts to play with my toes.

'That would be cool. There's a church in the village. We

could get married there and walk down to the beach for photos and stuff.'

'We could have a picnic reception!'

'Yeah!'

'I'd have to wear flats, though…' I say out loud, shrugging. 'That'd be alright, wouldn't it?'

'Course. Wear what you like.'

'Are you doing "This Little Piggy"?' I ask out of the blue; he's been wiggling my toes, one after the other.

'Sorry,' he replies, sniggering.

I laugh and turn to April. 'Come on then, my little prune. Time to get you out.'

Charlie follows us into April's bedroom, switching off the big overhead lights and turning on the nightlights. He leans against April's chest of drawers, watching as I get her dressed.

I still remember the first time I tried to put a nappy on her – I made a right pig's ear out of it. She still wears one at night, but I could probably put them on blindfolded now.

'I love you,' Charlie whispers, and I meet his eyes, glinting in the low light.

'I love you, too.' I smile at him and then direct my smile down at April. 'And I love you, too, darling girl. Do you love me?'

She grins up at me and nods, then yawns.

'She's so tired,' I say with amusement tinged with sympathy. 'I hope her teeth don't bother her again tonight.' I think that's what was keeping her awake last night. She didn't have a temperature or anything.

'I'll get up with her tonight if she wakes up,' Charlie promises.

'I feel fine, actually. I never even thanked you for my lie-in.'

'Well, you sort of did,' he says with a cheeky grin.

I laugh lightly and scoop April up for an all-too-brief

squeeze before walking over to the bed. Charlie pulls back her covers and tucks her in once I've laid her down. We stand side by side and he strokes her curls away from her face. She smiles up at us, one after the other.

'Can you say, "I love you"?' Charlie asks her.

'Lub you,' she replies, in the cutest little voice imaginable.

'I love you, April,' he says.

'I lub you, Daddy,' she complies.

'I love you, April,' I say, trying not to giggle.

'I lub you, Bidget,' she says in turn.

Beside me, Charlie hesitates. 'Can you say Mummy?' he asks quietly, and suddenly I'm the one to feel tense.

'Mummy,' April replies, pointing at the photo frames of Nicki on her side table.

'Yes, that's Mummy,' Charlie replies, and his voice is thick with emotion. 'But would you like Bridget to be your mummy, too?' he asks her. 'You're allowed to have two mummies,' he adds.

April grins at me and nods, and I blink back tears.

'I would love to be your mummy, too, April,' I say, hardly able to get the words out past the lump in my throat.

'Mummy,' she says to me, and I only just manage to gulp back a sob. I don't want to freak her out by crying so I bend down and press a kiss on her forehead, teardrops falling from my eyes and staining her pale pink pillow as I retreat. I turn to face Charlie and smile at him, hurriedly drying my eyes.

'Sleep tight, sweetie,' he murmurs, bending down to kiss his daughter as I struggle to compose myself.

'Sing,' she states, holding her hand out to me.

I take her hand and sit down on the chair beside her bed, glancing at Charlie. He shrugs at me and smiles, gently rubbing my back and leaving me to it.

I don't know how I manage it, but I make it all the way

through 'Somewhere Over the Rainbow' without crying. April is almost dozing off by the end of it. I give her one more kiss and then walk out of her room, starting with surprise when I see Charlie sitting on the floor outside her bedroom, his back leaning against the wall.

'What are you still doing here?' I ask in an alarmed whisper.

He smiles up at me. 'I didn't want to go.'

I blush. I wouldn't have sung with quite such abandon if I'd known he was listening. He gets to his feet and pulls me into his arms, holding me close until the heat on my face fades and my insides expand with happiness once more. I withdraw and place my hand over his chest, staring up at him as his heart beats against my palm.

'It's yours,' he whispers, completely seriously.

I feel slightly surreal as I take his hand and place it over my own heart. His lips tilt up into a smile.

'If my brother could see us now,' he says.

And then we both crack up with silent laughter, stumbling into our bedroom and grabbing pillows to stifle the sound as we really let rip.

He makes me laugh, he makes my heart feel like a hot air balloon that's lifting me off my feet, and he makes me cry – but rarely with anything other than joy. He really *is* the best person I know – and I can't wait to spend the rest of my life with him.

A Christmas Wedding

Never has an ending divided my readers more than that of Thirteen
Weddings. *So many readers have told me Bronte should've ended
up with Alex that when I asked members of* The Hidden Paige *to
vote for Lachie vs Alex, it actually surprised me when Lachie won.*

*I wasn't sure who Bronte was going to end up with when I began
writing* Thirteen Weddings *– I'd more or less decided to let the
ending write itself and had even wondered if Bronte might end up
alone… But then loveable Lachie appeared on the scene and I just
adored him.*

*I absolutely stand by the decision I made when I wrote that book –
there was no way Bronte and Alex could have had their happy-ever-after
considering everything they'd just been through. However, I did wonder,
if enough water went under the bridge and they met again one day,
what would happen?*

*Of all of my ebook short stories, this is my longest at almost half the
length of a full-length book. It was so much fun to write, tying in* The
Last Piece of My Heart, One Perfect Summer *and* One Perfect
Christmas, The Longest Holiday *and even* Lucy in the Sky, *but
it did break my heart at times. No spoilers, though. Here's Bronte,
three and a half years after the end of* Thirteen Weddings…

The sight of his name in my inbox causes flu-like symptoms to wash over my body in quick succession: hot flush, cold flush, prickling all over, dizziness, nausea...

Alex Whittaker

It's been three and a half years since I called and told him to stop emailing me, but it has been impossible to wipe clean the memory of his last words: '*I love you. I'm not giving up.*'

But then he *did* give up.

He let me go, just as I asked him to. And he hasn't contacted me since.

Until now.

With my heart in my throat and a shaking hand, I hover over his name with my mouse, feeling surreally shocked that he can still have this effect on me after all this time. What does he want? *Click...*

> Hi Bronte,
>   Sorry to land in your inbox out of the blue like this but I'm going to be in Sydney next month at the Tetlan offices. It's unlikely I'll be coming into *Vivienne*, but I thought I should let you know

in case we bump into each other in the lift or
something.

I hope all is well with you.

Alex

My heart thumps hard against my ribcage. Alex in Sydney?
Next month? In the same building as me?

Alex and I used to work together at a celebrity weekly
magazine in London – he was the head of the art department
and I ran the picture desk. I heard on the grapevine that he
has an even more senior role now, overseeing art direction for
the whole of Tetlan, the publishing company that produces
the women's style magazine where I work.

I read his email again. His tone is hard to dissect. I can't
tell if he's being cold and detached or respectfully distant.

How does he even know where I work these days? Does
he keep tabs on me? I shouldn't care about any of this, but
I'm alarmed to find that I do.

Massively.

My eyes come to a rest on his sign-off.

I hope all is well with you.

What was going through his mind when he wrote that?

'Hey, you ready?'

I whip my head around to see Christie, a colleague from
the style desk, smiling down at me expectantly. We're about
to do a casting for a photoshoot. Her face falls at the sight of
my expression. 'What's wrong?'

'Nothing,' I lie, pushing out my chair and getting to my
feet. 'I'm all set.'

Am I going to see Alex again? *Do I want to?* I'm not sure I should be pondering the answer to that question.

❋

As I gather my things together at the end of what has felt like a very long day, I overhear a group of people discussing their options for Friday night drinks venues.

'You coming, Bronte?' Louise, the features editor, calls from across the office.

I shake my head reluctantly. 'I can't. Next week, though, definitely!' I try to inject some enthusiasm into my voice and feel bad as she turns away. I had planned to join in tonight – I'm quite new to this job and I haven't fully integrated yet – but I need time to get my head together. The ferry ride home to Manly still won't be long enough.

Today has been a struggle.

I must've read Alex's message fifty times, but I haven't come close to formulating a reply. I need to talk it through with Lachie first. What will he say when he discovers that his old nemesis has been in touch?

Lachie and I still live in the same flat in the same northern beach suburb where we settled almost four years ago. Lachie was moving home to Australia permanently with his expended visa, but I was only supposed to be visiting for Christmas before returning to my job in London.

Then a certain someone rang and told me that he'd left the wife he'd married right in front of me and wanted to be with me instead.

Alex's declaration of love was everything I had hoped to

hear for months, but it was too late. I was happy with Lachie, and Alex had already caused too much pain.

I had a perfectly good plane ticket at the ready, but, rather than return to the UK to face my demons, I called my boss on the other side of the world and resigned so I could stay put in Sydney. I've been burying my head in the sand ever since.

I'm not proud.

Digging my phone out of my bag while waiting in line with the hordes of commuters at the ferry terminal, I type out a quick text to my boyfriend:

You coming home for dinner?

Lachie replies just as I'm boarding:

At the pub. Thought you were out with work tonight?

I wait until I've reached an empty space by the railings at the back of the ferry before I write back, '*Change of plan...*' I hope he's not up for a big one.

We're already chugging out of Circular Quay by the time he replies:

Just got the beers in. Come join me!

I sigh and slip my phone back into my bag, then tuck my long brown hair into my coat before zipping it up to my neck and bracing myself against the cold September wind. I don't want to be a nagging girlfriend, but Lachie is gigging at a wedding up in Newcastle tomorrow, a couple of hours drive away, so that rules out pretty much the whole of Saturday. I need to talk to him about this tonight. I need to talk about this, full stop. If I don't get it off my chest soon, I think I'll burst.

The Sydney Opera House is cast in golden light from the setting sun as we motor past. It was sunny today for the first time in I can't remember how long – spring is officially here, it seems – but I was too dazed at lunchtime to appreciate it.

Someone once said to me, you have to go back in order to be able to move on. Wise words, I'm sure, but the thought of seeing Alex again has always scared me.

I haven't returned to England since I left, and I still feel haunted by what happened. My boss, Simon, said he understood my decision to stay in Australia, but I'm mortified by how unprofessionally I behaved. Luckily, my career wasn't affected – at least, my *magazine* career wasn't; I haven't photographed a wedding since.

I thought that, with time, I'd start up that side of my work again, doing the occasional job on weekends, building up my portfolio, maybe even one day leaving journalism behind and going full-time as a wedding photographer. But, despite encouragement from Lachie, my mentor Rachel and my close friend Bridget, it still hasn't happened. Work has been so full-on; I haven't had the energy to pursue work as a weekend warrior as well.

Sometimes, though, I find myself daydreaming about all of those Big Days that I did… Not Alex's – I've buried that one too deep – but all of the others, and my head is full of images of beautiful brides and handsome grooms, flowers cascading from pews and the hands of pretty bridesmaids, sparkling champagne in crystal-clear flutes, and hazy blue skies and scented warm grass on perfect English summer days…

And then I miss it so much it hurts.

But I feel as if I left that part of me on the other side of the world and I'm not sure I could ever go back.

My stomach clenches. At this rate I won't need to go back in order to move on. Like it or not, my past might be about to catch up with me right here in Sydney.

✳

Lachie calls me as I'm disembarking at Manly.

'You coming to the pub?' he asks in lieu of a greeting.

'Not sure I feel like it,' I reply, shrugging my bag over my shoulder as I come out of the ferry terminal building into the darkening evening. I hang a right towards the beach.

'What's wrong? You okay?'

'Bit of a strange day.'

'Strange how?'

'I'll tell you about it at home.' *Hint, hint, don't stay out too long…*

'Er, well, El's just arrived,' he replies. 'He's at the bar,' he adds as my heart sinks. 'Seemed pretty rough. Said he'd fill me in once he had a drink down him.'

'Oh, right.'

'Come join us,' he says in a cajoling voice.

'Maybe. I'll keep you posted.'

'Okay.' He sends two kisses spiralling down the receiver and ends the call.

El – Elliot – is Bridget's ex. Bridget was my flatmate in England, and I missed her terribly when I moved back home. Luckily, she's a travel writer, and it took very little convincing to get her to agree to come and spend some time in Australia. Early on in her stay, she bumped into Elliot, whom she'd known as a teenager. They rekindled their relationship and we became an *awesome* foursome. It was *brilliant*. Until Bridget's visa ran out and she had to go back to the UK. She and Elliot managed long distance for almost a year, but Bridget broke it off when she fell for someone else.

I love Bridget to bits, but she's very up and down when it comes to men, a trait I recognise because I used to be a bit like that myself. And, even though she seems besotted with her new guy right now, I wouldn't put money on it lasting. I just can't believe she threw away everything that she had with Elliot – with *us* – for yet *another* infatuation.

The most gutting thing is, right before they broke up, Elliot confided to me that he was thinking about proposing. If they'd got married, Bridget could have settled in Australia permanently, and we *all* could've lived happily ever after...

But, clearly, El left it too late.

It was awful dealing with the repercussions of their break-up. Elliot was devastated. Lachie and I rallied round – Lachie especially – but El was a mess for months. Recently, he's starting dating again – well, *pulling* might be a more apt word. I don't love the idea of my boyfriend hanging out with a single man on a mission, but I know we need to ride it out until he's back on his feet.

Lachie and I live in a one-bedroom flat on the top floor of a two-storey building, a couple of blocks from the beach. There's a small balcony out the front, which in the summer hosts barbecues aplenty, but is currently being used only as a space for drip-drying Lachie's wetsuit. Lachie surfs almost every day – I'm a little envious that he has time to. His work takes place outside regular office hours – he plays the guitar and sings, mostly at weddings, but also at birthdays and other special occasions. I met him at a wedding in Scotland – he was gigging and I was taking the pictures. I thought he was so sexy, so far from my idea of a typical wedding singer.

I unlock the door and walk in to find our home ever so slightly better off than when I left it: the breakfast things are gone from the counter by the sink and the mail has been cleared into a neat stack, but there's still a ring on the table from where Lachie sloshed too much milk into his bowl this morning, and breadcrumbs on the board from his lunch-time sandwich preparation. I scan the contents of the fridge, relieved to see that my boyfriend at least remembered to go to the supermarket. But, before I can ponder what to cook for dinner, I have a flashback to Alex's email and reach for an open bottle of white wine instead.

I really, *really* need to talk to someone about this. I *have* to talk to Lachie, but I don't really *want* to. I *want* to talk to Bridget, I realise. It's Friday morning in the UK – I wonder if she's busy. I grab the phone and go to the sofa, taking a large gulp of wine and kicking off my shoes before dialling her number.

❋

Alex and I met about six years ago at an eighties club night in London – he was on a stag do and I was on my Aussie friend Polly's hen night. We ended up talking and bonding over the course of the evening and he confided that he'd recently broken up with his long-term girlfriend, Zara – or, techni- cally, *she'd* broken up with *him*, labelling it 'a break'. Later, he walked me back to my hotel and we spent the night together. It all happened so fast, but it didn't feel that way at the time. I *really* liked him, way more than I could've thought possible, considering we'd only met earlier that night, and the feeling seemed mutual.

So we both felt torn and confused the next morning when Zara texted and asked to meet him for lunch, claiming that she'd made a mistake. I was only in the UK for a couple of weeks for Polly's wedding so the smart option seemed to be to say goodbye and go our separate ways, but it hurt.

A year and a half later, I went back to the UK, this time on a one-year work visa. I'd landed a job at *Hebe*, the afore-mentioned magazine. To say I was shocked when Alex turned out to be the new Art Director is an understatement. I was thrown to discover he was engaged to his former ex and set to marry her later that year. We formed a tentative friend-ship, but the chemistry between us intensified until it became overwhelming and he stepped right back. He didn't want to leave Zara, whom he'd been with for a decade. They had a shared history that felt too hard to walk away from.

Now Alex and I have history, too. Whether or not we still have chemistry doesn't bear thinking about.

❄

'Hello?' Bridget's tinny voice comes down the receiver.

'Bridget!' I cry, relieved that she answered.

'Bronte!' she cries in return. 'I was just about to call you, I *promise* I was!'

'Why?' I ask, confused at her slightly panicked, slightly guilty tone.

'Has Elliot not told you?' she replies.

'Told me what?'

'Oh! I thought that was why you were calling!'

'Bridget!' I exclaim. 'What's going on?'

I hear her inhale quickly and let her breath out in a rush, while I wait for her to speak.

'I'm getting married.'

I almost fall off the sofa. '*What?*'

'I'm engaged. Charlie proposed to me. I'm getting married,' she repeats. And then she bursts out laughing.

'What? *How?*' I ask with surprise. '*When?*'

'Next summer.'

'No, I mean, when did he propose?'

'Two days ago,' she replies. I can't see her face, but I know that she's beaming from ear to ear.

'Wow.' I'm astonished. She and Charlie met a year or so ago and have only been a proper couple for half that time. 'That was quick!'

'I know,' she replies, her enthusiasm dampened slightly by my reaction. 'But when you know, you know.'

'And you know?' I ask weakly.

'I've never been more certain about anything in my entire life,' she states calmly but firmly.

A belated bubble of excitement bursts inside me and I let out a squeal. She cracks up laughing again, relieved that I'm finally responding appropriately.

'I thought Elliot must've told you!'

Realisation dawns on me. 'He's out with Lachie. Lachie said he seemed pretty down. Is that why?'

'Yeah, I called him earlier.' Her tone becomes subdued.

'He didn't take it well?'

'No.'

I'm not surprised. I'm reeling, myself. Bridget has been in and out of love so many times, and, even though she's told me that it's different with Charlie, that he's unlike anyone she's ever known, I didn't really believe it. Now I know I underestimated their feelings for each other.

It's funny, I always thought of my friend as an open book: warm, outgoing and the best person to be around. But there's a side to her that I never got to know in the time that we lived together. She's never struck me as a particularly maternal person – she and Elliot were alike in their desire *not* to have children, I thought. But Charlie has a young daughter, April, and the way Bridget talks about her with such obvious adoration makes me wonder if I ever really knew her at all.

'Where did he propose?' I ask with a smile, determined to try to make up for my initial lack of enthusiasm.

'At the beach,' she replies. 'The one with the sea glass.'

'I remember. So you're thinking next summer for the wedding?'

'Yes. And, Bronte, please will you come?'

'Of course I'll come!' The thought of returning to England feels surreal, but I'm awash with nerves at the reminder that Alex will be coming here, well before then.

'I was kind of hoping I'd be able to persuade you to do the wedding photos,' she adds with slight trepidation.

'Oh... I haven't done any weddings since I left the UK.'

'I know.' She sounds uneasy. 'I still don't really understand why.'

'Work is so busy...'

'You managed to squeeze them in before, when you had a full-time job.'

'Anyway, I'm also a bit out of practice.'

'You've got almost a year before I walk down the aisle.'

I can't help but smile at her perseverance. 'You really want me to start doing weddings again, don't you?'

'Yes,' she states. 'You loved it. You were great at it.'

'It feels like a lifetime ago,' I say sadly.

'It *kills* me that he ruined it for you!' she snaps.

'Who? Alex?'

'*Yes*, Alex!' she cries.

Bridget is not Alex's biggest fan.

I sigh heavily. I don't really know what to say to that. I don't want to blame Alex. Yes, photographing *his* wedding set me back a bit, but it's my own fault for letting that part of my life slip through my fingers.

'He emailed me today,' I tell her.

'*What?*'

'Alex. He emailed me today for the first time in years to tell me that he's coming to Sydney next month.'

There's no reply from the other end of the line, so I keep talking.

'He thought he should let me know in case we bump into each other in the lift, or somewhere. He doubts he'll need to come into *Vivienne*, but he's going to be in the building. You know he's the Art Director for the whole of Tetlan now?'

'Yes, I did hear that,' Bridget replies quietly.

I don't remember passing that information on.

'Russ and Maria told me,' she answers my unspoken question.

Russ used to work with me at *Hebe* and Maria is the make-up artist who introduced me to Rachel, my wedding photographer mentor. Maria and Russ got together on a work night out and are now married with two children.

'When were you talking to those two about Alex?' I'm taken aback.

'They came to Cornwall on holiday back in June and we caught up. I was just wondering if they ever saw or heard anything of him.'

I feel slightly strange that she asked about him. 'Why didn't you tell me?'

'I'm sorry,' Bridget says gently. 'I was just curious, to be honest, but I didn't think you'd want that whole can of worms opening.'

'Oh.' Can of worms officially opened.

'How do you feel about it?' she asks. 'Him rocking up in Sydney?'

'I'm freaking out,' I admit.

'Oh, B,' she murmurs. 'What did you say to him?'

'I haven't written back yet. I thought I should tell Lachie first.'

'Good plan. Do you *want* to see him?'

'No!' My reply is instant.

'Are you sure?' she persists.

Butterflies cram my stomach. 'He was only telling me out of courtesy,' I say eventually, deflecting her question. 'He didn't ask to meet up with me, and Lachie would hate that, so I won't see him unless we really do bump into each other.'

My heart contracts, suddenly, inexplicably. Alex is going to be here in Sydney. The thought of *not* seeing him fills me with the oddest array of confusing, conflicting emotions.

I'm still feeling confused and a little miserable later that night when I've sunk half a bottle of wine and am fixing myself toast for dinner because I can't be bothered to cook. Lachie isn't home and I haven't heard from him again. He's no doubt helping Elliot to drown his sorrows. El may have moved on physically from Bridget, but it's clear he's still emotionally attached. I don't think he expected this thing with Charlie to last, either, so the marriage proposal will definitely have knocked him for six.

Could I really photograph Bridget's wedding? She's taking a risk in asking me – what if I'm rubbish these days? But, deep down, I know I'm not. I *was* good at it. Sure, I made mistakes, but nothing too major, and I always managed to get the one shot that Rachel told me was the most important: the groom's reaction to seeing his bride for the first time.

A memory assaults me from out of nowhere and my heart folds in on itself. Before I can think about it, I'm opening the wardrobe in our bedroom and digging out my old laptop. Guilt pricks at my gut as I wait for it to fire up, and then I'm searching the items in my documents, looking for a folder deceptively entitled 'Boring Bits'. Hidden right at the bottom of that folder I find three photographs called WA1, WA2 and WA3. *WeddingAlex*. I highlight and click on all three of them.

Alex's face appears on the screen, his blue eyes staring straight back at me. The look on his face is so tortured, so uncertain. He had just told me that he loved me, that he didn't know what he was doing, that he wasn't sure if he could go through with marrying Zara. I wasn't supposed to be photographing their wedding – Rachel had called me the night before in a panic because her regular assistant had caught the flu – but I agreed to do it because Alex had said that he'd be fine with it.

Lachie actually called things off with me when he heard that I'd consented – he'd been travelling around Europe and had phoned to ask me if I'd join him in Paris for the weekend. I told him of my alternative plans and he hit the roof. But he did an about-turn and was there, waiting for me, when I came out of the church. I couldn't follow through with the job – it was all too much – but I'd got the most important shot, the one Rachel had entrusted to me.

I still remember that totally surreal feeling of willing Alex to turn around and look at his bride-to-be coming down the aisle. I wanted to do a good job for Rachel – and for Alex and Zara. But he didn't look at Zara: he looked at me.

These are the pictures I took of him, staring straight down my lens.

Why have I still got them? I ask myself in a daze. Alex means nothing to me now. Lachie is everything. I should have binned them long ago, but I didn't. What's stopping me?

Nothing is stopping me.

I should get rid of them.

I *should*.

I close down the photographs, inwardly wincing at the sight of Alex's deep-blue eyes disappearing from my screen, one after the other. I highlight the three files and drag them to the trash, hovering over the icon. Feeling slightly sick, I let them go.

But I know they're still retrievable, so I force my fingers up to Finder on my desktop menu and scroll down to 'Empty Trash'.

Come on, Bronte. Just let go. Let *him* go, once and for all.

A cold sweat comes over me and I hastily click off the menu and go down to the trash to hunt out the photos, restoring them to my 'Boring Bits' folder.

I'm scared to discover he still has a hold over me.

Terrified.

❉

I'm in bed, trying to sleep, when Lachie gets home at close to midnight.

'You awake?' he whispers loudly, pulling his T-shirt over his head.

'Yes.'

'Bronnie!' he cries with delight, stumbling into the wardrobe as he attempts to take off his jeans.

'How drunk are you?' I ask with mild amusement as he flops his long, lean body onto the bed and gathers me up in his arms.

'Very,' he replies, pulling me against his muscled chest.

Despite how beery he smells, I love being in his arms. His warm, strong, *familiar* arms.

He slides one leg between mine and kisses my neck. Is he naked? I have a quick feel for his boxers and realise they came off with his jeans.

'How was Elliot?' I ask.

'Bad. Bridgie's getting married.'

'I know. I spoke to her.'

'Thought you might've.' He kisses my neck again.

'So Elliot's in a bad way?'

'He was. He's pretty happy right now, though. Fliss took him off to a club.'

'I didn't know she was out with you tonight.' I don't sound thrilled.

'Bumped into her and she stuck around.'

I bet she did.

Fliss – Felicity – is a friend of Lachie's from work. She and her older sister, Georgina, run a catering company and they've been putting a lot of weddings his way. I'm sure she wants to get into his pants, but Lachie insists she only sees him as a mate. He reckons I'd like her if I gave her a chance.

'I thought she was doing this wedding with you tomorrow.'

'She is. She's picking me up at six.'

'She's driving? And she's still out drinking? She'll probably still be over the limit when she gets behind the wheel!'

'She'll be fine,' Lachie mutters, while I have this horrible feeling I sound like his mother. 'Anyway, George will probably drive.'

'So Fliss is out with Elliot right now?' I ask as he kisses my neck again.

'Mmm.'

'Does she fancy him?'

Lachie shrugs. 'I don't know. He fancies her, though, so that's a good start.'

'Isn't she a bit young for him?'

'Says the cradle snatcher,' he snorts with amusement.

Lachie is twenty-eight, the same age as Fliss, while Elliot is thirty-five, just one year older than I am. My boyfriend has a point, but I shove his shoulder indignantly, regardless.

'Doesn't she care that she's his rebound shag?'

'Can we stop talking about El and Fliss?' he asks pointedly, rolling onto his back and pulling me on top of him. He runs his hands up inside my top and cups my breasts.

There are other, far more pressing things to talk about, but right now, there are also far more pressing things to do.

❄

I have to drag myself from bed the next morning when Lachie's alarm goes off.

'You don't need to get up,' he says in a deep, groggy voice.

'I'll make you a coffee,' I reply, stumbling into the kitchen. It's quarter to six. The shower turns on and, a few minutes later, Lachie joins me in the kitchen wearing black jeans, a grey T-shirt and a dark-blue beanie pulled over his blond hair. He never wears a suit when he gigs.

He presses a kiss to my temple. I turn and slide my arms around his waist and he pulls me close, engulfing me with his warmth.

'You okay?' he asks, withdrawing to gaze down at me with tired but beautiful blue eyes.

I sigh and place my hands on his face, running my thumbs across his stubble. After going clean-shaven for a year, he's growing back his beard.

'I wish you didn't have to go today.'

He looks dejected. 'Sorry, Bron,' he whispers. 'Fliss and George need to get there early to prep. I could've driven later, but it seemed crazy to pass up the offer of a ride.'

'I know. Don't worry.'

He reaches past me to grab his coffee from the counter, and, at the same time, we hear a knock on the door.

'I'll get it.' I open the door to find Fliss before me, looking a bit worse for wear, but still gorgeous. Her dark hair is pulled up into a high, tousled bun and her big brown eyes stare out at me from behind a thick fringe. We're around the same height at five foot seven.

'Hey,' she says in a huskier voice than usual.

'With you in a sec,' Lachie calls from the kitchen.

'Good night?' I raise one eyebrow at her and lean against the doorframe.

She smirks. 'Could say that.'

'Did you shag him?' Lachie asks with a grin, materialising at my side, coffee cup still in hand.

'No, I did not!' she replies mock-indignantly. 'What sort of a girl do you think I am?'

He shrugs and grins and my insides clench. There's something about this girl that makes warning bells go off in my head.

'I thought you were desperate,' he teases.

Has she been divulging to my boyfriend how much she wants sex?

She rolls her eyes at him. 'Not *that* desperate.'

'You could do worse than Elliot,' I chip in, feeling suddenly defensive of our friend.

She screws her nose up. 'He's way too old for me.'

Cheeky bitch! I know I said the same thing last night, but now I feel like she's implying that *I'm* too old for *my* boyfriend.

'Come on, Loch Ness, time to go,' she urges.

Lachie is actually pronounced Lockie, and, somewhere along the line, Fliss got the idea of nicknaming him after the Loch Ness monster. Lachie and I met in Scotland, while Fliss has never even been to Europe, but that's not why I find the nickname irritating. I hate how familiar and cutesy this girl is with my boyfriend. And Lachie, who has always been a flirt, doesn't discourage her.

Lachie downs his coffee and plonks the cup on the table, picking up his guitar case and bending down to peck me on the lips. 'Have a good day,' he says.

'You too,' I reply.

I watch him follow Fliss down the external staircase. The frown is still etched onto my forehead when I return indoors.

Elliot texts me at eleven, wondering if I'm free for brunch. I reply that I am, glad to have something to take my mind off yesterday's email. I went back to bed after Lachie left, but couldn't sleep for my mind ticking over.

We meet up at a café across the road from Manly Beach. Elliot is already at a table when I arrive, looking decidedly worse than Fliss did at six o'clock this morning. His normally tanned skin is washed out and pasty and he's resting his darkly stubbled jaw on his hand. He smiles up at me, wearily.

'Hungover?' I ask the obvious question.

'Not really,' he replies, to my surprise, as I take a seat opposite him. 'Miserable more than anything.'

'Oh, El,' I say with sympathy, reaching across to touch his hand. His eyes fill up with tears.

'Christ!' he mumbles, averting his gaze with embarrassment. 'I should've stayed at home.'

'No, it's good that you came out. Have you ordered yet?'

'Just a coffee.'

On cue, the waitress brings it over. I order a latte for myself and turn my attention back to Elliot, who's in the process of upending three sachets of sugar into his drink.

'How was last night?' I ask, trying to lighten the mood.

He shrugs. 'It was alright.'

'Anything happen with Fliss?'

'Nah, we just went dancing. She's not into me like that.'

'I think she has a crush on Lachie.'

'He only has eyes for you,' he replies without missing a beat.

'So she *does* like him, doesn't she?'

'I don't know, Bron.' He looks awkward, all of a sudden.

I try to ignore the niggling feeling in my stomach as I pick up the menu.

'Have you spoken to Bridget?' he asks when we've ordered.

'Last night,' I reply quietly.

He shakes his head and picks up his coffee, taking a large,

scalding mouthful and wincing. 'It's too soon,' he states, putting his cup down a little too firmly on the wooden table.

'She seems pretty sure about him.'

'Yeah,' he says bitterly. His blue eyes dart up to meet mine. 'Why didn't she ever tell me she wanted a kid?' He sounds anguished.

'I'm not sure even *she* knew it. But would it have made a difference? I thought you were set on not having children.'

'Yeah, I was. I am. I just... I don't know. We could have at least talked about it.'

'And said what? She *was* happy with you, El. She *was*. But maybe she didn't know what she *really* wanted until it was right there in front of her.'

'I should've proposed to her sooner.'

'Do you think it would have made a difference?'

Elliot doesn't answer, but he looks downcast.

'Maybe this is what you needed to hear to move on,' I say gently, my thoughts jumping unwelcomingly to Alex.

I wonder if he's moved on... Did he remarry? Does he have a girlfriend? Children?

'Yeah,' Elliot mumbles after a long pause, bringing my focus back to him. He doesn't sound convinced. 'I guess I just miss her.' His voice is racked with emotion.

I reach across the table and cover his hand with mine, giving it a small squeeze. I don't need to say it out loud. He knows I miss her, too.

❋

I wake up stupidly early on Sunday morning. I don't know what time Lachie came home because I was too tired to respond when he whispered hello. He's still out cold, his full lips parted in sleep and his dark-blond stubble another milli-metre closer to being called a beard. The next few months will see his shaggy blond hair lighten further under the sun. I reach out, but stop short of pushing a wayward lock off his forehead.

He rolls away from me, the duvet slipping down to reveal his toned, muscular back. I can't resist. I press a kiss onto the dent at the top of his shoulder and rest my cheek against his warm back. He stirs.

'Alex emailed me,' I whisper, feeling guilty for waking him, but unable to hold it in any longer.

His whole body tenses.

'What?' He rolls over to face me.

'Alex emailed me,' I repeat. 'He's coming to Sydney next month.'

His red-tinged eyes are full of an emotion I can't decipher. Anger? Trepidation? Concern?

All of the above?

'He needs to do some work at the Tetlan offices and thought he should let me know he's going to be around,' I explain. 'I guess he didn't want to freak me out.'

'Has he asked to see you?'

'No.'

'Do you want to see him?'

His eyes widen at my split-second delay. My ensuing 'no' sounds false on my tongue.

'Great,' Lachie says sarcastically as he falls onto his back and stares up at the ceiling. 'All these years and we still can't escape the guy.'

'I have no intention of seeing him,' I state firmly, placing my hand on his chest. 'I haven't even replied to his email.'

He turns his head to look at me. 'But you will.'

'Well, yeah,' I reply uncomfortably. 'I wanted to speak to you about it first.'

'What did his email say exactly?'

I recite it, word for word.

'Jesus, Bronte,' he mutters, that indecipherable look back in his eye.

'What should I say?' I persist.

'Just write back and say thanks for letting me know.'

We stare at each other for several long seconds.

'Really?' I ask.

'Yes,' he replies, and I have this odd feeling he's testing me.

'Okay.'

Neither of us brings up Alex again that day, and on the surface it's a perfectly pleasant Sunday, but underneath is an underlying tension that we both choose to ignore.

✻

Back at work on Monday morning, I fire up my computer with a niggling feeling in the pit of my stomach. I don't want this to hang over me for any longer, so I open up Alex's email and type out a reply.

Thanks for letting me know.
   Bronte.

The words look so stark. Is that really the best I can do after all this time? He's only letting me know out of decency that he's coming here.

I try again.

Hi Alex
Long time no speak!

I quickly delete that sentence, still shaking my head. Too
jaunty. Too... *wrong*.

Hi Alex
Thanks for letting me know. All's well here – hope
you're okay too.
Bronte

I suddenly remember that I don't even know exactly when
he's coming – I don't want to be on edge for the entire month
of October. I ask the question and then press send, safe in the
knowledge that it's the middle of the night in England and
he won't be checking his emails for hours.

❄

His reply is waiting for me on Tuesday morning.

7th October – I'll be there for three weeks.

That's all he says.
I don't reply.
When I walk through the door that evening, I find Lachie
sitting on the sofa, strumming his guitar. His long legs are
encased in tattered denim jeans and his bare feet are up on
the coffee table, beside an open bottle of beer.
'Hey,' he says with a small smile, going to put his
guitar down.

'Don't stop.' I grab his beer and take a swig, squeezing between him and the armrest. His eyes drift to my lips and his own curve up into an amused smile. 'What's that you were playing?' I ask.

'Nothing. Just messing. How was your day?'

'Fine.' I lift my shoulders into a shrug.

'Has he replied?'

I forgot that Lachie is like a sniffer dog when it comes to Alex.

'Yeah. He's coming on the seventh of October for three weeks.'

'He volunteered that information himself?'

'No.' I shake my head, feeling uneasy. 'I asked when he was coming.'

'Ah.'

If he *was* testing me, I have a feeling I've failed.

He puts his guitar down on the floor. I kick off my shoes and rest my knees against his lap, edging my shoulder into the crook of his arm. He takes the hint and pulls me close. I kiss his neck and he turns his head to stare at me levelly. His expression is unreadable, but I'm reluctant to ask what he's thinking.

He soon makes it clear. 'Do you want to see him?'

'No! I've already told you that.'

'You just ran away. Four years ago, from England and Alex. I've never really known if you were taking the easy option by staying here in Oz with me.'

I pull away from him and stare at him, shocked. 'How could you even *think* that? *You* are *why* I stayed in Australia. I wasn't running *from* Alex. I love *you*. I chose *you*. And, thankfully, you let me.'

A long moment passes and then Lachie's lips quirk up

into a smile. Full of relief, I lean forward and plant a kiss on them.

'I don't want to see him,' I repeat firmly, grabbing his super-soft T-shirt with my fingers. 'That part of my life is done with. If I never set eyes on him again, it'll be too soon.'

I mean the words as I say them.

It's only later that I doubt their truth.

✳

The closer it creeps to Alex's arrival date in Sydney, the more on edge I feel. On the morning of the 7th of October I consciously spend no more time on my appearance than usual, but I find myself reaching for my favourite skinny jeans, teaming them with the top I bought at the weekend when Lachie was working.

I know my boyfriend hasn't forgotten the significance of today, even if he's not bringing it up.

People have a habit of underestimating Lachie – I did, too, at first. He comes across as so carefree and young at heart that it's easy to mistake how much he actually *sees*; how shrewd he is. When I go to kiss him goodbye and he tells me that I look nice, I can't help but wonder at the hidden depths in those summer-sky eyes of his.

'Thanks,' I reply, choosing to take the compliment at surface level and not read into things.

I'm jumpy the entire day. Every time I step out of the office, my nerves ramp up a notch. Crossing the landing to go to the communal kitchen, taking the lifts, walking across the lobby, even going for a wander at lunchtime, I'm racked with tension, half expecting to see Alex at every turn. I spy him in every tall, slim, dark-haired man who passes me by – just for a split second, but it's enough to make my heart skip a beat.

It's the same the next day. And the next. By the end of the first week, I tell Lachie to stop asking me if I've seen him, vowing to divulge the information if I do. But the tension never leaves me.

By Wednesday of the following week, I begin to feel oddly fretful. It suddenly seems like a very real possibility that Alex could return to the UK without us laying eyes on each other. And this doesn't make me feel happy. In fact, I feel the opposite. Do I *want* to see him? Do I *need* to in order to be able to move on?

I try not to overthink it, but I find myself venturing out of the office more, finding excuses to go and see friends or colleagues at different magazines, just in case we cross paths.

On Thursday, Lachie calls me at work to say that he's invited Elliot over and is getting some steaks in.

'Seen him yet?' Elliot asks with a raised eyebrow as soon as I walk through the door shaking my umbrella.

He and Lachie are sitting at the living room table with the adjacent balcony doors wide open to the elements. The barbecue is smoking.

'No,' I reply firmly, rolling my eyes and casting a look over at the four empty beer bottles on the kitchen counter.

'El thinks you should,' Lachie stuns me by saying, in a flippant tone.

'What?' My eyes dart between my boyfriend and our wayward friend.

'You need closure,' Elliot states adamantly as Lachie jumps up and pecks me casually on my cheek. He's wearing shorts and a T-shirt, despite the heavy rain.

'You want a beer, Bronnie?' he calls over his shoulder as he heads into the kitchen.

'Sure,' I call back distractedly. 'Well, Alex has been in the building for two weeks and I haven't bumped into him yet,' I say to Elliot. 'I'm not sure I will.'

'Then why don't you email him to arrange a catch-up?' Elliot suggests easily as Lachie returns to the table, chinking our bottles as he passes them over.

'Maybe he's right,' Lachie chips in with a shrug.

'Are you serious?' I stare at him in shock, unable to believe what I'm hearing.

'Lay it to rest, once and for all,' he continues. 'You've been tetchy as hell lately. This is your one chance to see him and move on. Once he's gone, he's gone. Hopefully for good,' he adds drily.

I put my bottle to my lips and tilt, deciding to get as drunk as I can in as short a time as possible.

✳

The next day, I'm still mulling over our conversation when I walk into the Tetlan lobby and press the button for the lift. The doors open, I step in – and *freeze*.

'Sorry!' I exclaim, quickly coming to my senses and moving off to the side as the person behind me crashes into my abruptly halted frame. I breathe in deeply to be sure, and a kaleidoscope of butterflies flutter inside my stomach.

Alex has just been in this lift. I'm sure of it, because I can smell his aftershave. There's only the faintest trace of musk, but it used to be like catnip to me.

By the time I've reached my desk, I'm in pieces. Devastated. I don't understand how he still has the power to do this to me. I *have* to lay what happened between us to rest, and, if that means seeing him, then that's my only option.

I pull out my chair, sit down, and send a text to Lachie, giving him one last chance to back down.

He doesn't.

'I'm sure,' he replies. 'Good luck.'

I text back that I love him, but don't get a reply.

Opening up a new email, I type out a brief message to Alex:

Are you here? Want to go for lunch sometime?

He replies within minutes.

Yes and yes. Today?

We agree on 1 p.m. but I shirk his suggestion to meet downstairs in the foyer, naming a coffee shop a few blocks away. If I'm going to see Alex again, I don't want anyone I know to bear witness to our reunion.

I leave early and walk quickly, hoping to get there first and settle myself in before he appears. But, despite my best efforts, he's already there leaning up against the stone wall outside the coffee shop with his feet crossed at the ankles and his attention fixed on his phone screen. His posture reminds me of how he looked on the night we first met, leaning up against a pillar at the eighties club, playing Angry Birds on his phone.

He's wearing a red and black checked shirt with the sleeves rolled up, layered over a white T-shirt with black jeans and black boots. He glances up and instantly clocks me. My stomach does a somersault and his eyes widen.

'Hi,' he says, his face breaking into a grin as he stuffs his phone into his back pocket.

'Hey.' I force a smile in return, but my insides are going haywire as I come to a stop two feet in front of him.

He's suddenly awkward, not knowing how to greet me. I make the decision for both of us, stepping forward to give him the briefest of hugs. His hands only just touch my back before I retreat, but there's time enough for his catnip to hit me, full force.

'I hope they have a table,' I mumble, blushing as I turn away to push the door open. I'm hyper-aware of his proximity as he follows me inside.

There's a table right at the back and I brace myself as I sit down and come face to face with him again.

He rakes a hand through his dark hair to push it back from his forehead and then rests his elbows on the table between us.

He hasn't changed a bit.

'How are you?' he asks, studying me. His eyes are ocean blue, several shades darker than Lachie's.

'Really well, thanks,' I reply, reaching for the salt shaker to play with. I'm nervous. 'You?'

'Good.'

I lie. He *has* changed. The lines at the corners of his eyes are deeper than they once were, and now there's a hint of grey in the hair at his temples. He must be thirty-six – two years older than I am.

'Let's order and then we can chat,' I decide, picking up the menu.

'What do you usually go for?' he asks, his eyes levelling mine over the top of our menus.

'I don't. I've never been here before.'

There's a query in his expression.

'I've been to the gift shop next door,' I reveal.

'Ah.'

I think it's just dawned on him that I've chosen somewhere no one else I know would go to.

We need to order and pay at the counter, which I insist on doing, refusing, to his dismay, the note he tries to press into my hand. I go for the soup of the day – pumpkin and sweetcorn – while Alex opts for a baked potato with cheese.

'So…' he says when I return to the table. He's grabbed the salt shaker. 'This is weird.'

'Just a bit,' I agree. 'It's been a long time.'

'Almost four years.'

'How's it going at work?' I ask.

'Good, I think.' Small talk can be a blessing. 'It's sometimes hard to know, but the team seem to be responding well to suggestions.'

'That's good. Jet lag?'

'Terrible for the first week. I think I'm over it now.'

'Is it your first time in Sydney?'

'Yeah, first time. I'm cramming in my sightseeing at the weekends. After work I'm going straight back to my hotel and crashing out. The room-service staff and I are on first-name terms.'

Although he's gently jesting, I feel a stab of pity. It sounds like a pretty lonely experience in a new city.

'I would offer to have you over for dinner sometime, but…' I don't need to point out that he wouldn't be welcome.

He looks down at the table. 'How *is* Lachie?' he asks after a moment.

Does he know for certain that we're still together? Has anyone told him? Has he asked?

'He's great,' I reply, forcing what I hope is an easy smile, despite my nerves. 'Still the same, still gigging. He's got so many weddings on these days.'

He leans back in his seat and folds his arms, his foot accidentally kicking mine. We both quickly move out of each other's way.

'What about you?' he asks. 'Are you still doing wedding photography?'

I wrinkle my nose. 'Not really. Not at all, if I'm honest.'

His eyebrows pull together. 'I'm sorry to hear that.' He sounds genuinely regretful.

'Bridget is getting married next summer. She's asked me to do hers.'

'Oh, wow!'

'Yeah. I should probably get some practice in before then.'

'Surely it's like riding a bike…'

I shrug. 'Maybe.'

Neither of us says anything for a long moment. I avert my gaze only to come back a second later to meet his eyes again. He smiles a small smile. 'It's good to see you. I wasn't sure we'd get to catch up.'

I shake my head. 'Me neither. Lachie persuaded me, actually.'

His eyebrows practically hit his hairline.

I can't help but let out a little laugh. 'Apparently I've been tetchy as hell and this is my one chance to put it all behind me. I think his actual words were, "Once he's gone, he's gone. Hopefully for good."'

Alex winces and looks away. 'Fair enough.'

Another long silence ensues.

'I'm sorry if my trip here has stressed you out,' he says eventually, glancing at me.

'It's okay. It's actually nice to see you.'

His look becomes disbelieving, and then he makes a frustrated sound and leans forward again. 'Yeah,' he says quietly, biting his lip.

Luckily, the waitress brings over our food at that point, so we have something to distract us.

We talk about little things as we eat – about the people we know, the magazines that have closed down and the ones that aren't doing too badly, and my old boss Simon, who's apparently married now with a baby on the way. Eventually, I feel at ease enough to ask about his personal life.

'How about you? Marriage again? Kids?'

He shakes his head. 'No. Zara remarried, though. Had a whirlwind fling with some hotshot American advertising exec last summer. She's settled in New York.'

'You okay about that?'

'More than okay. I'm pleased she's happy.' He sounds completely sincere.

'Still got the guilts?' I say this flippantly, but we both know there's nothing glib about the events of four years ago.

'You have no idea.'

He doesn't meet my eyes at all as he says that last sentence. His voice sounds laden down with the weight of remorse.

'If we'd never met—' I start to say, but he shakes his head and doesn't let me finish my sentence, wherever it was going.

'Zara and I had been coasting for a while. We'd been together so long, I don't think either of us could face starting again, even though things weren't right. She told me she'd also been having doubts but, like me, opted for the easy option.'

'The easy option?' I ask with astonishment.

'Going through with a wedding that we weren't sure about seemed less horrendous than letting everyone down. At least, that's how it felt at the time when we were in the midst of it. But, Christ, I wish I'd done it differently. There are so many things I regret.' He shakes his head again. 'I'm so sorry, Bronte.' He looks pained as he meets my eyes. 'I fucked everything up badly, and then, like a dick, I kept emailing you.' His face twists in disgust. 'I should've just backed off. I arrogantly assumed that I could make up for past mistakes if I told you enough times I was sorry, but you were happy with Lachie and I was an idiot. I'm so sorry,' he repeats, his blue eyes shining.

I shake my head, my own eyes pricking with tears. 'It's okay. We were both pretty messed up with it all, weren't we? It all worked out okay in the end. I love Lachie. He's like a ray of sunshine.' I say this with a proper smile.

His own smile is tinged with sadness. 'I'm glad things worked out for you. *Both*,' he adds.

A few moments pass. 'Anyone significant in your life?' I find the courage to ask.

'Not at the moment, no.' Alex makes a dismissive gesture with his hand as he continues. 'I've been on a couple of dates, allowed myself to be set up to appease certain friends.' He says this last bit with mild amusement. 'But nothing serious.'

'I'm sorry,' I find myself saying.

'Don't be!' He frowns. 'When it's right, it's right. I'd know. I don't see the point of wasting time – hers or mine – when it's not going to go anywhere.'

'But then you're never giving anyone a proper chance. Just because you don't click on a first date doesn't mean you have nothing in common and you won't grow to love each other.'

He grins and rolls his eyes. 'Now you're sounding like my mate Ed.'

'Best man Ed?'

He breathes in sharply, nodding, as he remembers that we've met.

❋

The first and only time I met Alex's best friend was just before he married Zara. Alex was late to the church, so I went to look for him. I found him in a dark alleyway where Ed was giving him a pep talk.

'We'll be there in a minute,' Ed had said to me firmly when I'd asked if everything was okay.

But then Alex turned and whispered to him, prompting Ed to stare at me in shock.

'What are you doing here?' he asked.

'I'm photographing the wedding,' I told him, holding up my camera.

The look on Ed's face was incredulous. '*She's* photographing the wedding?' he asked Alex.

'I'm Bronte,' I said, unsure of what was going on.

'I *know* who you are.'

And it was clear from his tone that he knew *everything*.

Alex wanted a minute alone with me, but the hard look that Ed gave me as he stalked past still haunts me to this day.

Of course, Alex did go through with marrying Zara, but it all came crashing down just weeks later. To know I was the cause of that breakdown fills me with shame.

But, even if I hadn't been in love with Lachie, I'm not sure Alex and I could have picked up the pieces. I would have been the woman who broke up a decade-long relationship. Zara had been an integral part of Alex's life for so long – accepted by all of his friends and family. The easy way his mother spoke to me when she thought I was just Bronte, *there to do the photos*, would have transformed into something altogether more suspicious and disagreeable. It would have been the worst possible start to a burgeoning relationship. We never stood a chance.

❄

So yeah. That was the first and only time I met Alex's mate Ed.

'I guess we should be getting back,' Alex says after our short stint of mutual reminiscing.

'Yes.' I gather my things together.

We walk back, side by side. Neither of us speaks until we're a block away from the office.

'Maybe we could go for lunch again next week?' Alex suggests, casting me a sideways glance.

I hesitate before answering. 'I don't think that's going to be possible.'

'Oh.' He sounds taken aback. 'Okay.' And disappointed.

'Sorry, it's just… Lachie wouldn't like it.'

'Oh! Okay. Sure,' he says quickly. 'I wasn't meaning—'

'No, I know!' I cut him off, self-consciously. 'It's just, you know, this was supposed to be a one-off. Closure.'

'Fine. Sure, I get it.'

How awkward?

He rolls the sleeves of his shirt down as we walk. There's a proper chill in the air today. Not that I'd know, because my face is burning.

'I'm sorry,' I say again, feeling bad.

'Don't be,' he insists, protesting. 'I totally understand. It was good to see you. Give my best to Lachie too, please.' His voice sounds strained, but only from embarrassment, I think.

'I will.'

We walk into the building together and he presses the button for the lift. The doors open immediately and we step in.

'Floor?' I ask him.

'Seven.'

I press seven, and five for me. The doors close, leaving us alone in the confined space together. My chest feels constricted as I breathe him in. I'm not sure this has really worked. I don't feel better for seeing him – if anything I feel worse. There's so much we still haven't covered. But I'm not sure it's appropriate to say any more.

'Come and say goodbye before you go home?' I blurt as the doors open to let me out on level five.

'Okay,' he replies.

I step out onto the landing and turn around, feeling suddenly panicky.

'See you,' I say.

'Bye,' he replies with a small, sad smile. His eyes drop just as the lift doors close.

He never does come to say goodbye.

❋

Two months later, Lachie and I head to Perth for Christmas. Lachie has a big family – two loving, happily married parents, four doting older sisters who each have families of their own, plus multiple cousins and aunts and uncles, most of whom still live in the suburbs surrounding the city. So, when I say big, what I really mean is *enormous*.

Lachie's parents live in a four-bedroom house, but, on Christmas Eve and Christmas Day, three of his sisters and their families choose to cram into it rather than go back to their own homes, so Lachie and I take to the backyard in a tent – not just to give them all more space, but to give us some, too. Lachie's nieces and nephews will still hunt him out in the morning – they absolutely adore him. *And* me. I'm very good at choosing Christmas and birthday presents, as it turns out.

I love being around Lachie's family. It's so completely different from mine. My dad passed away a couple of years ago, so it's only Mum and me now, but she and her new husband, David, have belatedly discovered a love for travelling. This year they're going on a cruise that will end up in Sydney Harbour to watch the fireworks on New Year's Eve. We'll see them on New Year's Day, so I'm blissfully free of the usual guilt that comes when trying to decide who to spend Christmas with.

Right now, it's late on Christmas Eve and I'm squeezed in beside Lachie on the sofa, holding the newest addition to his family: ten-week-old Ella. Lachie's parents have gone up to bed, but his sisters and their partners remain. Bea is Lachie's eldest sister at thirty-seven, Maggie is slightly older than me at thirty-five, Tina is thirty-three, and Lydia – Ella's mother – is thirty. She's the only sister not staying over tonight and the one who is closest to Lachie both in age and spirit. She's been to visit us in Sydney a few times.

Last year Lydia finally tied the knot with her long-term boyfriend Mike, and despite their recent sleepless nights, they seem reluctant to go home to bed.

'Suits you,' Bea says to me with a smile, nodding at Ella.

'Okay, time to hand the baby back,' Lachie jokes.

'No way,' I say, snuggling the little bundle closer and smiling down at her angelic, sleeping face. 'She's adorable.'

'*Definitely* time to hand the baby back,' he says.

I glance at Lachie and narrow my eyes at him with not entirely mock annoyance.

'Aw,' Maggie says, the corners of her lips turning down as she gazes at her brother. 'I thought you wanted kids?'

She has three boys upstairs – all asleep and ready for Father Christmas.

Lachie shrugs. 'Yeah, one day.' He pauses. 'I think.'

I shoot him a quick look. He *thinks*?

'But not for a few more years,' he adds.

'You shouldn't leave it too long,' Bea advises, avoiding my gaze.

The fact that I'm six years older than Lachie has escaped no one's attention, I'm sure, but they're too diplomatic to mention it.

'We've got plenty of time for all that,' Lachie replies calmly.

'I hope you haven't been hanging out with Elliot too much,' Lydia chips in drily.

Lachie rolls his eyes at Lydia, while Maggie tactfully changes the subject, but his youngest sister's comment is still playing on my mind later when we've retired to our tent.

'Lachie?' I'm lying in his arms, tracing my fingertips across his ribcage.

'Mmm?' he replies sleepily.

'Is Lydia right? Has El's anti-kids stance rubbed off on you?'

I expect him to sigh or scoff or dismiss the conversation, but when he doesn't immediately reply my fingers freeze in their tracks.

'I love my nieces and nephews, but being around them just reminds me of how much work it all is.' Lachie yawns, not seeming to notice how tense I suddenly feel.

'I know, but everyone says it's different when it's your own,' I point out.

He stills and then cranes his neck to look down at me. 'Are you getting broody?' He sounds apprehensive.

'I don't want to wait *too* much longer.'

'How much longer are we talking here?'

'I don't know. A year or two?'

He slowly rests his head back onto his pillow and scratches his chin.

I wriggle onto my tummy and prop myself up on my elbows so he can't escape my scrutiny. He looks pretty uncomfortable.

'Lachie?' I prompt.

'I'm only twenty-eight,' he replies eventually. 'But thirty still seems way too young to me.'

I always wondered if our age gap would come back to bite us.

I think it just has.

'I just… I don't want to be an older mum. I'm already thirty-four. I thought I'd have children by now.'

'I thought I'd get married one day, but you don't believe in marriage, so that's that, then…' His slightly shirty voice trails off.

'I'm not *totally* against it,' I say with a frown. 'I just don't really see the point. Wait. Do you *want* to get married?' I ask with surprise.

He doesn't meet my eyes. 'No. That's not what I'm saying.'

His tone triggers a wave of nausea and I find myself sitting up in my sleeping bag.

'But you *do* see a future with me, right?' I ask cautiously.

'Yeah. You know I love you. But...' He's not meeting my eyes.

'What?' I ask warily.

He sighs and my nausea ramps up a notch. 'I guess I've felt a little... stifled lately.'

'*What?*'

'You never want to go out anymore,' he says. 'We're becoming boring.'

'You mean *I'm* becoming boring. You've been going out plenty,' I snap.

'I'm only twenty-eight, Bronte! We should be out every other night, having a laugh with our mates, not sitting at home relentlessly watching telly on the sofa.'

'Do these mates include Fliss?' I ask irately.

'Don't start that again,' Lachie snaps.

A couple of weeks ago, I got a nasty surprise when I overheard Elliot asking Lachie if Fliss was okay.

'What's this?' I interrupted, and it may have just been my imagination, but Lachie seemed to tense up.

'Her ex has been harassing her,' he divulged, reluctantly, I thought at the time.

'Lachie's been her knight in shining armour,' Elliot teased.

'It's no big deal.' Lachie brushed it off.

'In what way?' I persisted, forcing a smile, despite my unease.

'He's just been giving her a bit of shit, always ringing her, turning up at her flat uninvited, wanting her back. He rocked up at that wedding we were doing last weekend, so I told him where to go.'

'Pow!' Elliot interjected, smacking his fist against his other hand.

'You punched him?' I asked my boyfriend, shocked.

'I didn't punch him,' he snapped infuriatedly, shooting Elliot a look. 'I just gave him a bit of a shove.'

'Why didn't you tell me?' I asked.

'It wasn't a big deal.'

Out of the corner of my eye, I caught Elliot pulling a face, as though he'd belatedly realised he'd landed his mate in trouble. I chose to drop the subject, but couldn't let it lie.

'Why didn't you tell me what was going on with Fliss?' I asked later.

'I told you, it wasn't a big deal.'

'Elliot knew. How was that, then?'

'He came out that night with us, remember? You didn't feel like it.'

'Only because it was eleven o'clock by the time you finished that wedding!' I exclaimed. 'I was already in bed! I thought you were going to come home!'

It was not the first argument we'd had in recent months.

'Do you find her attractive?' I ask Lachie now. It's time we got to the bottom of this.

'Of course she's attractive – any bloke would think so.'

'No, do *you* find her attractive?' I repeat.

'What do you expect me to say?' he responds eventually, his eyes glinting in the darkness.

'Oh, shit,' I mumble, fighting back tears as I unzip my sleeping bag.

'What are you doing?' he mutters, reaching for my arm.

I snatch it away from him. 'Getting some fresh air.'

I sit on a garden bench in the damp night, staring up at the stars. Lachie is snoring lightly by the time I return half an hour later. At some point during the night, he tries to spoon me, but the distance between us is real, and not just because we're in separate sleeping bags.

The next day, five children pile into our makeshift bedroom at seven in the morning and we manage to feign excitement as we vow to come straight in and open, or, rather, dish out our presents.

Once they've left us to get dressed, Lachie meets my eyes directly. 'I don't fancy Fliss,' he states adamantly. 'I fancy you. Only you. Just… chill out, okay?'

I try to, but the tension between us doesn't dissipate.

A merry, merry Christmas it ain't.

❄

'Say hello to Bronte!'

'Hello, Bonty,' a sweet little voice comes in reply before Bridget's face is obscured by a small, chubby hand.

It's a Saturday evening in late March and Bridget and I are FaceTiming.

'Give that to me, you cheeky monkey,' Bridget chides, wrestling her phone back. 'I'll get you one of these when you're twelve and not a year younger.'

I smile at my friend's face, lit up with love as she grins down at her daughter. It still feels surreal, but Bridget is, without a shadow of a doubt, this tiny person's mummy, now. They haven't quite completed the adoption process, but April has been using the moniker for months.

'How are you?' Bridget asks once April has run off to amuse herself with some toy or other.

'I'm okay.' I nod.

There's sadness in her eyes, which I know mirrors mine.

Things haven't been right between Lachie and me, not since Christmas, and, if I'm being honest, not for some time before that. Bridget is as clueless as I am about a solution.

'So he definitely can't make the wedding?'

I shake my head. 'Aside from the fact that he refuses to let people down, we can't afford to both fly over at the moment.'

'Is today's wedding with Fliss?' she checks.

'Yep. And the two in July when I'm over with you. She sees more of him than I do.' I miserably put my feet up on the coffee table. 'He reckons we should be thankful to her for getting him so much work.'

'Yeah, I'm sure her heart is in the right place.'

I love it when Bridget is sarcastic.

I grin at her. 'Miss you,' I say.

'I miss you, too,' she replies seriously. Her expression suddenly becomes anxious. 'Am I making a shitty mistake asking you to do the pics?'

Now I'm worried. I haven't managed to line up any other weddings since she asked me to do hers. Lachie said Fliss could ask around – she is very well connected, apparently – but I decided to cut off my nose to spite my face, where that one was concerned.

I'll probably live to regret it, but I can't face her being involved in my career. It's bad enough that she's so entwined with Lachie's, although I do know deep down that I should be more appreciative of all the work she gets him. He'd much rather be playing his music than working on a building site or behind a bar.

'Are you having second thoughts?' I ask apprehensively.

'No!' Bridget cries. 'Of course I'm not! I just want you to kick back and enjoy yourself, not have to work.'

'I will *absolutely* enjoy myself. Anyway, Rachel will be there, too.'

I was thrilled when Bridget managed to line up my

former boss after I voiced concerns about my current lack of experience. Luckily, Bridget and Charlie are getting married midweek, so Rachel was free. She gave them a whopping great discount and was delighted to hear that I would be assisting her.

'I spoke to her last week,' I say with a smile. 'I can't wait to work with her again.'

'I assure you, the feeling is mutual,' she replies. 'With Maria doing my make-up, it'll be like old times.'

'Any more thoughts on your hen night?' I ask.

Last I heard, she still hadn't made plans. Her friends have put forward so many suggestions – mostly involving European getaways – but so far, none of our ideas have been received with enthusiasm from our bride-to-be.

Now our *blushing* bride-to-be, I notice.

'I'm not sure I really want one,' she reluctantly admits.

'*What?*' Bridget, turning down the chance to go out with her mates and get shitfaced?

'I know this is really, really sad,' she continues bashfully, 'but I just don't want to be away from Charlie and April, even for one night.'

'What has he *done* to you?' I cry.

Her cheeks brighten further and I can't help but laugh.

'How do you cope when you have to go away for work?' I ask, genuinely curious.

'Charlie and April come with me,' she replies, still sheepish. 'I know I'll have to work away from them sometimes, but I wouldn't choose it,' she reveals.

I laugh again. 'I never, ever thought I'd see the day.'

'Me neither,' she replies.

❄

It's Lachie's twenty-ninth birthday a week later. He wants to go out in Sydney for a big night, but at the last minute he's asked to do a gig at a popular Manly haunt after the booked artist drops out. His friends are only too happy to go to his gig first before carrying on locally, so I head home straight after work to get ready and join him at the venue. I find him having a beer with a couple of his former builder buddies.

When we settled in Sydney, Lachie lined up a stint on a building site to help pay the rent, but he has enough gigging work now to get by. He's stayed in touch with the guys he liked the most, though, including his former boss, Nathan, who's propping up the bar with him now.

'I didn't know you were back,' I say to Nathan with a smile, after kissing the birthday boy hello. 'Is Lucy coming?'

Lucy is Nathan's wife and we became friendly almost instantly. She and Nathan have been over in the UK for the last few months, working and visiting Lucy's family. They try to split their time between the two countries.

'Yeah, as soon as she's got Finn down,' Nathan replies, referring to their not-quite-two-year-old son. 'Jet lag is a bitch for toddlers. His sleep is all over the place.'

'When did you get back?'

'Only a few days ago. We'll have to have you over to ours for a barbie soon.'

'That would be great.'

We tend to go to theirs more, just because it's easier with Finn. Plus, they have a really cool old house, just up the hill from here. It was pretty much derelict when they bought it, but now it has modern touches and loads of glass and natural light. Nathan did all of the work on it himself.

I turn to Lachie, pleased to see that he's wearing the new watch I bought him. 'How was your day?'

'Pretty chilled,' he replies with a warm smile.

'When are your days *not* chilled,' I tease, slipping one arm around his waist. He does the same to me, pulling me against his hip.

'What do you want to drink?' he asks.

'I might get a glass of bubbles.' I try to flag down the girl behind the bar, but she's not looking my way.

'Prosecco?' he asks, raising an eyebrow.

'Yes, please.'

He twists away and leans over the counter. The girl looks his way immediately and attends to him within seconds.

This always happens. Not that I'm complaining.

A few more friends arrive, including Fliss, who walks in, laughing, with Elliot.

'Am I missing something?' I ask in El's ear when he comes over.

He brushes me off. 'No. She was at her sister's, so I offered to pick her up on my way from work. I had a meeting with a client this afty in Cremorne.' That's a suburb southwest from here, on the way to Sydney. Elliot's a civil engineer.

'Cool watch!' I hear Fliss say to Lachie.

'Bronnie got it for me,' Lachie replies, and he's already smiling at me when I turn to catch his eye.

'She's got good taste, your girlfriend.' Fliss flashes me a smile that doesn't reach her eyes.

'Too bloody right, she does,' Lachie jokes, grabbing my hand and tugging me towards him. He loops his arms around my waist from behind and plants a kiss on my cheek.

'Aw,' Fliss says soppily, smiling at us both before calling out to Elliot. 'Oi, El, are you buying me a drink or what?' She steps away to join our friend.

Eventually, Lachie has to go and do his set. It's been ages since I've seen him gig – obviously I can't go to any of the weddings he does, but I miss the days when we used to work together. As he takes to the stage, the venue fills with deafening cheers and whoops – his mates have got some lungs on them. I feel a wave of pride. Lachie looks so right up there, so at ease and sexy with his ripped jeans, dark T-shirt and shaggy blond hair. With his short beard, he looks a lot like how he did when we first met, albeit with broader shoulders these days. He's even more attractive, if that's possible.

He casts his eyes over the audience with a lazy, delightful grin as he sits down on a stool. Then he leans towards the mic and says a simple, affectionate 'Hi' before launching into a stripped-back acoustic version of The Killers' 'When You Were Young'.

'Ah, man!' I hear Nathan exclaim with dismay.

I cast him a sideways look.

'I can't believe Lucy's missing this. She loves this song,' he explains.

'Is she still coming?' She's pretty late. I hope she's okay.

'Finn was throwing a tantrum, but she's on her way,' he promises.

Lachie catches my eye during the first instrumental section and smiles, prompting a series of tiny shivers to spiral down my spine. I still fancy him. So much.

I remember the first time I saw Lachie on stage. It was at a wedding in Scotland and, when he appeared, both Rachel and I swooned. We couldn't take our eyes off him.

'*The hottest wedding singer I've ever come across, period*,' were Rachel's exact words.

He joined us for a beer during one of his breaks. He seemed so young and flirty to me at the time – not boyfriend material in the slightest. I was shocked when he later asked if he could come up to my room. He'd caught a cab back with us to our hotel and I'd naturally assumed he was staying there. We'd had a few drinks together and I thought he was sweet, but I wasn't about to sleep with him, the cheeky git, *or* let him crash on my floor, which was his next question.

He ended up kipping in his car in the hotel car park, where he'd left it earlier – he didn't have a hotel room booked, after all. I felt a little bad about that, but he didn't seem fazed. That was just what he was like – free and easy.

Not long afterwards, he rocked up in London and sought me out – I'd told him where I worked. We became friends, although he later revealed he'd had the hots for me from the beginning. I was so caught up in Alex that I didn't have room in my heart – or life – for anyone else, even though the situation with Alex was hopeless.

When Lachie and I eventually got together, it was after Alex had stepped right back. It's not that I hadn't been attracted to Lachie before, because I definitely had; I just hadn't visualised a future for us.

Four and a half years later, here we are.

After a few more songs, Lachie does 'Cocoon' by Catfish and the Bottlemen, one of our favourite bands.

When he gets to the part in the lyric about his girl staying to outdrink him, he smirks to himself and looks down at his strumming hands on the guitar. But the next time he sings these words he grins out at the audience. Something makes me search for Fliss in the crowd and, from the look on her face, I know straightaway that they're sharing a private joke.

My stomach turns over, and then a pair of hands land on my waist. I jump and twist around to see Lucy.

'Hi!' she shouts over the music.

'Hey!' I try to sound as enthusiastic as I would if I hadn't just witnessed what I'd witnessed.

She tilts her face up to Nathan, who obligingly presses a kiss to her lips. 'Hell?' he asks.

'Shocking.' She casts her eyes heavenwards, shrugs and nods.

Distracted, my eyes return to the stage. Lachie isn't looking at Fliss anymore, but another glance at her reveals that she's still grinning at him, rapt.

'Sorry I'm so late!' Lucy says in my ear, chinking my beer bottle with what looks like vodka and cranberry.

'No worries at all,' I reply, trying to ignore the sick feeling roiling in my gut.

Am I losing Lachie?

Is he already lost?

'Are you okay?' Lucy asks with sudden concern.

Her empathy has a powerful effect on my emotions.

'Bronte, what's wrong?' she asks with alarm as my eyes well up with tears. 'Is it Lachie?' she persists.

I'm mortified, but I nod as I swallow. I like Lucy too much to lie to her.

'Who is that?' she asks, following the line of my sight towards Fliss.

'Fliss,' I reply. 'She's the girl he's been doing all his weddings with.'

'You think there's something going on?' She's startled.

I shake my head. 'I don't know. I just have a bad feeling.'

'She looks young.' Lucy casts Fliss another surreptitious glance.

'She's Lachie's age,' I reply.

My friend meets my eyes with understanding.

'Sorry, this is not the time or the place.' I'm shocked and embarrassed at how much I've said. I really don't believe Lachie is cheating on me, but it hurts to think that his feelings may drift further than friendship.

'What are you up to tomorrow?' Lucy asks. 'Is Lachie working?'

I nod miserably. 'With her.'

'Come over for a cuppa,' she urges. 'I'll make sure Nathan's out of the house and will put Finn down for his nap so we can chat properly.'

'Okay,' I reply. 'Thanks.'

I know I'll be very glad of the distraction.

❋

'Sorry I had to leave early last night,' Lucy apologises the following day when our plan comes together.

Finn kindly obliged us by going down for his nap without any fuss. Flying halfway around the world to land in a completely different time zone used to knacker me out, but at least I knew why my body clock was all over the place. It must be very confusing for a toddler.

'But I had an excuse,' Lucy adds, smoothing her hand across her floaty top to reveal what I now see has been disguising a rather large bump.

'You're having another baby!' I cry. 'That's amazing news! How far along are you?'

'Five months,' she reveals with a smile, picking up her mug from the coffee table and taking a sip.

My eyes pop out of my head. 'How on earth have you kept that a secret?'

'We've been in the UK.' She shrugs. 'I wanted to tell people in person.'

'Wait, weren't you drinking last night? I thought you were on vodka cranberries?'

'Cranberry, no vodka,' she replies with a cheeky look.

'Sneaky! Do you know what you're having?'

She nods. 'A girl.'

I squeal.

She grins, but then her features grow sober. 'Sorry, I just wanted to get that bit out of the way first, but I do want to talk about you. How was the rest of last night?'

My mood takes a nosedive. 'We ended up back at ours with Fliss and a few others. It was… unsettling.'

'In what way?' She cocks her head to one side, causing her long chestnut hair to swing in its high ponytail.

'I know Lachie has hung out with Fliss in the past when I've been at work, but she was so comfortable at our place.' I shake my head despairingly. 'You should've seen her making herself at home, offering her pals tea and biscuits.'

'*What?*' Lucy pulls a face, outraged.

'She's obviously been there loads. Lachie clearly chose not to tell me how much because he thinks I've got it in for her. And he's right.'

'Does *he* think she fancies him?' Lucy asks, tucking her bare legs up underneath herself on the sofa and nursing her mug between her hands.

'He's adamant she doesn't, but he's wrong. I don't know if he's blind to it or if he's just kidding himself, but I've seen the way she looks at him. She absolutely adores him.'

'He is pretty adorable,' Lucy says, her eyebrows pulling together.

I smile at her, but then my face crumples. 'I'm sorry,' I say. 'I don't know what's got into me. Lachie and I have been together for so long and he's always been tactile with other women. I'm usually cool with it – in fact, I usually *like* it. I love how he was with Bridget, for example, but I've always been so sure about his feelings for me. Seeing Fliss jokily push him over the back of the sofa and then climb on top of him was—'

'*She did what?*' Lucy blanches.

'She sort of fell on him and they both cracked up laughing and he had his arms around her. They were just being silly and were both *really* drunk, but... Argh! I hated it!'

'I'm not surprised.' Lucy looks aghast.

'Like I say, I like that Lachie is tactile. It was one of the reasons I fell for him. But I don't like seeing him be that way with Fliss. There's something about her...'

'You have to tell him,' Lucy states firmly.

'I have!' I cry. 'He thinks I'm nagging him!'

'You're not,' she states firmly. 'You have to talk to him about this! If she makes you uncomfortable, then he should stop seeing her.'

'They work together,' I say. 'She gets him most of his gigs.'

'That's tricky,' Lucy replies with a grimace. 'But at the very least he should try to wean her out of his social life.'

'I couldn't make him do that.' I shake my head.

'Why not? Nathan doesn't have any female friends, not anymore. It's just... not necessary.'

'But Lachie has always had female friends.'

'People change and grow and adapt – they have to. We can't always stay the same.'

'That's just it, though. Lachie doesn't want to change. He likes his life exactly as it is. In fact, he wants *me* to change. He thinks I've become boring. But I don't want to stay out late and get hammered all the time. I want a more chilled life. I want a family. And he doesn't. Not any time soon. We're on completely different wavelengths and I can't help but think it's because of the age gap between us.'

Lucy appears thoughtful.

'Did you ever have this problem with Nathan?' I ask. He's two years younger than she is – they got together when he was twenty-four.

'Not really. He wanted to get engaged super-fast.'

'You're a catch,' I say with a grin.

Lucy laughs. 'And, anyway, we waited years to have kids. We wanted to be on our own for a while before bringing a family into the mix.'

I smile at her again, my eyes drifting to her bump. 'I'm so happy for you. You're right about Lachie. I need to speak to him about it. But let's talk about something else, now. How's your pregnancy been so far? And I want to know all about your trip!'

The rest of the afternoon passes by pleasantly.

❋

I wait up for Lachie that night, hoping he's too hungover from his birthday bash to go out drinking again. He appears at eleven.

'You're awake!' he says with pleasant surprise when I get up from the sofa.

He puts his guitar case down as I step forward for a hug.

'You okay?' he asks softly.

'I missed you,' I murmur.

I *miss* you.

'Aw,' he replies with affection.

'I thought you might go out drinking again.'

'Nah, I'm shattered.'

'Bed?' I step back and take his hands in mine.

His blue eyes smile down at me, and then he lets go of my hands and hooks his fingers through the belt loops of my jeans, tugging me forward so we're hip to hip. Bending down, he plants his lips on mine.

It is the sweetest kiss we've had in ages, but all too soon it grows into something more. His fingers find the hem of my T-shirt and our mouths are forced apart as the fabric comes up and over my head.

'Bed?' I repeat, breathlessly.

He shakes his head. 'Here.'

It's been so long since we've had sex outside the bedroom – the idea feels strangely illicit. We both get very busy unbuttoning each other's jeans and stripping down to our underwear. He pulls me against him again and now only the flimsy fabric of our underwear separates me from what is a pretty impressive show of how turned on he is.

Our lips lock together with increasing urgency as he lifts me onto the table and unclasps my bra. I wrap my legs around him, gasping at the intense sensation. A moment later, he steps away to wriggle out of his boxers, reaches between us to pull my lacy knickers to one side, and surges forward.

I grip his muscled back and hold on for dear life.

It is the best sex we've had in... I can't remember how long.

'Lachie?' I say the next morning as he sleepily traces circles on my arm in bed.

'Mmm?'

'I need to talk to you about Fliss.'

He sighs. Loudly. 'You've got nothing to worry about.'

'I can't stand her,' I state. 'I don't like the way you are with her. I hate the way she is with you. I don't want her hanging around the flat when I'm not here.' I say these three sentences without pausing, but, by the time I've finished, he's already taken his arm out from behind my shoulders and is sliding out of bed.

'You're being unreasonable,' he says, pulling on Friday night's jeans. Yesterday's are still out in the living room.

'I'm not. I'm trusting my instincts and I don't trust her.'

'What about me?' he asks emphatically. 'Do you trust me?' He irately tugs open a drawer and swipes a fresh T-shirt, pulling it over his head.

I don't answer.

'What. You don't?' he demands to know.

'No, I do,' I say reasonably. 'But I don't see why you have to be friends with someone who makes me so uncomfortable. I wouldn't do that to you.'

He rolls his eyes, unhappy about being backed into a corner.

It's true, though. I still feel unsettled by that whole episode with Alex. It might've helped me to see him again while he was here, but I didn't out of respect for Lachie.

'I saw the way you sang that Catfish and the Bottlemen song to her,' I state.

'What?' He recoils.

'You looked at her when you sang that bit in "Cocoon" about her out-drinking you and her friends all hating it.' I'm startled to see that he looks guilty. 'What was that about?'

'It's nothing,' he says.

'It's not nothing,' I bat back.

He can see I'm not giving in, but he looks sickeningly shifty as he speaks.

'What I mean to say is you have nothing to worry about,' he insists, his voice sounding forcibly calmer as he edgily meets my eyes. I wait for an explanation and eventually one comes.

'Last week, when you were out with work, I went for a beer with El and we bumped into Fliss and some of her friends. She invited us to join them, but I got the feeling that a couple of her mates wanted a girls' night, so, when Fliss ordered a bunch of shots for us to do, they refused to join in. It all got a bit silly.'

I feel ill. 'What do you mean, "silly"?'

'We just got a bit drunk and her friends ended up leaving and Fliss felt really bad about it the next day.'

'She can't have felt too bad, seeing the smirking look on both of your faces when you were singing about it.'

'Oh, for God's sake,' he snaps, but he knows I've caught him out.

'Bloody hell, Lachie,' I mutter. 'That girl is into you. Are you really completely blind or do you just not want to see it because you fancy her, too?'

'I do not!' He raises his voice.

'Bullshit!' I raise mine in return. 'I don't want you hanging out with her!'

'I *have* to hang out with her. I work with her!' he yells.

'Then get some fucking jobs off your own back instead of relying on her so much!'

He looks absolutely furious for a moment and then shakes his head rapidly. He's completely pissed off, but to my relief he doesn't storm out of the room.

A lump forms in my throat. 'Lucy's pregnant again,' I tell him.

He glances at me. 'Is she?'

My eyes well up and his expression softens.

'B,' he says quietly, sitting down on the bed and reaching for my hand.

'I want a baby, too,' I say past the lump in my throat. I've hardly acknowledged to myself how broody I am, but I can no longer deny it.

His hand goes limp in mine and he looks away. 'I'm not ready.'

'I don't want to wait much longer. I'm going to be thirty-five next month,' I say imploringly.

'I'm not ready,' he states again, shaking his head and letting go of my hand.

'No one thinks they're ready and then they have a baby and it's the best thing that ever happened to them.'

He stares at me directly. 'It's not going to happen. Not any time soon. I can't even *support* a kid.'

'I'd have to go back to work,' I say, feeling a pang at the thought of a horribly short maternity leave.

'What? And I'd be a stay-at-home dad?' he asks incredulously, getting to his feet.

'We're actually really lucky,' I say as he paces the floor. 'You work nights and weekends, while I work weekdays. One of us would always be with him. Or her.' I realise I have a battle on my hands in convincing him. He doesn't even *want* a baby, yet here I am suggesting he be its primary carer.

'We don't have room for a kid.' Lachie waves his hand around our poky bedroom to make his point.

'We'd have to move. Probably further out, but—'

'I don't want to move! I like it here!'

'We'll have to make some compromises.'

He comes to a standstill. 'Bronte, I am *not* having a baby. Not yet. Not any time soon.' His tone turns regretful with his last few words. 'I'm sorry, but you won't change my mind. Having a family is a long way off for me.'

'How long?' I ask stupidly, brushing away tears.

'I don't know,' he replies heavily, sitting back down on the bed and staring at me forlornly. There are only a couple of feet between us, but it might as well be a chasm of Grand Canyon proportions.

❄

Try as I might, I just can't bury my head in the sand about this one.

The weeks leading up to my setting off to the UK are overwrought with tension and arguments. There is no compromise to be found.

I want a baby; Lachie doesn't. It's as simple as that.

We're stuck. Stagnant. With nowhere to go.

What's worse, *Vivienne* gets a new editor who turns out to be a complete nightmare. She's disorganised and indecisive and I end up working longer and longer hours. Although Lachie's birthday gig at the bar turned into a fantastic regular stint, I'm lucky if I make it in time to see his last couple of songs.

But Fliss is always there, invariably. Lachie claims to have backed off from their friendship and has cut down the amount of time he spends with her outside of the weddings that they do together, but the message has not filtered down to her.

More likely, his signals are nowhere near strong enough.

A few days before I set off to the UK, Lachie and I find ourselves at opposite ends of the sofa, facing each other. The telly is muted and our dirty dinner plates are on the coffee table, but we can't find the energy to get up and drag ourselves to bed. I rest my cheek against the sofa and look across at him, my knees up in front of me.

'Will you think about everything while I'm gone?' I ask softly.

He sighs.

'I get it if you don't want a baby now or even next year,' I continue. 'But can we come up with some sort of plan, agree to some form of commitment?'

He swallows and dangles his arm over the back of the sofa, breaking eye contact with me. 'What if I can't?' he whispers. 'Is this a deal breaker for you?'

'What do you mean?' I ask warily.

'What if I don't want to have children?'

My jaw drops. 'Are you serious?'

He roughly drags his hand over his beard. 'I'm just... I'm so far off wanting to be a dad. What if I'm never ready?'

I shake my head. 'I can't bear to think about that possibility.'

'We might have to.'

I stare at him with horror. 'Then *yes*, it's a deal breaker!' I can't keep a lid on my emotions. 'I want kids! I've always wanted a family. Are you serious? You might do an Elliot on me?'

He looks hopeless. 'I don't know. But what if you *are* wasting your time with me? You said it yourself: you don't want to be an older mum. But that's the way things are heading if we stay together. And that's if we ever even get to that point.' He grows misty eyed. 'I love you,' he says in a choked voice. 'And I promise you this is not about Fliss.' I jolt at the sound of her name being brought into our intimate conversation. 'I like her as a friend, nothing more, but it's true that I have felt more on her wavelength than yours in recent months.'

I feel like I'm going to throw up. And he's not finished.

'Being around her has made me face the fact that things haven't been right between us for a while. We're not connected, not like we used to be. I feel like you're racing ahead in a different direction to me and I can't catch up with you. I'm not sure I *want* to catch up with you.'

My stomach continues to freefall. 'Do you just need some time and space to think? Because you're about to get it.' I'm going to be away for over three weeks. My new boss is none too pleased about it, but it was organised well before she came on the scene.

'I've had plenty of time and space already,' he says. 'We barely see each other.'

My voice sounds small as I ask my next question. 'Do you think we should break up?'

The devastation in his eyes as he stares back at me says it all.

❄

Bridget has invited me to stay with her for the ten days leading up to the wedding, but first I go to spend a few days in south London with my old Aussie school friend Polly and her family. Polly and I have had our ups and downs over the years, but, despite the fact that she now has two young children demanding her almost constant attention, she really comes through for me. She's a rock and I'm feeling much better by the time I set off to Padstow in Cornwall, where Bridget and Charlie live.

I still can't believe that Lachie and I are over, but it's real. The days before I came away were hell. We shed so many tears between us – I have no idea how I managed to drag my sorry arse into work.

He intends to move in with a friend while I'm in England, and when I get back I'll look for a place of my own. I could probably stretch to paying all the rent on our flat, but with our shared memories it would be too painful to stay. I'm thinking about moving out of Manly altogether. It's always been more Lachie's scene than mine, with his surfing lifestyle. But I'll miss Lucy. She was gutted when I told her that Lachie and I had split up.

❄

Bridget comes to collect me from the train station when I arrive in Cornwall and my mood does an about-turn at the sight of her beaming face. We throw our arms around each other and squeeze tightly.

'I've missed you so much!' she cries.

'I can't tell you how much I've missed *you*,' I murmur.

She withdraws to look me over, the corners of her lips turning down.

'Don't talk to me about it or I'll lose it,' I warn.

'Okay,' she complies, nodding.

She looks well and happy, her khaki shorts showing off her long, slim, tanned legs. They've been having a heatwave that we all hope lasts through the wedding celebrations.

'Your hair has grown!' I tug gently on a lock of her just-below-shoulder-length, dark, wavy hair.

'Yours is still exactly the same,' she replies with a laugh, her navy eyes smiling.

'I had a trim a couple of weeks ago, I promise. You can't see because I've tied it back.' I'm wearing it in a long fishtail plait, one of my favourite styles when I can be bothered to make the effort. 'Maybe I should lop it all off and have a proper post-break-up overhaul.'

'Don't you dare. It suits you like this. How was your journey from London?' she asks. 'It's a bit of a shit, isn't it?'

'Could've been worse.' The flight from Sydney to London was bleak, made a million times worse by my broken heart.

'I'm excited to see a part of the UK I haven't been to before.'

'I've got so many beautiful places to show you.' Bridget sounds like she can't wait.

'We'll have to cram it all in.' I'm determined to stay upbeat for her.

'I wish you could stay longer,' she laments. 'I feel like postponing my honeymoon.'

I laugh.

'I'm not even joking,' she says. 'Laura can't get here until Saturday.' That's four days before the wedding. Laura is her friend who lives in the States.

'Are you sure you'll have room for us all?'

'Definitely! It'll be a bit of a squash, especially when Mum and Dad get here, but I want you with me, *so much*. Are you sure you don't mind sharing a room with Laura and Max for a couple of nights before the wedding?' Max is Laura's baby. 'Mum was talking about getting a hotel room, but she hasn't managed to get organised.'

Bridget's parents are divorced, but their relationship is amicable enough for them spend a few days in the same house together. The same room, however, would be pushing it.

'Of course not,' I reply. 'I can't wait to meet everyone. So Marty's staying at a B&B?'

'Yeah. She and Ted wanted a proper mini-break. She can't believe we're getting married midweek and making them use up some of their holiday time.' She shrugs and grins.

Marty is engaged, too. Bridget thinks it's hilarious that she's beating her chief bridesmaid down the aisle. No one saw *that* coming.

'Why couldn't Leo make it?' I ask. That's Laura's partner.

'Too many bookings, and I didn't give them enough notice.' They run a guesthouse in Key West. 'It's probably just as well. I don't want anyone to upstage Charlie on our Big Day.' She giggles.

She's told me on numerous occasions that Leo is super-hot.

'I can't wait for you to meet Charlie!' She bangs the steering wheel with excitement.

I have a feeling that, if she weren't driving, she'd be clapping her hands like a three-year-old.

'Me neither,' I reply, and I mean it.

We're back at Charlie and Bridget's house in no time, a gorgeous four-bedroom detached house with a whitewashed exterior and a silver-grey slated roof. Charlie and Bridget have only recently finished renovating it after buying it late last year.

'This place is amazing!' I gush as we climb out of the car.

'We couldn't have got it without Dad's help,' she reminds me coyly, as we walk up the pretty, flower-lined stone path to the moss-green front door.

She's already told me as much. Bridget's dad 'invested' in a flat in Chalk Farm years ago, but it's obvious he bought it primarily to help his beloved daughter get onto the property ladder. Property prices in London have skyrocketed in recent years, so he made an absolute packet when he sold it and insisted on using the profits to help Bridget buy a family home with Charlie.

'He's so great,' I say, and I know this from experience. I met Bridget's dad many times when she and I lived together. I've never met her mum, but I will do in a few days when she's here for the wedding. Bridget said it was a complete faff trying to agree on a date that suited her.

She doesn't talk about her mother much, but I understand they've had a slightly strained relationship over the years, not helped by the fact that her mum chose to go back to work on a cruise liner, travelling the world, when Bridget was just six years old. Her dad raised her pretty much on his own.

'He's thinking about selling up the pub and retiring down here,' Bridget says of her dad.

'No way!'

'Yeah.' She grins and gets her keys out of her purse.

'What does Charlie think about that?' I ask in a low voice in case he can somehow hear me.

'Oh, he's delighted. They get along like a house on fire. Dad says Charlie's the son he never had.'

'That is so cute.'

'Yeah, it's lovely,' she says fondly, unlocking the door.

'Hey!' A male voice calls out, and, a moment later, Charlie appears from a door off the hallway, a big grin on his face. 'Hello, Bronte,' he says warmly, coming forward to embrace me. 'It's so nice to finally meet you properly.'

'You too,' I reply with an equally big smile as we hug.

He withdraws and ruffles Bridget's hair. She bats him off with a smirk, blushing. Has she gone all shy? She has! She really wants us to like each other, I realise.

Charlie's even better-looking in person. His eyes, which are a sort of golden hazel and are really striking, didn't come across on the small screen when Bridget has made us say hi via FaceTime. He's also taller and broader than I expected with shortish, dark-blond hair, the same sandy shade as Lachie's I think with a pang.

I haven't wanted to talk about Lachie yet, but I know that Bridget will get the whole story out of me later.

'You want a cuppa, Bronte?' Charlie offers, jerking his head towards what I assume is the kitchen.

'Yes, please.'

'April!' Bridget calls out. 'Where is she?'

'In the living room,' Charlie replies over his shoulder.

'She's quiet. What's she doing?'

'Go and see,' Charlie calls back with amusement.

'What are you up to?' Bridget asks in a high-pitched voice as we round the corner. There's a small, blonde-haired girl in a red-and-white-spotted dress lying on her tummy on the wooden floor. She's surrounded by about two dozen brightly coloured crayons and several sheets of paper covered with messy scribbles.

'Oh, wow, these are beautiful!' Bridget exclaims, crouching down beside her adopted daughter.

April grins up at her and then looks at me.

'This is Bronte,' Bridget introduces us.

'I see Bonty on phone,' April replies, pointing at me.

Oh, my goodness, she's adorable. She's not quite three.

'Yes, Mummy talks to Bronte on the phone quite a lot, doesn't she? She's Mummy's very good friend.'

'Hello!' I say to April, sitting down cross-legged and proceeding to act as if her artwork were worthy of Picasso's protégé.

She seems to like that.

❋

That evening, once Charlie has taken April upstairs to bed, Bridget and I retire to the living room with a bottle of rosé.

'How are you feeling?' Bridget asks, and I know it's time to talk about the break-up.

'I'm going to need tissues,' I alert her.

She passes me a box from under the sofa, followed by a pack of baby wipes. 'There are more where those came from,' she says.

I tearfully bring her up to date.

'Can I speak completely freely?' Bridget asks after a while.

'When do you not speak freely?' I reply with an emotional grin. 'I'd expect nothing less. I *want* nothing less.'

She smiles. 'Well, I'm kind of surprised that you and Lachie lasted this long.'

I'm a little taken aback.

'I never really thought he was your forever love,' she says. 'Did you?'

I shake my head. 'I guess not, if I'm also being honest with myself. He was there at the right time and the right place and I loved him to bits. But you're right. If you'd asked me back then if I thought we'd still be together four years later, I don't think I would have said yes. Lachie is still all of the things that worried me about him when we first met. Young and carefree and flirty. And I *did* grow to like that about him, but I've been getting increasingly tired of it. I just wanted him to grow up a bit, take things up a notch. But if anything, he's been hitting the pub more than ever lately, almost as though he's rebelling against getting older.'

'I don't suppose it's helped that Elliot's been free and single and a willing accomplice.'

'No.' I shake my head ruefully.

Elliot gave me a card to give to Bridget, actually. He's in a pretty good place now, I think.

'I wonder if you'd still be breaking up if Elliot and I had stayed together,' Bridget muses.

'Who knows? Possibly not.'

That's a slightly freaky thought. We all know that the people we meet shape us, but who knew that our friends' experiences could alter our entire destinies? Maybe I wouldn't be so broody if Bridget and Elliot were still a couple and resolutely child-free. And, if Lachie had never met young, fun Fliss, would he be so resistant to growing up?

'I could've fought for him,' I say. 'He wasn't sure about breaking up, you know. We did – do – still love each other, but I'm scared I'll waste some of the best years of my life with him and we'll still break up eventually. Then again, maybe he would have come around to the idea of having a baby. It terrifies me that I'm back to square one and might not meet anyone else. Who wants a single woman in her mid-thirties?'

'Erm, Charlie did,' she teases, and I blush, feeling like an idiot. 'You can't think like that,' she carries on. 'If you think like that, you've already lost. You've got to believe it will all work out. Throw yourself in headfirst and live positively and love will find you.'

I brush away another tear. 'I'll try,' I promise.

'Are you going to see Alex while you're here?' she asks discerningly.

I blanch. 'You've got to be kidding, right? As if I need another complication.'

She shrugs. 'I just thought…'

'What?' I'm astonished at the direction this conversation is taking. 'You hate the guy!'

'I don't *hate* him. I just hate what he did to you, how shit he made you feel. But I know there are two sides to every story and he was going through his own struggles.'

I'd told her how he'd apologised when he came to Sydney. I gave her the full lowdown at the time.

'I *know* you've never got over him,' she says. 'You thought *he* was your soulmate, not Lachie. I still remember the way you let him continue to email you after he left Zara, telling you he loved you and that he'd wait for you… I *know* you loved him back, even though you were happy with Lachie and loved him, too. It wouldn't surprise me if you still had the pictures of him looking at you on his wedding day.'

My face heats up.

'Ha!' She points at me. 'Gotcha.'

'No,' I state, trying to be firm about this. 'I'm not going to see Alex again. I'm sure he's moved on by now, anyway.' Despite everything, my heart pinches at the thought. 'I'm just not going there again,' I say adamantly. 'I'm not strong enough.'

She reaches across and presses my hand. 'It's all going to be okay. Failing everything else, there's always sperm donation. I bet Charlie's younger brother would help you out.'

We crack up laughing.

'I'm so happy to see you,' I reply, when we've both calmed down.

'We're going to have the best week!' she exclaims. 'I'll cheer you up.'

'Believe me, you already have.'

Bridget always was the best medicine.

※

Bridget's mates love her too much to force a full-blown hen weekend on her if she really doesn't want one, but there's no way we're allowing her to tie the knot without doing *something* together. So, on the Saturday night before her impending nuptials, we head into Padstow for dinner and a pub crawl. Apparently, one of the pubs is hosting a karaoke night, and Charlie has made me promise to video Bridget doing Eminem's 'Lose Yourself'. We've never done karaoke together before – he claimed with a grin that it'll be one of the funniest things I've ever witnessed.

Some of Bridget's local friends have joined us, including her former across-the-road mummy friend Jocelyn, who seems very likeable. Then there's Bridget's best mate Marty, Maria, who's doing Bridget's make-up and is also an old friend of mine, plus the lovely Laura, whom I'm so happy to meet after hearing so much about over the years. Rachel was doing a wedding in Hertfordshire today, so she couldn't make it, but she's coming here on Monday to catch up.

Poor Laura is a little jet-lagged after arriving from Florida only a couple of days ago. She's been visiting her parents in Cambridgeshire with six-month-old baby Max and came to Cornwall earlier today.

Max is unbelievably cute. He has a full head of dark hair, big brown eyes with ridiculously long lashes and chubby cheeks that expand twofold when he smiles. I keep picking him up for cuddles, and then struggle to put him down again.

Laura said I won't like him nearly as much when he wakes me during the night. In the words of Lucy's husband Nathan, jet lag is a bitch.

Charlie has very kindly offered to babysit, despite his hangover – he had his stag do last night, organised by his younger brother, Adam, who is hilarious and a complete flirt. He's been over a couple of times in the last few days to hang out with us, and, although Bridget has warned him quite vocally – albeit unnecessarily – not to mess with me, his attentions have done my confidence a few favours.

'Here's to Bridget and Charlie!' Marty exclaims, raising a glass to our bride-to-be. 'You guys were meant for each other!'

We all drink to that.

'You know what?' Bridget says later, when we've lucked into finding an outdoor table at a pub that seats us all. 'You say that Charlie and I were meant to be together, but it *terrifies* me how close we came to never crossing paths.' We lean in to listen as she speaks. 'When I look at the series of events that brought me to him, I feel completely freaked out.' She turns to me. 'If I hadn't bumped into Elliot when I did, he never would've given me the idea to write that book. And, although I didn't get a book deal, my writing landed me the job that brought me to Charlie. And if I hadn't met *you*,' she adds, still holding my eye contact, 'then you wouldn't have led me to Australia, which in turn led me to Elliot.'

'Well, if I hadn't met Lachie,' I say, 'then I probably would've come back to England instead of staying with him in Australia.' I even might've caved and gone back to Alex after he told me he'd split up with Zara. My head spins at the thought.

Where would Alex and I be now, if I'd given us that chance? Maybe we'd still feel tainted by how we'd got together. Would his friends and family be over it by now? Would Zara have felt happy enough to move on with someone else, or would she have felt so bitter about Alex getting together with me that it would have poisoned her, and in turn poisoned those who care about her?

Would Alex and I have lasted through all of the stress and the emotional turmoil? What if we had?

Would we have children by now?

Maria puts her arm around my shoulders, startling me back to the present. 'And if *you* hadn't agreed to cover Sally that weekend in Scotland,' she says, referring to Rachel's former unreliable assistant, 'then you never would've met Lachie.'

'Why did Sally cancel again?' Bridget asks.

'She had a new boyfriend,' Maria reminds her.

'So, basically,' I say, grinning at Bridget, '*you* are marrying Charlie, the undisputed love of your life, because Rachel's former assistant hooked up with a new man.'

'The world works in mysterious ways,' Marty says when we've all calmed down from laughing.

'I'll drink to that.' Bridget raises her glass and the rest of us happily follow suit.

❋

When Rachel arrives in Cornwall, she and I go out for a coffee together to catch up on old times, while Bridget stays behind to talk flower arrangements with her mum.

Bridget has been totally relaxed about the wedding on Wednesday, insisting on keeping it simple and doing a lot of the work herself and with Charlie – although I've also been helping out, obviously – but now her mum wants in on the action. Bridget is trying her best to indulge her, but I think she wants to tear her own hair out.

'It's so good to see you again!' Rachel enthuses when we're sitting opposite each other in a cosy café in Padstow with windows overlooking the sailing boats in the tiny harbour. The town is gorgeous, full of quaint buildings painted in shades of green, blue and white, narrow winding streets and a hilly backdrop.

'I'm so glad to be working with you again,' Rachel says.

'Me too,' I reply. 'Although I'm a bit nervous.'

'There's absolutely no need to be. You always were a natural,' she says, trying to reassure me. She furrows her brow.

'Why did you stop, if you don't mind me asking? Was it because of that last wedding? I was worried it had traumatised you for life.'

Rachel didn't know beforehand that Alex and I had a connection – she never would have asked me to step into Sally's shoes if she had.

'No.' I shake my head. 'Sure, I was traumatised, but I think I stopped pursuing wedding photography because it felt so intrinsically linked to England and my time here. I don't think I could bear to face up to how much I missed it. It felt safer to go back to what I knew, and, when I was offered the job at *Hebe* Australia, it seemed too good to be true. I guess life ran away with me after that.'

I glance out of the window at the estuary, titchy in comparison with Sydney's vast, beautiful, blue harbour, but, for some reason, I feel a pang at the idea of going home.

For a moment, I allow myself to imagine what it would be like if I stayed, if I didn't go back to face my horrible new boss and long working hours. What if I didn't have to deal with packing up the flat or finding somewhere new? What if I didn't have to see Lachie again and feel the intense pain of our break-up? What if I could just bury my head in the sand and run away from it all?

But no. I'm not doing that again. I need to follow through cleanly and properly so I might actually stand a chance of closure this time around. I want to move on with my life without a dark cloud hanging over me, and then, hopefully, I *will* meet someone new and wonderful and we'll do all of the things that I dream about doing.

This doesn't mean that I won't come back to England one day. There's nothing stopping me.

Apart from a visa, obviously.

But it's something I could look into, once I've picked up the broken pieces of my life and attempted to put them back together.

For the first time since Lachie and I broke up, the world feels full of possibilities.

✳

A day later, Charlie and Bridget tie the knot. I'm not the only emotional wreck at the wedding – I don't think there's a dry eye in the house. The shot I capture of Charlie at the altar, looking down the aisle to see Bridget coming towards him, is one I know they will treasure forever. His golden eyes are glistening with tears, and his face is lit with love and hope. I have no idea how I manage to keep my camera steady.

Bridget herself looks more beautiful than I've ever seen her. She's wearing a cream-coloured, crystal-studded, floor-skimming gown that hugs her stunning figure perfectly. She wanted her hair to be loose and natural, but, after a couple of trial runs, she asked me to braid the front section of her hair so it goes up and over her head, leaving the rest in long, lovely waves. On her feet are dusty-pink flats, which she needs to wear in order to be able to walk down the narrow, bumpy track to the beach where the picnic reception is being held.

The other sixty or so guests help carry chilled bottles of booze, Tupperware containers full of picnic food, armfuls of pink peonies, white and grey picnic rugs, cushions and camping chairs for those who need them. The children each hold bunches of pink and white helium balloons. It is such a glorious sight, the whole congregation walking down the track beside a babbling brook with dappled sunlight filtering down from the trees overhead. The photos are going to look amazing.

We come across the occasional set of playground equipment that keeps the children entertained on the long journey. I snap some shots of Bridget helping April to navigate her way across some wooden stepping stones, but rush to her aid when April slips and falls, bursting into tears.

Bridget scoops her up, and several people watching gasp at the sight of April's muddy feet streaking brown dirt across Bridget's dress.

Her mum loses it. 'Oh my God, darling, give her to me!'

'It's fine, Mum, it's only a bit of mud,' Bridget replies, completely unfazed.

'But it's your wedding dress!' her mum squeals.

'Yeah, and April's my daughter,' Bridget replies pointedly, carrying the little girl until she wriggles to get free again.

I lift up my camera and am just in time to snap off a shot of Charlie glancing sideways at his new wife as he takes her hand in his.

I think he loves her more, right then, in that moment, than he ever has.

✳

The day after I wave goodbye to Bridget, Charlie and April, who are off to France in their campervan, Hermie – formerly belonging to Bridget's dad, but passed down to them as a wedding gift – I travel to London to meet up with Simon, my former boss. I emailed him earlier in the week, hoping to say hello in person, and he asked me to come to his office for a cuppa.

I'm nervous as I walk into the big, marble-lined lobby, on full alert in case I see Alex. I know it's unlikely at this time in the morning – it's eleven o'clock, an unusual hour to be coming in or out.

Simon now heads up a men's lifestyle magazine in my old building and I'm taken aback to spy a couple of familiar faces as I walk in: Pete, who used to work on the news desk at *Hebe*, and Tim, who worked under Alex in the art department. They were both friendly with him years ago, and my pulse races as we all exchange hellos. Will they tell him I'm here?

'Bronte!' Simon exclaims from the other side of the office. I excuse myself and make my way over to my former boss.

Simon has worked with Bridget on and off over the years and wants to know all about her wedding while his assistant makes us tea. By the time we've moved on to him showing me pictures of his newborn baby, I'm feeling much more relaxed in his company.

When I'm ready, I take a deep breath and say what I came to say.

'I really am so sorry for letting you down when I left.'

He pulls a face. 'That's way back in the past. I hope you're not still stressing about it.'

'I do still feel bad,' I confide.

'Well, don't. It was a privilege to work with you while I did. In the end, you did what you had to do. And when you told me what had been going on...' He shakes his head in dismay. 'I'm not surprised you wanted to jack it all in and go home.' He pauses. 'Are you catching up with Alex while you're here?'

I'm surprised at his directness. 'I have no plans to. I saw him in Sydney when he was there last year.'

He nods. 'He mentioned it.'

'Do you see much of him?' I ask in turn.

'We have lunch about once a month. We met up a couple of days ago, funnily enough. He's been very preoccupied with his new business.'

My brow creases in confusion. 'His new business?'

'He set up his own design agency.' He opens a drawer in his desk. 'I've got a card in here somewhere.'

I feel a little funny inside as I watch him root around in his drawer, eventually pulling out a business card. 'Here it is.' He pushes it over.

It's a square-shaped design with a green, grey and yellow colour scheme. I turn it over and read Alex's name and contact details on the back.

'He's based in Camden now?' I glance up at Simon.

'Yep.'

So there never was any chance of me bumping into him today.

※

Rachel has invited me over to hers tonight to go through Bridget and Charlie's wedding pics – she lives in Golders Green in north London, so it's an easy trip up the Northern line – but I have hours to kill before then, so I decide to go for a wander around Covent Garden.

It's lunchtime and it's busy, the usual charity workers out in force as they call out to anyone who might have a minute. I look into the windows of shops without really seeing the contents, and, before I know it, I'm heading towards the market and the church where Alex married Zara.

There are buskers performing outside – two jugglers on

unicycles – but I ignore their antics and pass by into the churchyard, coming to an abrupt stop outside the alleyway where best man Ed tried to urge Alex down the aisle.

I drag my eyes away and walk up the steps to the front door.

St Paul's in Covent Garden is a beautiful church – it's known as the Actors' Church, its connection to the theatre illustrated by memorials to famous actors and actresses along the walls. My eyes drift up the aisle as I remember the sea of red winter berries and dark-red roses flanked by green pine hanging from the ends of pews. Up at the altar, I can still picture the dozens of pillar candles in tall clear vases, burning and flickering.

It should have been a beautiful wedding.

I sink down onto one of the pews and think back to the way his dark-blue eyes seemed to sear into my soul as I waited to photograph his reaction to seeing Zara in her wedding dress.

It hurt so much.

I loved him. A part of me still does, even now.

I feel wrong for even thinking that, considering how raw I am about Lachie, but I *haven't* managed to close the door on the past.

Bridget is right. I *did* think Alex was my soulmate. But it clearly wasn't meant to be. Every time fate has launched him into my life, the timing has been terribly wrong.

I met him at Polly's hen night, when I was only in the UK for a fortnight from Australia.

I saw him on the escalators going up when I was heading down, and, even though he didn't wait for me, our lives collided again that same morning when we discovered we were working together. He was already engaged to Zara.

And then everything with Zara came crashing down and

Alex finally declared his love for me but, by then, Lachie was embedded in my life.

Now I'm single. Is he?

The timing is still wrong. I know this. I've just broken up with Lachie and I'm nowhere near over him.

But still…

I never did get that closure. My meeting with Alex in Sydney was too brief, too unfulfilling. Am I really going to walk away from another opportunity to lay the past to rest?

I pull out the card that's been burning a hole in my bag and scan the address. I could call him, of course, but where's the fun in that?

With my heels clicking over the cobblestones, I head towards the tube station.

Time to kick fate in the balls and take matters into my own hands.

❄

Alex's new office block is in a quiet side street off Camden's hectic market centre. My heart is pounding in my chest as I walk up the stairs and pull on the glass door.

It doesn't budge.

My eyes drift to the intercom. Damn! So much for turning up unannounced. I take a deep breath and press the buzzer.

'Hello?' a male voice answers.

'Is Alex there?' I ask.

'He's just popped out. Is he expecting you?'

'Er, no.'

'Can I ask your name?'

I hesitate, my finger on the button.

'*Bronte?*'

My heart leaps into my throat as I spin around, coming face to face with Alex.

His eyes are wide, even more blue than usual, it seems.

'What are you doing here?' He looks shocked. He's holding two takeaway coffee mugs nestled into a single cardboard tray.

'I've just been to see Simon. He gave me your card.'

'So you thought you'd drop by and give me a heart attack?'

'Figured it was payback time,' I say with a smile that belies how on edge I'm feeling.

'I gave you three weeks' notice,' he says weakly, his lips tilting up with the faintest traces of amusement as he joins me on the top step and presses the intercom with his free left hand.

The crackly voice comes over the speakerphone again. 'Hello? Sorry, what was your name?'

'It's alright, Neal, I've got her,' Alex speaks into the receiver. 'Can you buzz us in?' He drops his hand and pulls the door open when it clicks. 'My partner,' he explains, holding the door back for me. 'You coming in?'

'If I'm allowed.' I raise an eyebrow as I pass.

'Yeah, I just wish you'd called: I would've got another coffee.'

'I prefer tea, anyway.'

He flashes me a proper smile and presses the button for the lift. 'We're on the top floor.'

'When did you decide to start your own business?' I ask as the doors close behind us. I decide to try breathing through my mouth.

'I've always wanted to,' he says. 'But it's hard to turn away a decent salary.'

'How's it going?'

'Really well.' He nods. 'Better than I could've hoped, to be honest.'

His black hair is shorter on top now, but a bit longer all over, curling at the nape of his neck. It's a little scruffy, but it suits him.

'What made you decide to leave Tetlan?' I ask.

'Nothing bad. I just felt like something needed to change. I'd been a bit stuck in a rut.'

'I know what you mean,' I say wryly.

'You're not happy?'

'My new boss is a bit of a nightmare.'

'I've heard that about her,' he comments.

'If her reputation precedes her, why do management promote people who can't cut it?' This annoys me immensely.

'Who knows? Politics of a big company. Can't say I miss it, even if I did like it while I was there.'

His new office is small but stylish, with big windows and far-reaching views across Camden to central London beyond. A slightly dishevelled-looking Neal jumps up to say hi, giving my hand a firm shake and taking his coffee from Alex with the enthusiasm of a caffeine addict. I find out that their business consists of just the two of them right now, but they're hoping to employ more staff. They've got more work than they can manage, but they know all too well that things could slow down again.

'How long have you got?' Alex asks me when Neal takes a call on his mobile.

'I've got to be at Rachel's at seven,' I say.

'In Golders Green?'

'Yeah.'

I shouldn't be surprised he remembers where Rachel lives – he always was good at stuff like that.

'That's hours away. Do you want to get a drink?' he asks.

I nod at the coffee he still hasn't touched. 'You've got one.'

'No, I mean a proper drink.'

'You can just leave?'

'It's Friday,' he says with a grin. 'And I'm the boss. One of them, anyway.' He pats Neal on his back. 'See you Monday,' he whispers, grabbing the denim shirt hanging on the back of his chair.

Neal nods and gives him the thumbs-up, his eyes growing round and his mouth stretching into a goofy grin when Alex places his untouched coffee in front of him. Neal waves a manic little bye at me as we leave. I like him immensely.

'Is there anything else you need to do in Camden while you're here?' Alex asks on the way back down in the lift.

'No. What are you thinking?' I cast him a look.

'Shall we go to Hampstead?'

'Hampstead?' Random.

'Yeah, it's not far from Rachel's. Less hectic than Camden. I brought my car in today and I live that way, so I could drop you to Rachel's front door.'

Not random at all, as it turns out.

'Are you sure? You really are finishing up for the day?'

'I can work from home over the weekend.'

Something that feels a lot like pride bubbles up inside me. He's so clever and talented.

Don't get carried away, Bronte… I need to keep my feelings in check.

Alex's car smells overwhelmingly like Alex. It's almost too much, being so enveloped by him.

'Where do you live?' I ask.

'West Hampstead,' he replies. 'I've been there for about three years now.'

'Are your parents still in Crouch End?'

He glances at me. 'Yeah, and Jo and Brian are in East Finchley, so we're all pretty close by.'

I remember that Jo is his sister, of course, but I've never met her. I have met Brian, however. It was at his stag do that I first came across Alex.

'They have a couple of kids now,' he reveals, making casual conversation.

'Do they? Boys? Girls?'

'One of each. It's my niece's first birthday tomorrow, actually.'

'Are you going?'

'Yeah. My whole family will be there.'

I steal a glance at his tanned, toned forearms, his hands resting on the steering wheel. His denim shirt is, typically, rolled up past his elbows.

I always did think he had sexy forearms.

Steady on, I warn myself.

But there's no ignoring my jitters.

He scratches his head and glances at me. 'How's Lachie?'

I turn to stare out of my side window. 'We broke up.'

The car jolts and I shoot my head around to look at the road, but can't see why he had to brake. Was it accidental?

'When?' he asks, stunned.

'Just before I came away.'

The silence stretches out before us, but his mind is ticking over.

'I'm sorry,' he says eventually. 'Are you okay?'

'Getting there.' I look out of my window again and clear my throat. 'How about you?' I ask. 'Any of those blind dates come to fruition?'

'No,' he replies, and, as I turn to glance at him, he catches my eye.

The jitters in my stomach intensify.

He takes me to the Holly Bush in Hampstead, a cosy pub tucked away up the hill and slightly off the beaten track. Luckily, a booth comes free, right by the window, as we walk into the room off the entrance.

'What are you having?' he asks as I slide onto the bench seat.

'Cider, maybe?'

He nods and heads off to the bar in the next room along. I look around, taking in the dark-wooden interior. There's a fireplace against the opposite wall, but it's not lit. It is July, after all. There aren't many people in here, but then again, I realise, as I check my phone, it's only four o'clock in the afternoon.

Alex returns after a minute with two pints. 'Shandy,' he tells me, nodding at his own drink to let me know he's not planning on getting blathered and driving.

We chink glasses and smile across the table at each other.

'I can't believe you're here,' he says.

'Do you mind? After your initial freak-out?' I add with a smirk.

'I didn't freak out,' he scoffs. 'But it was a bit bloody strange to come back to work and find you standing there on our doorstep. I thought I was seeing things. What if I'd been out at a meeting?'

I shrug. 'I don't know. I probably would've emailed you at some point to say hi. I'm flying back to Australia on Sunday, so I doubt we would've had another chance to catch up.'

He swallows and looks down, but not before I've seen pain flicker across his features. 'So soon,' he says quietly. 'So you've already been to Bridget's wedding?' He rests his chin on his palm and stares at me.

'Yeah, a few days ago. I've been down in Cornwall for a couple of weeks already.'

'How was it?'

'Amazing,' I reply with a smile.

'Did you enjoy doing the pics?'

'I loved it,' I enthuse, lighting up from within.

His smile is warm and genuine. 'You always did seem to feel at home behind a camera. What are your plans for the next couple of days?'

'I don't have any. I'm staying with Polly tonight and at a hotel near Heathrow tomorrow. I fly out first thing Sunday. Polly has to work tomorrow, annoyingly, so I'll probably go shopping or something.'

Polly is in hospitality, so her work doesn't stop at the weekends.

'Does she still live in Borough Market?'

I reel backwards and slap my hands on the table. 'No, but sorry, *how* do you do that? You remember *everything*!'

He laughs and shrugs. 'Only some things. Anyway, you can talk. You've also got an uncanny knack of remembering. How did you recall where my parents live?'

'I don't know. I forget to tie my own shoelaces most days.'

We smile at each other, neither of us looking away as the seconds tick by.

'Why didn't you come to say goodbye?' I blurt, the words spilling out of my mouth of their own volition.

He sounds bleak when he replies. 'I couldn't face another one.'

'It wasn't long enough, was it?' That time we spent in Sydney.

'It's never long enough,' he mutters. He sounds frustrated as he continues. 'I can't believe you're going back in two days. Why didn't you tell me when you were coming?'

I sigh. 'To be honest, I wasn't sure I could face seeing you.'
He flinches.

'It's just… Things have felt pretty raw recently,' I say.

He nods and reaches for his pint. 'I understand.'

'Tell me about your business,' I say as he drinks, abruptly changing the subject. 'How do you know Neal?'

After a bit, we order a couple of bar snacks, and later we get a couple more. I think I could stay there all night in that cosy pub, chatting and drinking, but I know I need to get to Rachel's.

'Jesus, it's already six thirty!' I exclaim, when I finally pull out my phone to check the time.

We share a mutual look of dismay.

'It's going to be a long way back to Polly's couch,' I say with a sigh.

'Where does she live now?'

'Croydon, south London.'

'That's miles away!' He looks alarmed. 'Why aren't you staying at Rachel's?'

'I didn't want to ask. Her boyfriend has just moved in and…' I shrug. 'It's not a big deal. Tube and train. I'll be fine.'

The atmosphere in the car feels heavier on the drive to Rachel's. I don't want to part company yet. It still feels too soon. There's so much we haven't said, so much ground we haven't covered. I don't even know what else I *want* to say, but I have this overwhelming urge just to *be* with him.

He pulls up outside Rachel's and cuts the ignition, tilting his chin in my direction without looking at me.

I don't make any move to get out of the car.

He groans suddenly and drags his hands across his face, then looks at me properly.

'I have a spare room,' he says.

I jolt with surprise.

'I don't live far from here. I could come back for you.' He pauses for my answer.

'Are you sure?' I ask in a small voice.

His face lights up with his smile. 'Yes, I'm sure,' he breathes with relief, tension visibly leaving his body. 'What time should I come back?'

'In an hour or two? Can I text you?'

We exchange numbers, but he doesn't drive away until Rachel has answered her door.

'Who was that?' she asks, her normally barely tameable blonde curls pulled back into a loose ponytail.

'Alex,' I reply.

She meets my eyes, agog.

'It's nothing. I'm just catching up with him while I'm here. He's coming back for me later. We're just friends. I might crash at his. He has a spare room.'

'You don't have to explain yourself to me,' she says laughingly as I dither about on her doorstep. 'Come in. Can I get you a glass of wine?'

'Better not. I think I need to keep my head tonight.'

She looks amused.

The photographs of Bridget and Charlie's wedding are out of this world. Their picnic reception took place on a pebble-and-shingle beach called Lansallos. The cove is horseshoe shaped, flanked by stunning greeny-grey rocky cliffs, and the aquamarine water makes the most stunning backdrop to the photos.

'You've still got it,' Rachel says with admiration, staring at the picture of Charlie with shining eyes as he waits for Bridget at the altar. She clicks on her mouse and moves her corresponding shot of Bridget so they're side by side. My friend's eyes sparkle with love and emotion.

'These are so beautiful,' I murmur.

'I don't need to ask you if you enjoyed yourself, because it's obvious that you did,' Rachel says.

'I loved it.' I'm awestruck looking at the work we produced.

'Honestly, I wish you lived here,' Rachel says wistfully. 'I could put so much work your way. The number of weddings I'm having to turn down because I'm too busy is unbelievable.'

'I'm so happy it's all going so well for you,' I say sincerely.

'Thank you,' she replies with a smile. 'Now, there's *one* wedding in December that I would *love* to have your help with.' The look on her face has me intrigued.

'What's that?' I ask.

'I'm sworn to secrecy.' She grins and my curiosity is properly piqued. 'But I need two assistants.'

'A celebrity wedding?' I ask with excitement.

She doesn't deny it. 'I'd give anything to tell you whose.'

'Go on!' I urge. 'I won't spill!'

'You used to work at *Hebe*,' she says with a laugh.

'I'm out of that world now,' I reply. 'Celebrity shelebrity.' I wave my hand dismissively.

'You. Would. Die.'

I crack up laughing. 'You're terrible!' I gasp. 'I can't believe you're stirring me up like this!'

'I'm still so shocked I've got the job.'

'So who have you got assisting?' I ask with a grin.

'Just Misha so far.' That's her regular assistant. 'I haven't lined anyone else up yet.'

We stare at each other.

'It's really well paid,' she adds beguilingly. 'It would easily cover your airfare back here…'

'Are you serious?' My insides begin to fizz with excitement, but then reality bites and the disappointment is crushing. 'I've already used up all of my holidays for this year.' I sound thoroughly fed up.

'I thought you hated your new job...' She raises an eyebrow, sassily, and I laugh. Who knew Rachel could be so persuasive? Surely she's not really suggesting I jack in my job and come back to the UK?

'You wouldn't regret it,' she says, still dangling her carrot in front of my nose. Dangle, dangle, dangle. 'The cred you'd get from this one job would set you up for life as a wedding photographer.'

Suddenly I'm no longer laughing. She *is* serious. Could this be my future? Could I be a wedding photographer? My own boss? Full time?

'I'll give you a couple of months before I ask anyone else,' she says knowingly as the cogs in my head turn. 'Think about it.'

Oh, I will.

❄

'Rachel has asked me to do a job with her this Christmas,' I find myself telling Alex as soon as I'm in his car.

'Really?' he replies with interest. 'Back over here or in Oz?'

'Here. All expenses paid. I'm seriously considering it. It's a celebrity wedding,' I whisper. 'But I don't know whose.'

He chuckles. 'Why are you whispering, then?'

I giggle, too. 'I don't know.' I glance out of the window and then back at him. 'Am I really going to stay at yours?' I've sobered up since leaving the pub and this fact is only just now sinking in. 'I don't have any of my things with me.'

'I'm sure I can find you a spare toothbrush and lend you a T-shirt.'

'Yeah, and I can set off back to Polly's early.'

'There's no rush, is there? I thought she was working.'

'True. Why, are you planning on cooking me a nice fry-up?'

'I'll cook you a fry-up if you like,' he replies with a smile.

I feel a tiny bubble of joy burst inside my stomach, but it's deftly followed by a hefty kick.

How would Lachie feel if he could see me now, in Alex's car, laughing away, without a care in the world?

He'd be shocked. Gutted. Disappointed.

The guilt is immense.

And then I wonder if Lachie also feels guilty spending time with Fliss. Is he seeing more of her since we broke up?

Probably.

I try to put him out of my mind.

I get out my phone and type a quick message to Polly, telling her that I'm staying 'up here'. I don't reveal who I'm with. She'll only flip out if I tell her I'm with Alex, not Rachel, but she's not my mother.

Even if she sometimes acts like it, bless her.

Alex lives only a couple of miles away from Rachel's and it takes us around ten minutes to get there. It's dark – almost 10 p.m. – so I can't really tell what his area is like, but, from the wide street and the trees growing outside on the pavement, I'm guessing it's pretty nice.

He lives in a maisonette in a Victorian terrace with its own entrance on the lower-ground level. I follow him down the steps to the front door.

Inside, his place is bright and modern, with some cool designer furniture and light fittings. The kitchen is to the front of the house; the living room to the back, overlooking a private garden.

Alex flicks on the outdoor lights when I ask to see what it's like out there and a mini-oasis is revealed, the surrounding walls almost completely obscured by ferns and bamboo and other greenery.

'Wow!' I say, looking at the round white table on the patio, surrounded by four differently coloured chairs. If it's sunny in the morning, that's where we're having breakfast. I'll insist on it.

The surreal feeling comes over me again, followed by another stab of guilt. What am I doing? Is this really just about closure?

Maybe there's hope for us as friends… We used to get on so well…

'Can I see upstairs?' I keep my tone light as I add, 'I want the full tour, Whittaker.'

He smiles and nods, leading the way. 'Spare room.' He opens the first door off the corridor. It's at the front, above the kitchen. 'Bathroom,' he says of the second room. I glance inside. Sparkling clean and white, with bright blue towels. 'And my room,' he says, opening the last door off the corridor.

I walk past him, into his room. It's very stylish and quite masculine with a black, grey and green colour scheme and a graphic bedspread. But I can't really take in my surroundings because I'm too distracted by the smell.

'Fucking hell!' I snap, looking around and spying another door that I'm guessing leads to his en suite. 'Where is it?' I storm across the room and open the door.

'What's wrong?'

'Your aftershave, Alex. I can't stand it any longer.'

I switch on his bathroom light and open the mirrored wall cabinet, scanning the contents.

'Christ!' he says, slightly affronted as he comes into the room. 'I didn't realise it was that offensive.'

'It's not offensive,' I retort. 'It drives me absolutely crazy. I can't bear it. What is it? What do you use?'

He looks bemused as he reaches past me and pulls out a small rectangular glass bottle with clear, caramel-coloured liquid inside, and hands it over. I put it to my nose and inhale, closing my eyes briefly before looking up at him, straight into his amused blue eyes.

The room suddenly feels very small.

And it *is* small. We're in his flipping en suite. I jerk my head towards the door. 'Let's go back downstairs.'

He leads the way out, but I quickly spritz his aftershave onto my wrist before following him. He throws a look at me over his shoulder, his pursed lips telling me that he knows full well what I just did. I shrug cheekily and he laughs.

'Well, you have a very nice place,' I say decisively when we're back downstairs. 'I like it. It's very grown up,' I add.

'That's a good thing?' he checks with a frown.

'Yes.'

He goes into the kitchen. I pull up a stool at his bar table. The whole of the downstairs is open plan with a countertop bar area separating the kitchen from the living room.

'Drink?' he offers.

'Sure. What are you having?'

'I fancy a beer.'

'What else have you got?'

He peers in the fridge. 'Beer,' he states, glancing over at me apologetically. 'Sorry, I wasn't expecting company.'

'I'll have one, then,' I tell him with a grin.

I have a flashback to Lachie cracking open a couple of bottles and chinking them as he hands them over. The image makes me wince and suddenly my nose is prickling. I quickly hop down from the stool.

'Is this a loo?' I call of the door under the stairs, hoping he can't hear the tremor in my voice.

'Yep,' he replies.

I go into the cloakroom and lock the door behind me, catching a glimpse of my reflection through blurry vision.

There's a lump in my throat the size of a golf ball and suddenly I miss Lachie so much, I want to sob my heart out.

I try very, very hard not to, but it's a while before my throat returns to normal and the pricking at the back of my eyes recedes.

I return to the living room.

'Are you okay?' Alex asks with concern.

I nod quickly and smile brightly. 'Fine!'

'You're not,' he states.

'Don't,' I cut him off. 'Please.'

He goes over to the sofa, running his hand through his hair and scruffing it up as he sits down.

'How did you break up?' he asks.

I swallow, the lump back in force as I join him at the other end of the sofa. I shake my head quickly.

'Was it you or him? Or mutual?'

'More him than me,' I reply unsteadily. 'I wanted kids. He didn't.'

'Ah.'

'I guess our age difference finally caught up with us.' I drag my fingers under my eyes to catch a couple of stray teardrops.

'I'm sorry,' he says softly.

'Yeah. It only happened a few days before I came away.'

'Do you think he just needs space?'

'No.' I shake my head. 'No, he's adamant. We want different things.'

He nods, scratching off the label on his beer bottle with his thumbnail as he stares at it in a daze.

'Sorry,' I say. 'Yours is not a shoulder I ever had any intention of crying on.'

He gives me a rueful look.

'Do you think you and I could ever be friends again?' I suddenly feel compelled to ask.

'Of course,' he replies.

I choose to ignore the fact that there was a moment's hesitation before he spoke.

❇

I wake up to the smell of bacon and freshly ground coffee. For a moment, I stare up at the ceiling, scarcely able to believe that I'm in Alex's home. I climb out of bed and sweep up yesterday's clothes, then walk through to the bathroom, glad of the oversized T-shirt covering me down to my thighs.

I don't look too horrendous, I note as I check my reflection. I had nothing to take my make-up off with last night, so I went to bed with it on and it's still pretty much intact this morning.

I say a silent thank-you to the clever people at Clinique who created their high-impact waterproof mascara and reach for the toothbrush Alex gave me from an unused airline travel kit. Then I drag the same kit's comb through my hair, take a quick shower and get dressed in yesterday's clothes.

'Hey,' Alex says warmly when I appear at the bottom of the stairs.

'Hi.' I smile back at him, my heart doing a funny little flip.

He's wearing faded black jeans with a tear at the knees and a light-grey T-shirt.

'Sleep well?' he asks.

'Surprisingly. Your spare bed is ridiculously comfortable. How about you?'

He screws up his nose. He looks tired, so I'm guessing that's a no, but I don't ask why.

'Tea? Coffee?' he offers.

'The coffee smells good,' I reply by way of an answer.

He grabs a mug out of a high cupboard, the bottom of his T-shirt riding up to reveal a brief glimpse of dark hair trailing from his belly button downwards.

I quickly avert my gaze, my heart quickening as I'm hit with a sudden flashback to the night we slept together. It was over six years ago, but it was pretty unforgettable.

'Can I open your outside doors?' I ask, feeling hot as I wander across the living room. His garden really is stunning. Compact, but gorgeous.

'Sure.' He comes over and unlocks the doors for me before pushing them open, letting a whoosh of cool air spill into the room. He goes back to the kitchen.

'Full fry-up, right?' he calls.

'Are you serious?'

'Deadly.'

'I'll get out of your way after that,' I vow. 'I'm sure you've got a ton of work to do.'

He doesn't respond.

Later, I help carry the breakfast things into the kitchen, looking around for a dishwasher.

'I'll take them,' he says, our fingers brushing as I hand

them over. I jolt, as though I've been given an electric shock, and his eyes shoot up to meet mine. Shaken, I walk out of the kitchen.

'Well, it was good to see you.' I'm attempting breezy, but my voice is wavering.

He clatters the plates onto the countertop and follows me.

'Bronte,' he says quietly, swiping my hand.

It happens again. The shockwaves quiver all the way up my arm. I pull my hand away.

He stares at me, helplessly.

'Why do you have to go?' he asks. 'Spend the day with me.'

I shake my head. 'I can't.'

'Why not? Polly's at work. Why are you rushing back?'

'I haven't got any clothes.'

'I'll take you shopping.'

'Really?' I ask with a laugh, feeling all of a sudden weirdly tearful.

'Really. We can go into Hampstead, go for a walk or something, have lunch.'

'Haven't you got to go to your niece's birthday party?'

His face falls and he stares down at the floor, lost. 'I forgot about that.' He glances up. 'Come with me?'

My mouth drops open. 'You've got to be kidding, right? Come hang out with your entire family for the day?'

'Why not? Anyway, it's not the whole day: it's a couple of hours.'

'Don't they hate me?'

He looks aghast. 'Of course they don't!'

'You never told them what happened between us?'

He recoils. 'Yeah, I did, but nobody *blames* you.'

'Your mum doesn't think I'm a complete hussy?' I can't help feeling a small spark of hope.

He rolls his eyes. 'My mum would give *anything* to meet you.'

'She has,' I say drily. 'On your wedding day. I was, "Bronte, there to do the photos".'

He looks pained. 'Yeah,' he says, looking away. 'I'm sorry about that.'

I sigh. 'You don't need to keep apologising.' My voice sounds leaden.

He stuffs his hands into his trouser pockets and hunches his shoulders.

'You really want me to come?' I find myself asking.

He glances up at me. 'Yes.'

'Okay,' I say.

What the hell am I doing?

❄

I end up buying new make-up as well as clothes, then insist we go back to Alex's so I can get ready properly. My nerves intensify dramatically on the short drive to East Finchley, where Jo and Brian live. I can't believe I've agreed to this. I stare out of the window with longing as we pass an Underground station.

'Don't even think about it,' Alex warns. 'They're expecting you.'

'Eek!' I reply with a gulp.

He smirks and reaches across to take my hand.

I'm so nervous the electric shock this time barely registers.

Alex ushers me up the garden path. 'I promise you they're lovely.' He presses the doorbell while I fight the urge to bolt.

A squeal comes from somewhere deep in the house. 'Jo,'

Alex murmurs. Then the door whooshes open to reveal her husband.

'Bronte!' Brian exclaims, greeting me like an old friend as he sweeps me up in a hug. A second later he's replaced by Alex's sister.

'I'm so happy to meet you at last!' she gushes, beaming from ear to ear. She's a bit taller than me with shoulder-length dark hair swept up into a tousled bun.

Alex's dad is a tad reserved, tall and slim like his son with a chiselled jawbone and a perfectly straight nose, but he offers me what feels like a genuine smile as he shakes my hand and retreats.

Alex's mum, Clarissa, however, with her startling, all-too-familiar blue eyes, greets me very amiably.

'It is *so* lovely to meet you,' she says, clasping my hand in both of hers. 'Alex has told me a lot about you.'

It takes all of five minutes for my nerves to dissipate. Alex wasn't lying. I'm amongst friends, not enemies.

The day is a revelation. Some of Brian and Jo's friends from their NCT group turn up with their little ones, and Alex and Jo's aunt and uncle also join in the celebrations. Clarissa takes me under her wing when Alex is called away to repair a broken toy, and I feel oddly at ease in her company.

The warm feeling that has been expanding inside me is threatening to burst by the time we leave that afternoon. I feel better and more at peace than I have in years. I turn to look at Alex in the driver's seat.

'Thank you,' he says, glancing at me.

'No, thank *you*.'

He gives me a quizzical look.

'I feel like a weight I didn't even realise I'd been carrying has lifted from my shoulders.'

Have I done it? Have I finally laid the past to rest?

We drive past East Finchley tube station and it occurs to me that I should be getting out.

'You want to come back to mine for a bit?' Alex asks.

'I should head to Polly's,' I tell him hesitantly. 'I need to get my bags and say goodbye.'

'I'll drive you.'

'Alex, you don't have to do that.'

'I want to. Honest. I'll take you to your hotel.'

'No! It's too far, I'll jump on a train.'

'Let me,' he says. 'Please.'

'Are you sure?'

He glances at me. 'I'm sure.'

I feel strangely reluctant to leave him, too.

It takes over an hour to get to Polly's, but we talk the whole way, and the atmosphere in the car is light and lively. I feel drunk with happiness after the day we've had.

'I really like your mum,' I say.

'She liked you, too. I knew she would. She gave me so much grief about letting you slip through my fingers.'

I stare at him, bewildered. 'Really?'

'Yes, really,' he says with a laugh. 'I just wish you could've met Ed this trip. Properly, I mean, under better circumstances. He feels bad about the way he spoke to you.'

I pull a face. 'It was understandable.'

'Maybe when you're back at Christmas,' he says.

'I don't know if I'm coming back yet.'

'You are.' He's jokily confident.

Polly is in the middle of bedtime madness, so she's happy to keep our farewell brief, assuming that I have a taxi waiting outside on the street for me. I shake my head at Alex as he makes to get out of the car to help me with my suitcase.

'You didn't tell her I gave you a lift?' he asks when I'm back beside him, cheerfully waving out of the window.

'No. Sorry. She would've given me shit about it.'

'Oh.'

I belatedly realise how this must make him feel. His friends and family are willing to have a fresh start, but mine aren't?

'It's only because I'm not going to get a chance to bring her up to date before I leave,' I tell him. 'You understand, don't you?'

'Yeah,' he says.

But I'm not entirely sure he does, and the journey to my hotel is more subdued.

Finally, he's pulling into a space in the hotel car park. He switches off the ignition and we sit there in the darkness, in silence, as the seconds tick by.

I'm the first to speak. 'Thank you. Today has been really nice. I didn't know how much I needed it.'

He nods, and then abruptly presses the heels of his palms to his eyes.

'Was this just about closure?' he asks after a while, meeting my gaze directly, his eyes glinting in the low light. I slowly shake my head and watch as a strange series of emotions wash across his features.

'Bronte,' he murmurs, reaching for my hand.

I let him take it, allowing his long, cool fingers to slip between mine while my insides go berserk.

But, once more, thoughts of Lachie assault my mind, my golden sunshine boy, my warmth, my heart for over four years. I can't let him go yet.

I extract my hand. 'I'll email you from Sydney,' I say, reaching for the handle.

'Fuck this!' he mutters. His expression is anguished when

he turns to face me. 'I'm damned if I'm going to let you walk out of my life again.'

My mouth falls open.

'I love you,' he says. '*Still*. I know you're not ready to start anything new. I know it's too soon. I know you're not over Lachie. But I can't let you leave without you knowing how I feel, even if it makes me look like a complete dick. Again.'

My expression softens.

'I love you,' he repeats, his eyes shining. 'I always have. I always will. I still think we're meant to be together. Our timing has seriously sucked in the past, and I know it's still not perfect, but I *will* wait until you're ready. Okay?'

I nod, my throat swelling up.

'I love you,' he murmurs, taking my hand and pressing a kiss to the tips of my fingers.

I blink back tears. But whether it's because of Lachie or because of my guilt or just down to goddamn timing, I don't tell him I love him back.

❄

My return to Sydney is hideous. Walking into a flat devoid of Lachie's things is unspeakably awful. It's the middle of winter in Australia and the cold, damp days don't help. I'm completely out of sorts when I return to work, but my horrible boss doesn't give a toss about my jet lag or my post-break-up trauma. She just wants me to deal with the work that's been piling up for me after she failed to hire full-time cover on the picture desk. And she wants it done yesterday.

Lachie comes over at the weekend to pick up a couple of stray items of clothes that I found in with my stuff.

It's acutely painful to stand in front of him and not be able to touch him.

'How was your trip?' he asks, his arms folded across his chest and his bulging biceps filling out the sleeves of his lightweight jacket.

'I caught up with Alex,' I find myself telling him, straight off.

He nods, not seeming surprised. 'I thought that you would.'

'You're not angry? Or upset?'

'I'm a little sad,' he admits. 'But I always knew you hadn't entirely closed the door on that one.'

I swallow, surprised that he's being so philosophical. 'How are things with you?' I ask.

He shifts on his feet awkwardly. 'I'm seeing Fliss,' he reveals.

Despite everything, the pain takes my breath away.

'I'm sorry,' he whispers. 'It just sort of happened. I feel so bad after everything I said about her, but I don't think I was being honest with myself. Or you. We just click. I still feel so guilty.'

I shake my head, not wanting to cry in front of him.

But I do later. A lot.

❄

Alex emails me soon after I arrive home to ask how I am, but he doesn't make another declaration of love.

One day, I come into work to find an email with a joke from him that he heard that morning on the radio and I find myself laughing out loud.

We begin emailing each other more often, usually just short, sweet, jokey messages that brighten each other's days.

A few weeks later, when I've finished packing up the last of my boxes, I have an overwhelming urge to speak to him. So I dial his number.

I like that I can picture him sitting on his sofa at home in his living room with a view of his garden while he talks to me about his day. I feel a million times better after that simple conversation.

August rolls into September and one day I realise it's exactly a year after Alex first got back in touch.

'Not coming to Sydney next month, I don't suppose?' I find myself asking him by email.

'Do you want me to?' he replies, almost immediately. It's late at night in England so he must be checking his emails on his phone.

'Yes,' I reply, my heart in my throat.

'I'll look into flights,' he responds.

A couple of days later, he tells me he's booked his ticket to come the following week. Just like that.

I ring Bridget in a panic.

'Why are you flipping out?' she asks bluntly. 'You wanted him to come, right?'

'Yes. I think. But Bridget, what if it all goes horribly wrong? I'm so scared he'll break my heart again.'

She doesn't say anything for a long moment and it's disconcerting because I can't see her face – we're not FaceTiming.

'I don't think you need to worry about that,' she says gently. 'I think this is your time. Embrace it.'

❄

The following week, I get up very early on Saturday morning and drive to the airport.

I'm a nervous wreck as I wait for Alex to come through the arrivals hall, but the look on his face when he spots me makes it worth it, a million times over.

'You came!' he gasps, engulfing me in a hug.

I didn't tell him that I would.

'Thought I'd better return the favour after you drove me around in England,' I reply with a smile, my stomach continuing to somersault as he pulls back.

He gazes down at me, his hands still resting on my waist. His dark hair is squashed half flat on top, his eyes are tinged red from lack of sleep, and he has five o'clock shadow gracing his chiselled jaw.

But he's still breathtaking.

He reaches up to brush his thumb across my cheek, leaving a tiny series of sparks fizzing electrically across my skin. I cover his hand with my own and realise his is shaking, ever so slightly.

'My car's this way,' I say.

Neither of us can stop smiling on the journey to his hotel. He checks in, and then I wait on his comfy double bed while he has a shower and a shave. He doesn't want to rest.

We've only got the weekend before I'm back at work – my office is around the corner from where he's staying. It's a flying visit – he's leaving next Sunday night. He and Neal have a big client meeting on the Wednesday after he gets home. This was his one free week for the next month and he didn't want to delay coming. He plans to work from his hotel room during the day and catch up with me at lunchtime and in the evenings. There is no way I'm staying late this week.

The bathroom door opens and Alex comes out, wearing nothing but a towel.

'Forgot to take my clothes in,' he apologises, going to his suitcase and dragging out jeans, a long-sleeve dark T-shirt and underwear.

My eyes track his return journey to the bathroom, watching the rivulets of water dripping from his wet hair and running down his leanly muscled back. He closes the door and I bite my lip, flustered.

It's probably a good idea we get out of this hotel room sooner, rather than later.

It is the *best* day. We wander around Sydney's botanical gardens and eat lunch at one of my favourite restaurants on the harbour, and, when it starts to rain, we head to a museum. At some point, he takes my hand and barely lets it go for the rest of the day.

But, by six o'clock, Alex is properly flagging, so we head back to his hotel to order room service. He sits on the bed to make the call while I stay on a chair by the window and, when he's hung up, he flops back onto his pillows.

'I'm knackered,' he admits, looking over at me.

I return his smile.

'Come here,' he murmurs after several seconds have passed, edging backwards to make room for me.

I hesitate momentarily before kicking off my shoes, then I go over and settle onto the bed beside him. We lie with our heads resting on the pillows, facing each other.

Neither of us speaks, we just stare, his lips tilted up at the corners as he mirrors my expression.

I feel a pull from deep within me, and it's almost as though strings are sprouting from inside me and are attaching themselves to him.

No, not strings.

Roots.

'I love you,' he whispers.

'I love you, too,' I reply.

He draws a sharp intake of breath and slowly reaches out to pull me closer. I'm happy to go to him, sighing contentedly as his fingers stroke over my hair.

As I rest my hand on his chest, I'm reminded of Lachie. He and I lay in this position almost every night for years.

Alex and I only had one night together.

Just one night.

He shouldn't feel as familiar to me as he does.

Lachie drifts out of my mind again and there's no anguish. I feel very much like I'm exactly where I'm meant to be.

Alex's stomach rises and falls slowly and his hand stills in my hair. I draw away to stare down at his sleeping face, his dark lashes creating miniature fan shapes across the tops of his cheeks.

I am so full of love for him.

He jerks awake suddenly, his poor, tired eyes hazy from sleep deprivation. 'Did I nod off?' he gasps, looking out of sorts.

I trace my fingertips along the side of his face as his eyes come back into sharp focus. The moment draws out, and then we very slowly inch towards each other.

Our lips connect and shivers ripple up and down my spine, extending outwards to every nerve ending. He twists his body towards mine, his hands tangling in my hair, and my head spins as our kiss deepens. I feel dizzy and weak and, if I were standing, I don't think my knees would hold me up.

He is an incredible kisser; he always was. His skilled tongue sweeps through my mouth, colliding with mine, and I feel delirious as I kiss him back.

Lachie flashes through my mind again, but it's without guilt or regret. I realise then and there that I'm truly over him.

Bridget is right. This is *our* time. Alex's and mine.

It took us long enough to get here.

I slip my hands up inside his T-shirt. He's broader than he was years ago, but his soft skin still encases hard muscles.

He draws away when my intentions become clear, pulling his shirt over his head. His pupils are dark and dilated as he stares down at me. I'm mesmerised by the sight of his ribs rising and falling with each heavy breath. 'Are you sure?'

'Yes,' I whisper. 'But I'm not on the pill right now.'

He gets up from the bed and goes over to his suitcase. I brought a couple of condoms with me too, just in case, but I'm glad he's also prepared.

My stomach is awash with butterflies as he hovers above me, pressing a gentle kiss to my lips. I pull him into me and we begin to move as one, staring into each other's eyes the entire time. It is intense. It is incredible. It feels like coming home.

We're lying, entangled, afterwards, when there's a knock on the door. We look at each other with alarm.

'Room service,' a voice calls.

We both laugh. We'd forgotten we'd even ordered.

'Impeccable timing,' Alex mutters with a grin as he drags on his jeans and goes to answer the door.

We don't make it as far as dessert before we're going for round two.

❄

It is devastating saying goodbye to Alex after what turns out to be one of the best weeks of our lives. We had a lot of heart-to-hearts while he was here, talking about the future and what we want from it. Ultimately, we decided that we want each other, and somehow we know we need to make it work.

He's only just set up his business, he loves where he lives and is very close to his family, but I know he would give it all up and move to Australia if I asked him to.

I don't ask him to. And I will never forget the look on his face when I tell him I'll quit my job, accept Rachel's offer and move back to England. He gathers me in his arms and presses kiss after kiss on my forehead before clasping my face in his hands and snogging me senseless.

As if I were going to give up getting one of *those* every day for the rest of my life.

My boss's face almost falls off a cliff when I resign.

I have a feeling I was more valued than she let on, but this does not work in my favour when she insists I work my full notice.

Rachel, however, is delighted and offers to sponsor my work visa. She promises to tell me whose wedding I'm doing when we're face to face. No amount of, 'Do they work on *EastEnders*, or *Corrie*, or have they been on *The X Factor...*?' sways her. She's staying silent until I sign my confidentiality clause.

Alex and I speak on the phone every day – sometimes twice a day – and, although physically we couldn't be further apart, by the time I'm packing up my things and walking out of my empty Bondi Beach studio flat, I feel closer to him than ever.

I do go for one last cuppa at Lucy's house in Manly, and it's strange stepping off the ferry and walking past our old home. I feel a pang as I cast a poignant look up at the balcony. There are no wetsuits hanging outside.

We did have good times there. But life moves on. I've moved on. Lachie has. Even Elliot has started seeing someone – a friend of Fliss's older sister, bizarrely. And Lachie is still with Fliss. I'm at peace with it.

I'm sad to say goodbye to Lucy, though. I'll miss her – and Nathan, Finn and now little baby Izzy, too. Lucy promises that they will all come and visit me next year when they're in the UK and I tell her I'll hold her to it.

'Are you going to see Lachie before you leave?' she asks.

I shake my head. 'I haven't spoken to him in months.'

Elliot was the one who told me that he's still with Fliss. I don't make a point of catching up with El, but he does work near me in the city, and sometimes we bump into each other and go for a coffee.

'I think you'll find him at the beach if you change your mind,' she says. 'He and Nathan have gone surfing.'

My head is still swimming with this information as I walk back to the ferry terminal via Manly Beach. I stand and stare out at the grey waves and the slick seal-like surfers sitting up on their boards. Pelicans fly low across the ocean as my eyes seek out Lachie. He looks my way and seems to freeze.

He catches the next wave in.

'Hey!' he calls, his smile hesitant as his feet pad across the sand towards me, his black wetsuit streaming with water.

'I was just saying goodbye to Lucy. She told me you were down here.'

He rakes his hand through his blond hair, several shades darker than it would be if it weren't wet.

'Nathan told me you're moving back to the UK,' he says.

I nod. 'The day after tomorrow. Rachel has asked me to do a wedding with her.'

His face lights up. 'So you're finally going back to wedding photography?'

'At long last.'

'Yeah, at long last,' he agrees reflectively. 'And Alex? Are things still happening there?'

I nod, managing a small smile. 'Yeah. We're good.'

'I'm happy for you,' he says after a moment.

'How's Fliss?' I ask.

'Good.' He smiles now too.

'I'm happy for you, too,' I say, and I mean it. I'm not sad, but emotion pricks at me behind my eyes as the years we spent together tumble away.

'Do you regret it?' he asks out of the blue. 'Choosing me?'

'No.' I shake my head, trying to hold back the tears. 'I loved the time we spent together. Most of it, anyway.'

'Me too,' he says, his voice husky. 'Good luck with everything, Bronnie.'

He steps forward to give me a hug.

'Argh, you're all wet,' I squeal, and he laughs, shaking his wet hair over me. 'Still so immature,' I chide, giving his chest a small, affectionate shove.

'The boy who never grows up,' he replies with a grin.

'I'll let you get back to your waves.'

'It was good to see you.' He walks backwards a few steps.

'You too.'

I watch him jog across the beach and pick up the surfboard he'd jammed upright in the sand, then I turn, the wind whipping tears from my eyes as I walk away. Just before I slip out of view, I cast one last look back at the boy who stole my heart when I most needed him to.

He's sitting up on his board, watching me, and lifts his hand in a half-wave. I do the same before letting him go.

❄

As is becoming tradition, Alex comes to collect me from the airport. We stand in each other's arms, holding each other tightly for I don't know how long as the other arrivals swarm around us and pass by. He rests his head against my forehead.

'I've missed you so much,' he murmurs.

'Me too.'

'I can't believe you're here.'

'For good, hopefully, if I can get that visa sorted out.'

'I've lined up an immigration lawyer,' he says with a smile, letting me go to take the trolley containing all my luggage.

We go straight back to his place.

'Are you sure you're happy with me staying here?' I ask with slight trepidation as he lugs the last of my suitcases down the stairs. I paid excess to bring what I could, giving away quite a bit before I left. Luckily, Lachie and I only ever rented and the flat was fully furnished, so I don't have a crazy amount of possessions.

'More than happy,' he says, digging into his pocket and giving me a key.

We spoke at length about this before I left Australia. He talked me out of getting a place myself, saying it was ridiculous when we'd probably end up living together anyway. Also, he has a spare room, which he says I can use as my own if I ever need a little space.

'I *will* pay rent,' I say firmly.

He sighs. 'You don't need to.'

'I want to pay my way.'

'I'm in a good place. I don't want you to stress about money.'

'I won't. Did I tell you that Simon has some work for me in January?'

'No?' He looks amazed and then a touch concerned. 'I thought you were going to focus on wedding photography.'

'I am. This is just a bit of freelance picture work until I get on my feet. I won't take another full-time job.'

He smiles and tugs me towards him until we're toe to toe.

'I'm so proud of you,' he says.

'The feeling's mutual.'

He leans down to kiss me, but I step away. 'I need a shower.'

He raises an eyebrow. 'Can I join you?'

I give him a cheeky grin and take his hand, leading him up the stairs.

I don't think I'm going to need to worry about digging out fresh clothes any time soon. I doubt we'll be moving from his bed.

❄

A few days later, I go to see Rachel. She looks like she's going to burst as I read over the confidentiality contract, finally signing my name.

'Spill it!' I say with a laugh.

'Joe and Alice!' she yells.

'Joseph Strike?' My eyes nearly pop out of my head.

She nods manically.

'No way!' I gasp. This is way, way bigger than I ever could have imagined.

Joseph Strike is a *huge* Hollywood star, like, proper

A-list. Alice was his first love – they met when they were eighteen, but lost touch. She married someone else, but she wasn't happy and, when Joe opened up about his feelings for her on a chat show years later, Alice's friend called in and the show put them back in touch. Everyone knows their story.

They've been engaged for donkey's years, but have had two children in the meantime, so it didn't seem like they were ever going to get around to tying the knot.

Funnily enough, I organised a Joseph Strike Baby Bump cover for *Hebe* once when my friend Lily in Adelaide offered me the pictures.

I was in Simon's good books big time after that. I've felt kind of indebted to the actor ever since.

'Where's the wedding taking place?' I ask Rachel.

'A country house up in Cambridgeshire,' she replies. 'It's all very hush-hush. Joe and Alice don't want the press to cotton on and harass them on their big day.'

'I can't believe it,' I say, shaking my head.

'I told you I think it'll set you up. It really will,' she says. 'I also wanted to ask you if you'd like to take on Misha's weddings from next spring?'

She's already told me that her assistant is having a baby and going on maternity leave.

'Do you really need to ask?'

'I know you'll go it alone eventually,' she says with a smile. 'But I do so love working with you.'

'I love working with you, too, and I'm in no rush to run my own show. Not yet, anyway.'

❄

Joe and Alice are getting married in early December and Alex and I decide to make a mini-break out of the weekend, heading up to Cambridge on the Friday night before the wedding. We stay in a hotel with a great view of the River Cam, and spend a cold but lovely evening wandering around the frosty streets of the fairy-light-laden city.

Early the next morning, I kiss Alex goodbye and leave him to a day of Christmas shopping and sightseeing, while I jump into a cab and head to a sleepy village a twenty-minute drive away.

Rachel told me that Joe and Alice wanted to prepare for the big day together at home with their two small children, and we need to be there to capture the proceedings.

I'm nervous. *Hebe* was great grounding, but you never get quite used to working with famous people. Joseph Strike is a *major* celebrity, and even Alice is almost as recognisable as her fiancé these days. I hope I don't balls this up.

To avoid any likelihood of the cab driver alerting the press, I get out of the car a good few hundred yards early and walk up the muddy country lane to the imposing gates at the end. I press the buzzer and they glide open after a moment, delivering a view of the stunning sixteenth-century Tudor mansion within.

I'm in awe as I crunch across the icy gravel driveway with my kitbag slung over my shoulder, looking around for Rachel's car. I'm alarmed to find that it's not there – she was supposed to arrive before me.

The heavy wooden front door swings open well before I reach it and a woman in a white fluffy robe and bare feet beams out at me.

Oh my God, it's Alice. *The* Alice!

'Hello!' she calls. 'You must be Bronte!'

'Hi!' I call back.

'Rachel's running a bit late. There was an accident on the A1.' She holds out her hand for me to shake as I reach her. 'She tried to call you, but couldn't get reception. It's a bit patchy round here.'

Despite her bare-faced appearance, Alice is stunning. Her complexion is flawless, the sort that would make Maria weep – what a shame she's not doing the make-up today – and her hair is jet-black and dead straight, falling to just below her shoulders.

'Do you need to see my credentials?' I ask, a bit taken aback that she's opening her own front door. Don't they have staff falling over themselves to do that sort of thing?

'Nah.' Alice waves me away and her green eyes seem to sparkle. 'Anyway, Rachel showed me a pic. I know it's you. You want a cuppa?'

'I'd love one.'

'Joe, this is Bronte,' I hear her say as I follow her into a large, warm country kitchen, complete with natural stone flooring and an Aga.

'Hey.' Joseph Strike jumps up from the table where he's spoon-feeding a baby. 'Joe,' he says, giving my hand a firm shake and smiling warmly.

Joe, not Joseph, I note.

He's a lot taller than I thought he'd be, with short, dark hair and dark-brown eyes. He's wearing casual grey cargo pants and a faded black T-shirt, but his biceps protrude from under his sleeves and I don't need to have seen his films to know how defined his abs are under that top.

I try to still my beating heart.

Don't be stupid, Bronte, they're just people.

'And who are you?' I ask in a sweet voice, bending to put my kitbag on the floor.

'This is Becca,' Joe says fondly, taking his seat again. 'Okay, okay, it's coming,' he chides his daughter gently, spooning another mouthful of soggy Weetabix into her waiting mouth.

I know her name, of course. And I know that she's seven months old. But at that moment, I wish I didn't. I wish this were just an ordinary wedding between two ordinary people. I don't want to ask questions that I already know the answers to, and I genuinely wish that I didn't already know the answers.

'You want another coffee, Joe?' Alice interrupts, filling up the kettle and putting it on the Aga.

Don't they have a cook to do this sort of thing?

At that moment, a small boy wanders sleepily into the room, dressed in Spider-Man PJs. Alice scoops him up.

'Good morning, precious,' she says softly, kissing him on his nose. The child rubs at his eyes and yawns.

Unsure if it's the right thing to do, but willing to take the risk, I quickly unzip my kitbag, getting out my camera and the lens I use to take portraits.

'Is this okay?' I ask Joe in a whisper.

'Go for it,' he replies.

I snap off a couple of candid shots so I don't miss the moment, then put my camera down and smile at Jack, Joe and Alice's son.

'Alright, little man?' Joe asks him. 'You slept well.'

Jack yawns again and buries his face against Alice's neck.

'Better than me,' Joe adds with a wry smile at his fiancée.

Alice smiles and taps her son on his back. 'This is Bronte,' she says. Jack lifts his head to look at me with his soulful dark eyes. 'She's taking some pictures of Mummy and Daddy's wedding day.'

'Hi,' he says in a cute, groggy voice. What a sweetheart.

Rachel arrives soon afterwards and the atmosphere remains laidback and lovely. Misha has gone straight to the country house where Alice's parents and the couple's close friends are getting ready. I really liked Misha when I met her earlier this week – we've never worked together before – but she has an easy-going, likeable nature, and apparently she and Alice have already bonded over morning-sickness woes.

It soon becomes clear that the Strikes don't have any staff, at least not in their home. There's a bodyguard next door who keeps an eye on security and who can be here at a moment's notice if necessary, but on the whole the family appear to strive to have as normal a life as possible.

By the time the morning shoot is finished, I have a little bit of a crush on all four of them.

Just as we're leaving the house, I notice a picture of Alice and Joe on the hallstand. Alice is holding a baby koala, and Joe has his hand placed protectively on his fiancée's pregnant belly. I know Lily's handiwork when I see it and make a mental note to tell my friend that they still hold dear the shot that she took – at their request, as it turned out – at the conservation park in the Adelaide Hills, where she works. The couple gave their permission for Lily to sell the pictures she took of them, hoping it might help her get established as a photographer – and it did. She regularly contributes to magazines, although she specialises in wildlife, rather than celebrities. Saying that, she has told me that a few Aussie soap stars have since visited the conservation park and asked if she can do some 'Joseph and Alice shots' for them, so I think that's given her a bit of a kick.

We go by hired limousine to the wedding venue a few

miles away. I travel with the Strikes, while Rachel follows in her car. I sit on one of the seats facing backwards and take some candid shots of the four of them, lined up.

Alice looks absolutely stunning in a simple, white gown with matching jacket and diamanté-studded high heels. Her hair has been styled up in an intricate but loose bun, with a few tendrils escaping to frame her face, and there are white orchids adorning her dark locks, which match the posy she'll carry up the aisle. The make-up artist has somehow managed to make the green in her stunning almond-shaped eyes look even more luminescent.

As for Joe, he's out-of-this-world gorgeous in a well-fitted black suit and cherry-red tie. He can't take his eyes off his wife-to-be.

'You're so beautiful,' he murmurs for the third time since we got in the car.

She smiles back at him. 'You don't look so bad yourself,' she whispers, casting me a slightly self-conscious look and giggling when I smirk at her.

Joe flashes me a grin.

I like this family so much. I wish we could be friends, I muse with an inward giggle at myself. I know damn well that everyone who meets them has that thought.

Alice is sitting between her two children, holding their hands. I put the camera back up to my eye and snap a close-up shot of Becca's tiny hand, entirely curled around her mother's forefinger.

Just because they're travelling to the venue together, it doesn't mean that we missed out on the shot of Joe and Alice seeing each other in their wedding outfits for the very first time. Rachel and I captured the moment when Alice came down the stairs and Joe was standing at the bottom. His chest expanded visibly and he looked utterly lost for a moment, completely blown away. Then his eyes filled with tears and he stepped forward to take Alice in his arms, cradling her tenderly.

Boy, does he love her.

Although part of me felt uncomfortable witnessing such a private moment, I know that, just as with Bridget and Charlie and all of the other brides and grooms we've photographed, these are two pictures that they'll treasure forever.

As celebrity weddings go, Alice and Joe's is massively understated. The day is clearly a celebration of love between two people among only their very dearest friends and family.

It was the same for Bridget and Charlie.

And, if I ever wanted to get married, it's how I'd do it too.

But I don't believe in marriage.

I doubt Alex does either, after what happened to him first time around.

I'm absolutely shattered by the time I get back to our hotel, but, as soon as Alex takes me in his arms, I feel better.

'You want something from the minibar? Tell me all about it?' he asks.

'In the morning,' I reply. 'Right now, I just want to go to bed.'

'To sleep?' He raises a dark eyebrow.

'Are you mad? I need to de-stress.'

He chuckles and starts to unbutton my fitted black shirt with his deft, skilful fingers.

We had to wear a uniform today so the guests knew who we were.

I turn my attention to his shirt, sliding my hands inside

and standing up on my tiptoes to kiss his lips. Very soon we're falling naked onto the bed, his warm, solid body colliding with mine. He rolls over, pulling me on top of him.

'Did you buy condoms?' I ask. We only had one left last night; Alex said he'd get more today.

His face falls. 'Shit, I totally forgot.'

I sink over his body with disappointment.

'We don't have to go the whole way,' he mumbles into my hair.

I turn my face to his.

Our kisses become increasingly heated, and, when it comes to the point of no return, I really, *really* don't want to stop.

He's panting heavily against my mouth, holding back from pulling me onto him.

'We both want the same things,' he utters out of the blue.

'What are you saying?' I sit up so I can look at him.

'I love you,' he says, 'so much.' He reaches up to push a strand of hair off my face, his fingers leaving behind a trail of sparks.

His touch *still* has that effect on me.

His eyes are full of adoration as he gazes up at me. 'You're my forever. I want to grow old with you. I want a family.'

I smile. 'We *do* want the same things.'

'Why wait?' he asks.

My head is spinning and I feel dizzy as I bend down to kiss him. I don't overthink it as he shifts beneath me, his hands on my hips, and I go with him willingly as we connect, skin to skin, just like our first time.

It's blissful.

Afterwards, however, as I lie in his arms, worry starts to eat me up.

'Are we moving too fast?' I ask.

He turns to look at me, his brow creased into a frown. 'I don't feel like we are. Do you?'

'No. But it *is* fast... I'm sure everyone else would think we're jumping ahead too soon.'

'I think we're where we'd be if we'd stayed together five years ago. It wasn't right then, but it is now. Yes, we're moving quickly, but it feels perfect. Doesn't it to you?'

'Yes.' I nod.

'When you know, you know,' he says.

I remember Bridget saying the same thing about Charlie. Not a bad example of things working out.

'But what if I don't get residency? Is it possible that I could fall pregnant and still be sent home?' I'm instantly full of horror at the thought. Why haven't I done more research about this?

He cups my cheek with his hand and stares at me levelly. My racing heart begins to return to normal. And then he speaks. 'Will you marry me?'

I almost jump out of my own skin. 'What? Did you just propose? You know I'm a nonbeliever, right?'

He smiles at me, unfazed by my reaction. 'I still believe in marriage,' he says. 'My parents have been together for almost fifty years. But, even if you don't, you've got to admit it would be a damn easy way to sort out your visa.'

'You're serious? You're really asking me to marry you?'

'Completely. I meant what I said. I want to be with you for the rest of my life. I know it shouldn't matter if we're married or not, and, obviously, it doesn't, not really. You could still divorce me if you wanted to.' He flinches as he says this, drawing on his own experiences of a broken marriage. 'But it would make things so much easier if we want to have a family, if you really do want to stay here. With me. You do, don't you?'

I nod, tearfully. 'Yes, I really do.'

'Then marry me,' he says simply. 'Let's just do it.'

A wave of love and emotion sweeps through me. I bend down and press my lips to his, then pull away. 'Fuck it. Okay.'

He laughs. 'I think that's the most romantic thing you've ever said to me.' But then he does a double take. 'Do you actually mean it?' he asks, now slightly breathless.

'Yes. I'll marry you.' I feel giddy. 'Want to have another go at knocking me up first?'

He doesn't have to be asked twice.

❊

The next morning, I wake up to find Alex lying on his pillow, staring at me. Sunlight is streaking through a crack in the curtains, hitting his face and making his eyes look lighter blue than usual.

'Hi,' I murmur.

'Hi,' he replies. He looks apprehensive. 'Did you mean it?'

I nod. His eyes fill with tears as he leans forward to kiss me.

'When?' I ask against his lips.

'I'd marry you today,' he whispers.

'Can we make it Christmas Eve?' I say, prompting his eyes to widen. I smile at him. 'I'm not winding you up. My mother and David are going to be here, remember?' They're doing a European cruise. 'She'll kill me if she's this side of the world and I don't invite her to my wedding. Not that she ever expected me to do something so out of character.'

Alex presses a hard, fast kiss to my lips. 'I'll start looking at venues.'

A shiver goes down my spine. Is this really happening?

❄

'You're pulling my leg,' Bridget says when I call to tell her.

'I'm not.'

'You are. I don't believe you.'

'I'm not,' I insist, laughing. 'Will you come or what?'

'To London for Christmas Eve? And then back to frigging Cornwall in time for Christmas with Charlie's family? Do you know what the traffic will be like?'

My heart sinks. I guess I wasn't really thinking when we decided on that date.

Bridget carries on. 'All to find out that this is some big joke and you're not getting married after all?'

'I *am* getting married. I'm marrying Alex. I need a visa.'

She falls silent. 'Are you serious?' she asks after a moment.

'Oh, *now* you believe me,' I say with a grin.

'Are you serious?' she asks again. 'You're marrying him? For a visa?'

'Sort of,' I reply. 'I mean, he wants to marry me. And I do want to be with him for the rest of my life. It makes sense.'

'How dreamy,' she says drily.

I laugh. 'Sorry, but you know what I'm like! I'm not going to change overnight.'

'You're really getting married? On Christmas Eve?'

'Yes, and I would love you to be my witness. My sort of matron of honour, even though you don't have to buy a special dress or anything. But I understand if it's too much of a hassle to drive from Cornwall.'

She screams.

Right. In. My. Ear.

'*HolyshitfuckinghellBronteyou'regettingmarried?*'

'Yes.'

'You love him. You really, really love him.'

'We've been trying to make babies together.'

'Holy fuck!' she gasps. 'This is real. This is happening.'

'Yes!' I'm laughing properly now. 'Will you come?'

'Yes, I'll fucking come! I wouldn't miss it for the world!'

❄

Alex and I both agree that we will not make a big deal out of this. But our friends and family seem to have other ideas. His mates – including Ed, whom I actually really, *really* like, which is just as well, because he's always popping over for post-work drinks – drag him out for a meal the night before we tie the knot. My friends do the same for me but, when we end up at the same tacky eighties club night where Alex and I met, I stamp my heels on the pavement.

'No way. No frigging way. I am *not* having my hen night here.'

Polly looks affronted. 'What's wrong with this place?'

Whoops… I never did tell her I wasn't a fan when we came her for her hen do.

'Just a couple of shots, I promise,' Bridget says. 'For old times' sake. It's where you met!' she urges, shaking my upper arms.

I dither. 'Okay, but just two shots,' I agree.

'And a bit of a boogie,' Rachel chips in.

I narrow my eyes at her. 'Okay, maybe one or two.'

Luckily, I'm already tipsy after all of the prosecco at dinner.

The joint is just as bad as I remembered but, damn, I feel full of affection for it. I look around, drinking in the cheesy eighties outfits as we walk down the stairs. Bridget takes me straight to the bar, putting her arm around my shoulders as we wait for the bartender to line up our shots. She looks over towards the pillar.

'That's where you met,' she says in my ear, letting me go and stepping back.

I feel a sudden wave of emotion. I remember looking over at Alex and him giving me this sweet, helpless little shrug. He didn't want to be here any more than me, yet somehow we ended up being the last to leave.

Familiar hands encircle my waist and I spin in his arms, unable to believe what I'm seeing. Alex smiles down at me as our friends whoop and cheer.

'Did you know they were doing this?' I'm amazed.

He shakes his head, his eyes sparkling with amusement. 'It took quite a lot for them to drag me in here.'

'Me too!' We start laughing and don't stop until our eyes are wet with tears, and then our friends are passing out shots and we're knocking them back, the alcohol going straight to our heads.

'Red, Red Wine' by UB40 comes on. Alex and I look at each other, incredulous.

This was the song we sexy-danced to, all those years ago. He doesn't say a word as he leads me across the lit-up dance floor and takes me in his arms.

A flash goes off and I look over to see Rachel winking at me, holding her camera aloft. She's coming tomorrow, doing the photos as a favour. I keep saying it's not a big deal, but no one is getting the message.

Maria has insisted on doing my make-up; Polly dragged me off to the shops, telling me I was mad to pass up the excuse to buy a pretty frock; and Ed organised an after-party in the upstairs room of a cosy pub in central London, just around the corner from the register office where we're getting married. Bridget, who has awesome taste in music, has sorted out the playlist.

I slide my hands up and over Alex's shoulders, smiling at him as his thumbs brush my hipbones. He bends down to kiss me, pulling me closer until we're flush to each other's bodies. He holds me tightly, and then we're both barely moving, barely breathing, just here, in this moment, together.

Until a man dressed up as Michael J. Fox from *Teen Wolf* crashes into us. Alex grabs me to steady me and glares after the werewolf-wannabe, and then we both meet each other's eyes and crack up laughing.

❄

I stay in a hotel near the register office and share a room with Bridget, who, despite her reluctance to be without Charlie and April on *her* hen night, convinced me it'd be fun to have a sleepover – for old times' sake.

She, Charlie and April are spending the festive period with her dad in north London after deciding to have one last Christmas in the house where Bridget grew up. In the New Year, her dad is putting his home on the market and moving down to Cornwall, ready to embrace the next stage of his life.

On the morning of my wedding day – MY WEDDING DAY – I wake up to Bridget playing 'I Do, I Do, I Do, I Do, I Do' by Abba on her tiny but loud portable B&O speaker. She follows this up with 'White Wedding' by Billy Idol and 'Going to the Chapel' by the Dixie Cups, while we sit on the bed, giggling and eating flaky pastries that she picked up from the bakery next door.

Maria turns up after a while to do my make-up, but I'm styling my own hair in my trademark fishtail plait. Then I get into my dress, a pretty, long-sleeved, lace, knee-length number that's the colour of crème caramel. I team it with brown cowboy boots.

Bridget shakes her head at me and starts to cry.

'Oh my *God*!' I exclaim, laughing. 'I can't believe you're *crying*!'

'I can't believe this is happening!' she blubs.

'Me neither,' I say, shaking my head.

And I really can't. It feels very surreal. I know I want to be with Alex for the rest of my life, but I can't actually get my head around the fact that I'm marrying him today.

I'm *marrying* him.

Nope. Still won't sink in.

We head to the venue in a black cab after Maria has retouched Bridget's make-up. Rachel joins us to snap some pics, bringing with her tiny bottles of chilled prosecco for the journey. We all still feel a bit rough after last night, but manage to knock them back anyway.

And then I climb out of the cab to see Alex standing on the steps outside the cream-coloured building.

I freeze, only very vaguely aware of Rachel and Maria clicking off shots. He looks so handsome. He's wearing a very dark-blue, fitted suit with a pale-blue tie.

Finally it hits me.

My legs feel like jelly as I come out of my daze. He jogs down the steps and takes my hand.

'Don't freak out,' he whispers in my ear. 'Visa, remember?'

'Yes, visa,' I repeat aloud. He casts me a sideways grin and squeezes my hand as we walk up the steps together.

'You look incredible,' he says seriously, and then he leads me inside the venue and down a corridor to two wooden doors at the end. Bridget, Maria and Rachel go in ahead, but, as the doors swing shut behind them, I catch a glimpse inside and breathe in sharply.

There are so many more people here than I'd anticipated.

'I thought we were keeping this small,' I whisper.

'It was a little out of my hands,' he replies. 'They all wanted to come. I hope you're not upset.'

I shake my head and then push open the door a crack and peek in, spying my mum up at the front next to David.

A lump forms in my throat.

'Hey,' Alex says gently, pulling me into his arms and holding me tightly.

'It's okay, it's okay,' I gasp. 'I'm not going to lose it.' I try to inhale, but my lungs refuse to fill with air.

He places his hand over my stomach and presses his lips to my temple.

I don't know how or why, but I suddenly feel calm. Like, *weirdly* calm.

He looks at me expectantly.

I nod and go to push open the doors.

As soon as we walk in, Starship's 'Nothing's Gonna Stop Us Now' pipes up. I start to laugh and look for Bridget, who's grinning back at me from the front of the room.

This is one of the songs they played at our first eighties club night, and I squealed when it came on again last night. She starts to melodramatically lip-sync to the words and I really want to join in, but then she suddenly seems to realise she's being completely inappropriate and gathers herself together.

Alex smiles at me when we reach the front.

'I love you,' he mouths, squeezing my hand.

'I love you, too,' I mouth back, tears filling my eyes. He's not letting me go, even though my hand is clammy.

And then we both turn to face the beaming registrar.

Ten minutes later, we're married.

Later the following year...

We're lying on our sides, facing each other, the lights in the room dimmed right down. It all happened so quickly, at the end. I can't actually believe we did it. *I* did it.

Alex runs his hand gently over the head of our tiny sleeping son, nestled between us. His eyes are blue.

'All babies' eyes are blue at first,' he said earlier.

'Our son's eyes will be blue,' I replied determinedly.

'Okay, I'll give you that, as long as our daughter's eyes are green like yours,' he stipulated.

I stare down at her now, emotion catching in my throat as I brush my finger across her tiny cheek. Not one, but *two* babies. *Twins.* Theo and Abigail.

I meet Alex's eyes, which are swimming with joy and pride as he stares back at me.

I tear my eyes away from my adoring husband and look down at the tiny sleeping bundles again, my heart threatening to burst with more love than I ever thought a human being could be capable of feeling.

Fate finally got it right.

And the timing was absolutely perfect.

Laura's Longest Day

I've thought about writing a mini sequel for Laura and Leo from The Longest Holiday *ever since I launched* The Hidden Paige – *inspiration has just been waiting to strike!*

In the epilogue for The Last Piece of My Heart, *Bridget reveals that Laura attended her wedding with her baby son, but there's no mention of Leo.*

In A Christmas Wedding, *Bronte tells us about Bridget's wedding in more detail, and this time we hear that Leo had to stay behind in Key West to run their guest house.*

Now, in this mini exclusive that I penned especially for this collection, it's time for Laura to tell us her side of the story…

'Godammit, Leo!' I press the button to end the call and throw my mobile phone onto the sofa, agitated with worry and frustration. Now neither the home phone *nor* his mobile is working.

'Still no word from him?' Mum appears in the living room, jiggling Max in her arms.

'No, they've already lost power to the island.' I open my arms for my son and Mum transfers him straight away. I think she can sense that I need my baby close right now.

'He'll be okay, darling. He's a tough cookie,' Mum murmurs as I stroke my hand over Max's hair. He has so much of it – it makes him look older than his six-and-a-half months. 'And it'll be lovely to have the two of you with us for a bit longer,' she adds.

'Mmm.' I don't mean to sound disheartened at the thought. I love my parents dearly, but I was ready to go home. We've already been away for two weeks and I've been missing Leo like crazy. He's had to manage Lorelei – our guest house – on his own, and now this tropical storm has been upgraded to a hurricane. The tourists have all been evacuated from the Keys, but my pig-headed partner has insisted on staying put with thousands of other locals. With the power lines down and the airport closed indefinitely, I have no way of contacting him *or* going home.

Not that he wanted us to return with all of this going on…

'The safest place for you both right now is in Cambridge with your parents,' he told me last night. I could hear the wind raging through the palm trees in the background.

I know he's right, of course. If I'd been in Key West, Max and I would have gone to the mainland for sure. But we damn well would've dragged Leo with us.

Carmen tried to persuade Leo and Jorge to go and stay with her in Miami – Carmen is Leo's sister-in-law and Jorge is Carmen's brother and Leo's best friend – but the two men were having none of it.

'Lorelei has withstood hurricanes before and I'm confident she will do again, but I need to do everything I can to secure her,' Leo said last night. 'I need more time to board up the windows and get our belongings in order.'

'Your safety is more important,' I stated adamantly.

'I'm sorry, baby, but it's too late now; I might not reach the mainland before the storm hits. But you wouldn't have changed my mind anyway,' he adds gently. 'This is my home. I'm staying. And once you leave the Keys you can't get back in.'

'That's because it's not safe!' I exclaimed angrily. 'They'll let you back in when it is!'

'I can't wait a week or more to find out if we still have a home; if we still have a dive boat. I'd go out of my mind.'

Jorge was in agreement. He used to only come to Key West during high season, but a year ago he moved down permanently from Miami to set up a dive centre with Leo – they're both scuba instructors.

Lots of our guests want to learn how to scuba dive and for a long time we've been giving business to the dive school where Leo and Jorge worked. The men thought it was about time they went out on their own, but the lease on their dive boat is cripplingly expensive.

That boat is their livelihood – as is our house. If the hurricane destroys either, we're screwed. Insurance pay-outs won't come close to covering all of the damage.

Lorelei was Leo's childhood home, rundown for years until I came along and urged him to do it up. Now that big old house is my home, too – and our son's.

It's gorgeous, with pale-blue shutters and gleaming-white weatherboarding and 'gingerbread' – the name for the patterned woodwork that hangs down from the eaves of many houses in Key West. Inside, the rooms are all styled in different, striking colours, from teal and emerald green to ochre and burnt orange. Brightly coloured, retro posters of old Cuba hang in large frames on the walls and colourful rugs adorn the newly sanded floorboards. The original intricately carved wooden banister has been varnished and polished to a dark shine, and there are leafy, green pot plants dotted throughout.

We've poured blood, sweat and tears into that house, not to mention our hearts and our souls. We have so much more invested in it than money. If anything happens to it, we won't just be screwed financially, we'll be heartbroken. It's going to be hard enough managing without the tourists in the wake of the hurricane.

Leo promised me that he'd hole himself up in the bathroom with plenty of food and water while the storm raged outside, and he'd better. They're saying there could be winds of 150 miles per hour or more, and one tin sheet from one house roof could take his head off.

I feel like I'm going to throw up.

Max wriggles and squirms in my arms, so I turn him to face me, bouncing his nappy-clad bottom lightly on my knees. He cracks up laughing, blissfully unaware of the danger his daddy is in.

Our son is adorable, his chubby cheeks expanding so far out from his face when he smiles that he reminds me of a chipmunk. He has the longest lashes: thick and dark and just like his father's, and aside from a small bald patch from where his newborn hair rubbed off on his pillow, he also has Leo's short, black hair.

My hair is light-blonde and my eyes are blue, so I don't think Max resembles me at all, but my parents claim his smile is mine. I assume they mean he looks like me from when I was his age. I'd be less than thrilled if they still thought I resembled a rodent.

Max and I came to the UK for my friend Bridget's wedding. Because of a holiday Mum and Dad had booked well in advance, we were only able to stay with them for a couple of days before we had to set off to Cornwall on an exhausting fourteen-hour round trip. I've been dreading our long-haul flight back to the States today, but now I can't wait to be allowed to step onto a homeward-bound plane.

I pick up my mobile and search my news apps for word of the hurricane. If Mum and Dad had Sky, I'd have CNN on constantly.

'Do you want me to take him, darling?' Mum offers.

'Thanks, Mum.' I distractedly pass Max back to her and return my attention to the news article on my phone screen.

Miami authorities are begging locals to evacuate the Keys, hours before Hurricane Jackie's arrival, warning

> that storm surges and high winds pose a particular risk to
> the string of low-lying sandbar islands tailing off Florida's
> southern tip.
>
>   Jackie's winds will hit Key West first in the early hours of
> Friday morning and officials worry there won't be enough
> time for residents to make what can be a three-hour-plus
> journey from Key West to the mainland.

I check the time this piece was posted and calculate the time
difference between America and the UK in my head. The
hurricane has already hit. I read the rest of the article with a
tightening knot in my stomach.

> We're very concerned about the residents who refuse
> to leave,' said Victoria Thomas, a county spokesperson.
> 'Storm surges could kill a lot of people. Once the water
> comes, there's nowhere to go.

'Dammit, Leo!' I exclaim out loud for the second time that
morning. Anxiety is pulsing through my stomach in waves.
Are you okay?

There's no way to know. We just have to wait for the
storm to pass.

A memory comes back to me as I think of those words…

Don't wait for the storm to pass; learn to dance in the rain.

It was written on a billboard outside a church on my very
first trip to the Keys, and it felt particularly relevant to me at
the time, considering everything that I was going through.

I'll never forget that long journey along the Overseas
Highway, the glittering ocean out of the car windows and

the pelicans flying low overhead as we crossed the forty-odd bridges on our way to Florida's southernmost key. In the driver's seat was Bridget, who I barely knew at the time, and next to her was our joint best friend Marty, who slept for much of the way. I was feeling nauseous with stress and misery because I'd recently found out that my husband, Matthew, had managed to get another woman pregnant on his stag do, a week before he'd married me. He'd made a terrible, drunken mistake with a girl he'd only just met: their seemingly harmless flirtation had led to a snog, and the next thing they knew, they were having it off in the club's toilets. The girl – Tessa – had tracked Matthew down seven months later to break the news that he was going to be a father. Their baby – *their* baby! – would be a constant, never-ending reminder of his infidelity to me, and Matthew would be expected to help raise the child that should have been mine. It's impossible to describe how humiliated I felt, how lost I was not knowing how Matthew and I could ever move on. We loved each other deeply, but our future felt like it would be forever tainted.

So I ran away to Key West with Marty and Bridget. I was only supposed to be away for a fortnight. But I stayed. I met Leo, developed a whopping great crush and decided to bury my head in the sand indefinitely. Everyone tried to get me to return to England to face the music, including Marty, who loaded on pressure for me to forgive Matthew and welcome his baby son into our lives. But I couldn't. What began as a crush strengthened to something more and I fell in love. I couldn't let Leo go.

Bridget was the only one who understood.

At first, she was just Marty's friend and I was the nuisance who gate-crashed their girly holiday and brought the mood down, but now she's the sort of person I'd fly thousands of miles for to attend her wedding.

She and Charlie got married in an old stone church in a place called Lansallos in Cornwall and then the entire congregation walked down a long track for a picnic reception on the beach.

It was such a beautiful day, but I missed Leo dreadfully, and not just because I had to manage Max almost entirely on my own. Charlie's lovely brother, Adam, offered to help carry him on the return walk up to the car park, but it was still a long day for him – and for me. It's not easy to breastfeed on a beach surrounded by dozens of people you barely know. Also, Bridget's wedding was the first I had attended since my own, and it brought back some surprisingly painful memories. I would've given anything to have had Leo sitting next to me, holding my hand and reminding me of how full our lives are, even though we're not married and never will be.

Leo doesn't believe in marriage. I don't blame him; his childhood was complicated. His father had another family back in Cuba – his mother was his father's mistress, and he and his brother their illegitimate offspring. Leo has half-siblings somewhere out there that don't know he even exists. But I still believe in marriage, even though mine ended in divorce.

I have another wedding later this year, too. Marty is getting married to her doting boyfriend Ted, and I'm going to be one of her bridesmaids, along with Bridget. Marty gave herself a headache, trying to choose between us – she was the chief bridesmaid for both Bridget and me, but only one of us can be her Matron of Honour. I'm Marty's oldest friend, but I won't be in the country much to help out, so I encouraged her to choose Bridget. Bridget was predictably thrilled, but on her hen night she did an about-turn and insisted we share the honour. I don't know how that's going to work, but it'll be fun, I'm sure. Things usually are where Bridget's concerned.

✳

After lunch, when there's still no new news, I decide to kill some time by taking Max out for a walk around the farm. It's a working farm, producing grain for local cereal manu-facturers, but my parents are pretty much retired these days, letting hired hands do most of the work.

Rather than try to navigate a buggy over the rough, tractor-shod ground, I hook Max into my forward-facing baby carrier so we're more mobile. He's not a big baby, but I won't be able to carry him in this for much longer, so I'm making the most of it. It's probably been my favourite piece of baby kit, allowing me to crack on with small jobs while keeping him close to me. Just before we set off for the UK, I had to wind lengths of rope lights up the two new palm trees that we'd bought to flank the gate at the end of the garden. Max watched me complete the entire task with avid interest and his whole face lit up when we turned on the lights. It made Leo laugh.

My heart pinches at the memory. What has become of our garden now?

When I think back to the overgrown shambles that it used to be, I can hardly believe how much we've done. It's been a work in progress and we've added to it as we've been able to afford it, but we now have a blissfully cool plunge pool and a separate hot tub set within wooden decking and surrounded by tropical flora and fauna. There are fragrant frangipanis and pink, purple and orange bougainvillea, fiery hibiscus, and even a Key Lime tree that produces the golf-ball-size yellow citrus fruit that gives Key Lime Pie its name. Along with numerous palm tree trunks that are strung with rope lights, we also have green uplighters shining through the leafy foliage of other plants.

Our guest house is not big by hotel standards, with only four double bedrooms and two shared bathrooms, but we have ambitions to build two more rooms down where the shed used to stand. It'll be a while before we can afford it – the proceeds from the sale of my London flat with Matthew are long gone – but we'll get there one day.

Because of the shared bathroom set-up, we tend to get families or groups of friends who know each other well, and my favourite part of the job is welcoming our new arrivals to the porch for afternoon cocktails and nibbles. Seeing them kick back and relax in our little oasis is very satisfying. Even Leo enjoys joining in. He used to be a bit… hmm, how shall I put this? Dark and brooding? Sullen and moody might be more apt. But he's chilled out a lot since we've been together and he's now warm and welcoming and surprisingly sociable. We make a good team.

We've been fully booked for the last couple of summers, so we don't get much time to kick back and relax in the garden ourselves as a family, but sometimes our guests go out on day trips, and as we organise a lot of these ourselves as part of the service, we know roughly when to expect them home. If Leo isn't at his day job, working as a scuba instructor, then we usually end up in one of the pools together. Sometimes Max is with us, and then it's all splashes and giggles. But sometimes Max is asleep, and then it's just Leo and me…

✳

I strip off quickly and pull on the red bikini that I found at the bottom of a drawer a couple of days ago – it's an old one, dating back to my early days on the island. I haven't worn it in ages – not since well before I fell pregnant.

Max has conked out after his night-time feed and the two families that are currently staying with us – two couples with four teenage children between them – are out together in town. They've gone on a sunset cruise, followed by dinner, after which they'll probably hit Duval Street, judging by what the teenagers were saying to each other earlier.

Leo and I finally have some time to ourselves.

Grabbing our beach towels, I walk out of the house into the darkening night. Leo is already in the hot tub. He hasn't switched on the outdoor lights, but I can see his dark eyes tracking my journey as I cross the deck towards him.

'I remember that bikini,' he says in a low voice as I reach the steps. 'It just about fits.'

'You look incredible.'

I smile and shrug, trying to take the compliment as I slip into the pool.

I don't mind that I haven't got my figure back after having Max. He's only five months old – it's hard to care about things like that these days.

Leo leans forward and holds his hands out to me so I take them and step forward into the deeper centre section. The water laps against my chest and Leo's jaw slackens. He stares at me. 'Do you really have no idea how hot you look?'

'With my bigger boobs?' I ask teasingly, knowing that the skimpy red fabric is now struggling to contain what it once could comfortably.

That's breastfeeding for you.

His expression remains deadly serious and his eyes are almost as black as his hair as his hands move to my hips and very slowly skim up my curves. 'Christ, Laura,' he mutters, his thumbs coming to a rest on my nipples. He pinches the tender skin and I gasp, my mouth falling open. It takes him all of two seconds to slip his tongue between my parted lips and pull me onto his lap so I'm straddling him. I can feel how turned on he is beneath me as we kiss.

We haven't had much sex since Max came along. None at all for the first six weeks. I had a difficult childbirth, partly due to complications arising from an accident I had a few years ago. Twenty-six hours of labour were followed by two hours of pushing and an eventual intervention in the form of forceps. I needed a fair few stitches and it took me a long time to feel okay again down there. Then with the sleepless nights and constant worrying that a crying baby will wake our paying guests, I've pretty much had to wave goodbye to my sex drive.

But, by God, it's returned in force.

I slide my hands over Leo's slippery, wet body, feeling the contours of his chest under my fingertips. He's still as ripped as he was when we first met: narrow waist, broad shoulders, muscled back.

'I want you,' I whisper in his ear, desperate for him to take me inside and ravish me senseless. No sex in the hot tub. That's the rule.

'You'll have me,' he whispers in return, nipping my lower lip. 'But not yet.'

'What? Why not?' I ask with alarm, withdrawing to stare at his face.

'Foreplay, baby,' he replies, a smile playing about his lips.

'Foreplay? What's that?' I stare at him blankly and he throws his head back and laughs. It's hard to keep a straight face.

'You've forgotten what foreplay is?' he asks with a deliciously wicked glint in his eye, knowing we've had no time for it recently.

I nod, feigning ignorance. I like this game.

'I'd better remind you, then,' he says in a deeply sexy voice.

Shivers rolls up and down my spine as he pulls me hard against him, prompting me to utter a small cry. He returns his mouth to mine...

❉

I'm so worried about Leo and what's going on at home that I'm barely able to appreciate the beautiful English summer that we're having as we walk out of my parents' big country kitchen, into the kitchen garden, vegetable patch and beyond. We do a loop right round the old stone farmhouse where I grew up, passing by Mum's roses out the front, which are baking in the afternoon sun. Their perfume wafts towards us on the breeze, mingling with the scent of warm grass. A big, fluffy bee buzzes by and Max looks after it, watching it go.

He's so much more alert these days: a real little man with a big personality. Mum thinks he's developed and grown even in the two weeks since we've been here. She doesn't think Leo will believe the change in him when we get home.

When will we get home?

Leo found fatherhood hard at first – Max scared him. He didn't know how to read his different cries, didn't know whether he was hungry or tired; he'd more likely hand him to me than try to settle him himself. But as Max has grown and become more responsive, the connection between them has strengthened enormously.

A few nights ago, we spoke on FaceTime...

❉

'I dreamt about him last night,' Leo tells me as I cradle Max in my arms. He's just had a feed and he's drowsy, content to snuggle.

'Did you?'

'Yeah.' He smiles sadly. 'I dreamt that I was in bed and it was morning, but he was still fast asleep. I was holding him on my chest and I swear I could feel the weight of his body. I miss him. I miss his chubby legs, his tiny ears, his fluffy hair, his little back…'

I can't help but giggle as Leo wistfully lists a few more random body parts.

'Aw,' I say gently. 'It's been a long two weeks.'

'I don't want to be away from you guys like this ever again,' he states seriously.

'What about Marty's wedding?'

'I'm coming.'

'Really?' I ask with delight.

'Yep. We'll block out those two weeks in the diary. I've missed you both too much.'

My heart melts. 'We've missed you, too.'

'I love you, Maxi!' he calls in a sweet voice, leaning in closer to the phone.

Max's eyes have been growing increasingly heavy-lidded, but now he perks up and looks at the screen.

'Hey,' Leo says to him warmly. 'I miss you, Maxi.'

Max reaches out, making a noise of dissent. I let him take the phone, but he cries out again, because it's not his daddy, just a piece of tech.

'Give Mummy's phone back, darling,' I say softly, trying to take it from him. But he begins to cry. 'I'd better go,' I tell Leo regretfully.

He looks utterly miserable as we end the call.

❄

That was the last time Max saw his daddy's face.

Max points towards the field where my old horse, Pandora, is kept. She's retired now and hasn't been ridden in years, but she ambles over to say hello to us. I forgot to bring an apple and the ones on the nearby tree are too green to eat, so I bend down and scoop up a handful of grass instead, making Max giggle with the dipping motion.

'Well, hello, there…'

Glancing over my shoulder, I spy Mrs Trust, who lives in the big country house next door, coming from the direction of the village church. She's wearing a tweed coat which is far too warm for this weather and is carrying a plastic jug in her right hand. The sight makes me think of something my mother said a while back.

'Hello, Mrs Trust,' I call.

I've known her since I was a girl and I dated her son for years, but she's still 'Mrs Trust' to me. I've always felt like a child putting on her best behaviour when I'm around her.

'Who's this, then?' she asks as we walk over to her and come to a stop on the small, dusty footpath.

'This is Max.' I'm sure my parents will have told her this, plenty of times. Mum said she's a bit doolally these days. It's not surprising, with everything she's been through.

I tickle my baby under his chin to try to tempt out a giggle. It works.

'My, aren't you a strapping, fine lad,' she says, her smile not quite meeting her eyes. I wonder if any of her smiles do anymore. 'How old?' She glances at me.

'Six-and-a-half months,' I obligingly reply.

She nods. 'Are you back for the ball?' Her question prompts guilt to streak through me.

I shake my head regretfully. 'I'm afraid not. We were

supposed to fly home today, but our flight's been cancelled.'

'Your fella here with you?' She looks around, thankfully not dwelling on the fact that it's been years since I last attended the charity ball I set up in her son's name.

I've had to let that part of my life go. I needed to, in order to be able to move on. It was the same with Matthew – we stayed in touch for a while after the split, hoping we could remain friends. He got in touch when he and Tessa decided to give their relationship a go, and he also informed me when it didn't work out. She's now engaged to someone else and Matthew himself is in a serious relationship, but I only heard that on the grapevine. We haven't spoken in years. Friends was too much of a stretch, sadly. But I'm glad it no longer hurts when I think of him.

I wish I could say the same for Will, Mrs Trust's son.

'Leo. No. He couldn't come with us this time, unfortunately,' I reveal. 'He had to stay in Key West to run our guest house.' My parents will have almost certainly told her this, too.

'Key West,' she repeats. 'Is that where you call home now?'

'Yes.' *Home is where the heart is*, I sing inside my head.

'Well, enjoy the rest of your holiday,' she says brusquely, making to leave. She seems to have forgotten that I said my flight was cancelled.

'Thank you,' I reply. 'Please give my best to Mr Trust!'

She gives me a curt nod in response and walks away, swinging the jug in her hand.

I stare at her departing back for a moment and then turn to look up the hill at the church. On impulse, we walk that way, and sure enough, there's a fresh bunch of red roses in the vase in front of Will's headstone, filled to the brim with clean, cold water. Mum told me that she replaces the flowers every couple of days.

She was so austere in life, cold and often disinterested. But how she cherishes her son in death.

Tears prick my eyes and I wrap my arms around Max in his baby carrier and give his small body a squeeze. *If anything happened to my son...*

I know Leo is right. The safest place for Max to be is here. But how I wish Leo were also here with us. *The thought of losing him...* I couldn't bear the pain of another loss.

I turn my face up to the sky and close my eyes.

Home is where the heart is.

Once my heart was here, with Will. A part of me will always love him, and I'll never stop mourning him. But now my heart is in Key West. If Leo was taken from us, would we go back there?

I try to picture myself living and working in the Keys, running Lorelei and raising our son singlehandedly, but I can't. I imagine putting Leo into a box in the ground and leaving America to live here with my parents and pain lances my heart.

How I wish you'd gone to Miami, Leo! This is no time to be dancing in the storm!

I need to stop torturing myself. I take one last look at Will's headstone before turning away, brushing my fingers against it as I go.

❋

It is the longest day. Every time I check my phone to see if there's any news of the hurricane, Mum tells me off because it's no way to distract myself. I feel chilled to the bone at the sight of one satellite image, which shows Key West in the eye of the storm. I stare at the angry red circle going around and around until Mum takes my phone away and replaces it with a cup of tea.

That night, I lay Max down in the cot in my old bedroom, which still has the nightlights I used as a child when I was scared of the dark. I consider climbing into my old bed so I'm close to him, but I'm drawn back to the guest room where Leo and I usually stay when we're here together. I lie down, my eyes on the ceiling and my hand on Leo's side of the bed, wishing I could feel his warm, solid body instead of the cool, empty sheet.

It's not long before my mind drifts back to the past…

The very first time I saw Leo was from the sun deck of our hotel, which was right next to Lorelei. It was late at night and I was restless with jetlag and misery over what Matthew had done. I heard music and laughter coming from nearby, so I went to investigate and saw Leo and his friends lazing on his battered old sofas in his untidy backyard, smoking one of his now long-gone cigars. I thought he looked like a film star with his olive skin, dark features and chiselled good looks. I couldn't believe it when he turned up on our dive boat a couple of days later – Bridget, Marty and I had gone on a snorkelling excursion. It inspired us to do a full scuba diving course and Leo was partnered with me. Jorge was our instructor – Leo was still only a dive master at the time – but now he's a fully qualified instructor himself.

I'm full of pride at the thought of how many people he's now taught to dive, how many minds he's opened to the astonishing underwater world that's all around us. It's been over a year since we dived together, but we'll go again when Max is old enough to leave with someone, and I know Leo will still hold my hand and the experience will still take my breath away.

Leo often used to make me feel breathless. My skin would spark under his touch and shivers would travel up and down my spine whenever he held my eye contact. He still makes me feel like that at times, but my love for him has risen to a whole new level.

When we first met, I was a mess. My heart was broken, I was beyond devastated that my husband had created a child with another woman, I had no idea what our future would hold, and on top of all of this, my attraction to Leo was very confusing. My head was all over the place.

But now we have a wonderful life with a little family of our own and I have never felt more settled or more complete.

I still remember the night we decided to take the next step in our relationship...

❋

'Let's have a baby.'

I lift my head from where it's been settled in the crook of Leo's arm and stare at him. 'Really?' I ask, my fingers pausing from where they've been stroking his chest.

'Yes,' he whispers. 'We're in a good place, aren't we?'

'A really good place.' The house is finally finished, bar a few things we'd still like to do to the garden, and Leo and Jorge are full of enthusiasm about the prospect of setting up their own dive school. Everything is coming together.

'I want a family with you,' he says.

I edge away from him slightly and he takes the hint, turning on his side to face me as I rest my cheek against my pillow and look into his eyes.

'*You still want to get married,*' *he notes regretfully.*

I don't say anything. I don't even nod. He knows what I want, what I'll never stop wanting. And I know that I'll never get what I want, nor will I ask for it. I respect Leo's wishes too much.

'*I'm sorry,*' *he says, his dark eyebrows drawing together.*

Now I do shake my head. '*Don't be. I understand.*'

'*I'm still sorry,*' *he says.*

I reach over and smooth the frown lines away from his brow. '*I understand,*' *I repeat.*

'*I swear, I'm yours until the day I die.*'

'*And even then,*' *I whisper.*

'*Even then,*' *he repeats, pulling me closer.*

He kisses me lovingly, tenderly, and then his lips move downwards, across my neck and my collarbone. He slides my vest top up over my breasts and kisses me again before continuing his downwards journey to my stomach, where he pauses. He kisses me slowly, three, four, five times, making me feel adored and cherished. I run my hands through his hair, feeling wave upon wave of love for this beautiful man.

'*I want to put a baby inside you,*' *he says in a low voice, and I lift my head from the pillow to stare at him. Seconds pass, and then goosebumps shiver into place all over my body.*

'*Okay,*' *I say.*

His eyes widen. '*Okay?*'

'*Yes.*' *I nod.*

He grins and hooks his fingers under the hemline of my knickers, pulling them down. I help to kick them off, but he catches my ankles in his hands and pushes my knees apart. He's not done with kissing me, yet, it seems…

❄

To our surprise, I fell pregnant quickly, but my pregnancy seemed to go on forever. I was so hot in the humid, tropical heat. I felt like a whale, waddling round the house, standing under the ceiling fans and wishing to God that we had prioritised air-conditioning over that blasted hot tub. I had to manage the guest house while Leo was at work, but he did what he could to help, coming home at lunchtimes and finishing work early whenever possible. But I was desperate for it all to be over. And then, not-so-suddenly, it was...

❄

'Hey,' Leo says softly when I open my eyes. I must've dozed off. He's sitting in the armchair next to my bed and is cradling Max in his arms. He's bare-chested, I realise, and our tiny baby is completely naked, not even a nappy adorning his backside.

'Skin on skin.' I smile with delight.

I told Leo that, if I had to have a C-section, he needed to have plenty of skin-on-skin contact with Max until I woke up. It's good for the baby, they say.

I didn't need to have a C-section, but I love that he's followed my advice, anyway.

'How are you feeling?' he asks, and there's an expression on his face that I don't recognise. He looks kind of shell-shocked, but in a good way.

'Okay,' I reply, although in truth I'm sore.

'Do you want him?' he offers, and I do, of course I do, but I can tell he's reluctant to let him go.

I shake my head. 'He looks happy there with you.'

He smiles, pleased, smoothing his big hand over the dark fluff gracing our baby's tiny head. He bends down to kiss him and when he straightens back up, I can see that the expression on his face has intensified. He's not shell-shocked, I realise; he's awe-struck. His mind has been completely and utterly blown.

My heart is so full at that moment that I'm not sure my ribcage is big enough to contain it.

❋

My nose prickles as I roll over onto my side and reach for Leo's pillow, pulling it close to my chest. It's no substitute.

The longest day is followed by the longest night – I can't sleep for the life of me – and then, at five o'clock in the morning, twenty-four hours after the hurricane struck Key West, my mobile phone rings.

'Leo?' I ask into the receiver, my pulse jumping unpleasantly.

'It's okay, I'm okay,' I hear his warm voice spilling down the line.

'Oh my God, Leo!' I cry, sitting up in bed, and then I literally *do* cry. *Sob*.

'Hey, hey,' he soothes. 'Baby, I can't talk for long. I've borrowed someone's satellite phone. But I'm okay. Okay? You just stay safe and I'll keep you updated when I can.'

'Have you spoken to Jorge?'

'Yes, he's fine.'

'How's Lorelei?'

'She's currently under several inches of water, but I boarded up the windows really well and managed to get most of our stuff upstairs.'

Relief surges through me. 'Well done. What about the boat?'

'It's a bit battered, but it survived.'

'Thank God!'

'We were lucky, very lucky. Others weren't. Listen, there's

a queue of people waiting to call loved ones so I've got to go, but I'll call you again as soon as I can.'

'When can we come home?'

'Not for a while. Weeks, at least.'

'*Weeks?*'

'It's not safe, Laura,' he tells me with regret.

'Then *you* be careful!'

'I will be, you don't have to worry. I love you. I love you *both*. I'll call again soon.'

'I love you too.'

The line goes dead.

❋

The longest day that was followed by the longest night is then followed by the longest month, because that's how long Max and I have to stay in the UK after the hurricane. I'm itchy with frustration and utterly miserable at being separated from Leo for so long, but he persuades me to remain with my parents so he can crack on with repairs without having to worry about us.

'The island was battered by 100-plus mile-per-hour winds for almost forty-eight hours,' he told me on one of our earlier phone calls, when I heard the airport had reopened and wanted to jump on a plane. 'Lots of stuff went flying. Boats crashed onto the streets with the storm surge and there was shit every-where – literally: the sewage systems failed. The rain hasn't stopped, the high winds are still blowing crap around, and there's rubbish and debris everywhere. I'm going to be boiling water for a long time to come, and the power's not even fully back on. You can't bring our baby son back to this mess.'

That was me told. But I felt so helpless, and I *hated* the thought of him going through that hellish time alone.

We fly into Key West on a hot, sunny afternoon. After clearing customs in Atlanta, we're able to walk straight off the plane and into Leo's arms. His face is a picture of relief at the sight of us.

Max fell asleep as we were coming in to land, and he's out cold in my arms, thanks to the kind lady who carried my not insubstantial hand luggage off the plane for me. I say a grateful thank you to her as she places my nappy bag at my feet and I drop my handbag beside it before stepping into Leo's embrace. His arms come around both Max and me, but it feels awkward due to the bundle in my arms. It nowhere near quells my craving to be close to him.

Leo pulls away to look down at Max, stiffening with shock. 'He's grown so much!' he exclaims in a whisper, meeting my eyes. A strange feeling of shyness comes over me then, like I hardly know him, which is ridiculous considering how long we've been together.

'Do you want to hold him?' I ask, and even my voice sounds funny.

'Will he mind?' he asks in return, and all at once, I realise he's also feeling unsettled, like *we're* the strangers and he's the outsider.

'Oh, Leo,' I erupt suddenly, as a wave of emotion crashes through me.

And then he pulls me back into his arms, cradling my head against his chest so I'm pressed against him sideways, and this time, we fit better.

Max opens his eyes and stares up at us both. I smile down at him and a tear splashes onto his cheek, which hasn't come from me. I glance at Leo to see tears streaming down his face and then I stand on my tiptoes and kiss them away, loving him like never before.

My actions make Max giggle, and then we all begin to laugh, beside ourselves with joy and relief at being back together again.

It's been a month since the hurricane tore through here, but the signs of its devastation are everywhere. Debris is piled up on the sides of roads, including furniture, washing machines and other appliances that were wrecked in the salt water storm surges. There are capsized boats in the water and wrecked boats on land; holes ripped in the sides of buildings and branches and leaves shredded from trees. The fronds of the palm trees – what's left of them – are still facing away from the direction of the wind.

'Jesus, Leo,' I murmur. I'm glad I flew into Key West because the journey down from Miami would have been even more heartbreaking, seeing the remnants of people's lives everywhere – some of the other keys were hit even worse than Key West.

I'd already watched a lot of footage of the aftermath of the storm: sandbanks washed onto roads, houses no longer on stilts, vegetation ripped out, broken signs and battered billboards, homes, sheds, cars and mobile homes destroyed.

Leo described the hurricane as like being in an earthquake – the whole house rocking and shaking. At one point, he realised that the boarding over the attic window had come off – he'd struggled to secure it in the first place because it had been too risky to use a ladder in the high winds. He'd ventured out of the bathroom to try to board it back up again, and moments before he'd entered the room, he'd heard the window glass shattering.

'I couldn't see for the rain,' he said. 'It was horizontal, and it was dark, like night in the middle of the day. You could just make out the trees swaying, like black ghosts. I got the hell out of there and went back to the bathroom.'

I dread to think what state the attic room was in after the storm. I have a real fondness for Leo's former bedroom. It was where we first took our relationship to the next level. But on the whole, we were lucky. Others weren't.

'How are Patsy and Alicia?' I ask Leo of our neighbours across the road, a lovely lesbian couple in their fifties who have lived in the Keys their whole lives, but only met each other a few years ago. Leo said their home was badly hit.

Leo sighs. 'Not so great. Alicia was sobbing out on the street yesterday. I was in the yard and heard her.'

'Why?' I'm aghast.

'A couple of tourists drove past and stopped outside their house to take a photo. The look on the assholes' faces is what broke her, like her hell was their entertainment. That sort of thing is happening all over the Keys. Disaster is *not* a spectator sport,' he spits with disgust. 'These are *actual lives*, not fodder for peoples' Facebook pages. Some people have lost so much.'

My throat swells at the thought of Alicia in tears. She's such a strong, spirited person. I can't imagine her breaking down. 'You wouldn't go and take pictures of people at a funeral,' I mutter. 'Don't do it here.'

'Exactly.' Leo shakes his head with disgust.

'I'll go over and see her tomorrow,' I say.

'She'd like that.'

Leo had already emailed me photographs, but nothing pre-pares me for seeing the garden in person. It's in a terrible state. Our two new, expensive palm trees were uprooted and blown clean away and most of our tropical plants have been shredded. The deck survived, and Leo has drained the plunge pool and hot tub and cleaned it out. MRSA and other infections are a big concern so everyone is being super careful. He hasn't got around to refilling the pools with post-boil alert water yet, and we'll have to shock the water before anyone swims in it.

'Everything is fixable,' Leo tells me, noticing my distraught expression.

I nod and force a shaky smile. 'It could've been worse,' I say, trying not to dwell.

He's replaced the damaged weatherboarding on the house, although it hasn't been painted yet, so it looks like a patchwork quilt.

'It could've done with a lick of fresh paint anyway,' I say. 'I'll have to get my paint brushes back out.'

'That's my girl.' Leo wraps his arm around my shoulders and presses a kiss to my temple.

I notice our two new leather sofas are outside on the porch and glance up at him. He shakes his head, his lips downturned. 'I put them outside, hoping they'd air out, but they're wrecked.'

'Maybe we can leave them out here for a bit,' I say. 'Make the most of having no house guests. It'll be like the old days.'

He nods and kisses me again.

It'll be another few weeks before tourists begin to trickle back. Most people cancelled in the wake of Jackie, but some were intent on sticking to their schedule. I'm glad we've got a timeframe to work to. It'll keep us occupied.

Inside, Leo shows me the watermark on the living room wall. It's remarkable how much of our furniture he did manage to protect, but the floorboards are warped and will have to be re-sanded before we'll know if they can be saved. Everything still smells of damp and God knows what else, but the house itself will come good.

'You want a nap or something?' Leo asks.

I shake my head. 'I'd rather push through until bedtime.'

'Why don't we go out for lunch?'

'Is anything open?'

He nods. 'A few places. Come on.'

I'm only too glad to get out of the house.

The walk into town is depressing. I keep averting my gaze, not wanting to stare at the state of other peoples' houses.

'Hey, Leo!'

An old guy I don't recognise is leaning out of a first-floor window of a house across the road, his white hair lifting from his forehead in the breeze. 'You got your family back with you?'

'I sure do. Hank, this is Laura and this is Max.'

'Thanks again for your help the other day,' he says to Leo, after we've exchanged greetings.

'Anytime,' Leo replies amiably.

The guy ducks back inside and I glance at Leo. 'Have you been making new friends?' I ask when we're out of earshot.

'Helped him rehang his back door,' he explains.

The same thing happens a block further on when a middle-aged woman, outside in her garden, calls out a hello to him and asks to be introduced to us. Max is now fast asleep in his buggy, but she comes over to have a look at him.

'He's a good man,' she says of Leo. 'Fixed my fence for me last week.'

Pride warms my insides.

'Have you been doing a lot of that sort of thing?' I ask when we've walked on.

He shrugs again. 'A bit.' And I know he's being modest.

My Leo. My handyman. He's come a long way since he took to the bathroom with a sledgehammer.

A family of chickens darts out of the undergrowth – a mother and a dozen tiny chicks.

'The chickens survived!' I exclaim.

Where London has pigeons, Key West has chickens: hundreds of them free-ranging all over the island, and roosters crowing, day and night.

'Of course, they survived,' Leo replies, returning my smile. 'They'd survive a nuclear bomb.'

'I think you might be thinking of cockroaches,' I say with a grin.

A gloriously resplendent rooster hops out onto the pavement in front of us and lets out a loud cock-a-doodle-do. I laugh and wince simultaneously. I don't want Max to wake up. It'll do him good to sleep a bit longer.

Key West is like a ghost town. Duval Street, normally jam-packed with tourists, is eerily quiet.

'People were driving boats down here after the storm,' Leo tells me.

I'd already seen the footage.

'Mallory Square is deserted, too,' he adds. Normally you'd never be able to get a parking spot.

It's surreal without the tourists, but I kind of like it.

Many of the establishments are still closed, but some are open. A lone guitarist is playing to a few chilled out locals in Sloppy Joe's, the famous bar that Ernest Hemingway once frequented – albeit when the bar was in a different location, a few doors down to the west, just off Duval Street.

'Mojito?' Leo asks.

I smile at him. 'Why not?'

It's a surprisingly lovely day, in the end.

❄

The next day, Max and I go with Leo to help rebuild the Tiki Hut outside the old dive centre where he and Jorge used to work. They've stayed friendly with the previous owner, who passes work their way when his own school is overbooked.

The dive centre is a couple of keys away – we pick up Jorge on the way.

'Man, were you missed,' Jorge says in my ear when we hug. It's great to see him again – I've been worried about his safety, too. 'I've never seen him so miserable and that's saying something.'

'We've been miserable without him, as well,' I reply. 'How are you? How's Lisa?'

Lisa is Jorge's girlfriend who works for them at the dive school. She's only been with them for ten months, but has become indispensable, captaining the boat and managing bookings, and even their accounts – jobs I used to help out with before Max came along. She's all-round awesome and Jorge, who has never been one to mix business with pleasure, was smitten from the get-go. I really like her – we're on our way to becoming good friends.

'She's fine,' Jorge replies with a cheeky grin. 'She's just about forgiven me for not evacuating with her.'

'Bet you had some making up to do?'

'Hell, yeah.' He smirks.

It's hardly surprising the Tiki Hut didn't survive the hurricane – it's an open-air bar with a roof made out of thatched palm fronds, so hardly likely to withstand high winds.

Marty used to call it Ye Olde Thatched Tiki Hut when we did our dive course here – she, Bridget and I would come here to prop up the bar for a bit after our lessons: they're days I'll never forget.

I can't do much with Max around, but I pop him into his baby carrier and pass twine, hammer and nails when needed. Leo is just happy to have us close – he keeps looking over at us and smiling, and I keep catching Jorge chuckling at the change in him.

Last night, as we lay in bed, arms and legs intertwined, Leo asked me if I still wanted to marry him…

❋

'Is that a proposal?' I ask with astonishment.

'If you'd like it to be,' he replies, staring at me seriously in the dim light.

It happens almost instantaneously – a strange lightness lifts me up, and I realise then and there that I don't need to walk down an aisle to feel like our relationship is set in stone.

'Oh, Leo,' I murmur, brushing my thumb over his lip. 'It means the world to me that you'd do that, but we don't need a piece of paper to tell us that we're in this for life.'

'Are you sure?' His eyes are shining.

'Yes.' I nod. 'But if I change my mind, you'll be the first to know,' I add with a smile, leaning in to kiss him.

He pulls away after one peck. 'I am so in this for life with you,' he says solemnly, and he looks youthful in that moment, full of promise and hope for the future. 'I want to make more babies with you.'

'Really?'

'Yes. I'd knock you up now, if you'd let me.'

I grin at him. 'You don't think it's too soon?'

'No, but you do. Don't you?' he asks with surprise when I say nothing.

I purse my lips and slide my hand down to my stomach.

His eyebrows jump up. 'You're kidding?'

I shake my head slowly. I've known since last week, but I've been waiting for the right time to break it to him in person.

'When did we manage that? How did we manage that?'

'That night in the hot tub,' I tell him, giving him a distinctly unimpressed look. Turns out some rules are made to be broken.

'Holy shit.' He exhales loudly.

'My thoughts exactly.'

I am nowhere near ready to go through that again. Luckily, I still have quite a few more months to prepare myself.

'Oh, man,' he says, pulling me into his arms and holding me tight.

'Are you happy?' I ask.

'You have no idea,' he replies. 'You, Max... My life was nothing until you came along. I don't want to stop at two. I want a big family.'

'Steady on!' I laugh.

'I mean it,' he says seriously. 'I want to fill this home with children.'

'What about leaving rooms for our guests?'

'Screw our guests.'

'How many Mojitos did you have again?' I ask with amusement. I opted for mocktails, but didn't tell him why at the time.

'I'm drunk on love,' he replies.

'Did you really just say that to me?' I ask with incredulity. 'Leo, that is cheese on Parmesan levels.'

He's laughing too, now, but when we both finally calm down, we're still in each other's arms.

'I love you,' he says.

How I waited to hear those three words, once upon a time. They still mean so much to me.

*

Lisa comes to join us at the dive centre later that day and it's great to see her again. She gives Jorge a lift home, so it's just Leo, Max and me on our return journey.

As we cross over the final bridge that takes us into Key West, I notice a big, hand-painted sign that I didn't see on our way off the island:

After the hurricane comes the rainbow.
Welcome home.

Tears fill my eyes and I reach over to take Leo's hand – we meet in the middle: he was already on his way to taking mine.

Suddenly, he pulls over on the side of the road, overcome with emotion. He leans across to cup my face in his hands.

'I'm so glad you're back,' he murmurs, kissing me on my lips.

'So am I.'

It's been the longest time, but my heart is finally where it's meant to be: home.

Author's note

At the time of this book's publication, it will be just over a year since Hurricane Irma struck the Florida Keys, leaving devastation in its wake. Hurricane Jackie is fictional, taking place at a different time of the year than Irma, but my research was drawn from real events, and my heart goes out to everyone who has been affected.

If you visit the Keys in the future, please support local businesses, tip big and be sensitive towards the locals. Don't ask about the hurricane; it was hard enough to live through it.

Q&A with Paige Toon

Sophie Kinsella, author: *When you write a short story, do you ever fall in love with the characters so much, you want to turn it into a full novel?*

I've done this once, with *The Last Piece of My Heart*. Bridget first appeared in *The Longest Holiday* as a friend character, then again in *Thirteen Weddings*. Both times, readers asked for a full-length book for her. I wrote her a short story – which is now the prologue for *The Last Piece of My Heart*. I think she's my favourite female character – I love writing from her perspective.

Lucinda Kirby: *Which of your characters would you most want to be stranded with on a desert island?*

As long as we're both single, I'd say Leo from *The Longest Holiday* because just looking at him would pass the time. Or Ben from *Pictures of Lily* because he's also fit and I reckon he'd be best in a crisis.

Rhiannon Baker: *What made you decide to write realistic love stories?*

Realism is really important to me – I get annoyed when reading books or watching films and thinking, *that just wouldn't happen.* Also, realism has a knock-on effect of making things unpredictable. You're never quite sure if the characters will end up where you want them to, and although an ending might break your heart, at least it's true and there's comfort in that.

Lindsey Kelk, author: *What's your favourite part of the writing process?*

The actual writing! Research is amazing because I usually visit the beautiful places that I'm writing about, but there's nothing like the thrill of catapulting towards a climactic scene when your fingers just can't type fast enough. It's like living in my own little movie inside my head – I love it.

Eva Duncanson: *If you could spend one day as a character in one of your books, who would you pick and what moment of the book would you choose?*

I put my characters through so much emotional turmoil that I had to rule out a few books straight away. I think it would have to be the day at the end of *Baby Be Mine* when Meg and Barney go with Johnny to the Goodwood Festival of Speed. I don't want to spoil it for people who haven't read the book, but I do think it's one of my happiest 'ever afters'!

Giovanna Fletcher, author: *What would you be doing if you weren't an author?*

Possibly acting – I went to Redroofs Theatre School as a teenager. Writing is a bit like acting because you have to get inside your characters' heads in order to be able to connect with them. I feel what they feel, whether they're laughing or crying.

Lila Grigoriou: *Why did you decide to connect characters from different books?*
I was inspired by Marian Keyes. After reading *Watermelon*, I was thrilled to get an update about the Walsh sisters in other books. When I came to write *Johnny Be Good*, I wanted to do the same for readers of *Lucy in the Sky* so I added Meg's small-part character into *Lucy* during the editing process. I've linked books ever since. *Five Years From Now* is the only exception, partly because of the novel's decade-spanning timeline – a link just didn't present itself and I'll never force it.

Milly Johnson, author: *If you could be any heroine from a 'classic' novel, who would you be and why?*
I wouldn't want to be any of them because they were so repressed, but I do have a soft spot for Marianne Dashwood from Jane Austen's *Sense and Sensibility*. She was so torn and heartbroken; she definitely inspired some of my plots!

Eva Kiss: *How do you say goodbye to your characters when you are done with a story?*
Sometimes I can't and I end up writing an extra chapter, as you've seen in this collection. It's part of the reason I came up with *The Hidden Paige* – I feel like my characters are all still out there, going about their lives, and I know I can drop in on them whenever I like to see what they're up to. *Five Years From Now* was the hardest to leave behind as it was so emotional. I had to take a break from writing afterwards.

Catherine Isaac aka Jane Costello, author: *I saw the video of you weeping when you wrote the stunning ending for* **Five Years From Now,** *but what book, by another author, has made you cry?*

Most recently, *While You Were Sleeping* by Dani Atkins, and before that, it was *You Me Everything* by you! A quick look at my bookshelf brought back many snotty-nosed memories: *The First Last Kiss* by Ali Harris, *The Notebook* by Nicholas Sparks, *The Fault in our Stars* by John Green, *Me Before You* by Jojo Moyes, *You're The One That I Want* by Giovanna Fletcher, *The Age of Miracles* by Karen Thompson Walker, *Wonder* by RJ Palacio, to name but a few.

Olivia Heys: *Why do you set so many of your books in both England and Australia?*

Because, like Lucy from *Lucy in the Sky*, I'm torn between two countries. I'm happily settled with my husband and children in the UK, but the rest of my family are in Australia, where I grew up, and I'd give anything to be able to pop over there more often. Australia is so far away, but writing about it brings it closer.

Louise Pentland, author: *I fantasise about writing in quaint tea rooms with giant scones and mugs of hot chocolate, but in reality I write most of my work in my 'soft office' aka My Bed!! Where is your favourite place to write?*

I actually did write a few books from a coffee shop, listening to music to drown out the clatter while my kids attended a nearby nursery. Now I write from my office or on my laptop if I feel like a change of scene. I wrote a chunk of *The Last Piece of My Heart* from my campervan at the end of our garden. Bridget, my heroine, was living in a campervan so I loved being able to picture her surroundings.

Hannah Clarke: *Which book was the hardest to write and why?*

Johnny Be Good was tricky because I was pregnant and my head was all over the place, but once my son was born, I flew through it while he slept in the pram beside me. *The One We Fell in Love With* was my most challenging because it's written from the perspective of three different sisters – triplets – and I had to make 'the twist' work.

Dani Atkins, author: *In all of your books, who has the best first kiss?*

The first kiss is probably my favourite thing to write. Rose and Toby from *The One We Fell in Love With*, Charlie and Bridget from *The Last Piece of My Heart*, Nell and Van from *Five Years From Now*... This is a difficult one! I think it's a toss-up between Johnny and Meg from *Johnny Be Good* and Leo and Laura from *The Longest Holiday*. I'll go with the latter because Johnny had just had a fag so I doubt he tasted very nice!

Molly Lucitt-Rees: *Do you know how your story ends before you write it?*

Usually, but when I wrote *One Perfect Summer*, about twenty thousand words from the end, I realised it wasn't going to be as clear-cut as I had envisaged. I basically decided to let the ending write itself and it was so liberating that I did the same with *Thirteen Weddings*. Those two endings might not have been straight-forward happy-ever-afters, but that wouldn't have been realistic for the characters at the time. I'm glad I got to revisit these stories, though.

Lucy Diamond, author: *Which of your characters is your favourite and who would play them in a movie?*

I love them all, don't make me choose! My characters don't look like anyone else inside my head, but readers have suggested Charlie Hunnan and Chris Hemsworth would make good Johnny Jeffersons, so I'll go with those options – but Chris would have to lose some of his superhero bulk first…

Victoria Ashford: *What piece of advice would you give sixteen-year-old Paige?*

'*Five years from now, you'll look back and understand why this happened*'. My dad gave me this same advice when I was seventeen and struggling with my A levels. He was right: I ended up going to a different university where I met my future husband – our two children would not exist if I hadn't messed up my exams. Most clouds have a silver lining, and even bad things have helped inspire my novels so I'd just say, soak up every experience and remember those emotions because one day you'll write about them. *Five Years From Now* is a good example of this.

Mesha Prout: *Which book did you most enjoy writing?*

The Sun in Her Eyes and *All About The Hype* were the *easiest* to write, possibly because the settings were already familiar to me, but *Lucy in the Sky* will always have a special place in my heart because it was my first. I was deliriously happy to have been given a book deal after dreaming about being an author since I was a small child. I loved every minute of the writing process.

Millie Tyerman: *Was there a specific moment in life that inspired you to write romance novels?*

I wrote what I most enjoyed reading at that moment in time: chick-lit! Now that term is considered by many to be derogatory, but that annoys me. To me, it's the literary equivalent of a romcom movie: a gorgeously warm love story that makes you feel a rollercoaster of emotions as you fly through the pages. I've lost count of the number of readers who have told me that my books helped to get them into reading; that they couldn't finish a book until they read one of mine. How can that be a bad thing?

Look out for the brand new novel from the
Sunday Times **bestselling author Paige Toon.**
The perfect summer read for 2019!

IF YOU COULD GO ANYWHERE

Angie has always wanted to travel. But at 29, she has
still never left her small mining town in the Australian
outback. When her grandmother passes away, Angie
finally feels free to see the world – until she discovers
a letter addressed to the father she never knew and is
forced to question everything.

As Angie sets off on her journey to find the truth –
about her family, her past and who she really is – will
enigmatic stranger Alessandro help guide the way?

COMING 2019

SIMON &
SCHUSTER

DISCOVER MORE FROM

paige toon

Paige Toon is the *Sunday Times* bestselling author
of over thirteen novels.

To find out more about Paige and her writing, or to
join The Hidden Paige newsletter and receive
free short stories, visit her website:
www.paigetoon.com

@PaigeToonAuthor

Facebook.com/PaigeToonAuthor
#TheHiddenPaige